"There is no greater agony than bearing an untold story inside you."

- Maya Angelou

Dedicated to all whose story is found in this one...
past, present, and future.

letters from

Ocracoke

J.M. Styron

Entry 1

The weather was blustery, the sky steel gray, the swells unforgiving as we arrived at the Cedar Island ferry for my return voyage north to Ocracoke. The cool spitting rain made me feel as though I had brought Seattle weather back with me to the Outer Banks. The white caps breaking along Cedar Island beach made the inland waters of Pamlico Sound resemble a pre-hurricane Atlantic. Yet, off in the distance the sky was lightening, stirring hope that the front would soon pass.

The ferry horn startled me as it sounded with piercing finality, heralding the end of one chapter of my life and the opening lines of a new and very different one. Though I sought to prevent any outward disclosure of my trepidation, my silence was no doubt an obvious sign that, though my mouth may have been still that morning, my mind was racing with anxious thoughts. The Ocracoke I left held a conglomeration of fearful and painful memories. The thought of returning to the place of my deepest woundings left me uncertain how to handle this new transition in life. Nevertheless, circumstance had left me little choice in the matter. Life had dealt me some rather unbeneficent hands and I had few options aside from returning to the small, secluded maritime village, which would be a crucible for facing my past and future simultaneously.

It was nearly ten years ago when I made my first voyage to Ocracoke. Prior to that time I knew of the village only from my North Carolina history course, or an occasional sound bite on the evening news each September. The eyes of the entire state would turn to the region every Fall as hurricane reports sounded from our local news stations, tracking storms which seemed to be as much a part of Autumn living in coastal Carolina as the beginning of the new school year. And, nestled midway on the string of barrier islands stretching from Wilmington to Duck lay the village of Ocracoke. This little, tucked away, obscure

hamlet stretching northeast into the Atlantic would provide me with some of my life's most monumental experiences, ones which would serve to alter the course of my
existence and my beliefs forever.

I was twenty-two years old when I drove my brand
new 1982 Honda Civic onto the Cedar Island ferry, heading for my very first appointment after graduating from
college. I was to be the interim pastor of a small independent church on the edge of the village. As most young
and immature pastors, I was full of answers. I had taken
hermeneutics, passed my courses in Greek and Hebrew,
and received formalized training in the exegetical disciplines; however, I knew I was not a great orator. There
were guys in my class at Bible College who could preach
with impeccable eloquence and grace, achieving a type of
rhythm and flow in their preaching that is characteristic
of many great holiness preachers. My style of speaking,
on the other hand, was more conversational. I tried to
mimic their patterns for a season, but it never felt natural.
Finally, a mentor gave me some advice which changed
how I viewed life and ministry. One day he looked me
squarely in the eyes and said, "Holden, just be yourself
and God will use you." From then on I began slowly
cultivating a sense of comfort in my own skin, though the
fullness of self-actualization would take many years to
reach fruition.

This sense of self-assurance was hard won. I learned
early on that if I wanted love it had to be earned. Love
and acceptance were not free gifts in my family of origin.
Though I do not doubt that I was loved by my mother
and my brothers, perfect performance on my part always
seemed to sure up their affection and approval. It was in
these moments of approved performance that I could find
the tangible trappings of a love that all families claim to
possess for their children, but often fail to show.

On my return crossing, as the waves of Pamlico Sound
curled and crashed against the forward momentum of

the steel hulled ferry, I smiled in melancholic sentimentality as I reflected upon the marriage of naiveté and deep understanding which existed within that younger version of me. I was ready to face the world and love them into the Kingdom of God. Ironically, as I make this journey back, nearly a decade after my exodus from the island, I am terrified. I am terrified at the thought of returning, and hoping that somehow, in the end, there will still be a place for me here and in God's Kingdom.

Entry 2

It was a sunny fall afternoon on that maiden voyage to Ocracoke, nearly ten years ago. As the ferry left its moorings and pulled away from the dock, I was struck with the reality that I was leaving everything comfortable and familiar behind for a world of newness, evoking feelings of wide-eyed anticipation coupled with deep ripples of diffidence. My life had been spent in a close-knit farming community in the piedmont, and leaving home and family was placing me far outside my comfort zone.

That afternoon, just before five, a tree line appeared on the horizon and I made my way to the bow of the vessel to survey the first evidence of land I had seen in well over an hour. As I recognized the pinnacle of the small white lighthouse dominating the skyscape, I drew in a deep, anxiety filled breath, realizing that I was staring into the face of my new life. Standing there with the cool sea breeze blowing through my hair, a thousand questions began to flood my mind. Was I ready for such a responsibility? Did I have what it takes? Would these people like me?

Within a half hour we were entering the harbor at Silver Lake and the late afternoon sky was casting its vibrant orange and pink hues upon the glass-like waters of the sand bounded haven. The harbor's mirror-like surface hosted reflections of the island homes, fish houses, boats, and cedars nestled about the harbor, interrupted only by

9

the wake of the vessel upon which I stood. This was like something out of a book, but better. Our North Carolina history text had failed to capture the quaint beauty of the island. To this day there are few visions that I cherish more than an Autumn sunset over Silver Lake.

My serene gaze was disrupted by the piercing wail of the vessel's horn as we pulled into the dock. Being woken from my wonder-induced trance, I made my way back to my little silver Honda, the back seat filled clear to the headliner with clothes, bedding, books and lamps. Like a line of automated dominos, the glow of brake lights began to appear in the dusk, as the vehicles began cranking their engines. Slowly we made our way from the ferry, the metal ramp making its clanks underneath the cars as we each pulled gently from the deck of the vessel onto the sand dusted asphalt that wound through the interior of the village.

Entry 3

I made my way around Silver Lake slowly in one of multiple parades which would converge upon this section of highway twelve with every ferry landing from morning until night. As the other cars were taking in the sights of the local shops, Oneal's fish house, and the Jolly Roger pub, I was looking for a narrow road on the left, departing the main thoroughfare just beyond the island post office. This was the first direction given by the deacon with whom I would be lodging with during my tenure on the island. At that time, there were no street signs on Ocracoke; therefore, my directions were simply comprised of landmarks and the counting of lanes and cottages, a rather precarious situation for someone who had never before stepped foot on Ocracoke. I was nervous enough as it was, without the added fear of ending up on the wrong doorstep.

Finally, I recognized a path meeting the description given by my host. Veering slightly to the left, I exited the paved highway onto a small cedar flanked lane. I couldn't help but chuckle upon noticing a wooden speed limit sign someone had posted at its entrance, which read: "Drive Real, Real Slow."

The narrow path was paved with two strips of what I would learn were oyster shells, just large enough for each set of tires, with a line of grass and weeds down the center. The lane was only wide enough for one vehicle, and was flanked with hedge rows and white picket fences, within arm's reach of my car window.

I counted aloud in muttered tones as I drove down the lane, keeping tally of the string of island cottages on my left until I came to number twelve. I pulled slowly into the driveway at about a quarter past six, parking behind a full sized Chevy pickup, its bed piled with mounds of green netting. The tail gate was missing and the dinted, rusty bumper boasted a noble collection of campaign stickers. Names like Whitley, Hunt, Jones and Morgan let me know immediately that this deacon was a strong Democrat, as most of us southerners were in bygone years.

Emerging from my car, I could see the glow of lights through the window panes of the one and a half story white wooden cottage. The exterior, like many of the other older homes I had passed on the lane, was covered with white clapboard siding. The weathered cedar shake roof was capturing the blue cast of the evening sky which was settling in about the island oaks and myrtle bushes. I made my way through the whitewashed picketed gate, down a narrow brick walk towards the front steps. The corner of the front yard held two massive fig trees mulched with mounds of the same type shell I had driven on as I made my way down the path. Mrs. Guthrie would later tell me the reason for this unusual type of mulch, unusual to me at least. For those on the island, mounding oyster shells at the base of one's fig trees was how it had been done for generations. It was one of many nuances indigenous to Outer Banks culture that I would learn over

11

the coming years.

The gate had not long shut behind me when the Guthries made their way through the screened door, onto the deep front porch which was furnished with white rockers and a wooden swing suspended by rope from the rafters. Climbing the front steps, I looked up into the faces of the couple with whom I would reside. It was my first encounter with two people who would forever change my life.

Mr. Guthrie was a tall, broad-shouldered man, who dressed most days in khaki pants and cotton shirts with sleeves rolled up just below the elbow. As I made my way onto the gray planked floor of the front porch, Mr. Guthrie reached out his large, rough hand in welcome, hands weathered by salt, sun, and the immense labor of the commercial fishing industry.

"You must be Holden!" he said with a large smile, "We're so glad to have you here on the island".

"This is my wife, Emilis", he said, placing his arm around her shoulder.

Mrs. Guthrie was a beautiful woman; to this day she ranks as the classiest woman I have ever met. Emilis and Robert married back in 1948, after which she moved to his family home on Ocracoke. By the standards of metropolitan business men and stock brokers of the Northeast, Emilis' family of origin would not have been considered upper class; however, in comparison to most of the other fine, hardworking natives of the Outer Banks, she came from considerable means. Emilis had grown up in the home of a well-established commercial fishing family that made a small fortune in the crab business. Her upbringing was evidenced by the way she kept herself and her home. Emilis may have grown up in rural Carolina, but Wedgewood, Bergdorf, and Cartier were also a part of her vocabulary.

As they welcomed me into the living room to have a seat, they were so eager to hear my story. How had I come to the ministry? What had my family done for a living? Where was I from originally? While all three were of great interest, the latter two are of special significance in southern culture. If you know the place and type of family a person comes from, you typically have a pretty good foundation for assessment. Had my answer been that I was born and raised in downtown Charlotte by a mother who practiced law and a father who worked in real estate development...Well, I won't say that they wouldn't have loved me just the same; however, they would most likely have held their breath until the cultural differences made themselves painfully known. Much to their relief, my response was nothing of the kind. I shared with them that I had been born and raised in rural Johnston County, that my father had been a tobacco farmer, and that my mother stayed home to raise my two brothers and me until she later took a job in a local mill to help make ends meet.

From that answer the Guthries could deduce, on some superficial, introductory level, that I came from country folk, not too dissimilar from the people in a rural Carolina fishing village. My father was a tobacco farmer, so I came from hard working people who knew what it was to labor and at times scrape for a living, much like the commercial fishing fraternity to which Mr. Guthrie and all his male ancestors had belonged. You see, in the South we have the most interesting and polite ways of making judgments where others are concerned.

After our introductions and a large, cool glass of sweet tea, we made our way into the dining room. I had never sat down at a more regal table before that night, certainly a far cry from the speckled formica top that my brothers and I had gathered around all our lives.

On the dark mahogany table were silver candelabras, linen hem-stitched place mats and napkins, layers of blue willow china, more forks and spoons than I had ever seen at one setting, and a collection of glasses at each of our three seats straight from Tiffany & Co. in New York City.

The crystal had been a wedding gift from Emilis' mother, and I must admit that I was nervous even sitting in front of them, much less drinking from them. Interestingly enough, fine as the table may have been, the mood in that house was never stuffy. Emilis had the most incredible way of putting people at ease, of making me feel not just welcomed, but rather like royalty. For a boy who had felt his whole life like he was nothing special, such treatment made a lasting impression.

I must say that, in the beginning, Emilis Guthrie was an enigma to me...and I'm afraid to a great many others on the island as well. However, in time I would come to see her as the epitome of a great southern woman. In my book she is Audrey Hepburn, Queen Elizabeth, Ruth, Esther, and Mother Teresa all rolled into one. I climbed the brick steps of their clapboard cottage that first evening to find a woman in navy plaid dress slacks, a popped collar on her starched white shirt, sleeves cuffed and linked with golden crests, and a red sweater draped across her shoulders, sleeves tied carefully mid-chest.

Emilis only wore a few pieces of jewelry, but you couldn't help but notice those she did wear. I cannot think of Emilis without, at some point, having a mental image of her gold set, smoky topaz ring, which has to be every bit of seven or eight carats. As November babies, it was both our birthstone.

She was a portrait of southern class and gentility. Yet, as the years passed I came to see in her a work ethic missing from many of the girls of my generation. Emilis had the ability to hold gentility and arduous labor in a perfect tension. I've watched her work along-side Robert on his shrimp trawler, the Miss Emilis, culling the catch and heading shrimp. It wasn't unusual to observe her standing at the conveyor belt in the fish house, grading fish, tossing slimy mullets, trout, and blue fish into their respective baskets on the cement floor. She would weed-eat in a pair of knee boots on their rear ditch-bank from

Spring till Fall, and scrub down the exterior of the house twice each year with Clorox bleach and a power washer. Nevertheless, in all of those settings she would have on her signature starched, popped collar shirt, dress slacks, and belt. Granted, these were no doubt older and well-worn items from her closet, reserved for such work, but the point is that Emilis was always fixed.

Unfortunately, the way she carried herself attracted the criticism of many women on the island, largely through jealousy as is often the case. Seethe as they may in unfair assessment, I came to know Emilis intimately over the coming years and she was as far from hubris or shallow conceit as any person I have ever known. Emilis Guthrie was simply the product of another place and never felt the need to adjust who she was in order to indulge the good humor of those too concerned with the latest gossip to engage in any type of genuine friendship. Emilis spent her time between her home, the fish business, her Church, and her family down the sound in Carteret County.

In addition to being the classiest woman I had ever met, she has proven to be one of the most loving, humble, and spiritual women I have ever had the honor of knowing. When life's hardships befell the same women who criticized her so viciously behind her back, while being the picture of cordiality to her face, Emilis was one of the first on their doorstep with a pie, a fig cake, or a pan of her famous yeast rolls. There were many times when she would quietly and respectfully pay someone's electric bill for them when she knew they had fallen on hard times, requesting that the clerk maintain her confidence in doing so. She believed deeply that her good fortune in material blessings was meant to be shared with those struggling to get by. And, in addition to everything she and Robert did throughout the year, it's untold how much money they would spend at Christmas in making sure that their workers' families were taken care of.

15

During my first Christmas with the Guthries, Emilis included me on her annual trip to Beaufort and Morehead, loading down their 1980 black Lincoln Continental with clothes and toys, hams and turkeys, and pretty much anything else a family needed for Christmas. Then she hauled it all back across the ferry to Ocracoke and distributed it to the families who worked on their boats, and any others in the community who came to her attention as needing a hand. I remember how she made me walk away when it came time to ring up the merchandise, how she never disclosed who was getting what. In fact, I recall that she would always call those on her list and have them come to the house at night to pick up their gifts. Many faces would come and go during those late night hours in the weeks leading up to Christmas, after little ones were tucked into bed. I would come to know some of these people more fully as my time on the island stretched into years.

One morning over coffee I asked if she would like for me to help deliver any of the gifts. I just figured it would speed the process up if we loaded down Robert's pickup and drove around the island one afternoon delivering to everyone's door. Her response gave me an insight into a depth of compassion and care for others that I have seen little of in my lifetime.

"No Holden, I don't take the gifts to their houses, because I don't ever want to embarrass anyone."

She then slipped into preaching mode, as only Emilis could do, but it was a sermon that I needed to hear. "Every person on this earth is created in the image of God, and deserves to be treated with dignity. Now, if I pull up in their driveway and knock on their door with boxes of food and toys, their children, their neighbors, and pretty soon the whole village will know where those gifts came from. Those parents' dignity will have been robbed in the eyes of their children. I don't want that, Holden. The Scripture teaches that we don't do things to be recog-

16

nized, we do them out of pure love. And pure love allows these people to slip down our path under the cover of night, without being seen by other islanders and especially their children...they get to maintain their dignity."

In all my life, I don't think I ever met a more unselfish couple or heard a more sincere desire to consider the feelings of others. Whatever the price tag, Robert just let Emilis go ahead and do what was in her heart. He would simply give a warm, sheepish grin as he watched her helping those families load their cars in the middle of the night. He had found a jewel and he knew it, and in a quiet way he reveled in all of her inventions.

Not only was Emilis full of grace and compassion, but also full of wit. Once, as we discussed finding the right girl for me to marry, Emilis looked at me and said, "Holden, if you have a hard time picturing the girl you are dating standing down at the fish house, cleaning a mess of fish, or heading shrimp, you don't need her." What she was saying, underneath an analogy that made me chuckle at its simplistic nature and truth, was that a woman who thought she was 'above' that type of work would be more trouble than she's worth.

Though Emilis' unique since of humor and words of wisdom brought me great joy, it would be her humility, her kindness, and her ability to reach out in love to those whom the rest of the world discarded which would become the feast upon which my weary and dejected soul would feed, finding strength and encouragement to go on living. That first night at the Guthries' table was my introduction to Ocracoke, as well as my introduction to a family that would become a surrogate to me for the rest of my life. As we feasted on baked flounder, deviled crabs, scallops wrapped in bacon, light rolls, and sweet potato pie, I came to feel a sense of home that I had seldom before experienced; a sense of belonging that left Ocracoke forever, deeply etched on the tablets of my heart.

17

Entry 4

The next morning I awoke to the sound of Robert's truck firing up well before daybreak. Raising my head from its rest, my forearms and hands still nestled under the warm, soft down pillow of the twin bed they had provided, I peered out of my upstairs window overlooking the driveway.

Through blurred, fresh from sleep eyes, I could see that Robert had moved my car up between his truck and the little white shed, allowing him to get out of the drive. I would come to know this shed as the 'little house', the title typically given to such structures by the island-ers. This building contained the Guthries' chest freezer, stocked to the brim with frozen shrimp, blue crabs, sea mullets, soft shell crabs, bay scallops...you name a seafood indigenous to the Carolina Coast and it was probably in that freezer; and more than likely, Robert had either caught it himself or purchased it from one of the local fisherman whose catch he dealt on the wholesale market. The building also contained most of Robert's tools and lawn equipment. The rafters provided ample space for storing a few extra gill nets. The bare stud walls were adorned with all sorts of flounder gigs, fillet knives, fish scalers, shrimp deveiners, yard rakes and coils of rope. The shelves under Robert's work bench were lined with paint cans, five gallon buckets, containers of net leads, and baskets of corks and crab pot buoys, a secondary stash to the more extensive one housed at his seafood business on Silver Lake. Yet, with all of these trappings of the sea, there was a corner filled with remnant bolts of fabric, braided edging and upholstery tacks. Here Emilis would work for hours on end transforming second hand, tattered furniture into pieces for their home. She once told me, "Holden, I've spent most of my life making a silk purse out of a sow's ear." She loved doing it, she said it gave meaning to each piece. The stately wing back chair

18

in their living room, the one that looked like it belonged at 1600 Pennsylvania Avenue rather than a sleepy oyster paved lane on Ocracoke, began as a battered, barren frame tossed on the side of the highway. Emilis stuffed it into the trunk of her Continental and brought it home to the little house. She had a gift for seeing treasure in unwanted things, a gift that would, in the end, save more than just discarded furniture.

Mr. Guthrie was an incredible man in his own right, the second generation owner of Guthrie and Son's Seafood Company. His sixty foot, white, wooden Shrimp trawler, the Miss Emilis, had become the flagship of his fleet. Robert was a hard worker, leaving home well before day and, most evenings, returning well after dark. His only reprieve was his lunch hour at noon, which he always sought to spend with Emilis. At nearly sixty years of age and after thirty four years of marriage, they still captivated each other. The romance and dedication I witnessed in those two was unlike anything I had ever seen in a marriage, giving me hope that true love really did exist, even today.

The only other hiatus Robert took from the demands of the fish house and the fleet he managed was Sunday. Robert refused to work on Sunday. No matter the cost to the business, he had determined twenty years prior, a few months after surrendering his life to Christ, that he would seek to honor the Sabbath by not conducting any business on that day. For Robert, Sunday was a day for rest, a day for worship, and a day for family; and nothing would persuade him differently.

For Robert, his faith was not about rule keeping; it was a genuine conviction in his heart about how to live his life. If Robert quoted a price to one of the local fishermen for shrimp, or crabs, or scallops, or whatever the seasonal fare, he stuck to it, even if he had to absorb the hit. It was this type of conviction, Robert's commitment to being a man of truth and integrity, that had gained him the respect of the commercial fleet that docked in Silver Lake.

Robert got saved in one of the great holiness revivals that had taken place on the island in the sixties. Prior to his salvation experience, or so I came to hear from those in the community whose greatest joy in life was divulging others' secrets, Robert was what the locals referred to as a Rounder. He enjoyed drinking, dancing, and women, and by the time he met Emilis, he had his fair share of all three.

Emilis' father owned a crab plant on Core Sound and had come to Ocracoke on business to meet Lynwood Guthrie, Robert's father. From all reports, Lynwood could be shrewd, but Emilis' father had somehow struck a chord with him and the two became life-long friends. On one particular trip to discuss a business venture with Lynwood, Emilis' father had brought her along.

I remember the night on the Guthrie's front porch when Robert told me of the first time he laid eyes on Emilis.

"Holden, I was stacking boxes of soft crabs on the back of a truck that we were sending to Fulton Fish Market up in New York, when I heard a truck pull up." He recounted as he whittled on a piece of tupelo with his pocket knife.

"I recognized the truck right off, it belonged to Clifford Davis, 'the crab king" as we all called him, from down the sound. Clifford and Daddy had been friends for years. He had been buying about every hard crab we could gather up and was haulin' em back down the sound to Davis where he steamed and picked 'em."

"Anyway," he continued, "before I turned back around to those boxes, out stepped the purtiest girl I had ever seen. She was just like something out of a movie" he said, giving a youthful grin.

"I just stood there. I couldn't move, couldn't speak..." His words trailed off for a moment as he stared off

20

and smiled, then turning to me he continued, "You see, Holden" he said in a serious tone, as he pulled a few more layers off of the wood with his pocket knife, "most of the girls I had been hung up with to that point were, well, kinda rough."

"How did y'all start talkin'?" I pressed eagerly.

"Holden, I couldn't get myself together enough to speak for a while." He said with a chuckle, "Luckily, Clifford broke the silence, "Robby, Where's Lynwood?"

I told him he was in the office doing payroll and then Mr. Davis said something that changed my life:

"Robby, I want you to meet my daughter, Emilis."

"Well, Holden." He continued, "from that moment on there was nobody else in the world for me but Emilis Davis, and within a year she was a Guthrie."

By the time he had finished telling me the story it was near dark and we turned into the house for the night.

"Holden, have you ever been shrimpin'?" he asked as he held the screen door open behind him until I caught it to follow him in.

"No, Mr. Guthrie, I sure haven't."

"Well, son. Keep your schedule free Monday night and we'll go," he said with a smile.

"We best get ready for bed, I don't want to keep you up all night telling you stories, you've got a big day tomorrow." Robert said, patting me on the back.

We made our way to the living room and I sat down in the White House chair as Emilis sat on the sofa, hemming a pair of Robert's dress slacks.

"Your first sermon at the Church! Are you nervous?" Robert asked.

"Yes sir, I have to say that I am."

"You're going to do just fine." He said, "We'll be praying for you. Won't we Emilis!"

"Honey, I've prayed for you all week." She said never taking her eyes off of her needle work.

"Are you going to come hear him?" Robert asked.

"Of course I'll be there." She said with a smile, this time looking up at me from her sewing.

I remember being rather confused and perplexed at this interchange. "Does she not go to Church?" I thought as I sat there amid this confusing dialogue. Robert must have read the look on my face.

"Emilis goes to the Methodist Church, Holden."

There was much more behind that story than I could ever conceive of in my youthful naiveté. But as I faced my own dark night of the soul, I would come to learn a great deal about the complexities of personal convictions and varied theologies.

Entry 5

I was up and out of the bed before daybreak on that first Sunday morning, the deep indigo sky beginning to lighten gently in the east. I gingerly crept down the old wooden stairs, trying not to wake my hosts; however, the sound of the percolator in the kitchen and the unique aroma of Eight O'Clock Coffee filling the first floor of the cottage revealed that I was not the only one stirring in the pre-dawn fall morning. I gently opened the front door and made my way onto the front porch, desperately need-ing some quiet time of reflection and prayer to calm my anxious soul.

After pulling the door to behind me, I took my place in a rocker at the south end of the porch. The island was still sleeping, and the morning calm seemed to settle deep into my soul, a comfortable weight of silent reverence. I just sat there, still, the only interruption to the peaceful morning was my breath, making a slight fog as I exhaled into the chilly autumn air. After a few moments of com-plete calm, the familiar sounds of a flock of Canadian geese broke the silence as they flew low over the house, heading towards Oyster Creek.

There is something about the sound of geese honking as they fly over in v-formation that comforts my soul. I delight in that sound. I can't quite describe the effect it has upon me, bringing back good memories of childhood, which were a precious commodity. The house mama had bought after leaving daddy, the place that we came to know as home, was nestled next to a wildlife refuge with a large pond. I remember so many autumn evenings playing in the yard with John, my older brother, after getting off of the school bus. As the fall afternoons grew increasingly shorter, before mama would open the carport door and call us in for supper, our play would often be temporarily suspended as we paused to watch rafts of Canadian geese fly in toward the pond. I was always fascinated by them.

Something about their sound, the blend of majesty and melancholy in their voices, something about seeing and hearing them just seems to take me back to a warm place, a place of simplicity and childhood innocence. In some way it serves as a reminder to me of God's goodness and His constant presence in my life. I cannot tell you the times when I have been down, anxious, or scared, and a flock would fly over. This may sound extremely silly to some folks, but in those moments I felt like God was sending me a message, a message that He was near and that everything was going to be fine. And here again, on the morning of my first sermon at my first Church, God had sent me another reminder of His care and presence.

I rose from my seat and made my perch upon the porch railing, leaning out until the porch eave no longer blocked my vision, looking up, watching, listening, reveling, until they disappeared from sight behind the tree line. A gentle peace settled over my heart and soul.

My gaze was still fixed on the southern sky and the tree line that had eclipsed my reminder from view when I heard the screen door slowly creak open. I looked over to find Robert backing quietly through the door with a cup of coffee in each hand, steam rising from them and catching the first few rays of warm, golden light as the sun began to peek across the Atlantic.

"Coffee?" he said with eyebrows raised as he offered me a fresh cup of morning brew.

"Yes, sir!" I responded. The chill of the morning had seeped into my core, and I welcomed something warm to ward it off.

"How are you feeling...about the sermon and everything." Robert asked as he sat down in the rocking chair nearest my perch on the porch railing.

"I've been a nervous wreck" I responded. Then I shared with Robert my experience that morning with the geese, and the way it made me feel that God was near.

"I know that may sound a little hokie," I said.

"Not at all, Buddy." Robert replied, "I believe that God knows each of us so well that He knows just how to speak our language." Then he continued...

"The Bible says that 'As a father has compassion on his children, so the Lord shows compassion on those who fear him' and a good father knows just how to show his children love."

"You're right," I replied with a gentle smile.

"It doesn't sound hokie to me at all" Robert said reassuringly, "You got a few minutes to spare?" He asked.

"Sure."

"Now I don't want to mess you up this morning or interfere with your prayer time." He continued.

"No, I've got a few minutes to spare. Church doesn't start for a few more hours"

"I want to take you somewhere real quick". He said.

With that, he got up and headed down the front steps and towards his pickup as I followed curiously.

He cranked the engine of the aging, rusted truck and off we went, down the little oyster shell path and out onto highway 12. We headed north on the road towards the Hatteras ferry and then took a sand path on the right that ran right down the edge of the island's small landing strip. Slowly we made our way through the soft sand, requiring

24

Robert to slip the truck into four wheel drive. The truck
edged closer to the seashore in a strained but determined
fashion and before long we emerged from the dune line.
All that lay on either side were miles of sandy, barren
beach and the Atlantic before us. The water was calm
that morning with just the occasional sea lopping gently
onto the sand, as shorebirds tried to out-dance sheets of
earth covering seawater while gathering their morning
meal.

Robert cut the engine off and we sat there with the
chilly breeze wafting through the truck cab.
"This is my reminder, I guess you could say, Holden."
Robert said. "This is where I come when I especially need
to feel God near."
"This is amazing" I replied, encompassed by a sense of
awe at the majesty and tranquil beauty of the secluded
beach. I had never seen a beach so peaceful. My whole
experience with the ocean was built around Spring Break
in Myrtle Beach, and it was a far cry from the peaceful serenity of the beach at Ocracoke. This place was so pure,
so untouched, so secluded that I felt like we were com-
muning with God as we sat by the shore and allowed the
melodies of the ocean to drown out the chaos and tension
that often hijack life.
"I can't tell you the times that I have had to slip away
and come down here to recharge." He said, his eyes fixed
upon the ocean as he rested his left arm on the windowsill
of the driver's side door.

We sat in silence for probably fifteen or twenty minutes. In some strange but welcomed way I felt as if I
was having a genuine father-son moment for the first
time in my life. That feeling permeated my heart with a
deep sense of gratitude for being in this place with these
people.

Eventually, we made our way back to the house, showered
and dressed for Church. I rode with Robert and Emilis
to the little white, wooden, clapboard Church that would

serve as my first pastorate.

The building was a humble one, but it certainly served the purposes of worship for the islanders who called that congregation home. For those families whose ancestral blood, sweat, prayer, and tears had helped construct the building some seventy years prior, it held a reverential respect, with roots reaching deep into their hearts and religious identity. It was a place where parents and grandparents had prayed, served, celebrated, and been laid to rest. This little white church, though humble and no doubt unimpressive to many tourists passing by, was tied to eternal significance in the lives of the fifty or so islanders who gathered here on the first day of the week to worship Christ, the risen Lord.

The Church was designed as one long rectangular room with its front facing the narrow side road that led to it from highway 12. There was a single large window in the center, directly below the apex of the ridgepole, and an entryway in the bell tower nestled on the right corner of the building. There were three Churches on the island, all of similar style and size. The Methodist Church was nearest to the Guthrie house, adjacent to the island school. There was an Assembly of God Church near the lighthouse in the center of the island. Then, on the north edge of the village was Grace Chapel.

Others could preach whatever types of messages they wished, but in my heart, all I was ever comfortable preaching was grace and compassion. I felt like that was the message of the Gospel, and I was increasingly aware of my own weaknesses and need for such mercy. I always felt really uncomfortable when people talked more about sin than about what Jesus did to fix it. The way I saw it, we were all sinners in need of a grace bigger than our faults and mistakes, deeper than our own misguided attempts and motives, broad enough to wrap us up in a love too deep to really fathom, a love that accepted us warts and all, a love that transforms us.

26

On that first Sunday in my new parish, I preached from one of the best examples of love found in the pages of Scripture, the parable of the loving Father found in the fifteenth chapter of Luke. I remember in college studying Rembrandt's The Return of the Prodigal Son, and feeling that somehow he hadn't gotten it quite right. In all of the versions of this that he had designed, whether etched or painted, it always struck me that the son was kneeling before the father in what always appeared to be the father's domain. But based on Scripture, this reunion happened somewhere away from the house, possibly in a field, possibly on a dusty lane leading home, but the reunion happened as the father left home and ran to meet his returning, hurting son. Why didn't the painting show that? Why didn't we see a picture of the two on a rugged road as the father embraced and kissed his son? This is the type of love that Jesus was telling us our Father has for us. I never understood why we couldn't ever seem to get a good grip on that, why we always viewed God as unmoved rather than as a loving Father Who cared so deeply that He would break a sweat to get to us, then embrace and kiss us before we ever had a chance to speak. I guess it's because most of us have had too little experience with that type of love. At least that's my excuse.

Late on the night before my first sermon, I had enlisted Emilis' help in gathering up some extra white sheets she had in her linen closet. Before we turned in for bed, I had asked Robert to help me with a project. Shortly after ten o'clock we were out in the Church yard hanging white sheets from the gnarled branches of the island oaks. I could tell that Robert was hesitant, but I kept assuring him that it was part of the message.

That Sunday morning as the congregation arrived at the Church, I could hear the low rumbles of people wanting to know what in the world those sheets were all about. As a matter of fact, when we arrived at the Church, locals and tourists alike were riding slowly by, looking out of

27

the windows at all of the white sheets flapping in the sea breeze. Robert kept telling some of the more vocally skeptical members to sit tight, that there was indeed a purpose. That morning I preached from the depths of my heart, but as I always found in preaching, I could never quite tell it the way I felt it; I could never quite get out the fullness of what was in my heart. I told the congregation of an all-loving Heavenly Father who runs to embrace every life-wearied child who yearns for home.

Years before, I had heard an illustration that I felt fitting for the day. The story was told of a young man who left his mother and father, traveling away to live in a distant town. The young man wanted to be free to live as he pleased, and so he left his home and family to embark on a journey of self-discovery. In the end, wearied, dejected, hurting, and alone, he wrote his father, expressing a desire to return. The son indicated that he was going to catch a train home on a particular date and asked that if the father indeed still loved him, and if there was still room for him in the father's arms, the father should hang a white sheet onto the clothes line in the back yard of their little bungalow. The train passed right by the back of the house, and the son had told the father that if he passed by and saw no sheet he would understand and not even get off at the station. As the day came and the train got closer to the house, the son was overcome with anxiety. He explained his situation to a fellow passenger and asked him to look in his stead. The son couldn't take the suspense, eclipsed by the fear of final rejection from his father. As they approached the town, the son closed his eyes, relying upon his new traveling companion to be his scout.

"What do you see?" he asked impatiently, his eyes tightly closed.

"I think you need to see this for yourself", the friend replied.

The son opened his eyes to see white sheets hanging

from clothes lines, fences, tree limbs, and porch railings from one end of the little town to the other. The message wasn't just that he was welcome to sneak back home, enter the back door, and take up a reclusive, shameful residence in the basement. The sea of sheets shouted a message directly from the father's heart, a message that he didn't care what anyone else thought, "You are my son, and with all my heart I want you home in my embrace."

I concluded the sermon that morning by instructing the congregation that, when people asked them the following week, "Why were all those sheets hanging in the Church yard?", that they should tell them that they were welcome home banners for every person who ever feared that God had given up on them. I looked down from the pulpit at my host family, and from the smile on Emilis' face and the tears in Robert's eyes, I could tell I had hit a home run that morning. As parishioners shuffled out of the side bell tower door, there was a sense of a holy hush amongst us. The type of silence that often occurs when God is massaging human hearts.

The message of God's grace and unending love seemed to strike a deep, resonant chord with a number of people in the small congregation. However, I would come to see that there were those in the Church who would not be satisfied unless I preached people into hell every single Sunday, and sounded excited that they were going. Little did I know at the time, but I was about to have my rose-colored glasses slapped from my face and mercilessly smashed on the ground.

Entry 6

The Monday evening following my first sermon, Robert took me on my very first shrimping trip. He had invited a couple of the younger men from the Church to join us, the youngest of them still fifteen years my elder. Just after supper we headed to the community store where

29

Robert gathered up two large paper bag fulls of provisions for the night: honey buns, moon pies, glass bottled Pepsi colas, pretzels, sweet sixteen donuts, and almond joys. By daylight I was thankful for the steady stream of sugar, as I tried to stay awake with the other men in the all-night excursion. As the sun set over the Pamlico I watched in awe as the crew moved in choreographed fashion, lowering the rigging and plunging the trawl boards and nets into the salty water. After an hour of towing, we began the process of hauling back.

I stood in the rear doorway of the cabin and watched the winches on deck spin violently, winding the ropes through blocks attached to the outriggers. Robert told me horror stories of young men who had lost their lives getting their oil skins or gloves caught in those ropes and winches, the cables either crushing them or cutting them in two; and, I didn't budge from inside the cabin door until those winches were shut off.

The smell of the boat's exhaust, mixed with the unmistakable scent of the salt water that dripped from the cables and ropes as they were wound tightly through the steel blocks, was a completely new experience. The cool fall breeze blew across the sound, making me glad that Emilis had packed me a hooded sweatshirt.

In time the trawl doors emerged from the water near the ends of the lowered outriggers, which protruded out eight or ten yards from the sides of the boat. Next came the large green tail bags. Hoisted from the Pamlico, these pregnant nets swung gently back and forth above the culling trays with every roll the Miss Emilis made in the gentle swells. Soon one of the men made his way over to one of the tail-bags and yanked on the cord beneath the large bulge in the webbing, unleashing a rush of seafood that flooded the culling tray, as sting rays lashed their black, whip-like tails in the air. A few blue crabs fell unto the deck, backing their way towards the waist of the boat with claws raised in angry defiance.

I remember how fascinated I was by the catch as it lay in the culling tray. To the boys of the island this was old news, just another night of shrimping on Pamlico Sound. For me, this was an introduction into a completely foreign way of life, a fascinating adventure for a young man who had only ever known life in the tobacco fields of the piedmont.

Once the nets and trawl boards were lowered back for another haul, Robert came out of the wheel house, sliding his gloves on, and we split a culling tray to ourselves. He patiently taught me how to pick up a hard crab without getting pinched, and what to watch for so that I didn't get injured by a sting ray. Robert was as eager to teach me his way of life as I was to learn it. There for the first time in my life I helped cull shrimp, filling galvanized buckets to overflowing with green-tails, some as long as my hand and as big around as a fifty cent piece. After the culling tray had been emptied and washed down with the deck hose, Robert motioned for me to come over to his side at the culling tray.

"I bet you've never headed a shrimp before, have you?"

"No sir, I haven't." I replied.

Robert grabbed a handful of shrimp from the top of the bucket and began showing me how to pinch their heads off.

"You try it!" He urged.

At first it felt a little weird squishing their heads off between the side of the index finger and thumb, but after the first couple I settled into the experience, feeling a sense of accomplishment as I mastered this new skill. After Robert and I headed several pounds, he quickly peeled, deveined, and threw them in a Ziploc bag, which he pulled from the chest pocket of his flannel shirt. Next he headed into the cabin, calling for me to follow him. As I entered the galley Robert was firing up the gas stove.

"Holden, these restaurants on the island advertise fresh seafood. Well, this is what you call fresh seafood." he

31

said as he hauled a large cast iron frying pan out of the cabinet.

Before long he had seasoned and breaded those shrimp, which just thirty minutes before were swimming in the salty waters of Pamlico Sound, and tossed them into the sizzling hot grease of the frying pan. I had never eaten fresh shrimp before, and certainly not at 2:30 in the morning. This new chapter of my life would see many firsts.

By daylight and our return to harbor, I was exhausted. The expedition had been long for one not used to being up all night, fighting blue crabs and heavy eyelids. After we got back to the cottage, I showered, crawled into bed, and didn't rouse until about four o'clock that afternoon.

As my eyes cracked open, I could smell dinner cooking downstairs. I got up, dressed and made my to the kitchen table, wiping the sleep from my eyes.

"So, what did you think about it?" Robert asked me, as I sat down next to him at the dinner table.

"I loved it!" I said, yawning.

"Would you want to have to do that every night?" He asked with a smile.

"No, sir. I don't believe I loved it that good!"

At this, Robert let out a hearty laugh.

"I don't either, buddy." Robert said. "I've done it a many a year; now I'm more than happy to let the young guns take her out for me."

It didn't take me very long after moving here to realize that the men of the island refer to their boats and their trucks with feminine pronouns.

Life on Ocracoke was an adventure. Learning all the nuances that make coastal living such a fascinating existence was a constant and enjoyable task. I enjoyed my life on the island so much in those early days. It was an adventure that would take me into many uncharted territories.

Entry 7

With the progression of Fall came Thanksgiving, and I dutifully drove home to spend the holiday with my family in Johnston County. Being with my family, after moving to Ocracoke, always came with mixed emotions. It was good to see my mother and siblings, although I must admit my trips to Johnston County were more often elicited from a sense of obligation than desire. My older brother, John, would be home from NC State. He had already graduated with his Bachelor's Degree a year prior and was completing the first semester of his MBA. My younger brother, Samuel, still lived at home with Mama and was preparing to enlist in the Navy after the first of the year.

When we were young, as far as I was concerned, the sun and moon rose and set upon John. I guess it's not a terribly uncommon sentiment for one to hold with regard to his big brother. The lack of attention given me by Dad was supplemented by the attention that John provided me in the turbulent world of our childhood.

While Dad was a hard-working man, and a decent financial provider, he was also an alcoholic. I had carefully and conveniently omitted this detail from the familial description I presented to Robert and Emilis on our first evening together. Not only was father an alcoholic, he was a mean drunk. We never knew what would be the igniting spark, the catalyst of his drunken rage following an afternoon with his whiskey out in the tobacco barn. It could be something as minuscule as mom browning the meat more than he liked; and ultimately she would find herself gathering the meal she had prepared from the kitchen floor, along with shards of broken glass and china. More often than not, those soiled morsels of food would be mingled with drops of blood, falling tragically from Mama's nose and lip, mixing themselves with the puddles of sweet tea, coffee, gravy, grits, or whatever else had been wiped from the kitchen table by my father's fear-evoking forearms. I came to know this sight well. My tender nature, combined with my deep affinity for my mother, placed me at her side on those evenings, helping, comforting, cleaning, and crying.

John found his coping mechanism in retreat. When things became tense, John disappeared. He would excuse himself and find respite in the forest beyond the tobacco farm, along the brook that wound around the back of our property. Over the years my big brother had constructed a camp there, a refuge from slamming doors, breaking glass, mom and brother's cries, and the haunting creaks from our parents' room, after the drunken left-overs of our father would drag Mama in there, slamming the door behind them.

After mom became pregnant with Samuel, the dynamic changed a bit. Perhaps even in his drunken state Dad knew that mother's condition was fragile. During those long months before Samuel was born, father's alcohol induced rage found another victim in its crosshairs.

In some ways our personalities reminded me of Jacob and Esau. I had always been a momma's boy, staying more around the house, while John was the All-American jock. Needless to say, I was usually near when father staggered through the kitchen door.

There are so many things that I have sought to block out concerning those early years. After Samuel was born, instead of going back to abusing mother exclusively, Dad kept us both as the objects of his derision. The effects of that time in my life have been deep and long-lasting. To this day my anxiety reaches almost uncontrollable levels whenever I find myself in volatile situations, or witness a father being heavy handed with his kids. There are some experiences of life too vivid to will from remembrance. Such was the evening of my seventh birthday.

On that chilly November night, mother and I were in the kitchen putting the finishing touches on my birthday cake. She had been teaching me a little bit about cooking and had helped me mix, bake and ice my own cake that year. I was so proud of that chocolate cake with strawberry icing. Ever since childhood that has been my favorite type of cake, a standing request for every birthday.

John was at the other end of the table finishing up my homemade birthday card, and Samuel must have been in the other room sleeping. It had the makings of a perfect birthday. I had mama at my side, my perfect work of art was receiving its last touches of pink frosting, and John, my hero, was sitting just feet away engulfed in his coloring, cutting, and pasting.

I would come to realize through the progression of those early years that, on some level, we were all holding our breath. Dad was always the wild card that could change the entire trajectory of the game, and it was never for the better. We were all, in varying levels of awareness, hoping that this one perfect evening could escape disruption. However, true to form, father would not allow this special time to exist without his famous signature of destruction.

I remember Dad coming in the back door, slurred of speech and staggering. Before I knew it John was gone, taking my card with him. Mother, in her usual careful and fearful way, tried to make peace and disengage hostility before it had a chance to explode.

Dad wanted to know what the cake was for, a painful disclosure of my worth in his eyes. Mother tried to play off his oversight, gently reminding him that it was my birthday. Instead of an apology, a hug, or a birthday wish from this stranger who lived in my house, came a drunken tirade.

"A pink birthday cake?" he retorted, "Only a sissy would have a pink birthday cake."

"Johnny, please..." mother tried to gently, fearfully intervene.

Dad was undaunted, "Is that what you are Holden, a sissy?"

35

"No", I mumbled through tears of pain, insult, and shame. With his words he had not only crushed the pride I had in my work of art, but had annihilated my self-esteem and shamed me concerning my personhood. "What's that?" he continued, unrelentingly, regardless of mother's attempts to intervene, "Are you a sissy? Boy, answer me! Huh? Are you?"

At this mother moved between me and the monster with whom I shared a last name. I shuddered in fear and anticipation of what was coming. Mother's frame was too frail to stand against the grotesque weakness of the horrific genie that emerged from every bottle of Wild Turkey he consumed. Before I knew it, he had pushed mother out of the way and into the corner cabinet. Within seconds he was breathing his hot, liquor tainted breath in my young, flushed face, as I sat there with my chin tucked into my chest, shaking, looking down, trying desperately to avoid eye contact.

"Look at me, you little sissy," he ordered through slurred speech.

I raised my little blue eyes without lifting my chin from my chest, cautiously making eye contact with the person I feared most in the world.

"No son of mine is going to have a pink birthday cake!" With that, he hurled my cake across the room. I winced. Opening my eyes I found pink icing, intermingled with bits of the chocolate layers, smearing the wall. The bulk of the cake lie on the floors, a pile of mangled confection to match the broken spirit which lay bleeding on the floor of my seven year old soul. Mother tried again to intervene, but this time it was a back hand across the face, leaving her curled against the corner cabinet holding her jaw as tears and sobs erupted from deep inside. She begged frantically for him to stop.

At that moment something happened inside of me. I don't know if what came next was based on language I acquired from eighth graders on the school bus, or from some of the soap operas I would watch with Mama on days when I was home from school, 'sick', waiting for bruises which clothing couldn't conceal to disappear. Irregardless, in that moment I lost all timidity for the first time in my life.

"You go to hell!" I said in a low but deliberate tone. "What did you say to me?" he snarled as my moment of bravery quickly passed and I settled back into mute terror. "Don't, please!" I heard Mama scream just before father snatched me from my seat, throwing me to the floor.

Then it happened.

At that moment I heard a sound that still sends shock waves reverberating through my core whenever I am presented with the slightest semblance of it. Father's belt made a dreadful hissing sound as he pulled it violently through his belt loops with one violent yank of his arm.

Either he meant to kill me that night, or he was too drunk to realize which side of the belt was in his hand as he went to work on my back side. The feeling of his belt buckle as it beat and cut me from the base of my neck to my upper thighs is still a haunting memory. I just remember feeling completely helpless. There was nowhere to go, no way to escape, no chance of fighting back, and so I just lay face down on the cold linoleum, crying as the lashing continued.

My whole life I have tried desperately to hide those scars, taking the shower head nearest the wall in my college dorm, or wearing a tee shirt even at the beach. Still, there were moments when a buddy or girlfriend would catch a glimpse and I would use my standard, masked statement. To inquiring minds, those scars were a result of my falling onto a piece of farming equipment from the seat of my father's tractor as a child.

Somehow Mama managed to regain enough strength to wedge herself between me and my assailant, absorbing some of the blows herself. Amidst the reprieve secured by Mama's frame, John reappeared and helped me up

37

and into our bedroom, locking the door behind us. After John pulled me up from the floor, all I remember is a mix of Mama's pleas for reprieve, dad's drunken curses and threats, the sound of Samuel crying from the other room, breaking glass, the warm, wet sensation of blood trickling down my young back, and the feeling of John's arms holding my weight as he partly led, partly dragged me through the room, out of our bedroom window, and onto the back porch.

That cold, clear November night, beneath a deep sapphire sky and low hung moon, two young brothers, one seven and one ten, hurriedly made their way through the frigid air in silence. That night John saved my life and stole me away to the only place of solace he had known, his little camp deep in the woods.

I can almost feel the chill that crept into my bones as John cleaned my wounds with his shirt, which he dipped into the frigid waters of the brook. All I remember of the rest of that night was my breath turning to smoke in the cold night air, the moonlight cascading through near bare red oak trees, and the cover of a blanket that John must have secured from our house at some point during the construction of his safe haven. John simply held me that night beneath the leaf linted blanket, drawing my head in close to his chest.

The events of that evening cemented a long-standing, impenetrable bond of brotherhood. Somehow, in those earlier years, not even Samuel was able to press his way into our alliance. A fact that for years brought tinges of sadness and regret to my heart, wondering if his chronic unsettledness in life and his propensity towards social deviance may have been tempered had the two of us been more closely engaged with him. Both John and I were secretly hoping that Samuel's upcoming involvement in the military would help him find his way. Nevertheless, no matter the regret where Samuel was concerned, the wounds of those early years forged a deep bond between the two brothers who lived to tell of them.

The next morning we were awakened by the sounds of breaking twigs and a host of male voices echoing through the woods, beckoning our names in repeated succession. The sight of a little boy's blood speckling cold linoleum from the kitchen table to our bedroom window was enough to unleash previously untapped resources of strength welled deep inside our frail little mother. Once father passed out that night, she made her way through the same cold, night air with little Samuel on her hip, bound for our preacher's house three miles away. Following Mama's brave exodus, our world became much safer and a little happier as we adjusted to our new normal, no longer walking on egg shells or cowering under beds.

The local sheriff gave mother the choice between dad or us kids. She chose us. Dad was apprehended, and a search was launched. The men of the community frantically combed the tobacco fields and woods surrounding our farm, searching for two little boys who they prayed had survived the long cold night.

My lacerations were deep and I had sustained two cracked ribs. I remember the Sheriff carrying me from John's camp to an ambulance parked in our driveway early the next morning. In all, they put fifty two stitches in my back and we were sent to live with a foster family until the courts teased out the details.

The sight of my beaten and scourged backside so moved the sheriff and the judge that our father was never allowed to return to our home. Dad was incarcerated and eventually moved to Georgia to live with family. Beyond that I have no clue as to what happened to him. For years I was plagued by a recurring nightmare of waking to find him at my bedroom door. After quite a few years, many prayers, and therapy, that dream seemed to dissipate.

Mama found meager work as a seamstress in a local textile mill to support us, supplemented by help received from Social Services. The local Church also took us in their embrace, feeding us in about every way one can imagine. This combination of arms into which my family fell on the first day of the rest of our lives helped to foster in each of us a great love for Christ and His Church, and a sense of loyalty to the democratic party that seemed to extend help to lost causes such as single mothers with three young mouths to feed.

That same year we left our tobacco farm, with all of its painful memories, and moved into government housing in town. While it was a much better arrangement than what we had known prior, we young country boys missed the forests and tobacco fields. Eventually, Mama secured a small brick ranch style home in the country, with a yard all our own. It's to this little brick home that we return each year for the holidays.

Try as we may to escape the pain of those early years, it still lingers. Those events did something to mama, robbing her of some deep sense of identity and confidence, reducing her to a quiet and withdrawn woman, a mere shell of the vibrant, fun loving woman she was reported to have been prior to marrying my dad. People really understand too little about the deep and far reaching effects of abuse. It's like most other things, until you have an apple out of that bag, you really don't understand.

That Thanksgiving was spent like most others we had celebrated after becoming teenagers. John, Samuel and I camped out on the couch telling stories of college pranks, dating fiascos, and dreams for the future, while mama slaved away in the kitchen. We no doubt loved each other; however, I came to see that my relationship with my family had somewhere along the way become an obligation rather than a joy. Our collective story was based in the stark realities of dreams shattered and abuses too brutal for timid ears. It was as if a subtle yet heavy cloud hung over our table as we shared holiday meals, the only reprieve coming during periodic escapes when John and I would run into town on an errand. On these

40

excursions John and I were lifted above the weight that seemed to surround our time with Mama and Samuel. Maybe it was Samuel's unspoken resentment at always feeling an outsider in his own family. Maybe it was Mama's unescapable regrets concerning the life to which we had been exposed, or the stark juxtaposition of hopes for our future against the inability to provide any material support in making those a reality, or maybe the haunting memory of her little boy's blood dotting the floor of that long-left dwelling. Maybe it was the haunting image of her two young sons making their way, slow and wounded, across the tobacco field that cold November evening, a glimpse she silently caught from the kitchen window as she absorbed her last night of physical, verbal, and sexual abuse from my father. Maybe it was mine and John's secret resentment of Mama for the sadness she lived under, or our frustrations with Samuel for always finding new ways to screw up. Whatever the underlying current, the nightmare of those early years robbed something from all of us that we were never able to regain.

After a couple of days in Johnston County, it was time to make my way back to my new island home, which persistently, inwardly beckoned my return. After our belabored goodbye and Mama's ritual of offering a prayer of blessing and protection over us before we left, we each embraced and expressed our love, each in his own unique way. John would take Samuel in a great big bear hug, leaning back and lifting him off the floor, a tactic he had been employing since we were kids, one which he refused to give up even though Samuel had actually grown a few inches taller than he was. John would always take me under his right arm and tousle my hair with his fingers.

Each of us would give mama a kiss and a strong hug before we left. She would always ask us if we had enough money, even though we all knew that if our answer were "no" she could have done very little to have helped. Yet, I don't doubt for a moment that she would have given us

41

her last dime of grocery money if she thought we were in need.

While John was always quick to lecture Samuel, my love seemed to take on a different, more nurturing role. I always tried to make sure that Samuel had what he needed. I wanted him to have as normal of a high school life as possible.

Mama provided all she possibly could, but luxuries were hard to come by in our house. Therefore, I would set aside money from my summer work in the tobacco fields, and my winter job at the Piggly Wiggly, in order to ensure that Samuel had the things he needed. I distinctly remember Samuel's first middle school basketball game and how the events of that morning were the beginning of my mission to look after my little brother in more tangible ways.

He was so proud of his uniform and the fact that he was on the team; however, the enthusiasm was soon eclipsed by the cruel realities of poverty and class divisions. Mama was barely making ends meet and had only been able to afford a pair of generic high tops from the local K-Mart, though Samuel had his heart set on a pair of converse sneakers like the other boys wore. I sat in the bleachers, my eyes welling with tears, my heart hot with indignation as I watched boys from more affluent families pointing, whispering and snickering at Samuel's shoes. He just sat there, a vulnerable target for their unjust amusement.

I never mentioned what I had seen to Samuel. After the game I came home, took the small television I had worked all summer in the tobacco fields to afford, and sold it to a kid down the road for the price of a pair of new converse sneakers. At the next game Samuel had just as good as the other boys, and I made an internal commitment that my little brother would never experience that type of humiliation again. In my heart, as long as I had a dollar to my name or a piece of bread to eat,

42

Samuel did as well.

Before I left the house that November day, I walked
with Samuel back to his bedroom and made sure that
he had some cash. I was paid a meager salary at the
Church, and Robert had been paying me rather gener-
ously for helping him around the fish house throughout
the week, so I was doing the best I ever had financially.
I slipped Samuel a fifty dollar bill, hoping and praying
that he would use it wisely and not spend a dime of it on
alcohol, though I feared that's exactly where some of it
would end up.

After giving each other a hug, I made my way back
to my car and headed east, eager for the smell of salt air,
Emilis' fig cake, and the comfort of my long talks with
Robert on the front porch swing. Mama stood on the
front stoop waving until I was out of sight. I loved my
family, in the way a child whose family has caused him so
much pain does love his family; but I must admit that as
my relationship with Robert and Emilis grew, my connection to Johnston County began to wane. I was so hungry
for love and belonging; and that's exactly what I was finding in my new home at the end of the oyster paved lane.

Entry 8

I caught the afternoon ferry from Cedar Island and
arrived back on Ocracoke just before nightfall, the days
growing shorter as December approached. I loved winter
evenings on Ocracoke, with rafts of ducks flying in off the
Pamlico at sunset leading to calm starlit nights. I often
drove down to the Guthrie's fish house when the winter
nights were especially still and clear, lying with my back
on the wooden dock, looking towards heaven in mute
meditation.

I pulled off of the ferry and made my way to my island refuge, parking in my spot beside Robert's truck. As
I made my way onto the porch, my duffle bag of laundry
in one hand and a pecan pie Mama had sent in the other,

43

I could hear music coming from inside the cottage. Holding my duffle bag between my knees, I opened the screen door and then the heavy wooden plate glass door which now stayed closed as the winter chill permeated the air. As soon as I entered the door I heard Emilis' voice above the Christmas record swirling on the turntable in the corner of the living room.

"Holden! You're just in time!" she said as she made her way across the living room, a Christmas ornament in each hand. In the background Karen Carpenter was singing of chestnuts roasting on an open fire.

"Did you have a good Thanksgiving, Darlin?" she said as she gave me a hug, being careful not to drop the blown glass ornaments she was holding.

"What do you have there?" she said, casting her gaze on the pie I balanced in my right hand.

"Mama wanted to send you one of her pecan pies."

"Well, let's have a piece right now!" She said as she took it from my hands and headed towards the kitchen. "Would you like some coffee to go with it, Holden?"

"Sure." I replied.

"Robert, do you want some of this pecan pie that Holden's mother made?" She asked.

"That I do!" Robert replied with a grin. "I wish you'd have been here an hour ago, so I could have lucked out of this job." He said with a smile, getting down from the stool he was using to finish the lights on the top of the tree. Before long I was on the step stool next to the tree they brought from Beaufort the day before, helping Robert finish stringing the lights.

Every Thanksgiving Robert and Emilis would drive one of the smaller fish trucks onto the ferry and head for Davis to spend a couple of days with Emilis' parents and siblings. Before returning, they would drive into the old port town of Beaufort and purchase some North Carolina Fraser Firs from the Rotary; and on the Saturday following Thanksgiving, Christmas decorating at the Guthrie cottage shifted into high gear.

I had known nothing of this kind of Christmas. We were fortunate to get a tree the week of Christmas, when the local grocer would put the dried out, picked over ones on clearance. To the Guthries, Christmas was the crown jewel of the year, and their excitement and love of the Season was infectious.

It took about a week of constant work for Emilis to get everything in order. The seafood market seemed to slow a bit as Christmas approached, with the exception of the numerous bushels of oysters Robert would buy and sell for the host of Christmas and New Year's oyster roasts conducted throughout the region. This allowed him a little more time at home, completing a steady stream of honey-do's in preparation for the coming weeks of enter-taining.

Robert's demeanor was so different from what I had witnessed in my dad. I watched as he quietly, and seemingly joyfully completed the list of tasks that Emilis outlined for him on those cold and often wet December days. There was always a parade of trees for him to bring in from the little house. The one we finished decorating upon my return to the island was just the first of many. Before the first dinner party, there would be one in the dining room, one in the foyer by the narrow wooden staircase, and a small tree in the breakfast room decorated with tartan ribbon and gingerbread cookies which filled the entire first floor of the cottage with the warm scents of ginger and cinnamon.

Robert had the task of getting all of those trees trimmed and secured in their stands throughout the house. Sometimes having to drive a nail in the wall, steadying the tree by tying it up with a piece of twine that he would pull from one of his net needles, always careful to do it in an inconspicuous location away from the sight of onlookers, since Emilis would have a steady stream of those from now until the 23rd of the month.

45

Early one Monday morning, in that first December on the island, there was a knock at bedroom door.

"Holden."

I recognized Robert's voice calling quietly through the wooden panels.

"Yes." I said, still half asleep.

"I'm getting ready to run around the back the of island and get some cedar for Emilis, do you want to go?"

"Sure, just let me get dressed."

"It's right smart cold this morning. You might want to put on some long-handled drawers," He instructed. To most people where I was from these particular items of clothing were referred to as long johns or thermal underwear, but somehow in the coastal region they had come to be known as long handled drawers, one of many colloquial expressions making this culture and its dialect so unique.

I got up and dressed hurriedly, washing the sleep from my eyes in the pedestal sink of the small bathroom at the head of the stairs. From the bathroom window I could see frost on the back lawn, glistening in the first few rays of sunlight.

After making my way downstairs I sat down with Robert at the breakfast table, spread with light rolls, bacon, and fried mullet roe. Emilis had made the bacon just for me, since I was never able to stomach the taste of mullet roe. I couldn't understand how Robert could eat that stuff, especially for breakfast.

I spread my light roll with the salted whipped cream that Emilis had fixed for us, the buttery roll almost melting in my mouth. As we ate our breakfast, Emilis was busy measuring flour and spices, her white and blue check apron slightly dusted as she stirred a large ceramic bowl containing the batter for her famous fig cake.

Robert finished his last swig of coffee as he rose from his seat.

"Well man, are you ready?"

"Yes sir" I replied as I finished my last piece of bacon and

46

grabbed a light roll for the trip.

"Now you all leave those dishes right there, I'll get them cleaned up in just a minute." Emilis interjected.

Robert walked over and kissed her.

"Now you all be careful out there on that water." She instructed.

"We will." Robert replied.

"Thank you for breakfast, Miss Emilis." I said before leaving the table.

"You're welcome, my Darlin." She said.

"All right," Robert interjected, "we'll be back about lunch time".

We headed out to the pick-up, still cold and frosted in the early December morning. The beams of the morning sunlight offering gentle warmth and illuminating the frosted windshield, revealing the web-like designs in the ice that obscured our vision. Robert started the truck and cranked the defrost to high. After a few minutes Robert backed from the drive and we made our way to the fish house, the defrost securing just enough visibility above the dash to navigate. It was a cold calm morning as we wound around the east side of Silver Lake, the old white lighthouse standing sentinel on our left.

The fish house was down on the shore almost directly across from the ferry dock, accessed by a sandy road that led through scrub oaks and cedars. I wondered why we didn't just get the cedar from right there, but I would soon learn that Emilis wanted juniper with its frosted blue berries; and Robert had a special spot where he could get her all she wanted.

We made our way into the fish house, quiet in the early December morning. The unique smell of salt water, seafood, and damp cement floors permeated the air inside of the white plywood walls. We made our way to the room housing the conveyer belt, where fish were sorted and weighed.

If the white cottage minutes away was Emilis' masterpiece, then the fish house was Robert's domain. He walked ahead of me to the wall adjacent the fish conveyor, where a row of nails in the wall provided ample hanging space for a collection of Helly Hansen oil skin jackets and overhauls in white, green, and orange. Robert inspected the labels until he found a pair he thought would make a decent fit on my smaller frame.

"Here you go partner, I think these will do." He said. "I'm gonna have to get you a pair of your own."

By the end of the next week, Robert came into the house toting a large cardboard box he had just retrieved from the post office. He smiled as he sat the parcel on the kitchen table in front of me. Once the seals were broken and the packing paper moved aside, I found that Robert had made good on his promise, my very own set of white oilskins.

After putting our gear on and hopping gingerly from the dock into Robert's twenty foot white wooden skiff, we made our way out of the harbor. I couldn't believe how clear the water got that time of year. I could see clear to the bottom, to sand spotted with shells, oyster rocks, and the occasional conch. The sky was Carolina Blue with only a few pure white clouds dusting the horizon. The sound was near 'slick-cam', the phrase used by the local fishermen to describe the water when it appeared slick as glass.

We wound around the Northeast side of the Island, past Northern Pond and Oyster Creek, to the marshland beyond Gap Point where a series of canals lay sprinkled with a mixture of scrub oaks, junipers, and yaupon bushes. It was so peaceful out there, away from all sounds of cars and ferry horns. Granted, Ocracoke village was not writhing with the sounds of a big city, but out there in the marshland behind the island, it was perfectly still.

I hadn't grown up in this culture and I didn't share the sentiment of having salt water in my blood, a trait ascribed to the local boys; nevertheless, there was something captivating about being out here on the water, the cold wind cutting at my cheeks as the boat coasted across the sound, sending tears trickling from the corners of my eyes. Out here with Robert, drinking ice cold Pepsi colas, eating moon pies, and taking a leak off the leeward side of the boat was like a dream come true for me. This kind, compassionate, hardworking man was all I could have ever wanted in a father. Every outing, every word of affirmation he gave, every time he taught me a new skill, it was like cool water on parched ground, nourishment to a soul that had searched its whole life for a father who cared.

We made our way towards shore, Robert shoved the bow of the skiff into the edge of the marsh near a cluster of trees, and I jumped from the bow onto the cord grass, anchor in hand. After securing the anchor in the muddy earth, we made our way to the cluster of trees, clippers and hatchets in hand.

Sure enough, they were laden with the blue berries Emilis was so fond of and we began clipping. In just under an hour we had enough juniper and yaupon, with its silver bark and bright red berries, to fill Robert's skiff from bow to stern, leaving just enough space for us to stand beside the steering stick on the way back to the dock.

The hull of the boat gently skipped across the face of the cold, slick water on our way back to Silver Lake, leaving a stream of white water churned by our propeller and a v-shaped wake curling out from the edges of the stern. Passing Oyster Creek, a raft of red heads flew over and landed off shore, their fast winged flight and distinctive calls as much a part of winter on the island as snow to New England. Once the skiff was hitched securely back at the long wooden dock, we began our series of trips from skiff to truck, transporting armfuls of clippings at the time. Once the skiff was emptied and swept of debris, we fired up Robert's pickup and headed for home.

49

For the first time in my life I felt I belonged somewhere.

Entry 9

"We'll haul all of this into the little house, there, Hold-en." Robert said, nodding his head in the direction of the squatty structure as we climbed out of the pickup and slammed the heavy doors in succession. Robert had already cleaned off his work-bench for Emilis and we placed the clippings in their respective piles on the concrete floor. The work bench, which one week prior had been laden with wrenches, screw drivers, and drill bits, now held spools of red velvet ribbon, floral wire, and wreath forms. Over the next week Emilis would whittle those mammoth piles of greenery into nothing more than scraps of bare twigs. By the weekend live juniper wreaths and crimson bows adorned each window of the little cottage and live garland swags draped from the porch railings. The front door boasted a large cedar and yaupon wreath, the bright red berries interrupted only by swags of grey cotton netting and the occasional scotch bonnet that Emilis had combed from the beach through the years. On either side of the door were galvanized buckets, like the ones Robert and I piled with shrimp on my first night aboard his trawler, which Emilis had draped with netting and filled with evergreens and gnarled bare dogwood branches from the side yard. The decorating spree didn't end with the cottage either. There were wreaths and red bows for the bow of every boat in Robert's fleet. And just in case anyone dare discount her taste in doing so, those wreath clad trawlers had appeared in the pages of Southern Living and the National Fisher-man.

It was as if I were living in a dream, like this was all too happy, too perfect, too good to be true. Eventually, I found myself wrestling with jaded envy to accompany the deep love and respect I had for the Guthries, the emergence of those feelings producing massive internal conflict. Why were their lives so perfect? How could they hover here on this plain of happiness and wealth, while my family and I had suffered such destruction and need? I began grappling with feelings of resentment regarding the very ones I loved so dearly. I resented them for their lack of suffering in life, indignant that I had suffered more than I felt was my rightful share.

One evening at dinner I grew weary of their conversation of plans for the upcoming string of Christmas parties, wrestling through my private internal accusatory dialogue. While they talked of the Methodist Women's circle brunch, Robert's men's ministries oyster roast, and the employee Christmas gathering, I was stewing guiltily as I thought of my poor mother scraping to get by and the sad Christmases of my childhood. I concluded that these people lived in some type of dream world, that they had no clue what life could really be like. Finally, I excused myself from the table and went to my room.

That night at about twelve-thirty I woke to a sound of muffled cries coming from below. I lay there motionless for a few moments. The sobs continued, interspersed with low tones of conversation. I quietly got out of bed and made my way downstairs. Something was wrong, something bad must have happened. Down the narrow staircase I came, walking softly so as to avoid any creaks in the old wooden steps. Upon reaching the cold wooden floor of the foyer, I slowly leaned forward, peeking around the door frame into the living room. My eyes adjusted slowly from the dark of the foyer to the light of the Christmas tree in the corner of the den.

Robert was slumped over with his head buried in Emilis bosom, weeping. Tears were rolling silently down her cheeks, falling onto his blue oxford cloth shirt as she held him, gently rubbing his back. I was hesitant to make my presence known, but Emilis caught sight of me leaning against the doorframe and motioned gently for me to come in.

51

I had no clue what was happening, I simply knew that they were devastated and I wasn't quite sure how to respond. I placed one hand on Emilis' shoulder and the other on Robert's back and silently began to pray for them both. Had someone died? What was happening? Robert was a gentle, compassionate man, but I had never known him to wear his emotions loosely. As I placed my hand upon his back he erupted into sobs even deeper than I had heard from my room. As I looked closer, I saw that Robert was clutching something against his stomach.

Eventually, the emotions slightly ebbed and I took a seat in the arm chair across from the sofa where Emilis and Robert were seated. Robert sat there, head in hands, while Emilis gazed solemnly at the tree. In the somber quietness, I followed her gaze toward the tree as I fought back my own tears, evoked from seeing Robert so devastated.

Through sniffles Robert broke the silence, still looking down at the coffee table that separated us.
"Holden, I'm sorry you had to see me like this." He said.
"It's okay, Robert." I replied. No apology was needed. I was just curious as to the catalyst.
"As much as we love Christmas," he continued, "it's a hard time for us."
I sat in silence just respecting his right to share as much or as little as he wanted without the intrusion of my questions.
"We had a son," he spoke these three words and once again was reduced to sobs, Emilis biting her bottom lip to keep back the tears.

That night emotions oscillated between heaving sobs and tear stained laughter, as they shared the story of their late son, his good looks, his level head, his loving ways, his gentle spirit, his wit and fun-loving charisma, his love of the water. Then they told of the cancer that robbed him of his youth and the Guthries of their wide-eyed dreams regarding his future. As they continued, I recognized

the object which Robert had been clutching so tightly.
Beneath his arm was a small black teddy bear, worn, ratty
looking, and missing one of its arms. It went without saying that this love wearied lump of stuffed fabric had been
the traveling companion of a little boy whose life had
been ripped from him far too soon.

What I saw in Robert and Emilis that evening would be
echoed in the faces of many others in years to come, the
pain that comes with the unfair task of having to bury a
loved one before it seems time. That night, my misgivings
towards the Guthries were replaced with empathy and
renewed respect. They had not existed in some painless,
privileged dream. They had indeed drunk from the well
of human suffering, which provides unwanted nourishment to most all of us at some point in life. The loss had
been devastating, and the shattered dreams borne to the
cemetery with their sixteen year old son were too many
to name. The saltiness of tears were not foreign to their
palate; however, the Guthries possessed a resolve I had
never seen. Suffering had awakened resiliency in them,
an appreciation for what they had been given, for the
time they had with their son, brief as it was. That night I
learned some valuable lessons: Life often isn't fair, pain is
inevitable, but we have a choice in the wake of the storm.
The choice to be made is whether we will persevere or
surrender to the devastation.

Entry 10

The morning after I learned of Robert Jr., we gathered
around the kitchen table for breakfast, just as we did most
every morning. Robert had already been to the fish house
at day break and given instructions to the crew. He was
taking the day off to help Emilis around the house. After
breakfast, we headed out onto the porch to hang garlands.
Robert and I would hold our respective ends of the
greenery, while Emilis stood off in the front yard giving us
instructions.

53

As we stood there, taking orders from our foreman, my concentration was broken by a dark green Cadillac pulling up in the driveway, eclipsing my little, silver Honda. I raised myself from my half-bent stature over the front railing, making eye contact for the first time with a woman who would come to impact me more deeply and spiritually than possibly any other person in my entire life.

Jane Anne was Emilis' younger sister and had come to spend a few days with Emilis and Robert, mainly to help Emilis get things in order for her annual Methodist Women's Circle Christmas party. As the wide, heavy door of the shiny new Cadillac swung open, out stepped a tall, slender, stately woman. She was dressed like Jackie Kennedy, her tall, slender frame accentuated by her black heels and bright red finger nails. As similar as they were in some ways, I would come to see that Emilis and Jane Anne were no more carbon copies of one another than Suzanne and Julia Sugarbaker. While both knew how to carry themselves, sharing the same social etiquette and impeccable taste in clothes, Emilis and Jane Anne had very different personalities. Emilis was the quintessential southern magnolia, a soft-spoken, delicate woman with poise and decorum. Jane Anne was larger than life. She had a sense of humor and dry wit that left us all weeping with laughter, our sides aching from the deep chuckles that at times threatened to take our very breath. She could tell jokes better than anyone I had ever met, but her real-life stories were even more hilarious. Nevertheless, there was a very deep side to Jane Anne. She possessed a deep faith that took her into completely different channels than many who become pharisaical in their religious expression. Even Robert, as well as myself in those early years, had a tendency to become rather legalistic. Sadly, we can often become more concerned with the splinter in our brother or sister's eye than the plank in our own.

If Jane Anne was ever going to err, it would be on the side of grace and love. It was these streams of compassion, pouring from Jane Anne like a river, which would be my lifeline in a time when I was afraid all hope for me was lost. Jane Anne never cast aside anyone that she loved, and she was convinced beyond persuasion that God felt the same way.

If there was one thing of which Jane Anne was convinced, it was the complete work of salvation that Christ had accomplished on the cross. Unlike me, who lived an existence of fear that I would somehow make a mistake too great for forgiveness, Jane Anne was more assured of the security of our salvation than anyone I have ever known. It was a concept that I had trouble accepting as a result of the years of performance based religion to which I had been indoctrinated, but one that would settle into my soul as the years went by, bringing with it such grace and peace, leaving me to wish only that I could have embraced it much sooner.

"Hey, my Darlin!" she called to me from the driveway. She raised her hand to her mouth, placing a cigarette between her lips as she closed her car door. Robert loved Jane Anne like his own sister, but he despised cigarettes with a passion and found a deep sense of enjoyment in giving her a hard time about them.

"Haven't you quit smoking them things yet?" I heard him call from behind me on the other end of the porch.

"Now Robert, don't make me kick your ass right here in front of the preacher," she replied with a mischievous grin. She and Robert had such a fun relationship and he let out a hearty laugh at her response. There was always some form of jeering and banter between the two of them. Banter as they may, Robert had a deep respect for Jane Anne and an appreciation for the deep bond of sisterhood she and Emilis shared. When Robert Jr. was diagnosed with cancer, it was Jane Anne who moved in and helped keep them all afloat throughout the sickness. She kept the house, made the meals, anointed her teenage nephew with oil, fasted and prayed for him, and helped get Emilis out of bed on days when she would have rather not faced reality. In the midst of the darkness that hung over the Guthrie house for the seven months during Robert Jr.'s illness, and the years ensuing his death, Jane Anne's particular brand of humor, her ability to bring laughter into even the most somber moments, became a mainstay of strength and recovery for Robert and Emilis.

Jane Anne made her way up the steps toward me and gave me a hug. Then, she backed away from me slightly and exclaimed, "Well, you're the purtiest man I've ever seen".

I must admit that I didn't know how to take such a compliment right at first, nor did I understand that, in the coastal brogue, pretty was pronounced purty. She was, in fact, giving me a compliment. I must have blushed because Robert interjected.

"Jane Anne don't embarrass him." He interceded.
She continued undaunted,
"Robert, now some men are handsome, but some are just down right purty, and that's a purty man." She said as she squeezed my arm.

In those first few encounters with Jane Anne I was both flattered and a little embarrassed. I wasn't sure if she was a cougar or just flattering me out of politeness. However, as our relationship grew deeper, it was just such affirmations and playful humor that served to lift me above a heaviness of mind that was becoming a pervasive, constant companion. She was always reminding me: "Now Holden, the Scripture says that a merry heart does good like medicine." She held a conviction of not letting life get too serious. She always reminded me to keep everything in proper perspective.

Legalistic Jane Anne was not. I remember Emilis telling me once about an incident that happened at Grace Chapel, soon after Robert had gotten saved during a summer tent revival. Jane Anne was visiting with them that particular weekend and both of them had accompanied

Robert that Sunday. The Church was having revival and
Robert had been very impressed with the speaker.

One has to understand that Robert embraced a different faith tradition than Emilis and Jane Anne. These sis-
ters were raised in a segment of Christianity that focused
more on the transformation of the heart than strict dress
codes, while the faith tradition to which Robert and I
belonged held very different beliefs. Even now it's embar-
rassing for me to admit that I ever subscribed to some of
those ways of thinking.

The tradition to which Robert and I belonged did not
approve of women wearing jewelry, cutting their hair,
wearing make-up, pants, or shirt sleeves above the elbow.
Even writing such a list gives me a tinge of shame regarding the way we thought back then, especially in how we
viewed all those 'worldly' Christians that didn't adopt our
dogmatic ways.

I came to learn that Robert never fully prescribed to
that way of thinking, and never sought to impose those
strict codes upon Emilis. I assume it's just as well, for
Emilis was strong in her own convictions and wasn't to
be swayed or stuffed into a mold that she didn't espouse.
What Robert enjoyed about this tradition was a freedom
in worship he hadn't found elsewhere and an openness to
the Spirit of God, which he craved.

Both Emilis and Jane Anne had worn long dresses
and had left their jewelry at home out of respect for the
convictions of the people with whom they were worship-
ing, but neither were willing to forego their make-up.
Evidently, as is often the case, even the sacrifices of love
which had already been made that morning were not
enough for some. At the conclusion of the service, as
Robert and many others gathered around the altar for
prayer, a member of the congregation made her way
back to Emilis and Jane Anne, who had remained in
their pew. For a moment it seemed like a kind gesture of
welcome, but before long the mood changed. The lady

57

began to criticize Emilis, calling her a stumbling-block and insinuating that her 'worldliness' was holding Robert back in his spiritual journey.

Emilis was horrified, she couldn't believe that this was indeed happening to her in worship on a Sunday morning. Her face was hot with embarrassment and her eyes mounding with tears that she fought to quench. She couldn't speak and didn't know how to respond. And as the discomfort of the encounter mounted, Jane Anne came to the rescue of her big sister.

Evidently, Jane Anne knew a little more about this woman than Emilis. Jane Anne had attended high school with her across the sound, and later revealed how promiscuous she had been during her teenage years and early adulthood. Evidently she had risen so high above her past that she had become a bastion of holiness for the rest of society. But, Jane Anne hadn't forgotten her former reputation.

Emilis may have been too genteel, shocked, and hurt to offer a rebuttal, but Jane Anne had taken all the hypocrisy she could stomach. Standing to her feet, she looked the woman square in the eyes and, with face red and nostrils flaring, posed one question that shut the woman's mouth and sent her stomping off towards the Church door: "There's none so righteous as a converted whore, is there?"

Jane Anne later told how awful she felt for saying such a thing, especially for bringing up a past the woman was obviously seeking to overcome; however, Jane Anne could not tolerate injustice. She was all for someone having a sincere experience and relationship with the Lord; but, she just could not tolerate anyone who was more pharisaical than Christ-like. Needless to say, Emilis and Jane Anne had not been back to Grace Chapel since.

Entry 11

Emilis and Jane Anne worked tirelessly, getting everything in order for the annual Methodist Women's Party. There was silver to polish, windows to wash, food to pre-pare, floral arrangements to be made and luminary bags to fill with sand. Jane Anne and Emilis worked inside while Robert and I folded and filled the dozens of white paper bags.

The night of the Methodist women's circle party went off without a hitch; and as dusk settled on the island, Robert and I lined the brick walk and oyster shell lane with the luminaries we had spent the better part of the afternoon working on. At about six o'clock, after lighting the last candle, we slipped away and left the ladies to their entertaining. Robert didn't have much interest in being stuck inside the house with two or three dozen women for the rest of the evening, so we made our way down to Albert Styron's General Store, just a baseball's throw from the lighthouse.

Entry 12

After Christmas' end, the winter months dragged by with bleak grey skies and icy white caps. Fishing season was in full swing and the island was a ghost town, as far as the tourist industry was concerned. And although we listened to Bing Crosby sing of White Christmases from November till the first of the year, it was an extreme rarity to ever see one on the Carolina coast.

With shortened days and freezing temperatures, the social hot spots of the island were its hand-full of general stores. On those winter nights after supper, many men and women of the community gathered in those quaint stores, huddled around large oil heaters with exhaust pipes rising up through the bead board ceilings. Just as on the night of the Women's Circle party, Robert would make his way down to Albert Styron's. Of all the gather-ing places on the island, this was Robert's go-to.

Emilis preferred to stay at home on those cold nights, but Robert took me in tow, initiating me into the fishing fraternity of which he held a lead position. Though I usually didn't say much, I enjoyed every minute. While the fishermen told their stories, I just sat there soaking it all in.

Joseph Wicker, a local fishermen and one of Robert's boyhood school mates, would usually take the floor. Joseph was a natural entertainer, and his weekly stage was the wide planked pine floor of the old store. He would really get on a roll, telling "yarns" as Robert called them. Whether they were true or embellishments of lore passed through the generations, they were some of the funniest stories I had ever heard. The men and women gathered within those walls would often find themselves bent double with laughter, trying desperately not to spill their glass bottled Pepsi colas or cups of steaming black coffee.

Joseph once told of an uncle who went to enlist in the service following the bombing of Pearl Harbor. The story goes that His uncle became upset in his stomach on the bus ride to New Bern and had to make his way into the woods at one of the stops to relieve himself, the only problem being that the only wiping tool he could find on the forest floor were handfuls of pine straw. Joseph Wicker recounted the events that followed as only he could in his thick Ocracoke brogue.

When Joseph's uncle arrived in New Bern he went to receive his physical for enlistment. During the prostate exam, the doctor instructed him to bend over the table. Reportedly, the doctor looked down at Joseph's uncle's rear end and replied, "Son, I've seen a many a tail hole in my life, but this is the first one I've ever witnessed that had a built in bird's nest."

This was just one of the probably thousands of "yarns" Mr. Wicker could recall from memory as the occasion warranted. Occasionally, he told stories of experiences he and Robert had in their younger, partying days. Robert would just laugh and shake his head. I could tell he had rather not relive those less than sacred moments in

60

his life, but the humor of those stories demanded laughter and Robert was a good sport and humbly obliged. My favorite story was of one winter evening during their teen-age years.

After a drinking binge, Joseph and a couple of the other island boys dared Robert to streak onto the ferry and beat on the pilot house windows. Evidently Robert couldn't pass up a dare in those early years; he headed aboard the boat, stark naked. The only problem was that Joseph and one of the other boys waited until Robert had climbed up to the pilot house and was pounding on the crew's windows, at which point they closed and locked the gate behind him.

After beating on the windows and rousing the crew, Robert turned to make an escape, finding his exit blocked. Faced with the fear of having to be taken home naked by the ferry captain to Lynwood Guthrie, whom the entire ferry crew knew well, Robert jumped overboard and swam the frigid waters across the harbor to the family fish house, only to find that his daddy was there working late. In the end, Robert had to sneak past the fish house door and down the street toward their home, ducking into hedges and behind fences as random cars approached. "Yes, and I almost died of pneumonia from it." Robert interjected with a smile.

Stories like that were fascinating to me, a glimpse of a younger, fun-loving, mischievous version of my mentor.

Entry 13

Spring of '83 came on slowly, but by late April the temperatures were reaching the upper eighties and the stream of cars pouring from the ferries began to slowly grow in size. One Saturday afternoon that May I ac-companied Robert and Emilis to the wedding of one of the native island girls, Lizzy Taylor. Lizzy had been a classmate and dear friend of Robert Jr.'s. No matter life's changes, Lizzy had always remained close to the Guthries, even after moving away from the island. After completing her degree at Peace College, Lizzy remained in Raleigh; but, when it came time to marry, she wanted her wedding at home on Ocracoke.

Ocracoke was an interesting mix of people. There were those who didn't believe in dancing, or drinking, or any other form of worldliness. There were those who were more moderate in their convictions and lifestyle, like Emilis and Jane Anne. And then there were those on the island who lived to party. This event was a conglomeration of all three.

After the nuptials at the small white Methodist Church, we made our way to the reception. By the time we left the ceremony it was dusk and the road leading from the Church was lined with luminaries that Robert and I, along with Lizzy's father and uncles, had spent the better part of an afternoon folding and filling with sand at Emilis' request.

The reception was hosted down on the grounds of the old lighthouse, a sea of luminaries guiding the way. The white tower and the ancient wind-swept oaks were illuminated from below with flood lights. The linen clad serving table, boasting an untold amount of seafood, seemed to stretch for a mile. The mounds of shrimp and blue crab claws were no doubt a wedding gift from many of the fisherman on the island, a concession of the island fishing fraternity to one of its own whose little girl was marrying.

The wedding was a mix of Lizzy's two lives, a blending of her thick brogued, spirited family and friends from the coast and the Raleigh socialite friends from her new home in the capital city. Lizzy wanted everything to be perfect. She didn't want her capital city colleagues to make fun of her Ocracoke roots or feel that this group of Outer Banks fisher men and women were any less cultured or astute. I've learned that when it comes to the sons and daughters of the Outer Banks, it's fine for them poke fun at aspects of their homeland; but, if someone from "off" makes those same remarks, they quickly become fighting words.

To ensure that everything was done to perfection, Lizzy had enlisted the help of the one woman on the island whom she trusted with such details. Emilis had no problem serving sweet tea from mason jars at oyster roasts in her back yard, but she had also entertained Governors and Congressmen on Wedgewood and Tiffany crystal during Robert's terms in the legislature. If there was anyone who could bridge the gap between Lizzy's two worlds, it was Emilis Guthrie.

The little white cottage had been stripped bare of its silver the week before the wedding. Walking through the picketed gate at the lighthouse, I quickly realized where it had gone. No Wake countian, nouveau riche or old money alike, was going to poke fun at Ocracoke on Emilis' watch. It was an evening for which the women of the village were glad that Emilis was one of them.

The historic white lighthouse served as a majestic backdrop for an evening of white linens and polished silver, crystal and candlelight, Oysters Rockefeller and Dom Perignon. Emilis was in her element as she produced the social event of the year, and I enjoyed watching her flourish, the perfect hostess, making her rounds through the sea of wedding goers. After an hour of eating and toasting the newly-weds, the band began its opening chords.

Emilis had booked the Chairmen of the Board, a wedding gift from her and Robert to their little boy's best childhood friend. As deep blues began dominating the late evening sky, the band opened their first set with 'Carolina Girls'. This was Coastal Carolina in all of its glory: cool late spring evening, sea breeze, gull's cry, lighthouse beam, island oaks, seer sucker and bow ties, beach music on the wind, and shagging beneath the low full moon. With dinner ended, and the band getting cranked up, it was time for the exodus of those who did not approve of

63

dancing, as well as the elderly who were nearing their bed time. I stayed near Robert for the better part of the evening, listening as he discussed politics and fishing with the men of the wedding party, his glass of sweet tea in hand.

Jane Anne had worked herself to a frazzle over the past three days, helping Emilis with the cooking, silver polishing, and flower arranging. With all the work behind her, Jane Anne had no problem declaring that it was time to let her hair down. Onto the dance floor she went, champagne flute in hand, as the band began its rendition of "It's Alright". I couldn't help but grin as I watched her. Catching my eyes, she began giving me her signature mischievous grin as she shimmied her way to the edge of the dance floor, motioning for me to come out and join her. Dancing to beach music was one of my absolute favorite things. The problem lie in the backlash I feared from the Church when certain members heard that I was out there on the dance floor.

Maybe it was the warm spring night, the moonlight and sea breeze seeping into my veins, or the fact that I was a twenty two year old young man who was tired of rigidity. Whatever the inspiration, I decided that it's sometimes easier to ask for forgiveness than permission. Within seconds I was in the midst of the crowd, having the time of my life as I led Jane Anne around the dance floor with all the feet shuffling and hip swaying that make dancing the shag such an art form. The girls of my generation seldom had the same knack for shagging to beach music as those who grew up on records of the Impressions, like Emilis and Jane Anne had done.

Before I knew it the crowd on the floor had made a space in the center for us, standing around us clapping to the music and swaying as they cheered us on. I think I was probably the first preacher in the history of Ocracoke who had ever joined the ranks of the "sinners" on the dance floor; and quite possibly the first time the women of the island, old and young alike, had been schooled by

someone like Jane Anne on how to really do the shag.
"Well, I probably won't have a job in the morning," I said
to Jane Anne while laughing over the music.

"That's all right, you can work at the fish house." She replied, and then leaned her head in close to my ear to add,
"And, if Robert says anything to you about it you just let
me know and I'll kick his ass."

I couldn't help but cackle, the kind of laughter that leaves
your cheeks sore and your heart so much lighter. For
the first time since crossing the Pamlico I truly felt free,
authentic, like I was being myself.

As the evening stretched on, Emilis busied herself with
gathering dishes and serving pieces and counting the
silver. Her work wasn't done until everything was cleaned
up and accounted for. When the Chairmen of the Board
began the last song of the evening, Robert distracted
Emilis from her work, leading her to the dance floor for
their one dance of the night. It was incredible to watch
from the sidelines as this couple floated across the floor,
laughing, smiling, shagging as the band played "You're
Still the One". They seemed so in love and lively. Their
dancing seemed a message to life, "You will not get the
best of us."

Sure there would be back-lash from some members
of the Church that Robert was dancing. Emilis would
likely be branded as a "heathern", if not for her jewelry
and makeup, then certainly for the cases of champagne
she had hauled to the island for the event. However, the
Guthries just danced above it. Robert had settled this account in his heart and knew he was doing nothing wrong.
Emilis had long ago retired from seeking the approval of
the Pharisees. She knew the content of her own heart
and had arrived at the mature, partially jaded sentiment
of knowing who her friends were and refusing to worry
herself with the criticism of those outside of that circle.

That night after the curtain closed on Emilis' carefully crafted production, it was left to the few and faithful

to clean up. Among the hand-full who stayed to help was a young man who would become my dearest friend. Parks Eason had moved to the island as a child from Kitty Hawk to live with his grandparents. From all reports, he was brilliant. After graduating valedictorian of Ocracoke School, he attended the University of North Carolina in Chapel Hill as a Morehead Scholar.

Though he definitely could have pursued a more lucrative career, his heart was in education. Parks was graduating cum laude from Chapel Hill that May and Robert had called in some political favors to ensure a position for him at the small K-12 school on the island. He would be teaching History and English to the fourteen students who made up the ninth, tenth, eleventh, and twelfth grades of Ocracoke school.

Robert brought Parks over to me as I broke down tables and chairs, placing them in the back of Robert's fish truck.

"Holden," Robert began, "here's a young man I want you to meet."

I think that Robert knew I was in desperate need of a friend on the island, someone my own age. After a brief introduction, Emilis called for Robert from across the yard and he excused himself to go assist her.

"Need a hand here?" Parks asked.

"Sure thing!" I replied.

"You had some pretty good moves out there on the dance floor, preacher man." he said with a chuckle. "I've got to give it to you, that took some balls."

"Yeah, I probably won't ever live this down." I said. "I told Jane Anne I probably won't have a job come day-light."

"Oh, well, this Island needs a little shaking up every once in a while." Parks replied.

When all was done for the night and we disbanded to head our separate ways, Parks invited me to go surf-ing with him the next week. I accepted his invitation, although I was honest that I had no clue how. Regardless, I was grateful to have found someone my own age on the island to befriend me. Though my first seven months on Ocracoke had no doubt been full and productive, my social life had been lack-luster. There were very few people on the island my age, and those who were didn't seem extremely excited about befriending the new preacher. The only social engagement I received, for the most part, were superficial interactions around the fish house docks, or on the Church steps following Sunday service. The one exception to this rule seemed to be the plethora of matchmaking ploys by the well-meaning ladies of the Church who seemed to have found their calling in life in seeking me out a bride. Needless to say, Parks' invitation to go surfing was a much needed reprieve to the polite, arm's-length interactions to which I had grown accustomed.

Entry 14

Parks was the quintessential Carolina surfer with long wavy blonde hair tucked behind his ears and a laid back, easy-going personality that seemed completely incapable of being rattled. I had to double check with Robert and Emilis to make sure that I wasn't confused, that the uber-intelligent honors graduate and the soft spoken, laid back, long haired surfer were indeed one in the same person. I guess I expected a Morehead scholar to be, well, nerdy.

Early one morning, a few weeks after the wedding, Parks appeared on the fish house dock as I was helping unload shrimp from the Miss Emilis.

"Holden," I heard someone call over the roar of conveyor belts, generators, and fork lifts.

I looked up to find Parks on the dock in his board shorts and flip flops.

"How much longer are you going to be?" he asked.

I looked at my watch and then peered down into the hull of the boat to see how much more work I had left to do,

"Probably another hour, maybe less."

"Man, the waves are perfect this morning. Do you think you can go?"

"Yeah, I think so, just as soon as I finish up with this."

"Ok, well I'm going to go get my extra board and run by the store to get us some snacks. What kind of drink do you like?"

"I'm ok, man. You don't have to get me anything."

"Holden, what do you want? Dr. Pepper? Mountain Dew?..."

"Pepsi," I replied.

"Ok, I'll be back directly."

I had come to learn that directly in island speech meant after a while, not immediately as one may suppose.

I finished up my work and double checked with Robert to make sure it was okay with him if I slipped away for a few hours, after we finished packing out. Of course, it was. After getting cleaned up a little, I made my way through the fish house and into the rear parking area to meet my ride.

Parks drove a small red Nissan pickup truck, the tailgate plastered with stickers ranging from Quicksilver and Billabong to Carter/Mondale and a host of others which were a collection from his time in Chapel Hill. I climbed into the cab and after running by Robert and Emilis' to grab my swim trunks we made our way down Highway 12 towards the Hatteras ferry. We pulled onto the side of the road about three quarters of a mile past mile marker 78, grabbed the boards from the truck bed, and made our way through a well-worn path in the dunes to the edge of the Atlantic.

Once we came to the water's edge, Parks began teaching me how to wax the board and what type of wax to use in warmer weather verses cold. We finished waxing the boards and he started giving me lessons on how to position my body on the board, how to paddle out, and how to pop up.

"Holden, just lay on the board and pop up to your feet

like you've just caught a wave."

"What? Right now?" I said, feeling rather awkward to be going through this exercise here on dry land.

"Just lay on the board and then pop up to your feet like you are riding the wave," he repeated, "I've got to see something".

I obliged, only to have him make an observation that I was unsure how to take.

"You're goofy footed." He said in a very matter-of-fact manner.

"What?" I responded, slightly perturbed and obviously offended.

"No, no, no, Holden," he said with a slight chuckle as he realized how I had taken his comment, "...there's nothing wrong with you man, I'm goofy footed too!"

He then explained the surfing lingo of being "goofy footed", the natural inclination to surf with your right foot forward, rather than regular footed or left foot first. I remember telling Parks, "You mean to tell me that I not only have to learn Ocracoke English, but surfer lingo, too." We had a good laugh over it. He was always making fun of my Johnston County accent, and though he had dropped a great deal of his Outer Banks brogue during his time away at Carolina, every once in a while it would surface and I would take full advantage of the opportunity.

We had a blast that first day and I actually got up after a few tries. The feeling of catching that first wave was addicting. There's something magical about being caught and driven by the momentum of the surf. It was incredible. Of course it would take years of practice before I could even remotely hang with Parks' level of mastery, but from that day on he never left me out. Whenever he went surfing he would come looking for me, and once I finished my work around the docks I would head up the beach to join him.

Just being out there on those waves, sitting behind the

69

breakers on the board with my feet dangling beneath me in the water, did something deep in my soul. The ocean became an escape for me from the troubles of my world, a place of therapeutic serenity where I could commune with God and ruminate on feelings and thoughts I couldn't visit anywhere else in quite the same way as I did on that longboard beyond the breakers. Parks was generous enough to loan me his extra longboard until I could save enough money to buy my own. Some days, when anxiety sought to overwhelm me, I would finish my days work and slip out beyond the breakers until well after the sun had set behind the island, leaving me out on the water in the dusk air. Here, the most present sound was the gentle lapping of the water against the board as the swells would gently lift and lower me.

I had the best tan that summer I probably have ever had, and the most time I had ever taken to think about my life. Something about the trance invoking rhythms of the ocean just seem to foster meditation. It was during this time that I first began journaling, which for me was a way of externalizing the tides of my thoughts, getting them out so that they could be managed. It was on the surfing excursions of that first Ocracoke summer that I began, in a more deliberate manner, processing the past, dealing with the present, and pondering my future.

Entry 15

Wednesdays and Sundays were mainly spent at the Church and around Emilis and Robert's table. I worked at the fish house on Tuesdays, Thursdays, Fridays, and Saturday mornings, whether it was driving one of the trucks, long hauling in Pamlico Sound, or grading fish and shrimp dockside. Saturday evening was a time of polishing the sermon I had crafted throughout the week. Mondays were my day to rest.

As the summer progressed my social circle increased a little. A couple of Parks' best friends found their way

70

back to the island on summer break, waiting tables or
working on the ferry to save money for the coming year's
tuition. Suzy had been Parks' dearest friend since their
grade school days. She was up at Meredith working on
her psychology degree and passed the summers waiting tables at the Back Porch Restaurant. Rann, Suzy's
boyfriend, was a Hatteras boy. Though they had been
acquainted for years in the surfing circles of the Outer
Banks, he and Parks had become closer friends as the
tenure of his relationship with Suzy stretched into years.
Rann had gotten a job on the Hatteras Ferry and crashed
at Parks' house every other week when his shift placed
him of the Ocracoke side of the inlet at night. None of
them were associated with the Church, though both Suzy
and Rann had been raised in Christian families. They
were respectful of my convictions, even if they didn't
share them all, and never made me feel uncomfortable or
pressured me in any way. In fact, when I was around they
wouldn't drink or smoke weed out of respect for me. We
had some good times that summer, building bonfires on
the beach, swimming off Parks' skiff, and passing afternoons down at the inlet soaking up the summer sun.

At least a couple of times a week we would grill out
at Parks' house, or Robert and Emilis would have them
all over for supper. And surf, man did Parks and I ever
surf. We were out just about every day there were swells,
except for Sunday.
One evening, about a month into our surfing expeditions,
while sitting out on our boards in the swells, Parks interrupted the silence,
"Holden, I've been wanting to ask you something."
"Sure, anything." I replied. I couldn't imagine what it
was, but it sounded serious.
"Now, if it's too personal, I don't want you to feel obli-
gated or pressured to answer me."
"Ok," I said, a little concerned and uneasy about what
was coming next. I had a tinge of those butterfly feelings

I always get in my stomach when conversations are approached in such a foreboding tone.

"The day I was teaching you how to surf, I noticed some pretty nasty scars on your back...."

"Oh, those. I...."

For a moment I started to interrupt, masking the truth by giving some fabricated account, just as I had done all of my life. But there was something about our friendship, a sense of safety and loyalty, that made me want to be honest about my scars for the first time in my life. For the first time I didn't want to make excuses anymore, I was tired of hiding.

"Parks, you're the first person I've ever told this to, other than a counselor years ago."

I could tell that he was bracing himself for something deep. His usual jovial countenance was replaced with one of seriousness. I continued,

"When I was young my father came home drunk one night and beat me pretty badly...horribly actually."

With this, I began to recount the fearful existence of my childhood and the night of pink frosting and Dad's belt buckle.

When I finished telling my story and removed my gaze from the horizon to look for Parks' reaction, I found him sitting there on his board, the summer sunset over his shoulder, tears streaming silently down his face as he stared at me with eyes full of pity.

Words were few for the remainder of that evening. We caught a few more waves in the pervading silence and then made our way back to the little red Nissan, parked on the edge of highway 12. After drying off with the towels we had left folded in the bed of the truck, we climbed into the cab. Parks just sat there, keys in hand, staring down the edge of the sand dusted pavement stretching north to Hatteras Inlet. I couldn't help but wonder if my story had been a little too much for my new friend to handle. After a few moments Parks broke the silence, his gaze still set northward.

"Holden, I think I'd like to talk to you sometime about some stuff."

"Of course, buddy." I responded, trying to provide both empathy and space, "Any time."

Those were the only words shared that evening between the swells and the supper table. Parks started the truck and we headed back to the village, windows down, radio on, and the warm sea breeze blowing through our damp, salty hair.

Entry 16

The summer of '83 was one of those seasons of life that will be replayed in my mind for as long as I live, forever memorialized as some of my very best memories. Days of laughter and cold Pepsi colas around the docks gave way to afternoons of surfing, clam bakes, and oceanside bonfires. When there wasn't any surf, Parks and I would spend the afternoons clamming off of Portsmouth, trolling for bluefish out in the inlet, or diving from his skiff into the deep, cool waters of Teach's Hole. Rann and Suzy would join us as often as possible, whenever work and their love life allowed.

There were many evenings spent gathered on the Guthries' porch, eating bowls of homemade ice cream and listening to Marvin Boyd, a dear friend to Robert and Emilis, play his guitar. My heart was so full of gratitude for it all, and I felt the closest to God, then, that I may have ever felt. This is what life was supposed to be like, enjoying the fellowship of God and others. My young life had been so full of tears, but the summer of '83 seemed like a parting of the clouds.

The summer was so perfect that even the hurricanes knew better than to threaten it. Late in September Chantal and Dean skirted by, way off shore, but the only effects felt on the island were gentle breezes and the best surf we had seen all year. It was also during that sum-

mer that Parks and Robert introduced me to flounder
gigging. We probably went about a dozen times before
the fall chill set in. Of everything they ever taught me on
the water, I loved flounder gigging the most, floating and
poling gently around the shoals off the island with our
lights illuminating the bottom. More than anything, I
enjoyed the fellowship. Now don't get me wrong, if we
came home with a couple boxes of flounder it was all the
better, but even if we came back empty handed, being out
there in the summer night, laughing and telling stories,
eating honey buns and drinking Mountain Dews with two
of the people I cared for most in the world was all I really
cared about.

The village was swamped with tourists that July 4th,
renting out every room at the Pony Island, the Island Inn
and every other lodging place available, with the ferry
bringing new crops of people every hour. We always got
a kick out of how some of these tourists dressed, with
their huge hats and white socks with sandals. Most of the
local boys' summer attire was board shorts and flip flops,
wearing a shirt only if they absolutely had too. Parks was
the same way. I, on the other hand, usually wore slacks
and a shirt. A number of people in our Church didn't
look kindly on shorts or even short sleeves, so to go shirt-
less in the village proper would have sealed my fate. I
only went bare chested from the shore to the ocean and
back again, or when swimming from Parks' boat. I guess
I figured that I wouldn't see any of those old women in
either place so I could go for it without offending anyone.
The Church seemed willing to put up with my boyishness,
so long as I didn't go parading around half naked or letting my hair get long like "those hippies", as they would
pointedly refer to a number of the surfers on the island,
Parks included.

I had to be around the fish house in the morning of
the fourth, as there would be a steady stream of boats at
the docks and locals in their pickups at the loading ramp,

74

filling their coolers with ice from Robert's freezer. He
never charged any of them for it, just wanted me there to
make sure that nothing but the free ice left the fish house
that day. By about two in the afternoon all of the locals
were either down at the inlet or out in their boats, and I
was free to chain up the freezer door, grab my board and
head for the surf.

The beach was flooded with locals on the fourth, a
fair number of which enjoyed celebrating the occasion
in ways I didn't approve. The internal scars of my dad's
alcoholism went deep and being around people who were
drinking made me very uncomfortable. I also feared
that I may have more of my Dad's genes than I wanted,
terrified that taking a sip might ultimately turn me into
what he had been. However, Parks was right at home in
the midst of all of it. In fact, by the time I broke away
from the fish house he had been down the beach with the
home-folk all day.

Parks loved to have a good time and was a social drink-
er, but he understood the complications I had with it. My
terrible childhood experiences with a father lost in the
bottle allowed me to whole heartedly embrace the position of our Church against all forms of consumption. In
those early years I had no tolerance for even a social drink
and disdained it as much as a bender. As my friendship
with Parks continued, and especially after my revelation
to him that evening on our boards concerning the scars,
he stopped drinking around me for a while. Although he
did not profess any faith at all, and did not attend any of
the Churches on the island, he was understanding of the
fact that I, in my position, could not be around people
partying. I knew he had gone down the beach that morning with Tommy Brewer and a bunch of his childhood
buddies; so, I didn't expect to see him anymore that day.
I could only imagine that by this point none of them were
feeling any pain.

After getting off from the fish house I went home to

75

grab a bite for lunch. Emilis had fixed a huge bowl of shrimp salad before she and Robert left to go to the fish fry fundraiser being put on by the Methodist Men. I mounded a cereal bowl full, grabbed a glass of sweet tea and headed into the living room to see if there was anything on television besides soap operas.

I hadn't been sitting down very long when there was knock at the back screened door. Before I could get up to answer, I heard it creak open and Parks's voice call from the rear of the house.

"Holden?"

"I'm in here," I called back.

In just a few seconds he made his way into the living room.

"So what are we going to do today?" He said as he plopped down in the white house chair in his board shorts and tank top, his bare feet still showing remnants of beach sand.

"I really don't have anything planned, man." I replied, "I figured you'd be down the beach all day."

"And leave you here cooped up in this house on the Fourth of July?" He replied.

"Well, Parks, you know I don't want to be down the beach in all of that drinking!" I replied.

"I know, that's why we're going to Hatteras." He interjected. "I called a buddy of mine in Buxton and he said there was a pretty good swell at the lighthouse jetty".

"What are you eating?" He asked.

"Some shrimp salad Emilis made. You want some?"

"Is Reagan a Republican? That I do want some!"

I fixed him a bowl and a glass of sweet tea, and after eating we threw our boards into the back of Parks' pickup and headed north. We boarded the ferry for Hatteras, windows down, and Billy Joel on the radio. Parks loved music as much as I did and the soundtrack of that summer is forever burned in my memory: the Police, Bonnie Tyler, Culture Club, and Billy Joel's Uptown Girl. Parks loved Billy Joel and whenever Uptown Girl came on the radio I knew it was time for talking to cease, as Parks cranked the volume and sang to the top of his lungs. Today was no different. Shortly after boarding the ferry, which was full to capacity of tourists heading up towards Kitty Hawk, Billy came on the radio and Parks began his usual personal concert. I think it was mostly for my embarrassment, and if that was his intention...mission accomplished.

It was a really good day of surfing for the most part, the only downfall being an altercation with another surfer from a little further up the coast. I was still learning and wasn't as astute in my surfing skills as Parks or a lot of the other guys on the Outer Banks. For one thing, they had been doing this since childhood and I was only in my third month. In one of the sets I had accidentally cut off one of the local guys. He just wouldn't let it go, so I paddled in and decided to sit on the beach for a while until he cooled down, but he followed me in and began cussing me out and getting in my face, trying to fight me. I was trying to be a peace maker and turn the other cheek, but that was getting me nowhere with this guy. Before I knew it, Parks had paddled in and was up in this guy's face, repaying him in kind. After the guy recognized Parks and realized that I was with him, and especially after Parks told him that I was a preacher, he couldn't apologize enough. I accepted his apology. Parks, on the other hand, looked him square in the eyes and said, "You should be sorry, asshole!"
With that Parks headed for the surf and called back, "Come on Holden, forget about this douche bag."

We paddled back out and enjoyed the rest of the day surfing just down the shore a few yards from where the rest of the guys were clustered on their boards, bobbing in the swell and calling their respective sets. We headed back to the truck as the sun started to set, wanting to give ourselves enough time to get home and shower before meeting everybody down at Robert's docks for the fireworks.

We hurried back home and got ready for the night. This was one of those social events that drew out everyone on the island, locals and tourists alike, so most of us younger guys and girls tried to look our best...without trying too hard, of course. I slipped on my khaki pants and the mint green Lacoste shirt Emilis had bought me, and made my way to the fish house.

The businesses around Silver Lake were buzzing with people as I walked down the highway framing the water's edge. The last ferry had made its delivery and the road was more like a sidewalk by this time of the evening. I could tell by the banter and the calls from college girls on hotel balconies that many of these people had started celebrating early in the day. By this late hour they were free of inhibition.

I arrived at the fish house and made my way out onto the dock to join the Guthries. There were large tables set up on the deck of the Miss Emilis with buckets of homemade ice cream, a mound of ice with spears of chilled watermelon, pans mounded with boiled peanuts, and galvanized wash tubs filled with ice and glass bottled colas. People from all over the island, different families, different denominations...anyone with a connection to the Guthries were there. Children were sprawled out on blankets on the top of the boat cabins, teenagers sat on the end of the dock with their legs dangling beneath them, and the older generation sitting back in their lawn chairs, while others stood around enjoying the company and waiting for the show to begin. Parks had gone over to watch the fireworks with some of his boyhood friends at the Jolly Roger Pub.

Shortly after dark the fireworks began. I sat there on a blanket beside Robert and Emilis as the flashes illuminated our faces and cast reflections upon the harbor, a perfect ending to a perfect day. It was good to be a part of something, part of a community, part of a family.

Entry 17

I was raised to, above all else, be a polite southern gentleman. I stuffed pretty much everything, feeling as if I were doing something sinful by voicing my disgust or disapproval of anything or anyone. Therefore, I didn't talk...about much of anything.

As the friendship between Parks and me grew, my silence and fear of expressing my own thoughts and opinions was something that he pressed me on. I don't know why I found it so difficult to be open. Somewhere along the way I had become a hoarder with regards to my thoughts and emotions, keeping everything stored up inside. Looking back, I can see now how truly unhealthy it was.

I remember Parks saying, "Holden, just get it out. Just say what's on your mind. I'm not going to judge you. Just get it off your chest, man."

In time I took his advice but it was a learning process for me, a learning process that revealed the nature of my problem with speaking my mind. I came to see that I was terrified of rejection and did everything possible to make myself agreeable to those with whom I interacted. I was the proverbial old shoe, the nice guy that everyone loved, the sweet boy that didn't speak out of turn and tried desperately not to offend.

Parks continually tugged at what was eating me inside. Not only did he seek to know what I was thinking, he was free in sharing his thoughts with me about everything from politics, to people on the island, my taste in music, and even some of the defining characteristics of those who were members of my Church. He didn't hold back. Parks was a straight shooter and his unbridled honesty was refreshing, even if it rubbed me with discomfort at times. Such was the case when he would make observations regarding some of the rules of our Church.

79

The independent Church that I was pastoring, much like the Church in which I had been raised in Johnston County, was an old-school brand of holiness. We may not have been so presumptuous as to say aloud that we were the only ones going to Heaven, but inwardly we were convinced that we would at least go a little ahead of everyone else. There was an underlying feeling that we were more spiritual than the Presbyterians, Methodists, or Baptists. And as such, there were characterizing features that set us apart from all the other "worldly" believers out there. Parks had grown up on the island but never attended Church, aside from the occasional summer Vacation Bible School, but even those were rare instances.

I had grown up in Church circles and I had a full grasp on all of the dos and don'ts, regardless of whether I found them agreeable. I never really questioned them and tried my best to fit in. Parks, on the other hand, wasn't afraid to challenge the status quo.

One day while we were fishing in the inlet he launched on a rampage, posing questions about why we did and believed certain things. His main points of objection had to do with things he observed as he grew up around the Church goers of the island.

"Holden, how come the women in your Church don't believe in wearing makeup, but it's okay for them to dye their hair?"

I didn't have an answer.

"Or," he continued, "How come wearing wedding rings or earrings is a cardinal sin, but they can wear gold or silver wrist watches and that's ok?

Again, no answer.

"I just don't get it, Holden."

"Well, Parks, that's just their personal convictions."

"I understand what you're saying Holden, but it's not just their personal convictions. They think that women who wear jewelry, or cut their hair, or God forbid wear pants, are going to hell."

This was an extreme case, but I couldn't deny the truth he had revealed regarding the beliefs of some in my Church. "I mean, why is it that men can't wear short sleeve shirts, but they can wear long sleeves and roll them up to their elbows, and that's ok?" He continued.

I was silent.

"Are you ok with me asking you this stuff?" He questioned, obviously aware that the conversation was making me uncomfortable.

"Yeah, I'm listening."

"I mean, I just don't understand what all these rules are for, or what purpose they serve. If it's somebody's personal conviction then great, but don't tell me I'm going to hell because I have long hair and wear shorts. I mean, I've grown up around this stuff Holden."

"I have too, Parks." I replied with an air of indignation.

"It just boggles my mind. I mean I know women who keep the dress code to the letter, but they're mean as snakes, they think their better than anybody else on the island."

I just listened. He was making a valid point. The discomfort I experienced was the rub between what I had been told was true Christianity since I was a child, and the hypocrisy that Parks was uncovering. Nevertheless, the rub had left me raw, and from that chafing discomfort I offered my rebuttal.

"Aren't you just as wrong in your judgment of them, in saying that their faith isn't real because they aren't perfect. I mean, who is, Parks? At least they're trying."

Parks just grinned.

"What?" I replied, in a tone that I'm sure betrayed just how pissed off I was with him. "What is it? What are you grinnin' at?" I pressed.

Parks grin morphed into a broad smile.

"What is it?" I posed the question, again.

"Finally." he said with a broad smile.

"Finally, what?" I blurted out in utter exasperation.

81

"You finally pushed back." He replied, "you're human after all."

"Shut up." I said, annoyed more at myself for allowing my anger to get the better of me.

"And you're a little feisty too," he said with a chuckle.

"I'm sorry man. I shouldn't have gotten so aggravated." I apologized, riddled with guilt that I had damaged my witness in my outburst or attitude.

"Holden, don't apologize. You have feelings just like the rest of us, and it's okay for you to have them. Stop keeping everything so pressed down and bottled up. Just be real man. I want to know the real Holden."

"I am real." I buffeted.

"Yes, I think you are." He said with a smile.

As minuscule as that conversation may seem, it was the beginning of me being able to have a voice, a voice that had been silenced for so long, silenced in fear of my father's backhand, silenced in fear of finding my mother's disapproval for not being her sweet little boy, silenced in the self-eclipsing desire to be accepted, approved of, and loved by the people in my life. Parks gave me permission to speak without fear of repercussion, to push back, to have an opinion...especially if that opinion was contrary to his. That experience was so freeing for me. For the first time in my life I was able to own my own space in this world, to own my own position on issues and ideologies without having to worry that I would be punished or ostracized for them. The summer of '83 found me more fully alive than I had ever been. I didn't realize it at the time, but it would serve as the turning of a page, the beginning of a new era.

Entry 18

Parks had some friends in Chincoteague who had been asking him to come up and surf ever since he returned to the island. In September he decided to take a long

weekend to drive up and invited me to come along. The
Church allowed me a couple weeks of vacation time a
year, so I took four days and joined him. I had set aside
enough money from working at the fish house to purchase
my first board earlier that summer, a 7'8" 1982 Parks
Richards Swallow Tail Single Fin Gun. It was bright red
with lime green stripes from nose to fins. The Thursday
before Labor Day we strapped our boards in the back of
Parks' truck, along with back packs and tent bags, and
then headed north for Virginia.

We made our way up Highway 12, through Buxton,
Oregon Inlet, and Kitty Hawk. From there we took 158
North through Coinjock, and then Virginia 13 through
the Chesapeake Bay Tunnel. We drove through towns
I had never heard of, like Cheriton and Machipongo.
Finally, we saw the signs for Chincoteague and made our
exit onto 175.

The similarities in culture, dialect, and way of living in
the fishing villages of Virginia and North Carolina were
unmistakable. The guys we met in Chincoteague and
Assateague could have just as easily been boys I worked
with on the docks of Robert's fish house. The way they
spoke, the way they dressed, their hobbies, their commercial fishing heritage, it was as if there existed some
form of ancient kinship linking the two islands together
unaware. And, like some of the guys I worked with at the
fish house, these boys liked to party.

It was on this trip that I had my first up close and personal exposure to pot. I had attended a Christian college,
and though I was under no grand delusion that marijua-
na didn't exist on our campus, it was not something I had
ever seen with my circle of friends. I could sense Parks'
discomfort as he tried to navigate the weekend, caught
between the buddies he had known since high school and
his new found friend who vehemently opposed all substance use. Respectful as he was, Parks didn't share my
conviction and I knew it.

83

The first night out with the guys he didn't drink anything, even as his buddies downed their consecutive bottles of beer around smoky pool tables in the little waterside bar where we had gathered. Based on a few of their comments I knew that Parks had talked to them before we came about not pressing me with anything. I'm not sure that they knew what to make of me. I'm pretty sure it may have been the first time they had spent a Friday night shooting pool with a preacher.

I enjoyed their authenticity, their freedom to just be themselves. I couldn't help but chuckle at their frequent apologies after curse words or dirty jokes. I just loved those guys and couldn't help but laugh at their stories and verbal jabs at each other. Later, we headed to one of the guy's house to crash for the night. When we were leaving the bar that night the guys all gave me hearty handshakes and even a few hugs. I remember one of them saying, "Holden, you're alright!"
"You come hang with us anytime, man." said another of my new acquaintances.
It felt so good to just be one of the guys and enjoy the camaraderie.

That night Parks tapped on my door as I was lying in bed, reading my Bible. He came in and sat down. I could tell by his countenance and the way he was acting that something was weighing heavy on his mind.
"What is it, Parks?" I asked, curious as to what his nervousness was all about.
"Holden, I need to talk to you about something."
"Okay." I said, a little concerned.
"Tomorrow we're gonna set up camp out on Assateague for the rest of the weekend, and I'm going to want to have a couple of drinks with the guys around the campfire at night."
I didn't respond right off, partly because I didn't know what to say. I knew he did it when we weren't around each other and I guess I was okay with that, but I wasn't

84

really okay with this. There was a wash of emotion going on in my heart and head at that moment. All I ever knew of alcohol was physical violence and verbal assaults, and it scared me to death for Parks or anyone else I was close with, friend or family, to drink when I was around. Being around alcohol elicited some serious flashbacks, which I sought desperately to avoid. Parks' disclosure led me to settle in silence.

"Holden, talk to me."

"What do you want me to say?"

"Are you going to be okay with that? I don't want to offend you." he continued.

Silence.

"Holden, talk to me."

"I told you, I don't know what to say."

"Say anything." he pressed.

"It doesn't matter." I said, the distance in my response betraying the walls that were being erected in my heart.

"I'm not buying it." He interjected.

"What does it matter, it's a free country, do whatever you want to do."

"I don't think you mean that. Tell me what you think about it."

"I don't like it one bit!" I said in a short tone, "It makes me nervous."

"I know, and I respect that."

"Then why are you going to do it?" I rebutted.

Silence.

"Holden, I'm not your dad."

"I know you're not my dad." I said with a slight air of hostility.

"I don't think you do." He continued, "I will only drink about two beers, just enough to relax. I promise. I won't get drunk."

Silence.

"I don't like it, Parks, I'm sorry," I said matter-of-factly.

"I know you don't, man, but I just want you to know that

I am going to drink a couple with the guys this weekend. I just didn't want to catch you off guard with it, because I know how you feel about it."

I could tell that he was as resolved in his position as I was in mine, and neither of us were going to budge on the issue. I appreciated his concern, but in the end he was a grown man and certainly didn't owe me any explanation, nor did he need my permission. We would have to agree to disagree and make the best of it. I would just be the only one around the campfire that night drinking Pepsi cola.

It has been interesting for me, in my adult life, to see the way the issue of alcohol affects me still. I can be around shallow acquaintances that are drinking and it doesn't bother me as much, but when it's someone dear to me, someone close, then I have a really hard time with it...some residual fear from childhood scars, I guess. Maybe I'm just a neurotic mess. Whatever.

The next morning we drove out to Assateague Island and made our way down to the hook of the beach, just to the south of Tom's Cove where we made camp. The waves were really good that day, so we hurriedly set up our tents and paddled out as quickly as we could. It was probably the best day of surfing I have ever had. I dropped in on my first wave that day, which completely psyched me up.

The guys treated me like I had been one of their inner circle for years. Anson, the guy who we had crashed with the night before, brought along some surf-fishing rods, so when we took breaks from surfing, which were scarce, we would try our hand at the rods in quest of some fresh seafood for supper. By nightfall we had a handful of blues and trout which we cleaned and cooked on a small charcoal grill Anson had brought along.

After eating, we sat around the campfire talking for hours, the beam of the red and white lighthouse flashing periodically above the tree line. The conversation was ac-

companied with beer, a substance I had grown first to fear
and later to hate. However, as I watched soberly, none of
these guys became violent. Anson got sloppy drunk and
stumbled off to his tent sometime after midnight. The
other guys followed through the next couple of hours,
and by about two thirty Parks and I were left in our folding beach chairs, as the new moon cast its white ripples
upon the face of the ocean.

The warmth of the last few flames and red embers
provided a warm reprieve from the chilly breeze blowing
in off of the Atlantic. With my feet near the fire's edge,
my bare legs were plenty warm; but, the day's sunburn
made the sea breeze that much cooler, sending occasional
chills through my neck and shoulders. I had made my
way back to the tent earlier in the night to grab a long
sleeve tee shirt in an attempt to combat the dropping
temps.

There's something trance evoking about a summer
bonfire in the sand. We sat there in silence just staring at
the flames, its orange flickers reflecting upon our salt and
sunburned faces. Parks had been true to his word and
only drank a couple.
"Are you having a good time, buddy?" He asked from
across the fire.
"Yeah, it's been good."
Silence ensued, interrupted only by the crackle of the fire.
"They're cool guys." I added.
"Yeah, they're pretty good old boys! We've been friends
for a long time." He said, his voice trailing off as he took
another sip of his beer.
"They're hilarious." I said, half laughing as I recalled
some of the stories they had told earlier in the evening.
"Yeah, they're a mess, that's for sure." He said, taking
another sip from the brown glass bottle. "I talked to them
about the weed."
"What do you mean?"
"I just feel like that's really disrespectful to you, so I asked

them not to smoke it around you anymore."

"Thanks."

"You're welcome." He replied. "I hope you're okay about the beer, man. I'm not drunk, I promise."

"I know, don't worry about it."

We sat in silence for a bit longer, watching quietly as the wood burned down to a ghostly white, the flames growing smaller and further apart

"Holden, you remember a while back when I told you I wanted to talk to you sometime?"

"Yeah."

"Well, I think I'm ready..."

With that, Parks began to recount the story of his life, a saga starring a soccer coach dad seeking to live vicariously through his only son. Parks had all of the unrealistic pressure of fulfilling his father's unrealized personal dreams, without any input as to his own goals in life. Whenever Parks didn't live up to those expectations he was told how stupid he was, what a pitiful excuse for a son he was, how his father wished he could have so and so for a son, constantly comparing Parks to his friends and teammates, placing scars upon his young heart just as horrifying as those marring my backside.

Parks found his refuge in the surfing fraternity of the Outer Banks, a brotherhood that temporarily served to temper the pain of his father's verbal abuse. As is often the case, there were times when the abuse became physical, but ever so privately. There were the midnight forced runs down the edge of highway twelve, beside his dad's pickup truck, until Park's legs buckled with exhaustion. Disgustingly, it all happened under the guise of making Parks a better athlete. But there were also the occasional bruises on the upper arm in the shape of his dad's fingers, or the excruciating sting of cigarette burns upon his shoulders. But the words...the words had left wounds and scars long after bruises faded and tired legs regained their strength. I understood exactly what he was

feeling, what he had been through, the type of empathy
that only comes from having walked a mile in similar
shoes.   Immediately, I understood the silence in the truck
that evening after I had told Parks about the scars on my
back. It had been the first time in my life that I had been
able to share openly. In my honesty Parks had found, for
the first time, someone he knew would understand exactly
what he had been through, someone sympathetic to the
emotional scars with which he still wrestled.

   Parks continued by telling me of a trip to visit his
grandparents in Ocracoke. It was then that the cigarette
burns had first been discovered. Parks was fourteen.
Sadly, Parks' mom chose to remain with his father. After
a nasty court battle, Parks' grandparents received custody
and Parks became a full-time Ocracoker. As is so painfully the case, those events did far more than simply change
Parks' mailing address, they shaped his view of the world,
of people, and of God. Parks had given me a precious
gift that night in the sharing of his story. I would guard
that gift at all costs. I realized more fully in those moments by the fading camp fire that vulnerability beckons
vulnerability, and authenticity welcomes the same.

Entry 19

   Autumn of '83 was beautiful as ever. While tourists
love Ocracoke in the Spring and Summer months, I always felt that the Fall sees the Outer Banks at its best. Of
all the scenes of coastal living, there's something ethereal
about an Autumn Outer Banks sunset, casting its warm
amber hues on the beach and illuminating the gray and
tan palette of marsh reeds behind the barrier islands.
The beaches and village seem to rest in the Fall from
the tiring influx of summer sightseers, inviting solitary
onlookers to rest as well.

   With the cooler temperatures come roe mullets. The
old timers on the island loved mullet roe. Salted, dried, or

fried, it was an island delicacy, one that Robert couldn't get enough of. I never could bring myself to try it. The long, fat orange roe looked to me like someone had lost a finger while wearing a pair of the orange gloves we used during summer shrimping.

Robert had geared up one of his skiffs for Fall mulleting and asked Parks and me if we would like to go a few days a week, mainly so he could get his yearly supply of roe for the freezer, as well as the supply he would give to the elderly residents of the island, trying to keep them stocked with fresh seafood. Part of being a true islander was having a freezer stocked with the bounty of the sea. Robert saw to it that the widows, and old salts of the island whose health kept them off the water, had plenty to eat and share with their families. I had learned to pull nets with Robert, while Parks was already well versed in how to operate the boats, a skill taught by his grandfather. It had been a few years since Parks had been mulleting, not since his grandfather's death of a sudden heart attack, but the skills were quick to return.

In early October we began taking the skiff out on Saturdays and weekday afternoons when Parks would get through with his last class at the island school. On weekdays we would stick close to the island, since the few hours between the end of school and dusk passed quickly, growing ever shorter as we moved towards December. However, on Saturdays we had more daylight and could be a little more adventurous in our excursions, heading north to Sandy Bay on the sound side of Hatteras, or south to Portsmouth Island, Royal Point Bay, and Daniels' Swash. The full flood tides of those chilly fall mornings are something my heart has longed for every autumn following. I loved heading out of Silver Lake on those still, calm mornings, the sun just beginning to rise in the east, clad in our Helly Hansen overhauls, hooded sweatshirts and ball caps turned backwards in an attempt to prevent them from blowing off our heads; the 150 horse power

90

Yamaha on the stern skipping us across the salty waters of Ocracoke Inlet.

The chill was warded off by a thermos of coffee, which Emilis had waiting for me on the kitchen counter each morning before daylight as I headed to the docks. The propellers left a trail of white water behind us, the bow occasionally crashing into the swells, spraying us with sea water. We would run down the back of the beach for miles as we looked for those signature ripples in the water, a promising disclosure to the trained eyes of local boys. The many nuances of the commercial fishing industry comprise a natural education much more scientific than many will ever give it credit.

Once Parks spotted the ripple on the surface he would lift his thumb, pointing over his shoulder towards the stern of the skiff. This was my silent cue to make my way to the rear of the boat and get the staff in hand, awaiting his next instruction. The staff was made of a solid wooden stake with pieces of steel fitted around it near the top and bottom. To these steel bands were welded metal rings that were attached to the gill net. When it was time, Parks would yell, "Now", and I would toss the staff, pointed end first, into the chilly salt water and brace myself as he gunned the skiff, hastily encircling the school of fish.

In the summer, when the water was warmer, we would get overboard inside the net and beat the water with our hands, or one of the oars, in order to drive the mullets into the marshes of the net. However, in the cooler months we just tightened up the net and used a couple of Robert's long, ash oars to beat the water from the edge of the skiff. Soon the corks would begin to bob around the circle, a tell-tale sign that the set had been successful. After a while we would begin pulling the net in over the side of the boat, clearing the fish from the marshes as they came over the side. The smell of those mullets as we pulled them from the sound and out of the

91

nets is still etched in my sensory.

By the time we reached the staff that I had thrown out, our oil skins, sweatshirts, and faces would be speckled with scales. Hopefully, we would have a couple of fish boxes filled with the fruits of our labors as well. Each set had its own feeling of exhilaration as we gave encore to our mechanical process, each set infused with the rush of the hunt and the hope of a good catch. The acts of our waterman's production were separated by an intermission of Mountain Dews, Honey Buns, and discussions on just about any topic one can think of.

Entry 20

There are dates in life that stand out from all others, some tied to births, some to deaths, or other monumental life events. Saturday, November 5th, 1983 was such a space in time, a day that in some ways forever altered the trajectory of my life. Parks and I had been down the sound, south of Portsmouth, all morning looking for fish. After clearing the nets and boxing just 17 mullets, we took it as confirmation of what we already knew, the season was well past its prime. After a couple more sets, with even poorer results, we finally decided to head back home and call it a season. Shortly after lunchtime we stopped off Portsmouth, silenced the outboard motor, and let the boat drift in the soft breeze as we un-wrapped our sandwiches. As we ate I looked over towards the old abandoned village, the black and white cedar shingled tower of the old Methodist Church peaking up above the cedars and scrub oaks.

"What exactly is over there?" I asked as I raised my can of Pepsi to take a sip, holding my half eaten bologna and mustard sandwich in my other hand.

"You've never been to Portsmouth?" Parks asked in a surprised tone.

"No." I replied, "I've only seen the Church steeple and a couple roof lines as we've passed by."

"Well," he said, jumping up with sandwich in hand to start the motor, "You'll see it today!"

He switched the boat into gear and we made our way up to the dock which ran off the back side of the island. After securing the skiff to the pilings with a few hitches of the cotton rope, we made our way down the pier and into the deserted village. Portsmouth Village seemed a type of coastal ghost town. We walked the grounds and stepped up onto porches, peering through old glass paned windows into homes that once bustled with activity, now a silent testament of a distant time. Parks, being the history buff, gave me the guided tour, telling me of a time when this mute hamlet once bustled with maritime shipping activity. This surreal place, far removed from the disruptions of the progress taking over the rest of the Outer Banks, was preserved. This collection of vacant cottages had once been the largest settlement on the banks, boasting a population of nearly 700 before the war between the states. The old wooden, clapboard homes and white picket fences allured me with a desire for such a simple and secluded existence, for a simpler time. The old Methodist Church that dominated the skyline of the island was simple and beautiful. Its interior was covered in bead-board, and there was an old upright piano near the altar rail which I couldn't resist playing. I made my way to the keys as Parks sat on the back pew hugging the aisle.

"They have a homecoming over here every year, you ought to come," he called from his perch in the rear of the Sanctuary.

"That would be great!" I replied, thumbing through the old Cokesbury hymnal for a familiar tune.

After a few songs on the piano, and a moment of silent prayer, I closed the lid over the worn keys and made my way back down the aisle towards the bell tower.

"You ready?" I asked, figuring it was time to get back.

"Sure, if you are," he said as he pulled himself up from

his seat, gripping the back of the pew in front of him.
It was a quiet walk back to the skiff. I was soaking in
the beauty around us and the quietness of it all, the only
auditory offerings of the island were the gentle lapping
of water on the shore, the breeze as it rustled the marsh
grass, and the song of cicadas from the maritime forest.

Parks hopped down from the dock into the skiff ahead
of me.

"You want a drink?" he asked as he reached into the
cooler and pulled out a can of Mountain Dew from the
icy water, wiping the ice and excess water from it."

"Yeah, I'll take one."

We sat there on the side of the boat looking back at the
island.

"So, what did you think?" He asked.

"I loved it!" I replied.

We sat for a few more moments in silent speculation as
the sun began its descent, the water lapping gently against
the windward side of the skiff. In that moment, before I
knew what was happening, I felt the warm, wind chapped
lips of my best friend gently against my own. As we sat
there looking out over the seascape, Parks leaned over and
kissed me, resting his hand against the side of my face.

In that moment I was overcome with a series of emotions that I'm still not sure I can adequately describe.
Surges of fear, anxiety and pleasure passed through my
stunned mind in rapid succession.

"Are you okay?" He said softly, a bit concerned after
he pulled away and gave me a few moments in silence.
I stared straight ahead, my insides trembling, as Parks
gazed at me from beside.

"Holden?" He said again, trying to break my panic induced trance.

I did not see this coming but the event had drawn back
the curtain on over ten years of questions and fears, and
a full-fledged fight to be normal. The kiss scared me to
death because it brought me face to face with a reality

94

I had tried to escape with all the tenacity that I could muster.

I had lived in a precarious form of secret pain for several years leading up to this unexpected encounter. As years rolled by, littered with failed relationships, anxiety attacks, and desperate attempts to suppress, deny and choke out any hint of this fearful reality. I made frantic pleas for forgiveness, for change of what I didn't feel I could control...but felt I had to before my whole life imploded.

I lived with a tightness in my chest that no young man in his twenties, or any age for that matter, should have to carry. My internal dialogue left my mind in a state of torment as I fought with everything I had not to be what I knew deep down that I was. For me, failure to escape this damned desire would lead to not just my eternal destruction, but total devastation of my life as I knew it. If I couldn't win out over this thing I would lose it all...I believed that. It's different for people coming to grips with their sexuality in rural areas. I feared this would end my life.

I fought thoughts of self-harm for years, trying desperately to come to grips with my warring desires: the desire to live for God, and the desire to be loved by another man. Even when Robert wanted to buy me a shotgun for duck hunting, I respectfully declined. Not that I had any objection to people bearing arms, but because I was scared to death to have access to a firearm...scared because I knew that I needed to keep means of suicide as far from me as possible.

I may have only ever disclosed this to one other person, but my life since college had been consumed with three major fears: 1. that I would not be able to beat these unwanted attractions and desires, walk away from my relationship with God and embark on a life that I felt was outside of God's will and blessing, 2. that I would have a complete nervous breakdown, or 3. that the pain would

95

become too much for me to handle anymore, leading me to take my own life.

Every match making ploy from the women of the Church only added to my mounting anxiety, knowing that with every passing year my situation would grow more risky as people began to wonder why I hadn't married yet, why I wasn't interested in any of the young women they were trying to set me up with. After many unsuccessful attempts I had left behind the tired ritual of trying to date away my problem. But in this moment I was face to face with what my heart had craved, and what my mind and spirit were forbidding. I couldn't be gay because I would go to hell. This was a belief as central to my existence as my very name. I had fought urges and desires ever since puberty and had tried with all my might to muster the strength and resolve to overcome feelings that sought to be my undoing.

"Holden, talk to me." Parks said as he placed his hand gently upon my shoulder, offering a gentle reminder of his supportive and concerned presence.

As I turned to look at him, tears ran down my scale speckled face.

"I'm sorry, Holden. I didn't mean..." his sentence trailed of as he looked at me with a mixture of fear and concern. I was sorry that it had happened, but glad that it had happened all at the same time. I wanted to run from Parks, but I also wanted to crumble in his embrace. I was torn in two, a feeling that had become a familiar component of my life as I came to grips with the gnawing reality of a sexuality that I had tried for years to change and snuff out.

At that moment Parks slowly reached over and held me, resting my head on his chest, his hooded sweatshirt a scented mixture of fabric softener and fish slime. In that moment, I breathed deeply, my insides still quivering, never feeling more right and more wrong in the exact same moment at any point in my entire life.

96

After a few moments I pulled away and looked at him.
"Why did you do that?" I asked, not indignantly, but out
of a deep curiosity of what kind of signal I had given off
to make him feel it was even safe to try. I had tried for
so long to divert any attention from my secret torment.
I labored to fit into the masculine world, to refuse all
semblance within myself of anything that suggested I was
anything less than the all-American alpha male I aspired
to be. Try as I may, I always felt a tinge of fraudulence.
I think I was as concerned with the fact that he had
discovered my secret as I was about what had actually
happened. Furthermore, I was finding it hard to accept
the fact that Parks liked men too. Parks, who in my mind
was the poster child of the Outer Banks man's man, the
surfer, the fisherman, the soccer jock...what in the world
was happening here?

"Why did you do that?"

"Because I couldn't take it anymore." He replied.

"What are you talking about?" I pressed.

"Ever since that first night at the lighthouse I have been
crazy about you and I just couldn't help myself."

"Do you think I'm gay?" I asked, scared to death that
someone may be able see my secret, and scared because I
still was not fully willing to admit that I was.

Silence lay heavily for a few moments as the sun began its
descent and the cicadas crescendoed.

"I'm hoping you are." He said solemnly.

"How can you be gay? You're not like that?"

"Like what? Effeminate?" He asked.

I just shook my head, affirming that he had filled in the
blank correctly.

"Holden, I'm attracted to men; that doesn't mean I have
to be prissy."

"But what made you think....What caused you to ..." I
couldn't formulate my thoughts very well.

"Holden, you are hands down the nicest guy I've ever
met. You're beautiful...or would you rather me say hand-

some? Why wouldn't I fall in love with you? I just felt like we were on the same page."

"Do I act gay?" I asked with a tone that suggested panic.

"No." He responded.

"Then why did you do that?" I questioned.

"Because, I hoped you would reciprocate." He said, annoyed that I was pulling away.

I can still remember the wash of emotions raging in my heart, like there was an internal spin cycle draining me of my delusions and bringing me face to face with the fact that, try as I may to deny, ignore, and run from this aspect of myself, I would have to deal with it in some way or another. Amidst the settling of this reality, there came the painful realization that I had never been just one of the guys, one of the heterosexual "in crowd". That day, more than ever, I awoke to the fact that I never would be. Parks challenged all of my preconceived notions and stereotypes. He was the picture of manhood, a picture that I wanted to emulate, a man that I wanted to be more like, and here I found out that we shared the same journey in more ways than one.

The kiss had also brought me face to face with the realization that I could no longer run from the fact that I was falling in love with Parks as well. Parks was handsome, strong, athletic and intelligent; but he was also gentle, compassionate, considerate and deep. That combination awakened feelings and attractions in me long buried, and long fought. He was the man of my dreams, forbidden as they were. The kiss made me admit to myself how I had been looking at him for months. My feelings were deeper than friendship. I secretly longed to be closer to him, but fought to keep an appropriate distance. I wanted to be free with him, but I was captivated by hypervigilance, afraid that if I allowed myself to be free with him that it would turn into flirtation or an experience that I both craved and feared. There was a civil war raging in my soul, and I worried that I would

98

ultimately be a casualty.

There were many times through my high school and college days that I had contemplated ending it all, so tired of the mental and emotional onslaught related to an attraction I didn't ask for and didn't want, yet one that was persistent in its prodding. It was during these times that I turned to my faith in order to give me comfort and serve as a protective factor against self-harm. The kiss had awakened me to a secular proverb that I had often heard: wherever you go, there you are. Run as I may, I would have to deal with this.

There was, however, one major difference between our two paths. Parks had long ago rejected any religious allegiance. His personalized sense of spirituality demanded only a sense of goodwill toward others, of caring for those less fortunate, and of being true to oneself. I on the other hand was a committed, conservative Christian and held the conviction that to give in to these feelings, to embrace what my heart and soul were screaming out for, would ultimately lead to my eternal destruction. Parks was set on go, but I was caught in a tug of war between opposing desires that both felt very central to who I was. What began as a routine day of mullet fishing in Pamlico Sound had proven to be one of the most monumental days in the story of my life. I sat there with Parks' arm around me, my body craving another kiss, a longer embrace, while my soul cried out to God for absolution, help, and remission of my sins.

Entry 21

We didn't speak much more that day. As we brought the boat in to the dock at Silver Lake my insides were literally trembling. The kiss and all it represented had shaken me to my core and I didn't know how to respond, other than to retreat into my own mind. I lifted the box of mullets we had caught and set them on the dock. I quickly climbed up onto the dock, lifted the box and

headed towards the freezer without saying a word. I left
Parks in the skiff, cleaning it of the few pieces of sea weed
and fish scales left from our sets. I didn't know where to
go from here. As I came out of the walk-in cooler Parks
was standing there leaning against the white plywood
wall, his arms folded, staring directly into my eyes.

"Holden."

I just looked at him, still reeling with an insatiable desire
to run, pack my things, and leave the island. I wanted
to pretend that none of this had happened, to continue
my life of denial; but as he stared at me with his crystal
blue eyes, I realized that something had begun that would
take every ounce of strength I had to overcome. Even
then, I wasn't sure that I had the strength to withstand
the weight of desire which plagued my heart and mind
for so many years. Here I was face to face with the man
of my dreams, and for once in my life that man actually reciprocated my feelings. Every time I heard Parks'
tender voice speak my name, trying to make sure I was
ok, I melted. No longer was it just a passing thought to
be banished quickly from my mind. I now had tasted lips
that I had studied secretly for months. The broad shoulders I had admired on surfing trips had now supported
my head, and the strong hands that threatened to knock
out an irate surfer at Hatteras had rested upon my cheek
in a gesture of intimacy. I was coming undone and I was
completely terrified.

"I can't do this Parks, I just can't." I responded, looking
down at the cement floor.

"Can't...or won't?" He replied.

"I can't."

With that I began to walk past him, I had to get away, I
needed to get back to the little cottage, to my safe place,
where I could process what was going on and what I
needed to do. I could feel my anxiety mounting, my
breathing becoming more rapid. He reached out to take
hold of my arm gently as I passed him by, but I pulled

away and kept walking. Prayers and confessions cycled through my mind as I walked alone down the side of the road towards the shell paved path of home. Before long I heard the little red Nissan pulling up beside me, and Parks calling gently from the driver's window.

"Holden, buddy, I'm sorry. I just thought..."

I just kept walking not even looking in his direction. My mind was a battlefield and I just kept looking down at the sand and grass as I walked. Eventually, he just pulled away. I made my way to the little cottage, which thankfully was empty, and locked myself in the bathroom. I ran the water as hot as I could get it and just sat there in the floor of the shower as the steaming hot water beat down on my scalp. Streams of hot bathwater and tears intermingled, running down my face into the crevices of my lips before dropping from my chin and swirling down the drain between my knees. The tears betrayed both a sense of guilt and trepidation related to what I knew would certainly be my eternal fate if I couldn't beat this. Yet there was such deep sadness as I considered how I had walked away from Parks. I thought of him, of what he was going through, of how I loved him. This patchwork of thoughts and fears gave way to a steady stream of tears, until the water morphed from scorching hot to lukewarm. I came face to face with the cruel reality of wanting so badly something forbidden.

Why? Why couldn't it be ok? Why couldn't I just love him? Why couldn't I just be with who I wanted to be with? Why did it have to be wrong? Why did it have to be condemned in Scripture? How could something that felt so natural, so right to me, be so detestable? I just couldn't understand, and for the first time in my life I questioned God as the anger and sense of unfairness intermingled.

I felt awful about how I responded to Parks, but I couldn't face him just yet. I needed some time to process all of it. I later came to learn of the private torture Parks

101

was facing in that four day period as I avoided him at all costs. He feared he had completely misread me, scared to death that I was going to out him on the island. I spent the days helping around the fish house in the mornings and sitting alone on the beach in the afternoons, trying my best to process it all. Parks spent his days at the school and his evenings at the Jolly Roger Pub or locked up in his house, encroached upon by the unalleviated stress of not knowing if I were going to out him to Robert, or even worse in his mind, if I would never speak to him again.

I knew that I couldn't live like this, but at the same time Parks had been my very best friend and every day that passed without him around felt like a death inside of me. I began mourning the loss of his companionship and finally decided that regardless of my own anxiety, I needed to try and salvage the friendship, to at least talk to Parks about everything. On the following Thursday afternoon I went out in search of him, I had been the one to abandon him and it was my place to build the bridge.

I went by his house that afternoon at about three-thirty, knowing he should be home from school by then. The driveway was empty and the house locked, but his board was missing from its normal perch by the back door. I got into my car and drove north until I saw his truck parked on the edge of 12 just past Molasses Creek. I pulled up behind it and got out, making my way atop the dunes in my kangaroos and corduroys. I could see his black, wet suit clad torso bobbing in the swells a good way off shore, leaning forward on his arms as he watched the horizon for approaching sets. I walked down to the shoreline and sat in the sand beside Parks' ball cap and surfboard wax, which he had set aside before entering the surf. I sat there for the better part of an hour, my knees raised to my chest in an attempt to shield me from the chilly fall sea breeze breaching the thin fabric of my track jacket. Sets came and went, but Parks never moved to catch them, a disclosure that he paddled beyond the breakers

102

that day to think rather than surf. Eventually, he turned his attention shoreward and saw me sitting there. Slowly, he began paddling in. In a matter of minutes he was just yards away, unleashing his ankle, wading through the shallows with the nose of his board under one arm, its tail dragging in the surf behind him. His long hair was wet and sprinkled with grains of sand, his face etched with a solemn, unsure countenance.

"Hey." I said, an awkward break to a four day silence.

"Hey." he responded in kind.

"We need to talk." I continued.

He just shook his head affirmingly as he laid his board down on the sand, sitting down in front of me.

"Parks, please forgive me for abandoning you the past few days, I just needed to think about everything."

"Holden, look. It was my fault, I'm sorry that I read you wrong, man. But please, please, please, promise me that you won't tell anyone, it would ruin me on the island." He said in tones bordering upon pleading.

"Parks, I would never do that to you."

There was a brief pause as Parks looked at me and then down at the sand around his feet.

"I just can't believe that I got it so wrong." He said, raising his eyes back to mine, "I just thought that you felt the same way. Man, did I ever miss it."

"Parks..." I began and then trailed off, trying to keep down emotions that were attempting to peak into outward visibility.

"What?"

"You didn't." I said.

"Didn't what?" He pressed.

"You didn't miss it."

A thin smile appeared on his face.

"You got it right, Parks...but I can't go there."

Silence.

"Parks, I know you don't believe like I do, but my faith will not allow it."

103

Silence.

"I don't want to be this way Parks, I want to be normal."

"Normal!" He retorted, "What's normal?"

"Parks, you know what I mean." I continued.

"Yeah, you want a wife, three kids, and a white picket fence, right?"

"Yes!...well... yes." I said, struggling with the reality that I really didn't want that either, what I wanted was sitting right in front of me, but I could not allow myself to embrace him.

"Parks," I continued, "Can't we just be best friends, like we've been all this time, without letting it go any further?"

"Do you really think that's possible?" He questioned.

"Isn't it worth a try?" I asked, "Or do you want to lose this completely."

He quietly looked down at the sand, then offshore, then back at me.

"No, I don't want to lose you, Holden." He said.

"Me either."

Silence dominated the minutes as we vacillated between looking into each other's eyes and then away at the horizon, or the waves, or the dunes...anything to quell some of the emotions that were so raw and powerful.

"So where do we go from here?" He asked me with a sense of sad surrender.

"Let's just take it as it comes."

"Ok." He replied in a resigned manner.

After a few more awkward moments of silence we made our way back over the dunes.

"I picked up a few oysters yesterday evening, do you want to come over and steam some tonight?" Parks asked as he strapped his board into the back of his pickup.

"Sounds good." I replied.

"Cool."

It was a relief to have had the conversation, the wall of separation now breached. It was as if we both had been holding our breath for the past four days. With the connection renewed and the red Nissan and silver Honda once again in caravan, we were both able to exhale and breathe in again. I left the ocean-side with hope that we could navigate this tension without losing each other.

After we arrived back at Parks' house, he jumped into the shower while I started the pot of water boiling. He soon emerged from his room in his jeans and long-sleeve tee shirt, still rubbing his hair with a towel to get the excess water out.

"What do you want to go with them?" He said as he walked over to the pantry to see what options we had.

"Doesn't matter to me, buddy." I replied.

"Well, let's see...I've got some dill pickles here, and some saltines.." He listed them off as he perused his stock of groceries, one hand bracing his weight as he leaned on the door frame of the pantry, still using the other to dry his hair.

I wouldn't have cared if we ate cold corned beef right out of the can that night, it was the fact that we were together, working through this together, and not letting it destroy our friendship...that was the real feast for me.

The oysters were great. Parks whipped up some of his special dipping sauce to go with them. Most everyone on the island made a sauce of Texas Pete, ketchup, and vinegar for their oysters. Parks' recipe was different in that he added mayonnaise, and I must say that I always liked it better. When the oysters were steamed, we sat down at his small kitchen table, covered in newspapers, and gorged ourselves.

We passed the night laughing, carrying on, telling jokes, and watching the Thursday night lineup of Night Court and Hill Street Blues. I always tried to be respectful of Robert and Emilis by being home at a decent hour, so as Hill Street finished up I made my way to the kitchen, turning on the kitchen faucet to begin washing up the dishes before heading home. As soon as Parks heard the water running I heard him call from the living room:

105

"What are you doing?"

"I'm just going to wash up these dishes."

"No, man, I've got that, you go on home and get some rest." He said as he made his way into the kitchen behind me.

"Parks, I'm glad to do it."

"I told you, don't worry about it, I'll clean up."

So I turned off the dish water and dried my hands.

"What are you up to tomorrow?" I asked, laying the hand towel on the counter beside the sink.

"If there are any waves I think I may try to catch some before it gets dark."

"Cool." I said, not wanting to press a self-evoked invitation, still unsure of how close we could or should be. I wanted to hang out with him all the time, but I was trying to navigate this new territory and wasn't really sure how to go about it.

"Do you want to go with me?" He asked, causing me to smile though I tried to maintain a suave exterior.

"Sure, that would be great." I replied, trying not to allow myself to be too eager.

We settled on a time and the next evening, like old times, he pulled up at the Guthrie house and I tossed my board in the back of the little pickup. Though my heart was ecstatic, I was wrestling with the complexity of trying to navigate a purely platonic relationship with someone I knew I had deep feelings for, and worse yet, who had the same feelings for me. It was like trying to perform a delicately choreographed dance without really knowing all of the steps; meanwhile, feeling that if I got a step wrong it would mean complete disaster. I was trapped in this chasm between wanting to just be free in my interactions with Parks and the hypervigilance that dictated my every move and every word, the fear of getting too close or too vulnerable.

106

Entry 22

As time passed, things seemed completely back to normal in our friendship, almost as if we had regained our pre-Portsmouth dance. We settled back into a level of ease with one another, the awkward uncertainty of how to act toward each other seemed to wane with each passing day of successfully navigating the tension. November dawned and brought with it my twenty-fourth birthday. I had already decided that I wouldn't be going to Johnston County, especially since I would be heading there for Thanksgiving in just a couple of weeks and could celebrate with my family then. Furthermore, I wanted to spend it on the island with the people I had grown to love. I cared deeply for my family, but going back to Johnston County seemed like a regression for me into a pit of painful memories and a reminder of Mama's depression, John's effortless happiness, and Samuel's newest antisocial tendencies.

My birthday fell on Tuesday that year, Election Day. Robert and Emilis were attending some political function that night and had already made plans to host a party for me on Saturday at the house, inviting a small number of friends and Church members that I had grown close to. The Church was to have a cake and ice cream party for me on Sunday, following the evening service.

With the day approaching, Parks asked what I had planned. I told him I wasn't doing anything on my actual birthday, but that Robert and Emilis were having a party on Saturday night. Unbeknownst to me, they had already invited him.

"Well why don't you come over and we can put some steaks on the grill." he said.

"You don't have to do that, man." I replied, though flattered that he had remembered and actually wanted to help me celebrate.

"Well, I wouldn't be a very good friend if I didn't do something, now would I?"

107

"I guess not." I replied.
"You just be at my house at about 5:30."

I pulled up to his place at about a quarter past five on my birthday to find the grill pulled out in the back yard a couple of feet from the porch steps, the flames rising fiercely from the charcoal mound. I could feel the warmth of the flames as I walked past them on my way to the back door. I knocked, even though I could see him in the kitchen working on dinner.
"Come on in." he said as he finished shoving a pan of potatoes into the oven. "Happy Birthday!" he said as he came over and gave me a hug.
"Thanks man, I appreciate all this!"
"You don't have to thank people for celebrating your birthday!" Parks answered.

We spent the afternoon grilling steaks, joking around, and watching television. It was a treasure to be cared for like that, to have someone actually remember my birthday and to go to all that trouble to celebrate it with me. Throughout my life and friendships I had always been the one to make sure that everyone else was celebrated, that everyone else was affirmed and made to feel special. However, too often it seemed, when it was my day, so many of the people whom I had worked so hard to care for were M.I.A.
We finished dinner, washed up the dishes, and I thanked him repeatedly for everything he had done.
"Well, hang on." he said, "It's not over yet!"

He pulled out a chair from the kitchen table and asked me to have a seat and close my eyes. As the years passed, I learned that one of Parks' greatest thrills in life was getting to surprise someone. He would get almost giddy with excitement when he had something special and secretive up his sleeve; he was like a child on Christmas morning. Sitting there at the table with my eyes closed I could hear the refrigerator door open, then a drawer, then foot-steps getting closer to where I was sitting.

108

"Okay, open your eyes." he said.

What I saw when I opened my eyes left me completely speechless. The evening to that point had removed all doubt regarding the value Parks placed on my friendship, but what he sat before me gave me a deeper understanding of the level of care and consideration he had for me. His gift afforded me a deeper understanding of his character and thoughtfulness, a level that went deeper than I had ever imagined.

"Is this what I think it is?" I said.

"Yes, sir!" He replied. "Happy Birthday!"

I couldn't speak.

"You see, I listen to you more than you know," he added. There before me was a chocolate cake with strawberry frosting. Parks had remembered that detail of my story ever since I mentioned it to him earlier in the summer.

"I can't believe you did this." I said, overwhelmed by this gesture. "Did you make it?"

"Sure did," he replied, grinning from ear to ear, "me and Betty Crocker."

It was one of the most touching things anyone had ever done for me. It was truly the greatest birthday gift I had ever received and gratitude welled so strongly in my heart that words escaped me. My awestruck silence seemed to be all the response Parks needed.

Never had anyone cared for me in this way. It was these types of gestures that helped me fall in love with Parks in the first place. Not only was it just a symbol to me of friendship, this gift was charged with all the emotion of when a young woman finds a long-stem rose on her pillow with a love letter from her boyfriend, the type of message received when a young man opens a card from his girlfriend to find a tape with a compilation of all of "their" songs. It was the stuff dreams are made of, but the problem was that my dreams were forbidden.

I sat there looking down at the dome of pink frosting, then over at Parks who had taken a seat next to me at the

109

table. Within a few silent moments I had leaned across the expanse and began kissing him, gently, passionately. But the moment I realized how comfortable I was with it, I freaked out and drew back.

"What?" Parks said as I walked over to the kitchen sink, leaning forward with my hands on the counter.

"I'm sorry, Parks, I can't do this. I just can't do this."

"What the fuck, Holden?" he said as he rose angrily from the table and headed into the living room.

"Parks, can't you understand?"

"Look, do you want to be with me or not?"

Parks had never spoken to me in this tone before.

"Parks, it's not that simple."

"Whatever, Holden. Whatever."

"Yes, I want to be with you..."

"Then be with me." he interrupted.

"Parks, I can't."

"Can't? Can't? Let me tell you what I can't do, Holden."

I was speechless by this point, never before had he lost patience with me, not like this.

"I can't keep riding this roller coaster with you, Holden! I can't do it anymore! I can't keep on just being your surfing buddy and your Friday night hangout, when everything inside of me just wants to be with you."

"I'm sorry, Parks."

I had been so consumed with my own thoughts and feelings in the midst of this war that I had never stopped to consider the toll this relationship was having on him.

"My life with you is like a yo-yo, Holden. One minute your head is on my chest, or you're kissing me, and the next it's, 'I can't do this anymore', and you're freaking out and talking about us going to hell."

"Parks, this is really hard for me."

"Oh, and it's a walk in the park for me? Just when I think we're finally getting somewhere, you're running away again. I can't keep this up, Holden. You're making me insane."

110

I guess it was only a matter of time until it all came to a head, and this was the night. How had an evening that started so well turned so sour?

Eventually the raised voices and flaring tempers subsided and we were able to talk civilly about our respective sides of the equation. For the first time Parks shared with me, in a deep way, what this was doing to him. I also shared with Parks my desires and fears, along with my understanding of where yielding to these temptations would land us. In the end, the consensus was as it had been since the afternoon at Portsmouth, we couldn't be together and we couldn't bear the thought of walking away...we would continue our tightrope walk for the foreseeable future.

Entry 23

The Thanksgiving and Christmas Seasons were a whirlwind of activities with a full Church calendar, trips back and forth to Johnston County, and annual traditions at the Guthrie house. On New Year's, Parks had an old college buddy come down to stay for a few days. They played soccer together at Carolina and had been suite mates there for a couple of semesters. Harrison was his name and he was everything I felt that I was not, the embodiment of everything my insecurities whispered that I lacked. He came down a couple of days after Christmas and stayed through New Year's Day.

Once Harrison arrived on the island things were a little different for me and Parks, a painful reminder of some of our differences. Parks and Harrison had plans to go out on New Year's to some of the pubs on the island with all the other local boys who were home for the season from college, work, or the service, whatever their ticket off of the island had been. Meanwhile, I was busy with the New Year's Eve watch-night prayer service at the Church.

Parks took Harrison up to Hatteras to see the light-

111

house, to the Wright Brothers Memorial in Kitty Hawk, and out on the boat...an itinerary that sought to cram the entire Outer Banks experience into a three day visit, to the fullest extent one could expect in the winter months. Between my schedule with the Church, the fish house, and helping Emilis and Robert around the cottage taking down Christmas decorations, I had very little time to spend with two of them. Harrison was taking the early ferry back across on the morning of the second and Parks had planned to go surfing on New Year's Day if the waves were conducive, an excursion which he asked me to join.

On January 1st, 1984, I donned my wetsuit, grabbed my board and headed out of the front door at the beep of Parks' horn in the driveway. Parks got out and helped me strap my board in the back of the truck.

"I'm glad you came." He said with a smile as he tightened the strap, holding the board sturdy against the tailgate, "I feel like I haven't seen you in a week."

"Yep." I said shortly, betraying the feelings of abandonment that I was trying to press down and keep buried. I climbed into the cab as Harrison scooted over in the middle and let me have the window seat. I was trying to be present with them but my heart was raging with emotions and I settled in silence as Parks sought to engage conversation that would connect his two friends.

"Harrison, Holden had never surfed till about eight months ago, and if I'm not careful he's going to be better than me before long." He said, obviously trying to lighten my mood and break down my defenses.

"It will be a long time before I'm as good as you are." I replied flatly, not biting his lure of flattery.

"Parks says you're a pastor." Harrison said, seeking to initiate a conversation with me. "When did you first sense a calling to do that?" He asked, launching us into a discussion about my life, my sense of calling, and my passion for helping others.

"I think that's awesome." He replied.

112

"Really?" I responded. Not many people our age referred to it in such a sincerely supportive way.

"Yeah, my grandfather was a pastor...spent his whole life helping people, teaching them about God."

"Wow. That's great!" I replied

"Yeah. I guess you could say he was my hero. He died a couple of years ago."

As the conversation progressed I realized that I had been very unfair in my ill feelings towards Harrison. He was truly a quality person, the kind of person with whom I could actually see becoming very good friends. We made our way down the island and out into the surf, only having a limited time given that the wetsuits still didn't totally protect the body from the effects of the cold January waters. There were times in the winter months when Parks and I would come in from surfing and not be able to start the truck for a few minutes because our hands were frozen to the point that we couldn't grasp the key.

The day turned out to be very enjoyable. Harrison caught his first wave, as Parks and I watched him from beyond the breakers. Yet, even amidst all the good times, I was beginning to wrestle with feelings and realizations that were painfully cut and dry. If I was not willing to be with Parks and he decided to pursue a relationship with another man, there was really nothing I could say or do about it. I tried to talk to myself and be rational about the whole thing, but my emotions refused to be curtailed with any form of rational self-talk. My mind may have been talking me away from the cliff, but my emotions were screaming 'no'. I had come face-to-face with the dilemma of refusing sexual intimacy with Parks, and yet not wanting anyone else to fill that place in his life. I felt like an immature, jealous school boy.

The next morning we saw Harrison off at the ferry dock. Even with all the tinges of jealously and misgiving I had towards his presence on the island, I truly had come to like him. He stood on the stern of the boat, waving

113

as the ferry made its turn out of Silver Lake and into the Pamlico. As the boat faded behind the cedars, Parks looked over at me.

"You want some coffee?" He asked.

"Sure!"

We made our way back to his cottage and Parks pulled his percolator from the bottom cabinet.

"How about some breakfast?" He asked.

"Sure, I'm starving."

We talked over breakfast about everything and nothing. True to form, Parks wouldn't allow me to evade addressing what was really going on inside. He could recognize the tension I was trying to hide. After persistent prodding, I finally opened up about what was eating at me. I told him of how I had wrestled with feelings of jealousy and how stupid I felt for having admitted it to myself, and now to him.

"Holden, Harrison and I are not like that. He's completely straight."

"Maybe so, but someday that won't be the case. Someday I'm just going to have to suck it up and wish you the best."

I had addressed a truth that we both had pondered in our private mental discourses. But here at Parks' breakfast table, for the first time, the idea had been laid bare. If I were not willing to pursue a full-fledged relationship with Parks, should he become weary of mere friendship, then there would indeed come a day when I would have to watch him live our dreams with another man. Neither of us knew what to make of that. Silence crept in after I acknowledged the elephant in the room, the only sounds for minutes were the low thuds of our coffee mugs on the formica table top and the screech of forks on our egg and bacon filled plates. Finally, Parks decided we had stewed on it for long enough.

"How about we just cross that bridge when and if we get to it?"

114

And so, we went about our day, our lives, our friendship, seeking to push back such clouds for as long as possible.

Entry 24

March came in like a lion that year, with gale-force winds working the sound into a murky sea of white caps and salt spray. The bleak, gray sky offered no solace from the piercing fierceness of cold wind, driving sheets of rain, and freezing sea mist. The ferries had been moored at the docks for three straight days, the waves too large and the winds too high for safe crossing.

Robert held a long standing order with Tipper Whitaker, a seafood restaurant entrepreneur from Calabash who had established a number of restaurants in the Myrtle Beach area. Robert was one of his chief suppliers.

We were three days late on our order because there was no way off the island. Even the shorter ferry north to Hatteras had ceased operation during the storm, since it had to pass in such close proximity to the Inlet on its northward course. Robert monitored the weather and maintained close contact with his connections in the Ferry Division, eager to move those fish south at first opportunity. Early on this particular morning that break came with a call from the ferry director well before daylight. He was calling to let Robert know there would be a test run at 7 am. The ferry wasn't going to be open to the public, but there would be a place for Robert's truck center stern.

At 4:30 that Saturday morning, the knock came at my door. Robert had just hung up the phone after receiving the news he had been anticipating.

"Holden." He called in a serious and deliberate manner.

"Yes, sir." I replied, still partially comatose.

"I need you to get up and get ready, we've got to get to the fish house right now. The ferry's running at 7." He instructed.

I made my way out of bed and got dressed with as much tenacity as I could manage in my half-conscious state.

115

At ten till five we were firing up the old pickup and backing out of the drive in the cold, driving rain. The past-prime windshield wipers slid across the glass, smearing the water more than actually removing it. We had just over an hour to load the truck and be in line to catch the trial run off of the island. The morning was lacking in conversation. It was time for business and a sense of urgency pervaded the air as Robert, the fish house crew, and I all moved in mechanical sequence, loading pallets and transporting them into the back of the refrigerated truck.

Shortly after six we were finished, drenched from the driving rain that took advantage of every breech in our oil-skin armor, soaking those areas in a mixture of frosty rain and fish slime. My underwear and tee shirt were wet with sweat, all my body heat trapped by the layers of long-handled drawers, sweat shirts and Helly Hansens. I had just a few minutes to spare before getting in line at the ferry dock, just enough time to swing by Parks's place with an invitation to join me.

Parks Eason was my one true weakness. In some way I knew my love for him promised to be my undoing, but like insects drawn to those glowing, blue bug zappers which illuminated almost every porch on the island on humid summer nights, there was a draw to him from deep inside me. Though the words were too much for me to own at that time, I had fallen in love with him. I was never quite as happy as when we were clowning around, diving from his skiff into the waters of Teach's Hole, surfing, or mending nets together on the shore of Silver Lake. There were also those times when we would sneak away on clear nights and lay on a blanket in the dunes, watching the skies above in silence, wondering what would become of us in this world and in the next. There was a sense of conflict always brewing within me as I wrestled between my faith convictions and the love that I had found in Parks. They were constant tides in opposition.

116

In the rare moments when I allowed myself to lie in Parks' embrace, my head resting on his chest, his heartbeat faint, his scent in my nostrils and his soft warm breath upon my hair as he rested his lips upon the crown of my head, I never felt a greater dichotomy of emotions. There was a sense in which this love reached to the very core of my being, that I was more alive with him than I had ever been in my life. Yet, there was a sense of fear, a real sense of danger, a deep river of confusion and inner turmoil at the intersection of my felt-experience and the Word I held sacred, which seemed to condemned the very thing I was. Maybe this is why I had such a hard time understanding the love of God for so many years, because I had a hard time understanding how He could love me when I had read of His condemnation of people like myself. There was a deep feeling of shame and guilt because of my double-life, an internalized disgust regarding my secret sin, and a deep sense of sadness at the prohibition of a love that touched me so deeply.

After pulling onto the edge of the road in front of Parks' house, I climbed down from the light green cab, bearing the J. L. Guthrie & Son logo, and pulled the hood of my oil skin coat over my head, shielding me from the cold rain. I eased through the front picketed gate and down the east side of the house to Parks' bedroom window. After a few taps on the glass, his sleep filled eyes appeared as he pulled the edge of the curtain slightly from the window facing. He motioned toward the back porch and I made my way around the rear of the house, as he slipped quietly onto the back porch, gently closing the door behind him.

"What in the world, Holden?" he said, still half asleep, crossing his arms and rubbing his biceps to ward off the cold.

"Come ride with me to Calabash!" I said still standing on the top porch step.

"When are you leaving?" He said, I could tell he wasn't

117

completely coherent yet.

"Right now." I replied, "Come on."

"Let me get dressed." He said as he wiped sleep from his eyes.

"Hurry. I can't miss this boat."

I made my way back to the truck and turned the heat on high, trying to ward off the pervasive damp chill. In a few minutes Parks made his way down the front walk and into the cab. After fussing with the clutch and finally getting the truck in gear, we made our way back onto the road and headed off of the island on the 7 o'clock boat.

The journey across Pamlico Sound was treacherous as the ferry rolled from side to side in the strong winds and large swells. Sheets of salt water beat a constant cadence upon the windshield of the fish truck. It was probably the closest I have ever come to getting sea-sick.

Finally, we made our way to the dock at Cedar Island and pulled from the steel deck of the ship onto solid ground, a welcomed friend after nearly two and one half ours of dipping and rolling upon the large steel vessel. We then headed south, down highways 12, 70, 24 and 17 until we came to Calabash. It wasn't anything glamorous, just a typical day of hauling fish; but, the companionship made it so much better. The foundation of our relationship was always a deep and abiding friendship, an appreciation of each other's company and the laughter that filled our lives when we were together.

As we were approaching Morehead on the way home, Robert called to tell me the ferries had been docked again due to another increase in wind-speed. He had made a reservation for me to stay at the Driftwood Motel, right beside the ferry dock at Cedar Island, so that I could keep the truck in the ferry line and wait out the storm. I would have to wait for the first ferry back to Ocracoke once the storm broke.

Robert's phone call filled me with a divided sense of anxiety and excitement. I was warring with the theological ramifications of what had happened between Parks and me up to that point. As a matter of fact, we had a serious talk after our second sexual encounter about what we were going to do. I did not want to live contrary to my faith convictions, and neither of us wanted to lose the friendship that we had. I decided, much to Parks' dismay, that I couldn't do it anymore. I didn't feel that it was pleasing to God and I just couldn't allow myself to go there again. From that point on we had sought to be best friends and nothing more.

Things had gone according to plan for the months which lapsed between that difficult conversation and our trip to Calabash, but as I processed the words Robert spoke to me over the phone, I realized that this would be an extremely difficult night. I tried not to betray my inner turmoil, but Parks knew me too well. He was always much more in touch with his emotions and had a much easier time expressing them. I, on the other hand, was hypervigilant in my every word or action, afraid to let my walls down, afraid to be known, afraid of coming undone. "What's the matter?" He asked, in a tone he employed when sensing that I was wrestling with something I didn't want him or anyone else to see.

"Nothing." I responded.

"Holden."

"It was Robert. The ferry isn't going to run tonight because of the weather."

"Gotcha", he replied, looking out of the window as we climbed the high rise bridge between Morehead and Radio Island, the dashes of white on the horizon revealing the turbulence of the sea at Beaufort Inlet.

"He reserved a room at the Driftwood." I said, settling back into silence with my eyes focused straight ahead, trying to keep my anxiety in check.

"The Driftwood." He said in a playful tone, "Man have I had some crazy nights in that place."

I didn't respond.

119

"Holden, lighten up!" He continued with a smile, "I was just trying to get a rise out of you."

"I'm sorry, it's just..."

"I know." He interrupted. "Look, you've got nothing to worry about. I'll be a perfect gentleman."

He had reassured me on a number of occasions that he respected my convictions, even if he didn't agree with them.

"It's just so hard, Parks. I mean, I guess, I don't know.."

I couldn't formulate my words, partly because I couldn't even tease out the complexities of my experience in my own mind. The one comfort being that I still had Parks in my life. But as anyone of any sexual orientation can probably attest, once you've been intimate with someone, it is difficult to return to baseline.

Entry 25

We arrived at the Driftwood around seven that evening, hungry and weary from the early start to the day and the miles logged in driving rain. Famished, we didn't even shower before going to eat. Once we checked in and got our key, we asked to be seated.

The restaurant was warm and dimly lit, with porthole windows overlooking Cedar Island Beach. The soft background music was interrupted only by the clinking of silver and glassware, or the occasional discourse of local brogues carrying up into the dining room from the lobby below, where a number of the local fishermen were congregated, recalling the events of the day.

Parks ordered a beer and smiled as I ordered my traditional sweet tea. Although I was wrestling with my sexuality, I still knew where I stood on the issue of alcohol. Parks just gave a soft chuckle, musing at my convictions.

I didn't realize it at the time, but Robert was a close friend of the owner. The two of them served together in the state legislature back in the late sixties and seventies, Robert representing Hyde and Dare Counties and Mr.

Fulcher representing Carteret and Onslow. The two of them together had fought hard to secure the funds necessary to make the ferry division what it was, constantly seeking to bring home the bacon for their local constituency. Robert and Emilis considered the Fulchers to be some of the finest people they had ever known. It wasn't until my return to the island that I got to know them, and I must say that I feel the same way. The two families had been very effective and extremely loyal to their home folk, and to one another. It was this commitment to constituent service that secured Robert's re-election for six terms, up until his father passed and the entire brunt of the seafood business fell upon Robert's shoulders. Robert first ran for the legislature in the years following the loss of his son. He once told me that the demands of the office provided a welcomed distraction from his own depression, that the constant demand for his time in political matters helped motivate him again. Whatever the catalyst, Robert had served the people of his village and district with tenacity and conviction.

In reading some old news clippings Emilis shared with me, I came across a statement made by the Lieutenant Governor at the time, highlighting Robert's determination in seeing that his constituents on the coast were taken care of. The Lt. Governor was quoted as saying, "When it comes to Robert's heart for the people of his district, the word in the State House is, 'When Representative Guthrie is determined to get something done for the people of the Outer Banks, you either help him, get out of his way, or get plowed over.'" Commitment and resolve where defining characteristics of Robert's life. Whether it was a commitment to paying fair prices to the fishermen who sold to him, or remaining loyal to a friend even when doing so cost him social capital in the end, Robert didn't shrink from his convictions. Mr. Fulcher, a fellow democrat, and Robert were a powerful duo in their political careers, looking out for the needs of their people in ways that few politicians have the guts to do anymore.

That night at the Driftwood, Parks and I ate until we were miserably full. After finishing up with two pieces of old fashioned condensed milk lemon pie, we paid our tab. The young girl who served us, a native of the island and a senior in high school, had shared with us her dream of going to college to be a pharmacist. As we got up from the table, Parks threw down a fifty dollar tip, more than the amount of our entire bill. Raised by his grandparents in a home supported by commercial fishing, Parks realized that this young girl would likely be the first in her family to have attended college.

After making our way down the staircase from the dining room and onto the motel porch, we walked over to make sure the truck was secure and then headed towards the room Robert had reserved for me. As I opened the door my eyes caught sight of two double beds, to which I let out a silent sigh of relief. I made my way to the bed closest the bathroom door and sat down on the edge of the mattress to slide off my boots and remove my damp, woolen socks. I placed my socks on top of the heater vents below the window to dry, as Parks turned on the television and began to search for something to watch. "You want to shower first?"

"No, you go ahead." he replied, engrossed in a movie he had found on HBO.

After locking the bathroom door behind me and getting undressed, I proceeded to take a long-hot shower, spending much of the time thinking about the war that was going on inside of me and praying for help and peace, as the water streamed over my face. I was tired of living amidst the onslaught of such a vicious and private war. After giving myself a good talking to, I proceeded to get out of the shower and dry off. I had brought no night clothes, I had fully intended on returning to the island that same day; so, I put my underwear and tee shirt from the day back on and headed back into the room where

122

Parks was sprawled across the bed, still glued to the television.

"Did you leave me a drop of hot water?" He said, jokingly.

I just laughed.

After Parks showered, he climbed into his bed and I curled up in mine, pulling the covers up around my neck in an attempt to fight the subtle chill that had settled into my bones that morning at the fish house and never fully left. We lay there for probably an hour just talking about life, our dreams, and questions for the future. Parks, understandably, wondered aloud about the trajectory of our friendship. I just listened, retreating inward, fleeing words for fear of saying the wrong thing, for fear of saying too much, for fear of allowing myself to drink deeply of the pain I was feeling.

People cannot imagine the turmoil of my existence at that moment. A Christian, a preacher of the Gospel of Jesus Christ, a young man who deeply loved God and yet found himself experiencing a sincere love for another man, a love that was exciting, refreshing, persistent, fearful and haunting, simultaneously. I was feeling like what Paul described as the chiefest of sinners. However, for me the feeling was a little different, I felt like the chiefest of hypocrites.

That night I shared with Parks how I felt like I needed to leave the ministry until I got a better handle on all of this. I felt guilty every time I stood behind the sacred desk and tried to share the Word of God with my parishioners. I became increasingly uncomfortable with the type of fire and brimstone preaching that some in the congregation desired. I didn't know where to turn or what to do. My world was unraveling. Just one week before I had knelt, looking up toward heaven, praying a one word prayer of desperation: "Help!" My whole life promised to come unglued if I could not win this battle over my sexuality, and I felt I had no one in which I could confide.

123

Parks listened quietly and respectfully from his bed three feet away, a distance that at times felt like a safe ocean, and at others threatened to overcome my resolve in its proximity. He had deep empathy and respect for the battle I was fighting, and his willingness to not abandon me, even when anything more than friendship was removed from the table, is still incredible to me. I was living a war which many people refuse to take the time to understand.

Eventually, the conversation had run its course. It wasn't that we ran out of things to say. More so, it was a time of weighted silence as we both pondered things from our respective pillows and points of view. With the lights in the room darkened, the only illumination a gentle glow from the outside porch light penetrating the curtains, I laid in bed staring at the ceiling, awash with anxiety and emotional pain. I just wanted someone to understand, to help bear my burden, and the only person I had ever known who really got it lay just feet away.

Hours passed after the break in conversation, but sleep eluded me. I called out in the dark, in hushed tones so as not to rouse Parks if he were asleep.

As I called his name, a tear flowed from the corner of my eye.

"Yeah." he whispered back, evidence that sleep had failed his eyes as well.

I rolled over onto my side facing his direction and saw him lying on his back, staring at the ceiling. I couldn't speak. I knew if I did it would be like unleashing a floodgate, and I was utterly terrified of losing control.

"What is it, man?" He replied, after not receiving an answer.

Try as I may to quench it, I began to cry. Here I was, a young man in his mid-twenties, and yet I felt like the same wounded little boy who made his way across that now distant, cold tobacco field. The only difference being that on that long ago night, the sheltering arms of my brother were holding me, helping me cope. Tonight the only human arms present to hold me also threatened to be my undoing. What began as low sniffles erupted into deeper sobs that, until this moment, had never been allowed full and unbridled expression. The pain and weariness of the struggle seemed too much to handle, and the fear of being alone circumnavigated all of my guards.

Sometime after two a.m. I crawled from my bed and made the journey of a thousand miles across the three feet of space that separated me from Parks. As I crawled beneath the covers I buried my head in his chest and wept. Parks simply held me. There was no sexual advance, no manipulation, he just held me and let me cry. As I wept, I felt the reverberations from Parks' chest, a disclosure that I wasn't the only one suffering. Never before had I allowed myself to be so vulnerable, so exposed to someone. A fact that Parks seemed to sense and respect. After the tears subsided and my breathing returned to a soft, rested rate, I fell asleep in Parks' embrace.

Entry 26

The next morning I awoke as Parks jumped up abruptly, causing my head to fall from the support of his chest onto the mattress.
"Hey, someone's in here." I heard him say frantically, nervously.
In the epic events of the preceding evening we had forgotten to set our alarm, sleeping well into check-out time. Parks had awakened to the sound of the door opening as a woman's voice called out, "Housekeeping". Parks tried his hardest to intercept her intrusion, but before he was able, she was standing there staring through the half opened door. She seemed in shock, her mouth gaping as she found herself face to face with two young men in their underwear, lying together in the same bed.
"I'm sorry, I'm sorry" she kept saying, until Parks went over and closed the door gently in her face.

Sometimes anxiety presents itself in hand-wringing worry and at other times it surfaces in nervous laughter, a feeble attempt to masque any sense of fear and foreboding. Surprisingly enough, laughter took over that morning as we conjured up all kinds of scenarios regarding what must have been going through her mind. We took solace by reassuring each other that we were across the sound, that the Pamlico would serve as a type of moat protecting our lives on Ocracoke from our accidental discovery on Cedar Island.

We hurriedly dressed and made our way back to the truck at the ferry office, trying desperately to dodge any additional encounter with the housekeeper. We cranked up the fish truck and pulled onto the next ferry bound for Ocracoke. Laugh as we may, there was an undercurrent of anxiety, the fear that this discovery would have far reaching consequences.

Entry 27

By mid-April the weather had warmed significantly. With the rise in temperature, college students on Spring Break were beginning to appear on the island, and the soft-crab season was getting well underway. I had come to learn over the course of my nearly two years on the island that peeler crabbing, as Robert called it, was one of the most taxing and time consuming seasons of the entire year. However, with flats of soft shells selling at Fulton Fish Market in New York for nearly forty dollars per dozen, it was also one of the most lucrative ventures of the seafood calendar.

The Spring of '83 had been my introduction to this around the clock work which began in early spring as the water temps on the Carolina coast began to rise. As with so many other new experiences on the island, it seemed there was an entire dictionary of terms for me to learn. Crabbing terms like buster, double decker, jimmy, and paper shell were common knowledge to the locals, but for me it was yet another learning curb.

At the peak of the season Robert, Emilis, and I were at the fish house pretty much around the clock, harvesting crabs from tanks inside the fish house and the from floats in Silver Lake, being diligent to get them out of the water before their shells began to harden. Early in the season we would get up in the middle of the night and make our way down to the fish house to cull through the tanks. At the height of the season, when their shedding rate became almost feverish, Robert and I would sleep on the old sofas in his office, since we would have to be up every couple of hours. Emilis usually stayed there with us until after our one o'clock harvest, and then return well before sunrise with thermoses of steaming coffee and anything from a fresh pan of rolls to a pot of steaming hot cheese grits.

The season was short, probably just over a month, but there were tens of thousands of dollars to be made in that small window. Robert had several boys selling peelers to him, but he also sought to teach me the trade. Early in the spring he had taken me off of the island and shown me where he placed his peeler pots, knowing that he was going to turn over this aspect to me once things shifted into high gear. Not only did I have to learn the nooks and crannies of the island waterways, Robert would have to teach me how to pull a pot, how to handle the crabs, and how to identify the peelers by the small red marking that appeared on their backfin just before they were ready to shed.

Life was back into its normal routine of fish boxes and sermon preparation. My struggle was always with me. I was a young man with all of the hormones and impulses that young men have. The only problem was that the object of my affection presented a host of moral, social, and spiritual dilemmas that I was unable to resolve. If there was ever a battle in my life, a cross to bear, I felt that this was it.

Periodically, the thought of being discovered by the housekeeper on Cedar Island would evoke overwhelming worry if I allowed it to linger, but I largely sought to push it from my mind. Parks and I had engaged in many long talks since that night and I had told him again that, no matter how much I may want more, friendship was as far as I could ever go. I had also spent a lot of time in prayer since that night, trying to escape my feelings. I began pouring myself more and more into my Church work and spent more time at home with Robert and Emilis.

On Thursday, April 21st, 1984, I spent the morning helping Robert secure a few more peeler crab floats to the stakes he had driven in the water just off of the fish house. It was a gorgeous spring day, warm enough to work in a tee shirt. At lunch I drove my car up to the village store to get a loaf of bread and some Dr. Pepper for Emilis before returning home.

As usual, I greeted several of my parishioners while inside, making small talk. After paying, I headed out of the door, the large brown paper sack containing my purchase cradled under my arm. As I stepped off the wooden plank steps onto the parking lot, I looked up in time to lock eyes with a woman I had hoped to never see again. Though my encounter with her was brief, I was almost assured that I was staring into the face of the housekeeper from the Driftwood. To compound matters, she was entering the store with Vicky Dare, the wife of Ryan Dare, one of the fish house workers.

In that moment I could feel my heart rate increase and my head begin to spin. My face became hot. I wasn't sure if I was going to faint or vomit.

My private torment was interrupted by Vicky's voice. "Hey, Holden! Are y'all already off for lunch?" She asked.

"Yes, Ma'am!" I said, trying not to break out in a cold sweat, trying desperately not to betray my trepidation to the lady who may be wondering if I was the boy from the room that morning.

"Holden, I want you to meet one of my best friends,"
Vicky continued, "this is Maddy Thompson, she's staying
with me for the week."

"Nice to meet you, ma'am." I responded. "Hope you
have a good visit."

I wanted to keep my eye contact to a minimum and get
away from her just as quickly as I possibly could.

"Same to you, son." She replied. It was her, no doubt. As
the seconds stretched into centuries I could see that it was
her. Indeed, I recognized her and wanted nothing more
than to flee from her presence before she remembered my
face.

"Well, good to meet you." I replied, "Ya'll have a great
day!"

"You too, man." Vicky responded.

I could hear Vicky telling her as I walked away that I was
preaching on the island and working down at the fish
house with Ryan. My stomach was in a knot. I tried my
best to shake the whole thing off and go on like nothing
happened.

The next morning at work Ryan was acting differently towards me, more distant. I tried to figure out if I
was reading the situation correctly, if he was privy to my
secret or if I was just being paranoid. I kept trying to talk
to myself, to decrease the level of anxiety I felt with every
glance he gave from across the docks, with every whisper
to another worker, causing them to look my way. But as
the rest of the crew slowly arrived and I watched them
whispering and glaring at me over the mounds of crab
pots, I became slowly convinced that a nightmare was on
the horizon.

Ryan and I had never been especially close. He was
a hard case. He stood about five feet tall and I always
felt that he had a Napoleon complex. He always had to
be the big man, always had to be right, to have the last
word...that kind of guy. Altogether, he just didn't impress

me.

Just before lunch he came over to me.

"Holden," he said, "I want to ask you about something I heard the other day."

"Ok." I responded as my heart began beating out of my chest, this was it and I knew it. It was the same type of feeling one gets as a roller coaster makes its eerie climb, just before it sends you reeling on your first horrific drop.

"Have you been staying over at the Driftwood lately?" He questioned with an accusatory air.

I had nothing to say. All I could do was stare him directly in the face with an expression that must have betrayed the panic I was feeling inside.

"So, it is true." He replied with disgust. "Wow." He said in such a way as to enhance the magnitude of his discovery...and my shame.

"Ryan," I began.

"Wow." He interrupted, "What is Robert going to think about this? His golden boy is a fudge packer."

"Ryan..." I began, again.

"You don't have to explain it to me." He said with a peculiar grin as he turned to walk away.

My mind was awash with racing thoughts. Shortly, I gained the clarity to realize that I needed to find Parks. I nearly ran to my car and sped from the fish house.

Upon reaching Parks' house, I pulled my little silver Accord off on the side of the road and made my way, shaking, through the front gate. I went around back and knocked on the screen door that led into the kitchen.

Parks came to the door with a peanut butter sandwich and glass of milk in hand, his favorite combination. With one look at me he knew something was terribly wrong and his entire countenance shifted.

"What is it, Holden?" He said with a worried, matter-of-fact tone.

I just stood there shaking my head.

"What happened?" He pressed.

130

"It's out." These are the only words that I could muster before breaking out in the first full-fledged panic attack I had ever experienced. I couldn't catch my breath. My entire life, my reputation, my calling, everything seemed like it was getting ready to crumble at my feet and I was crumbling with it. I was completely overwhelmed by the magnitude of what was happening, the weight of my world hurling to an end. I was bent double on Parks' back porch, heaving in an attempt to catch my breath. "Holden, look at me!" Parks demanded, getting directly in my face. "Holden, Holden...look at me, buddy...breathe, breathe...deep breaths." He instructed, as he put both his hands on my shoulders and looked me dead in the eyes.

I felt so helpless, so hopeless. After finally catching my breath, I curled up in somewhat of a fetal position by one of the back porch posts, which served as a type of tangible stabilizer in a world spinning out of control. I could see Parks pacing in the back yard right by the edge of the porch, rubbing his hand repeatedly through his hair from forehead to crown and back again. There was a look of disbelief and panic on his face. Both of our lives were about to change forever and the magnitude of that reality was engulfing us like the treacherous shadow of a rogue wave.

Though Parks didn't share my convictions and had expressed his desire to get away from the island in order to be who he was, preferably with me by his side, he was not prepared to be exposed like this. He was one of the last people on the island that anyone would ever suspect of being gay and this news would have far reaching ramifications, definitely ending more than a few of his friendships, and quite possibly his career.

"What are we going to do, Holden?" He said, still pacing and rubbing his scalp.

"I don't know." I said, now in a sense of shock and disbelief.

"Where are we going go, what are we going to do?" He

131

said again, as if he never heard my weak response.

After probably a half hour of vacillating between panic, fear, and disbelief, I decided to go to the little white cottage that had become the best form of home I had ever known, hoping desperately that its walls would prove impenetrable to the storm raging outside.

My chest was tight with anxiety as I drove hastily down the shell paved path and made my way up the front steps. Entering the house, I found Emilis sitting at the kitchen table alone, staring silently out of the window. There was no greeting, just silence. Not a cold-shouldered silence, not an "I'm disgusted with you" silence, but an "I can't get my mind around this"...an "I'm in shock" silence.

As the moments passed without a response, I realized that she indeed had heard the news. Her gaze was fixed in a blank stare out of the back window. I broke the silence.

"Emilis..." my voice cracked and trailed off as I began to cry. "I'm sorry, I'm so sorry," I muttered repeatedly in hushed, desperate tones as I braced myself against the door facing. At the moment, Emilis was too stunned, too hurt, too confused, too gripped by the private crisis this news had evoked to respond. She sat frozen in the chair with an occasional sniffle.

This was all too much. This was greater than all of my fears. I knew that my struggle threatened to end my ministry and my worth in the eyes of a great number of people. But I had never considered that Robert and Emilis would be unable to support me in the storm. I never considered, in a deep way, how all of this would affect them.

I misread Emilis' silence that day. We have had many occasions since to discuss the events that unfolded and the emotional state she was in for that first hour. However, in the moment, her silence only added to my incredible sense of isolation. My mind took her silence, in conjunction with all the other events of the day, the engulfing thoughts of eminent catastrophe, and formulated a narrative void of all hope. I was certain that I had lost everything and the pain was too broad for me to carry.

I was overcome. Parks, suffering his own besiegement of mental and emotional duress, seemed a thousand miles away. To further complicate matters, I quickly convinced myself that even GOD was finished with me. The little cottage seemed to close in upon me. I was drowning in relentless waves of fear. I headed out into the yard. I had to get some air. I needed to walk. I cannot describe what I was going through in those moments, but it was awful.

Emilis had not moved from her place at the table. She later recounted to me how she wept as she watched me pacing back and forth in the back yard, my arms crossed over my chest, my hands grasping my upper arms as if to offer myself the embrace that I felt no one else was willing to give in that belabored moment of sequesterment. I took a seat beneath the large old fig tree in the back yard, my legs pulled up to my chest, my head buried between my knees, crying from a place of complete brokenness. After a time, I rose from my seat and slipped into the little house.

Eventually, Emilis got up and headed outside to comfort me, realizing that whatever pain she was experiencing at the moment, mine far surpassed it. If the news she heard two hours before sent her reeling in shock and disbelief, the following moments would prove to solidify that day as one of the most traumatic of her life. As Emilis has told me since, she entered the little house that afternoon to find me curled up in the corner, next to her bolts of upholstery fabric, tears rolling down my cheeks and blood covering my tee shirt and khaki pants. The warm, wet liquid was emanating from slashes in both wrists made with one of the fillet knives that hung from the bare studs of the little shed. There are visual and auditory segments of that afternoon forever etched in my memory. I will

133

never forget the desperation in Emilis' voice, a verbal manifestation of the crisis in which we found ourselves.

Emilis got down in the floor beside me, switching into crisis management mode. Quickly, her voice shifted from one of fright to one of power and assurance, telling me that everything was going to be fine, that we would get through this, that she loved me. As she spoke words which were my only sense of grounding in those withdrawn, frightening moments, she hastily removed her shirt and ripped it into pieces, wrapping my wrists tightly in order to quell the bleeding. Rising to her feet, she placed an emergency call from the rotary phone that hung on the little house wall, then returned to me in my curled position on the chilly cement floor. She took me into her arms that afternoon and pulled me over into her lap, holding and rocking me back and forth like a crying child.

Before long the silent hell of those events was pierced by the howling of ambulatory sirens and the whirlwind of activity encompassing my transport to the humble air strip at the north end of the island, from which I was airlifted to the nearest hospital in Greenville. The paramedics tried to prevent Emilis from riding along on the ambulance, but she was not to be deterred.

"I'm going with him!" I heard her say in a stern, deliberate tone.

With that, she climbed up into the back of the ambulance and took her position beside me.

News travels fast in a small town, and an island setting only intensifies that rule. By the time the helicopter lifted off with me inside, the area around the landing strip was speckled with clusters of people watching as the tragedy unfolded, some with tears, some with ridicule. Gazing through the opening into which I was loaded, I could see Emilis, alone, standing at the forefront of the on-lookers. The woman who was always dressed to a T, the lady ridiculed and mistaken by many in the community as

134

being prideful, stood between me and the sea of onlookers. This woman that I loved like a mother, who had been such a source of comfort, encouragement, and care stood frozen between me and the crowd, her gaze fixed unwaveringly upon me. I can still picture her there in her slacks and camisole, her clothing, arms, and face smeared red from holding me, rocking me, and wiping away her own tears as she sought to soothe mine. She told me that it was at that moment God gave her a love for me and a commitment to me that surpassed all of her personal mourning, anger, or embarrassment. She told me that the moment she walked into the little house and saw me curled up in a ball, dripping with my own blood, she first understood how deeply and how badly I was hurting inside, just how tormented I had been. From that experience a seed was planted of loving me at all costs.

As the helicopter lifted off from the tiny village airstrip, I found myself caught between complete numbness and utter devastation, my weeping intermingled with moments of detached silence. Then, somewhere on our westward track toward Greenville, I looked down at my wrists. The reality of what I had done began to settle in, along with an emerging tide of shame, which further complicated my emotional and mental state. As I gazed down at those white rags, saturated in blood my eye caught site of one of Emilis' golden cufflinks, still attached to the torn sleeve she had used to bandage my wounds...a comforting and painful reminder that I wasn't in this alone.

Entry 28

I arrived at the emergency department of Pitt Memorial Hospital and was put through the necessary procedures to stabilize my condition and tend my wounds. I had lost a considerable amount of blood and was placed in the progressive care unit for observation, until my condition stabilized and I could be transported to Behavior Health.

135

I was also assigned a sitter, due to the way in which the injury had occurred.

I lay in the sterile and lonely room, isolated from everything and everyone familiar, the piercing and cold florescent lights above serving as ironic symbolism of how stark and exposed I felt before the world. The sitter didn't speak to me at all, she just sat in a chair in the corner of the room near the foot of my bed doing her crossword puzzle, occasionally glancing up at me. For the most part, I just lay on my back with my eyes closed, when I wasn't staring at the stark drop tile ceiling. I had no clue how this was all going to play out, but I was ashamed, scared, and lonely.

As I lay there, listening to the beep of the monitor recording my vitals and the metered clicks from the I.V. pump, replacing some of the blood that had been lost, my isolation and loneliness was interrupted by a familiar voice. I opened my eyes to the sight of Jane Anne standing at my bedside. Emilis had called her after she got home from the airstrip.

It was going to be an additional hour before the ferry would be leaving Ocracoke for the mainland and then four more hours of ferry ride and driving combined before Emilis could make it to Greenville. Jane Anne jumped in her car as soon as she got the call. In less than two hours she had made the trek from Davis Shore to Greenville and was standing by my side. Emilis had filled her in on what had unfolded and asked that she head on to the hospital, since she couldn't bear my lying in Greenville all alone.

Jane Anne didn't say a word at first. She just smiled and reached down to gently run her fingers through my hair, a silent sermon of her care for me. Jane Anne may have been the nearest thing to a real-life comedian I had ever known, but when calamity struck she could adopt a serious streak equal to her wit. She only spoke one sentence to me that entire afternoon, but it was poignant

136

and well placed.

"Holden, I will never stop loving you....and in time you're going to realize God will never stop loving you either."

That was it. She didn't preach, she didn't ask questions, she didn't shame me any further than I was already shaming myself. She just stayed with me and, whether it was stroking my hair or resting her hand on my upper arm, she fed me on one of the most essential relational needs of all mankind - the human touch. She knew it wasn't a time for words, that would come. These hours were a time for being comfortable in the silence and offering the only language acceptable in the midst of such circumstances, the silent assurance of unending love and of not being alone.

Later that evening Emilis made it to Greenville. I could see the worry on her face as she entered the room. The strain of the day's events were evident in her countenance, but she was there, nonetheless, to stand by me and advocate for whatever needs I had. I was very glad to see her, but a bit anxious as I gazed at the door behind her. I was caught in a tension between wanting desperately for Robert to be there, quelling my fears of his abandonment, and at the same time hoping in some way that he wasn't, because of a fear to face him. I feared his response worst, now that the word was out about the struggle that I had kept buried for so long. He didn't come, not that evening. The realization that he had remained on the island sent silent tears streaming down my cheek, as I felt the weight of what I internalized as abandonment. I didn't mention it right away, knowing that if I tried to speak my emotions would get the better of me.

"Where's Robert?" Jane Anne said, soft and low. With that Emilis shook her head slightly giving Jane Anne a look that ended the discourse dead in its tracks. Though she tried to allay the topic subtly, I could read her response for what it was, an attempt to guard my heart against the reality of Robert's absence and difficulty in

137

dealing with the unwelcome news he had received earlier in the day. It was a night of silence, as I drifted in and out of sedative induced sleep. Emilis and Jane Anne kept watch through the night, taking turns cat napping in the pitiful excuse of a recliner the nurses had brought in to them. The next morning, after the medical conditions related to my self-injuring were stabilized, I was taken from the unit to the behavioral health ward. At this point I faced the burden of being separated from the consolation of Jane Anne's humor and Emilis' doting, the only exception being a one hour window late each afternoon when they checked their bags at the front desk and joined me in my stark white room, a complete contrast to the island cottage I had called home for the past two years.

Emilis later told me how her heart was ripped from her chest every time she came and saw me sitting in that bare room, dressed in a hospital gown and the Sperry's they had given me the Christmas before, now void of laces. Though she was strong and encouraging during those hour-long meetings, years later she confessed that after leaving she would collapse into Jane Anne's sturdy embrace in the hallway beyond the locked door of the unit, crying the type of guttural sobs that are so raw and overwhelming that even the presence of passers-by fail to hinder the expression. Little did she know that often times I was reduced to the same flood of emotion as they pulled the door closed behind them to leave. It was in the remaining twenty-three hours, between vital sign checks, group sessions, grand rounds, and meals that I would sit and think about my life. In those lonely hours I pondered where I would go from here, and began facing the slowly emerging reality that I might have to leave the only place that ever truly possessed a sense of home for me.

One evening about four days into my two-week stay, there was a tap at my door from the social worker telling me that I had a phone call. I got up from my under-stuffed twin sized mattress, slipped on my Sperry's

138

and made my way down the hall to the phone that was
mounted just outside the nurses' station.

"Hello?" I said in a curious, nervous tone, unsure of who
it could be or what type of salutation I would be receiving.

"How are you?"

It was Parks.

I hadn't heard from or seen him since I departed his
house that colossal afternoon. I had wondered about
him, where he was, how he was, and when I would see
him again. I wondered and feared what his response to
me would be. In the days that followed my suicide attempt, he seemed the only ally who could truly grasp the
private hell turned public that I was now trying desperately to survive, yet not a word. With the warm, tender tone
of his voice echoing in my ears for the first time in almost
a week, tears welled in my eyes.

"I'm so glad to hear your voice." I said through low
sniffles.

"I'm sorry that I haven't called before now," he continued, "it's just been a rough few days and I really didn't
know how to contact you."

I sat in silence, glad to hear from him, yet processing feelings of resentment I harbored with each passing day void
of contact.

"Holden, you scared the shit out of me." He said in a
more deliberate tone.

"I know," I replied.

"Holden, when I heard what happened I literally got sick
to my stomach, like my whole world was coming unglued."

"Why didn't you come?" I posed in sincere inquiry, only
one of the many 'whys' that had plagued my mind in the
previous days.

"Holden, after you left the house I got in my truck and
parked down on the beach. I just needed some space,
some air. I couldn't be around anybody, I couldn't handle

139

what was happening."

He continued to explain how he sat in silence for the better part of an hour, staring out into the ocean, trying to get his mind around what was taking place and the life-changing ramifications it would have for both of us. Then he recounted how his gaze was interrupted by the sound of a chopper flying low and landing back behind the dune line towards the airstrip.

A medic chopper landing on the airstrip in Ocracoke is about as cheerful an omen as a "mayday" call over the trawler radio. Whenever you see it, you know something terrible has happened. With that morbid curiosity in full force, Parks headed back up the beach to see what was taking place.

By the time he made the several mile drive through the soft sand and pulled back onto Highway 12, the chopper was lifting off with me inside. He approached the airstrip as Emilis and Robert made their way back to the old pickup truck. Evidently Robert had gotten there some time after the door closed for takeoff.

Parks described how he found them that afternoon, holding each other, crying. As he approached them in utter terror, Emilis verbally unleashed on Parks all the emotions she had held in since finding me curled up in the corner of the shed. There in front of every onlooker, overcome with heartbreak turned to anger, Emilis blamed Parks entirely for my demise. Raw emotions and hurt feelings can often leave destruction in their wake and this was no exception. The encounter left a rift between the two of them for many years. Although Emilis sought his forgiveness soon after and tried frequently to bridge the divide, he was hardened against her and the hatchet wasn't easily buried.

The next day Parks came to see me. It was difficult because I only had one hour of visit time each day. In the end Jane Anne served as our advocate with Emilis and they yielded the hour they cherished so dearly so that

140

Parks and I could talk.

Initially, the sight of my stitched wrists was too much for Parks and he rushed to the restroom to throw up. One of the nurses thought it best for him to leave, but my social worker saw to it that he could stay, if he felt up to it. After getting himself together, we sat facing each other on the edge of the parallel twin beds. Like Emilis on the airstrip, I don't think it was until that moment, in the sterile white room of a psychiatric ward, that Parks really began to understand what a tormenting struggle this truly was for me. He had gotten so frustrated with me over the past year, not really understanding how mammoth the waves of this storm were in my eyes, or how truly frightened I was at all I was feeling. It was in this moment, as he stared at my unshaven face, at my hospital gown, at my healing wrists that he really caught the full weight of my dilemma.

"I'm so sorry for pushing you so much." he said, sadly.

"What are you talking about?"

"I've been so cold and unsympathetic to how hard this is for you."

I couldn't completely disagree, but it hurt to see him be so hard on himself.

"Parks, it's been hard for both of us."

"I know, but I never took the time to see just how serious of a tension this was for you. I'm so sorry, Holden."

"Parks, please don't treat me any different after this."

"What do you mean?"

"I don't want you to feel like you've got to walk on egg shells or that you've got to worry about me all the time. I don't want you to treat me like I'm sick, or like I'm crazy."

I knew that nothing else would be the same in my life from this point. The one thing that I desperately needed was for things with Parks and me to be normal. Everyone else was going to handle me with kid gloves, and whisper behind my back at what a basket case I was. I didn't want that from Parks. I wanted everything to be as it had been.

141

Entry 29

I felt my whole life had been spent void of a father figure and just when I finally found someone who seemed to fill that chasm in my heart, destruction hit. With every day of Robert's absent silence the feelings of separation and abandonment I felt from men my entire life were only reinforced. At the time, I had no way of knowing the full extent of the flash fire of gossip, slander, and bitterness that spread across the small island in the wake of such an earth shattering disclosure. Robert, being one of the head deacons, and the one with whom I had lodged since my first day on the island, found himself in the cross-hairs of many a disgruntled parishioner and village resident. Accusations were rampant, insinuating that the Guthries were aware of my secret, and even that they supported me in it, neither of which were true, but when the flood gates of unbridled tongues are unleashed it is amazing the spins that can be attached to a story.

On my second Sunday in the behavioral health unit, Robert came to see me for the first time. I was a bit surprised to see him, on this day especially. He never missed Church for any reason other than being deathly ill. Even after burying Robert Jr. on a chilly Saturday afternoon, Robert made his way to worship the next morning. The fact that he missed Church to be in Greenville was curious, and yet fear gripped me as I heard his voice in the hallway outside of my room. It is one thing to dream up and rehearse in my mind the scenarios and words which we might exchange in our first encounter. However, being faced with the reality that this conversation was getting ready to take place, one which may even further my sense of isolation and rejection, seemed to infuse my veins with surges of fear and feelings of nauseous dread.

To help shield myself from what I feared was coming, I took the only measure I had of guarding myself in that moment. Before he entered I turned my back to the door, feigning sleep. The door creaked open and

142

footsteps made their way to the edge of my bed. I heard Robert's deep voice speak in a soft, tentative tone, "Holden." It was reminiscent of mornings in my first weeks at their home, when Robert would come and rouse me for breakfast, trying not to startle me. But at this moment I couldn't respond, I just lay there staring towards the blank, white wall with Robert sitting in a hospital chair at my back.

"Holden?" He tried calling again, but I was too gripped with fear to respond.

The metal chair legs screeched on the tile floors. He was leaving. I was sick to my stomach, trapped between an overwhelming desire to call out for him not to leave and an ever increasing dread of what he had come to say or not say.

This barrage of thoughts was interrupted as I felt the edge of my mattress being pressed down just behind my back. I slowly rolled onto my back to see what was taking place. Turning my head I saw Robert kneeling beside my bed, his elbows bearing down on the mattress. His forehead was buried in the thin white sheet. He was praying.

I just lay there, not really knowing what to do or how to respond. In time he looked up to find that I was now 'awake'. After making brief eye contact with me he began to cry.

"I'm sorry, Robert."

Robert wasn't liberal with words, but his actions that day served to bring a deeper comfort to my heart than I had known since the day I tried to be no more. In the quiet of my room Robert just held me. He cried and I cried. It was a time of mending, a time of cleansing, a time for reassurance.

When the knock came at my door, signaling the end of the visitation hour, Robert pulled away just far enough to look me square in the eyes and make a promise he would spend the rest of our time together keeping. No other words spoken to me during that season of life meant

143

as much or touched me as deeply as the words Robert
uttered that day, reaching into my soul, meeting needs
long unfulfilled, and bringing absolution to any fear that
I would be discarded from his life because of this or any
other circumstance:

"Holden, I love you like you were my own son, and I'm
not going anywhere."

In the years that would stretch past that moment,
we came to discuss the reasons for his absence. What I
perceived as rejection was in-fact a time of soul-searching.
One evening the following summer, Robert finally addressed it.

"Holden, I don't like to just brush things under the rug."
He began.

I was bracing myself for the things I felt he had been
waiting to say until I was stable enough to hear them:
how I had disappointed him, how I had hurt him, how he
felt betrayed and lied to, how he thought I was perverse
or sick because of my attraction to men.

"Holden, I want you to forgive me for not being there for
you when everything happened like it did." He continued.

"It's ok." I responded quickly. Serious discussions like this
had a tendency to make me uncomfortable.

"No, it's not ok, Holden." Robert continued, "And whether you want to admit it or not, I really think I hurt you by
taking a whole week to come to Greenville."

I just sat in silence.

"Tell me the truth."

I quietly shook my head affirmatively.

"I knew it, and that's why I need to talk to you about what
was going on with me."

I have to admit that I had already rehearsed all of
those excuses in my mind as I lay in bed at the hospital.
To be honest, I had no desire to hear any feeble attempt
to explain away his absence. I secretly harbored a sense
of betrayal and indignation because I wanted Robert
to be there, regardless of what people thought or said, I

wanted to mean more to him than his own pride or position in the community.

"Holden, when Robert Jr. died, a part of me died with him. Not only did I bury my son, but also my dreams of a son, a friend, a father of my grandchildren, a business partner...they were all packed in that oak coffin with him. I laid them all to rest. Then came you."

I shifted my gaze from the sea to look across the front seat at Robert as he threw this curve ball across my bow.

"In the time you spent with us, some of those dead, buried dreams were slowly resurrected. You began to take a place in my heart that only one other person had ever held." he continued. "Emilis and I talked about it many times, how much you had become a part of us, how we both felt that God had given us a second son. When I got the news about you and Parks one hour, and the news that you had tried to kill yourself the next, I felt the weight of those dreams dying again and I knew that I didn't have the strength to handle losing two boys. And so I did what I do best, I pulled away. It's something Emilis has been on me about ever since we got married."

"What made you change your mind?"

"It took what it normally takes when I have my head up my rear end," he said with a slight smile, "It took a swift kick in the pants from someone who can tell me like it is."

"Emilis?" I asked, returning the same slight smile he had extended moments earlier.

"No, to tell you the truth, it was Jane Anne."

"Jane Anne?"

"Yep. After about four days of me not showing up she told Emilis she needed to run to Davis to get some more clothes. But, she never went to Davis."

"What did she say?" Knowing Jane Anne, I could only imagine.

"She told me exactly what I needed to hear to get my head on straight." Then he continued.

"I was in the office, trying to avoid conversation with just

145

about everyone, when the door swung open and there she stood. From the glare in her eyes, I knew immediately that she had come on a mission. She walked in, sat across the desk from me, lit up a cigarette, and didn't hold back. Just as she was getting wound up, the phone rang and I motioned for her to hold on as I answered it. She never said a word, just reached over, took the phone out of my hand, ripped the cord out the wall, opened the office door and chunked it down the stairs."

By now Robert and I were both laughing.

"What were you thinking?" I asked through a low chuckle.

"I was scared to death! Wouldn't you have been?" he replied, now grinning in hindsight.

"What did she say?" I pressed.

"She lit into me: 'Robert, that youngun laying in Greenville in that psychiatric ward, that young man that loves you like a father, that you love like a son, is more important than anything you've got going on here right now!'

"I tried to intercept the conversation but she was already in high gear, 'Let me tell you something,' she continued, 'I'm certainly glad that God doesn't give up on us as quickly as you've given up on Holden.'

"I tried to tell her she had it all wrong, but she wasn't to be deterred...

'Well then, you tell me what it is Robert, I'm all ears. Because it sure seems that way to me, like you've washed your hands of him and it breaks my heart! And if I feel that way, you can cool believe that young man is laying in Greenville Hospital feeling even worse."

She wouldn't let up...

"Go ahead Robert, you tell me what's going on. You tell me why that youngun has laid in that hospital for almost a week without a visit from you! Go ahead, I'm waiting. Because I think it's downright common of you."

By now, Robert was getting serious. His previous laughter was now a solemn, sincere tone.

146

"Right there is where I broke," he continued, "I shared with Jane Anne just what I shared with you a few minutes ago, how you had become like a son to me and how I was scared to lose another one.

She sat there for a few moments in silence, put out her cigarette, and then continued, much gentler than her initial tirade.

"Robert, don't forget who this is you're talking to. I helped you bury Robert Jr. fifteen years ago and I mourned right along with you. You were never the same after the day we put him in the ground. Not until Holden came along, and I watched that old spark come back, the laughter, the joy, things I nor Emilis have seen from you in a long time. Robert, God has put the two of you together for a reason and Holden needs you real bad right now! But I think you need him just as much!"

Then, she walked out and left me to wrestle with how bad I may have hurt you in the tunnel vision of my own pain."

That was a crucial evening for me and Robert. Sometimes the hardest conversations are the ones most needed. As night began to fall upon the island, we made our way back up the beach to the access road and headed home to the little white cottage that, thankfully, I could still call home.

Entry 30

My brother John and I had stayed in close contact throughout the years after I moved to Ocracoke. Periodically we would write, I would send pictures of the island, and we would call each other to catch up for about an hour or so every few weeks. He called Ocracoke during my hospitalization but Robert had protected my confidentiality, telling him that I wasn't at home at the time and that he would give me the message. Now that I was back and feeling a little better, a little stronger mentally and emotionally, I knew that an unwanted task stood

147

before me. I would have to disclose everything to my
big brother. You would think that the ones closest to you
would be the easiest people with which to share the dark-
est caverns of your soul; however, for some reason that is
not the case, at least for me.

I needed to tell John about the suicide attempt and
the hospitalization, after all, it would be hard to hide
the scars on my wrists from him for the rest of our lives.
Were the tables turned, I would have been furious had he
kept something so serious from me. As a matter of fact, I
would have been furious to have not known of it while he
was in the hospital, but I just couldn't face him then.

John had always been my hero. He was the one I
wanted to emulate, the big brother who could do no
wrong, the one who had saved my life. And, John was
also the big brother who wouldn't let my reporting stop
without a thorough explanation, he would want to know
what was wrong and how I got to the point of wanting
to take my own life. And, that is what made me most
anxious. I could not even begin imagining how to tell
John that I was gay. My sexuality was something that I
couldn't even admit to myself for so long. But tell him I
must, I knew that.

A couple of days later the phone rang. Emilis answered and then, holding her hand over the receiver,
whispered to me that it was him.

"Hello." I answered.

"Hey man! How are ya?" He replied in his usual joyful
tone.

"I'm doing ok." I replied amidst the onslaught of racing
thoughts.

"Holden, I called you two weeks ago and you never called
me back. Did you get the message?"

"Yeah, I got it."

"Well, why haven't you called me? I was starting to get
worried about you...Hey hold on a second." Then I
heard him speaking to someone in the background.

148

"It's Ashlyn," he said, as he returned his attention to our conversation, "She came over to do some laundry".

Ashlyn was the girl my brother had been seeing for the past nine months or so. He had sent pictures of them at Christmas, taken at some type of sorority formal.

"You there?" He said.

"Yeah, I'm here." I couldn't seem to come up with much more than three word responses to any of his questions.

"What's the matter?" He pushed again.

Silence.

"Holden?"

"Yeah"

"Are you ok?" I could hear the concern in his voice.

"John, I need to talk to you about some stuff, but I can't do it over the phone."

"What kind of stuff?" he replied, his tone a marriage of concern and nervousness. "Are you in trouble?"

"I just need to talk to you, face to face."

"Ok." He said in a somber tone. I think the seriousness of the conversation was sinking in and he knew there was something deeply wrong. Through the years John and I had shared everything with each other...well, almost.

"I don't think I can make the trip to Raleigh right now," I responded.

"You need me to come to Ocracoke?" John said in a manner that assured me he would be in the car within an hour if I would just say the word.

"That would be best." I replied, trying to hold back the tears.

"What time does the last ferry run from Cedar Island today?" he asked.

"Seven." I replied.

"Let's see, it's four right now," he paused in calculation, "Buddy, even if I walked out the door right now I don't think I could make it, with Raleigh traffic and all."

Silence....more thought.

"I could come on and just stay at that motel there by the

149

ferry and catch the first one in the morning."

"NO." I said with more vigor than I had used in the entire conversation. "No, man," I repeated a little softer, "you stay home tonight and head on tomorrow when you get up and going, I'll be ok." The last thing I wanted was for him to check in at the Driftwood and someone recognize our shared last name. I could just imagine John, true to form, striking up a conversation with someone at the motel, mentioning that he was heading to Ocracoke to see me, telling of the work that I was doing on the Island. I couldn't risk him hearing this through the grapevine.

"Ok. You're sure?" he pressed in concern.

"Yeah, I'm sure."

"What time is the first ferry?"

"Eight o'clock."

"I'll be on it!"

"Ok, I'll meet you at the dock".

Silence dominating the following seconds.

"I love you, Holden." I heard him say on the other end of the line.

"I love you, too."

   With that, we ended our conversation and I was faced with the reality that in less than twenty four hours I was going to completely rock the world of the person who had been my chief ally all my life. The majority of that night was spent in my room journaling. I filled pages with the thoughts that were cycling in my head. Periodically, Robert and Emilis would tap at the door to see if I was ok.

   I beat the sun up the next morning, which wasn't hard to do since I laid awake most of the night, watching the red glowing numbers change on my alarm clock. I starred sleeplessly as 2:00, 2:30, 3:20, and 4:45 all rolled around. Shortly after five I made my way downstairs to put on some coffee. I wasn't as quiet as I had hoped to be in fumbling for the parts of the percolator. Before long, Emilis came wandering into the kitchen, still tying her chenille robe around her, her eyes squinted and heavy with sleep.

"You okay, man?" she inquired, her voice still trying to find its bearings.

"Yeah, I just couldn't sleep".

She came over and joined me at the counter, handing me the parts of the percolator which I had plundered over without recognizing.

After the coffee was done, Emilis and I spent the first hour of that day sitting across from each other at the kitchen table, mugs in hand, talking about how scared I was to talk to John. She mainly listened, and being able to talk through the anxiety I was feeling really did me good.

She reached across the table and took me by the hand, assuring me that I had a home here with them, no matter what. I desperately needed to know that something in my life would remain stable. In a few moments she got up from the table and began pulling out pans, "French toast sound good this morning?"

"Sure does!" I replied.

The morning drug on, much like watching a pot of water on the stove, waiting for it to boil. The nervousness of telling John settled deep in my stomach, causing me to lose the french toast that brought such comfort an hour before. At ten o'clock I was standing on the dock by the old lifeguard station, watching the steel hulled ferry slowly approach as it navigated through the sand bar bounded channel. As the ferry docked I anxiously awaited the first sight of John, no doubt exhausted after a four hour drive from Raleigh, which must have begun around 3:30 that morning.

We tried to exchange small talk after he parked and met me on the dock, an awkward and empty pursuit. After a few moments I had him drive to the fish house so I could borrow Robert's truck and take John to the only place I knew where we could have the privacy needed for such a conversation. After driving onto the beach and

151

finding a section of smooth sand left by the receded tide-waters, I parked the truck and began a disclosure that was long overdue. I had rehearsed it in my head a thousand times since we hung up the phone the day before, but this was one conversation for which I would never feel pre-pared.

"Thank you for coming." I said, an admittedly feeble introduction to what I was about to say.

"Holden, what is going on?" He responded in matter-of-fact concern.

"There's something that I have to tell you, but I'm scared to."

John gave no response other than a silent stare of concern as he braced himself for whatever news was coming. The anxiety and tension in that truck cab was almost tangible. I slowly rolled up my shirt sleeves, turning my wrists up-right so he could see.

"Oh, my gosh, Holden!"

Panic covered his face.

"Holden, when did this happen?" he said, his eyes wide with concern.

"Three weeks ago."

"Why didn't you call me, why didn't Robert call me?"

"I didn't want them to. I couldn't face you right then."

"You couldn't face me?"

"John, I just couldn't have this conversation with you then, everything was too fresh."

"What are you talking about? What couldn't you tell me?"

I just sat in silence.

"Holden, I'm your brother. If you're dealing with depres-sion or whatever, you can talk to me about it."

"Not this."

"Not what? Is it that bad?"

"John, I'm gay."

John's lips were pursed and his eyes wide as he sat in silence processing my disclosure. Eventually he looked

152

away, shifting his gaze out of the passenger window, lips still pursed, jaw muscles flexing, betraying the gritting of his teeth.

"John?" I began after a long, awkward silence.

"I heard you."

More silence.

"John..."

"Holden, you're not gay." He interjected bitterly.

"Yes, I...."

"No, you're not." He said in a short tone, interrupting me again. "Now, I don't know what has happened down here in this God forsaken place to make you think that..."

"John, I've struggled with this for as long as I can remember."

"Holden, that's a lie. What about Caroline, huh? We all thought y'all would marry. How about that girl you dated in college? What was her name? Lisa?"

"Linda." I interjected quietly.

"Yeah, well, you all seemed pretty hot and heavy to me."

"John, you just don't understand."

"You're not gay!" He said forcefully.

"John."

"I won't hear of it, Holden. Now you just drop this. Whatever this is you're going through is going to pass. Have you even prayed about this?" he said accusingly.

"Oh, my gosh." I replied with obvious disgust, "Are you serious, do you really want to go there?"

"Yes, I do want to go there!" he retorted, "Holden, you know what the Bible says should happen to people like that!"

I was completely taken back and horrified at what was unfolding.

"Homosexuals are an abomination." he continued, "Do you want to go to Hell, Holden?"

"No, I don't." By now I was fighting tears. "John, if you only knew what I have been through."

"Holden, you're going crazy. This isn't you at all."

153

"John, yes it is me. This doesn't make me any different."
"No, I don't know this Holden". He said, cutting me off mid-sentence.

    I had never heard him speak like this to anyone, especially me. I was the younger brother he always coddled and protected. I didn't expect for him to be thrilled, or even accepting for that matter, but the detached coldness of his response was something for which I was completely unprepared.
"Now I don't know what this crowd down here has done to you, but I'm gonna tell you what you're gonna do," he began, "you're gonna get your things and you're going home with me and we're gonna get this fixed."
"John, I'm not going to do that."
"Oh, yes you are. You are not stable. I'm gonna get you in touch with our pastor and we're gonna take care of this."
"John, I've met someone and I'm not leaving."
The way John looked at me after I said that was like someone had just slapped him across the face.
"Holden, I don't want to hear it."
"But John, couldn't you at least listen. If you could just meet him, maybe you would realize..."
"No, I'm not gonna listen to this, and I'm sure as hell not gonna meet this queer that's got your head all screwed up."
"John, listen to the way you're talking to me. It's me Holden...remember me? Your little brother, the one whose life you saved?"
I hit a nerve at this point and John teared up, but the moment was short lived. Shaking his head in rapid succession, as if he was shaking away any emotion that may cause him to soften, he quickly regained his composure.
"Holden, you can't do this."
"John, I've tried to change, but I don't think I can."
"Holden, please don't do this."
Silence occupied the next minute or so, making it seem

154

like an hour.

"You're determined that you're gonna be with this fag-got." He retorted.

"John, stop talking like that. You don't even know him."

"No, and I don't think that I even know you anymore." He lashed out piercingly.

"Take me back to my car." He continued in a flat, cold manner.

"John!" I pleaded, my heart hanging between complete devastation and utter shock. He didn't respond.

Eventually I fired up the old pickup and gave heed to my big brother's request.

I don't know what I had expected, but this was definitely not it. I got out of the truck and stood by his car, while he sought desperately to avoid eye-contact with me.

"Have you slept with him?" He asked pointedly, looking down as he retrieved his keys from his jean pocket.

"Yes." I answered quietly.

He shook his head from side to side.

"You're going to hell, you know that right?" He replied, looking into my eyes for the first time in over ten minutes, "Is that what you want, Holden?"

At this juncture I began to cry, but the arms which had comforted me so often remained folded in guarded objection.

"No," I said through bitter tears of pain and disappointment. "No, I don't. I just don't understand. John, I have fought this for so long and I just don't understand anymore."

"When you're ready to repent of this, then you'll have your brother back. Until then, you are dead to me." And with that he got into his car, closed the door, and pulled away from the fish house. There was no embrace and no 'I love you.' I have never heard those words from him again. In fact, I haven't heard from John or seen him since that day.

There are hurts that go beyond tears, erupting in utter

155

silence and numb, surreal feelings of detachment. This was the sensation I had as I watched him pull away, the feeling I still have as I think of the miles and years that separate us. The one person in the world I had counted on to always have my back walked out of my life when I needed him most.

Entry 31

A couple of days after my encounter with John I tried calling Mama, certain that John had broken the news to her by now. I wanted desperately to avoid the whole thing, but she was my mother and I owed her a personal disclosure. After a week of leaving messages, with no response, I decided to make the trek to Johnston County and have a face to face conversation.

It was about quarter after five in the afternoon when I pulled into the drive of our little brick ranch home amidst the tobacco fields. It was supper time. Mama's Buick was under the car port and Samuel's pickup truck was parked under the large pine in the front yard. I slowly made my way to the side door under the carport, my heart pounding. Normally I would just have gone on in, but the storm door was locked. I knocked a few times and then stepped back down onto the concrete floor as I awaited one of their faces to appear from behind the glass.

In just a few seconds I heard foot-steps nearing the door from inside and then mama's face appeared from inside the glass. She opened the wooden door, peering through the glass of the storm door into the eyes of her middle son. This was a moment that I had dreaded for as long as I knew that I was gay.

For a moment we just stared into each other's eyes. I know the news had all but killed her. They say that the nearest thing to God's love is the love of a mother, so I stood there in silent hope that the love which carried me for nine months, raising me from knee socks and smocking to college graduation, would trump any sense of

156

shame. I hoped desperately that somehow her love for me would be greater than her own pain, shame, or disappointment. The answer to my wondering came as she closed the wooden door. Her shadow disappeared. The sound of her footsteps grew fainter with every step back down the hall towards her bedroom.

Of all the scenarios scripted in my mind over the four hour trip from Ocracoke, I never imagined this one. I found myself leaning up against her white Buick for what seemed like an eternity, eclipsed by the shock of what had just occurred. Hoping that maybe she had just gone to get something and would be right back. Eventually, I accepted the fact that she had literally just shut me out of her life. I made my way back to my car and pulled out of the drive to make my way home to Ocracoke, utterly, completely, numbly crushed.

How can a mother reject the very life she helped to bring into the world? My head was a fog as I put the car in drive and began to accelerate. Just then, I caught a glimpse of something in my periphery. It was Samuel.

He ran through the front yard trying to intercept me. I didn't know whether to stop or not. If this was to be a repeat of my encounter with John I just didn't have it in me, not today. After all, I was only two weeks out of the psychiatric ward. How much can one person take? But, after all, this was my little brother.

I pulled to the side of the highway as Samuel jumped the ditch and made his way around to the driver's window.

"Holden, get out of the car."

"Samuel, I can't do this right now." I said in sheer exhaustion, leaning my head back onto the headrest. I didn't have the energy to fight, to argue, or even to cry.

"Holden, please get out of the car." Something in his voice suggested that he wasn't looking to fight, and so I unbuckled my seat belt, opened the door, and slowly made my way to my feet. No sooner was I on my feet

157

good than Samuel caved in my arms, his head buried in my chest.

As it turns out, he was the one who needed to cry that afternoon. We just stood there on the edge of the rural route, cars and log trucks zooming by, with my little brother's tears soaking my polo. In all those years I had been too preoccupied with worrying about him and being frustrated with him to even realize the depth of love that he held for me and the level to which he had elevated me.

I guess there can be few things as painful as the failure of a hero. Somehow those tears were a relinquishing of all the unrealistic idealization he had attached to me through the years. In the end, I was human, struggling like everyone else to make sense of things, to find my way in life.

After Samuel's tears subsided and he raised his head from my chest. I placed my hand firmly on the back of his neck and looked him square in the eyes.
"I'm still your big brother. I'm still Holden."
"I know", he said, still sniffling.
"I love you, Samuel. Don't you ever forget that."
"I love you too." He said, his eyelashes wet.

With that I got back into my car and made my way back onto the highway, watching him in my rearview, standing there on the side of the road, his hands in his pockets. I was unsure what the future of our relation-ship would look like; however, in some gentle way I was encouraged by his willingness to still embrace me, to show that we were indeed still brothers. In the coming years I would see that this moment with Samuel was both a death and a rebirth, the death of my hero status, the death of a larger than life character which he had devel-oped in his maturing mind, and yet the birth of a truer brotherhood and friendship than we had ever shared to that point.

That day marked a change. From that point forward, Johnston County, North Carolina was permanently in my

158

rearview mirror, though not entirely of my own volition. As much as I love a sappy love story, we don't always get 'happily ever after', things don't always work out, and reconciliation sometimes eludes us, regardless of how much we would like to grasp it.

Through the years I have sent mama and John a host of letters, Birthday, Mother's Day and Christmas cards, but I have never gotten a response. For years I harbored a lot of bitterness in my heart because of how they had disowned me. In time I would come to see that my bitterness was a thin veneer masking a broken heart. Slowly, I have been able to relinquish some of that hurt. I have attempted to see things from their perspective, as difficult as that is. Unforgiveness is a soul eating disease and, by God's grace, I have been able to gradually let go. But there isn't a Christmas, a Birthday, or a Mother's Day that goes by that I don't think of them, pray for them, and wonder how they are...and how things might have been different.

Entry 32

It's painful to recall the magnitude of life change I experienced upon returning to the island from Pitt Memorial. Before I was outed I had been the golden boy of the island. I was the man all the mothers wanted their daughters to marry, and the guy they wanted their sons to emulate. But, after the tidal surge of my news washed across the island, I came to be despised by many of the same people who had claimed to love me so dearly the two years prior.

I couldn't walk to the community store without returning home in tears. I would run into those eager to tell me how disgusting and horrible I was, or I would have to face the equally painful silence and shunning of those who once offered warm smiles and ready embraces. I was now a leper in the village and it became painfully clear that I would not be able to live on Ocracoke any longer.

159

Parks had long wanted to move away. Now that everything was out and both our lives on Ocracoke were plagued with upheaval and hostility, all our former objections seemed to fade. It came as no surprise that, due to the fallout following our discovery, Parks was unable to retain his position at the island school. This was the last and most devastating blow, poising him with eagerness to close this long and painful chapter of his life. To Parks, Ocracoke was a place where he would never truly be able to be himself, at least without constant fear of rejection or retaliation. He tasted a semblance of freedom while at Chapel Hill and coming back to the island, by his own admission, made him feel as if he were suffocating. The constant pressure to keep his secret hidden, coupled with the drowning fear of discovery, wracked Parks with anxiety. He never shared this with me until after I got home from Pitt, but he had to be prescribed anti-anxiety medication shortly after returning home to teach.

Regardless of how resolved Parks was concerning a move, for me Ocracoke held the truest sense of home and belonging I had ever experienced. It was killing me inside to think that I would have to leave it all behind. But with each passing day I could see that I would have to go, though it would completely break my heart to leave Robert, Emilis, and Jane Anne.

In addition to the fact that sentiment on the island towards me was hostile at best, I was also having a crisis of faith that was driving a painful wedge deeper between the Guthries and me. I fought so hard for so many years against this struggle, against these attractions. I turned down so many advances and opportunities for relationships through the years because I felt that it was not God's will as I read in Scripture. To be what I felt I was, meant I was an abomination before God, and I couldn't be that, I couldn't handle that. And yet, the war raged unabated. My entire life and faith seemed in turmoil.

I had wrestled for so many years, but it wasn't until

160

that point that I could even conceive of being, or admit to being, angry with the LORD. I just didn't understand. I didn't understand why I had to struggle like this, why He would let me struggle like this when I was trying to give Him all of my life, to live for Him with all my heart. Why didn't He take these desires away from me after I prayed, and cried, and pleaded for help and healing? After years of struggle with no change in my attractions and sexual desires, the why's seemed to change a little. "Why do I have to suffer like this?" became "Why does this have to be wrong?"... Why? Why? Why?

It seemed to me that my questions outweighed answers, and no one could help me understand. Robert and Emilis, love me as they may, were very uncomfortable discussing the issue. They were still trying to wrap their minds and their faith around everything. My anger at God, my anger at some of the people on the island, my anger at myself for not being better or stronger seemed to poison my discourse with everyone but Parks.

I was also angry with God because I tried to do the right thing, I had called off all sexual encounters with Parks and was fighting this thing, I felt, with everything I had. After all of that, my life was still in shambles. I blamed God for not shielding us from this hell in which we found ourselves. I was so angry and hurting to my core. In those days I rode a pendulum, swinging from unbridled anger to torrents of tears and cries for mercy. I felt that God had let me down.

I had come to feel that He must hate me anyway, because of the struggle I had not been able to overcome. And so, I decided that God and I would take a break from each other. I was tired of struggling, tired of fighting, and saw no way of reconciling my faith with my deep love for Parks. I had a great man in Parks, a man who loved me, who cared for me, who made me happy and so I decided that I was going to drink deeply of this love, if it hairlipped congress.

161

Entry 33

That July, Parks and I packed our few belongings into the little silver Honda and made our farewell voyage across Pamlico Sound. With the island fading on the horizon behind us, we were standing on the precipice of a new life together, free from every external limitation. Parks had been in contact with a friend of his from Chapel Hill who had moved out to the west coast, who helped secure Parks a teaching position in Seattle. In retrospect, it seems that we were removing ourselves as far from our former lives as possible.

Once the ferry landed at Cedar Island we set our course for the Northwest Coast. The sentiment was bittersweet. The sadness of closing a chapter in life was intensified by the fact my leaving Ocracoke was more out of necessity than true desire.

In our journey westward, the reordering of our lives, we experienced all the anxiety and uncertainties that accompany such an adventure; however, our exhilaration was high with the anticipation of fresh beginnings and new faces. The money Robert had helped me save and invest became our cushion for this opening chapter of our lives together, paying for our trip across country and easing the financial pinch of getting settled into a brand new world some 3,000 miles from the village that had been home.

One week to the day after boarding the ferry from Ocracoke we caught our first glimpse of the Space Needle through a rain speckled windshield. The better part of the first week was spent in search of an apartment, buying second hand furniture from consignment shops, and me scouting for a job. The cost of living in Seattle was very different from what we were accustomed to on Ocracoke. We finally found an apartment near Pike Place and Elliot Bay, a small one bedroom on Virginia Street just across First Avenue. From what we could find, it was the cheapest area for rent in the city. Granted, it was a dump, but our excitement for our new life eclipsed such realities. We did our best to spruce it up and, after some deep cleaning and personal effects, what began as a cold dingy space quickly became home. In those earliest days of the move there was an engulfing sense that whatever hardships may come, facing them together seemed to somehow make them bearable.

The first full weekend in Seattle we spent exploring our new frontier. Since our apartment was down near Pike Place, we decided to take the morning to check out the Market. That Saturday morning, as we stepped in and out of shops on the waterfront, we first met Sara and Ty. They had opened their gift shop at the Market a few years prior after moving to the northwest corner of Washington. The four of us were close in age, and they had been living in the Emerald City for about five years.

Ty moved to Seattle from Boston after finishing a degree in philosophy at MIT. In Massachusetts he had been the quintessential clean cut, east coast prep, but by the time we met him six years later, he was donning a fisherman's sweater, Chuck Taylors, and blonde dreads. He told us he just wanted a change, and so he packed his car and made the drive westward. Sara had grown up in the Spokane area and moved to the coast following her graduation from Whitworth in hopes of securing a career in journalism. Ultimately, she landed a gig as an entertainment columnist for the Seattle Times, but not before several years of waiting tables atop the Space Needle. It was in this revolving restaurant above the city that Sara and Ty met.

They were good people. The four of us were products of very different cultures and backgrounds, but there was a genuine goodness about them, a sincere concern for the well-being of others which made Parks and me feel so at home in their presence. We probably stood in their shop talking for well over an hour that first day. They were fascinated with our accents and completely intrigued by the Outer Banks culture. Before we said our goodbyes, to continue our exploration of the city, they invited us out for dinner that evening. We gladly accepted and from that point forward the four of us became the dearest of friends.

One night in early September, after settling into our Seattle life, Parks and I went out with Ty and Sara to a little bar on the south side for karaoke. Sara really couldn't sing a lick, bless her heart, but she loved karaoke and you couldn't help but laugh at her. I mean, she was so bad that all you could do was laugh. She didn't come near hitting a note, it was awful and hilarious. After a couple dirty martinis we had to practically pry the microphone from her hand.

To my surprise, it was not just your usual cheap sound system and TV screen karaoke; this place had a live band, which explained the steep cover charge. I was amazed by the breadth of their repertoire. I had never done karaoke in my life and the only singing that I had done since leaving Ocracoke had been in the shower. We were all sitting around our little table, Sara with her martini, Parks with his Foster's, and Ty with his Miller High Life. I was nursing my glass of cranberry juice when Parks chimed in, feeling increasingly free of inhibitions as the night wore on.

"Holden can throw down on some singing." Parks blurted out to Sara.

"You sing?" Sara said, with an excitement that let me know I was in trouble.

"A little," I replied sheepishly, "it's been a while."

"How did I not know this already?" She exclaimed.

"Well, you have to sing one!"

Before I could offer an objection she was up grabbing a copy of the band's song list. She came back and plopped it down in front of me.

"Pick one." She said grinning ear to ear.

"No, that's okay. Maybe another time."

"Look, if I can get up there and do it, you can too." She
replied.

She definitely had a point there.

"Gimme that." Parks said as he sat his beer down and
reached over to pick up the list.

Before long he was grinning from ear to ear.

"What?"

"It's a surprise."

With that he jumped up from the table, putting my name
on the list.

"What did you put down?"

"Don't worry, you've got this." He said, lifting the Foster's
bottle to meet his mischievous grin.

After about twenty minutes of suspense, and some
drunk guy absolutely murdering Springsteen's Glory
Days, the MC called my name over the system and I
made my way reluctantly to the stage. With the first few
guitar riffs I began to laugh, shaking my head as I looked
out at Parks. He had fallen in love with The Outfield
after their album release that year, Your Love eclipsed
even Billy Joel's Uptown Girl on Parks' list of favorites. If
I had a dollar for every time he played their tape in our
living room with the volume cranked...Anyway, I was so
nervous as I started that famous first line, "Josie's on a vacation far away". With my three fans sitting there cheer-
ing, I gave it my all. Parks always changed the lyrics to
"I like my guys a little bit older." Though I was only two
years older than Parks, he always teased me about being
an old man.

Singing on stage that night was a blast, one of the
greatest memories of my life. It was a type of awakening,
the sense of elation which accompanies the dusting off of
long dormant dreams. After the music ended I rejoined
my comrades, now standing in ovation. We resumed our
roundtable banter, as Sara searched for her next rendition.

While the next guy in line gave his best attempt at

165

Carry on my Wayward Son, the MC made his way to our table. Before I knew what was happening, he was handing me his card and asking that I join a cover band that he was starting to perform in the bar scene of the greater Seattle area. Parks actually seemed more excited about the opportunity than I was and before long I had a booking to sing at least twice a month.

Seattle's night life was a far cry from singing in Church on Sunday mornings, and at first I was uncomfortable with the change. The sight of drunk people in the crowd brought back horrible memories, and I often closed my eyes to lose myself in the lyrics. I had always loved singing and this gig provided me an exciting outlet. Though Parks was always inviting some of his teaching colleagues to hear me, it was he, Sara, and Ty who were the old faithfuls. If I didn't know another soul at the venue, I could count on those three familiar faces smiling back from the crowd.

During set breaks I could steal away a few minutes to sit with them and then it was back for another round. I was glad the commitment only involved a couple of weekends each month. Though I enjoyed singing, I didn't want every weekend to be tied up with concerts. There was a time when being in front of all those people may have been extremely appealing to me, but I had grown weary of shallow interactions and longed simply for quality time with Parks. I think Parks was glad it was only a couple of times a month as well. He had signed up for a city soccer league that Fall, and between going to his games and my concerts our weekends were pretty busy. Every spare weekend moment that we could have to ourselves was precious and guarded.

We were always entertained by the volume of phone numbers I would bring home from the sea of college aged girls in the audience, obviously eager for some post show rendezvous. Parks and I would crack up as I spread them out on our coffee table before tossing them in the trash.

166

Bless their hearts, if they only knew.

There were several times in the course of my stint with the band when guys would approach me as well, offering an invitation for drinks after the show. It was flattering to me, but I had absolutely no intentions or desire of accepting. One night Parks walked up, after getting another beer from the bar, and overheard such a proposition...it didn't go well.

I had never known Parks to be a jealous person; but, based on that day surfing in Hatteras, I did know that he wasn't afraid of a fight where I was concerned. Parks didn't get physical until the guy insulted me and spit on Parks' shoes. By the time the bouncers broke it up, the guy had taken some pretty hard licks and Parks walked away dabbing his busted lip with the cuff of his shirt-sleeve. They were both thrown out of the club and I had to get the band manager to sneak Parks backstage until we finished our last set.

When we arrived back at the apartment that night we got into a serious argument. I was helping to doctor his lip, when he looked me in the eyes and began questioning me.

"Did you want to go out with him afterwards?"

"What?"

"You heard me!" He pressed.

"Are you being serious?"

Silence.

"Parks, I can't believe you would even think that for a second."

"Did you? Answer me!"

"Not at all!"

Silence.

"Parks, do you know how many of those invitations I've turned down?"

"Oh, so this happens all the time?"

The conversation continued this downward trajectory for the better part of an hour. I had never known him to be

167

so jealous, so paranoid, so untrusting. I can honestly say that I never gave any other guy a serious second thought. Of course I noticed attractive guys, I'm human. But never once did I ever consider pursuing any of them.

Aside from being completely in love with Parks, he was also my very best friend. For all my faults, I was loyal. Looking back on it, my love for Parks at times bordered on enmeshment, which is why I felt his jealous paranoia was so preposterous. My world revolved around him and our relationship. The way he was behaving was almost laughable; yet, he was serious, and that troubled me.

Finally, I just went to bed, wearied of the unproductive conversation that was looping around an unbelieving suspicion. Parks came and took a pillow, letting me know that he was going to sleep on the couch that night.

Before daylight he made his way back to our room and the pre-dawn hours brought apologies and expressions aimed at mending the rift he had created between us. Though more than ready to accept, I still found myself perplexed as to where all of this came from. I couldn't imagine where he would ever get any ideas of suspicion regarding my fidelity.

Entry 34

February 4th, 1985 was Parks' twenty-third Birthday. It fell on a Tuesday and it just so happened that the Outfield was playing a concert in Seattle that night. I picked up extra shifts for a month to afford the tickets.

I wanted it to be a complete surprise, so I constructed a cover story that I had to work a double shift that day at the coffee shop. Parks was to come by the shop after he got out of school and hang out with me there until I got off of work. I had a coworker clued in on the whole event. When Parks arrived that afternoon, she would tell him I wasn't feeling well and had gone home early. When he got home, I would have everything ready and waiting to surprise him.

168

I took the entire day off and spent the morning running around the city, picking up everything needed to make his surprise dinner perfect. Parks' grandmother, for as long as he could remember, always made a carrot cake for his birthday. Now that he was estranged from her, I saw to it that he had one every year after we moved to Seattle, made by the little bakery where we would get fresh beignets every Saturday. His other favorite meal was stewed hard crabs and yeast rolls, a coastal Carolina staple. I called Emilis to get the recipe and some inside tips. The main problem was the absence of Blue Crabs in Puget Sound, and so I had to use Dungeness.

The day was spent running from baker, to grocer, and to the Bay docks for crabs. I wasn't expecting Parks home until about four or four thirty, giving me plenty of time to get things in order. We would eat at about five thirty, then head over to KeyArena for the eight o'clock show. Parks didn't suspect a thing and I was giddy with excitement! He loved surprises and I couldn't wait to see his face when he walked in that afternoon.

At about a quarter after one I made it back to the apartment to begin cooking. Entering the apartment I found that Parks was already home, his school bag lying in the middle of the living room floor, his tie tossed upon the back of the sofa. I heard whispers coming from our room. Making my way down the hall, I learned that the voices I heard were those of Parks and Conly Rutherford, the guy who had helped Parks get the teaching job in Seattle, the guy Parks had called when everything fell apart in Ocracoke, the guy who begged us to move to Seattle, the guy who sat at my table with his own boyfriend just weeks ago. At that moment my world as I had known it was crushed and I realized that Parks had made birthday plans of his own.

The two of them heard me as I opened the door to our apartment. Our tiny little apartment didn't even have closets in the bedroom, and with the bath's only entrance

169

in the hallway, there was nowhere to hide. I stood frozen in the hall peering around the door frame, my eyes locked with Parks' as Conly braced his back against the headboard and waited to see what would unfold.

I didn't say a word. The wind was completely taken out of my sails. I just stood there, my eyes fixed, staring into the deep blue eyes I had formerly considered to be exclusively mine. Parks slipped from the bed, wrapping his waist in our sheet, making his way towards me. I dropped the bag of crabs, the flowers, the box with his carrot cake, letting them hit the floor right where I stood as I turned to leave, my head spinning, my hands shaking, my breathing rapid, my eyes wet. Parks called for me frantically from the top of our steps, clad only in our sheet, as I continued undaunted to the ground level and out onto the bustling street.

I didn't go back home that night. I couldn't. I couldn't face Parks at that moment; it was all just too much. How could he do this to me? How could he give himself to anyone else? How could he betray me like this? Was I not enough for him? Was I not good enough, strong enough, handsome enough? What was the problem? Questions, insecurities, and memories raced through my mind as I wandered the streets of Seatown that cold February night. Fits of crying gave way to intense anger and then the cycle would begin all over again.

I loved this man. He was my best friend and the one with whom I had vowed to spend the rest of my life. I knew him and all of his little idiosyncrasies. How, every morning, he ate dry Fruit Loops with his fingers from his cereal bowl, chasing them with a glass of whole milk; how he slept on his side with a pillow between his knees; how he would get a twitch in his left eye whenever he was completely exhausted or trying to hold back tears. I was the one who knew the story behind the round scars on his shoulder blades. I was the one who knew how he took his coffee in the morning. I was the one that washed and

170

folded his clothes, who took care of him when he was sick with flu or the mirage of seasonal allergies he battled each year. I was the one who walked away from my entire world to be with him. I had lost the most in pursuit of his love, and was glad to do it because in the depths of my heart I loved him. He was the only person I had ever been with and I loved him still, even amidst the flooding of anger in my heart, evoking a desire to hate as much as I had ever loved. Was this why we moved here? Was this his plan all along? Is this why we moved to Seattle, so he could be near Conly? What was their history? How long had this been happening? How long had Parks been living this double life? Was this the only time? Was this the only guy? My head was spinning and I wasn't able to be around anyone. I just walked.

That night I passed the hours walking through the city in a trance of devastation, the only comfort being the subtle warmth of my pea coat, my collar raised, my chin tucked low to my chest in a feeble attempt to fight the cutting winter air. From Pike Place, up Olive Way, across Interstate Five, through the trails of Cal Anderson Park I wandered for most of the night, occasionally stopping to lean against one of the lamp posts, gazing up into the clear cold night sky. I was trying to wrap my mind around this new and unwelcome reality. Was he looking for me? Was he worried? I hoped so! In fact, I wanted him to suffer. He couldn't worry or cry any more than I wished him to that night! If he could feel just one tenth of the pain that was causing my heart to burst at the seams, then he would be devastated.

From Cal Anderson I wandered on frigid feet down Denny Way and up Fifth Avenue, wandering as my world unraveled. Sunrise found me below the Space Needle, as park attendants and merchants began to file in for the day. Making my way back down fifth, I slipped into a small barista for a cup of coffee to warm my hands and burn off the fog of a sleep deprived night. I sat at the little

171

round wooden table, holding my latte mug in both hands, staring down into the froth and wondering where to go from here. Two girls at the next table talked of moving to Portland, sparked by gripes concerning their respective boyfriends. Two college aged guys in overstuffed chairs pontificated their last exam and their plans of conquest for the night ahead, all the while I was fighting the desire to stand in my chair and scream for everyone to just shut the hell up. Their conversations were so petty to me that morning. Seething from betrayal, I convinced myself that they wouldn't know real pain, disappointment, or drama if it jumped up and bit them on the ass. I, on the other hand, was amidst a living nightmare and wanted to vomit in disapproval of their petty discourse.

Finally, and not a moment too soon, they left for class or whatever other self-important item they had on their agenda. Meanwhile, I sat warming my hands on my mug, wondering what Parks was doing, what he was thinking? I hoped desperately that he was as miserable as I was.

I finished my morning brew and decided that I would have to go back to our apartment sooner or later, but decided to wait another couple of hours so that Parks would be at work. I wasn't ready to face him. How could he do this? How could he injure me like this? How could he even think of being with someone else? I just couldn't get my mind around the events of the last twenty-four hours. I had been so faithful to him. I was committed to Parks. We had been through so much together. We had lost our homes, our careers, our families, our friends. We had moved across country together, our only ally being one another. I supported us both financially in our move and in the weeks leading up to our first pay checks in our new city. I just couldn't understand what had gone wrong.

At a quarter after nine I made my way back to Pike Place and our apartment, slowly placing my key in the lock and hoping he wasn't at home. I opened the door to

172

find him sitting on the sofa in silence, his eyes red, his hair disheveled. I could tell that he was worried, and I was glad.

"Holden," he said in a desperate tone, rising from the couch and approaching me with his hands tucked into pockets of brown corduroys I had bought him the Christmas prior.

I never said a word, I'm sure I didn't have to. I have always worn my emotions and thoughts on my face, even when I didn't want to. This morning I just gave him a look that made him stop dead in his tracks, a frigid scowl that had never before been directed towards him. I walked straight past him without speaking and into the bedroom.

Entering our room, I saw the covers still mounded in the middle of our bed, the covers that he had crawled beneath with someone else, and sadness gave way to rage. I came completely unglued. What began as a quest to come home and gather up a few belongings morphed into a destructive tirade. I flipped the mattress and box spring off of the bed frame, wishing I had a baseball bat so I could beat the very walls out of that room. I saw all the pictures of us on the chest of drawers at the foot of our bed, pictures from the journey west, Birthdays, Christmases, beach trips, and goofy poses from a happier time. Those pictures, which I had looked at so many mornings after rousing from sleep, became missiles of disgust as I hurled them across the room, breaking our mirror and the bedroom window upon impact.

Parks came in and grabbed me in a bear hug to prevent me from doing any more damage. I fought him with every bit of strength I had, but his grip proved stronger than my wild objections and my rage subsided into deep sobs as I beat my fists into his chest. Through floods of tears I began crying out, repeatedly asking the most salient question of the day, "Why, Parks? Why?"

Though words were few that morning, tears were in

173

full supply. In the midst of infidelity, apologies and ex-
planations are worth little. After all, what can be said to
ease the pain of such a wound, what can be said to erase
the sense of betrayal, to explain the whys and the hows?
Nothing! Even so, Parks did apologize, begging me not
to leave him, pleading for us to stay together and work
through it. I said nothing. The wound was too fresh and
the mental image of him and Conly too intrusive. In the
end he said he would give me time to think, that he would
go and stay with friends while I sorted everything out.
"With whom...Conly?" I jabbed indignantly.
"No." Parks replied in the humility of realizing he deserved any verbal lashing he received.
 "I've already talked with Sara and Ty and they said I
could crash with them until we get this sorted out." He
continued.
"Do they know?"
"Yeah." He said softly.
"What do they think?"
"They're pretty pissed at me right now." He replied,
looking down at the shag carpet in dejection. I shook my
head in cold agreement with their sentiment.
"Ok." I said sternly, my tone drenched in betrayal.
"Ok, what?"
"Ok. You go stay with them until we figure this whole
thing out."
For the rest of the afternoon he slowly packed and put
our room back together while I sat in the living room,
quiet and dejected. He emerged with his duffle bag to
say goodbye, but I remained in my chair, my gaze fixed
out of the living room window, allowing him to depart in
all of the uncomfortable silence he deserved. I couldn't
look at him. I couldn't allow my feelings for him to hijack
reason. He had royally screwed up this time and I knew
it wasn't going to be an easy fix, if it were ever fixed at all.
Harsh as this separation may have seemed, I had to do
this for me.

174

Entry 35

The days passed slowly with Parks gone, the nights even slower. I couldn't believe that we had ended up in this place. I missed him so much, loved him so much, and yet waves of hatred washed over me as I thought of what he had done to us. How could he? This was the question that played in my mind like a skipping record.

I looked back on our first time together, how scared, nervous, and inexperienced I was, and how patient and gentle he had been. He had so often held me in warm assurance that everything was going to be okay as I would lie there, detached by an internal war. His smile, his laid-back way, his gentle voice, the compassion wed with strength that Parks embodied had captured my heart in the beginning and haunted me now in his absence.

I missed having his arm across my chest as I slept at night. I missed waking up next to him in the morning. I missed his soccer cleats by the front door and his dirty socks left in the living room. I missed toothpaste remnants in the bathroom sink and yesterday's underwear littering the bathroom floor, following his morning shower. Things that once annoyed me became sentimental hallmarks, creating a sense of longing for the one from whom I was estranged.

Parks had been true to his promise of giving me space, his only contact being the occasional note taped to our apartment door on evenings when I returned home from work. I used that time of separation to do some serious thinking about whether there would be a future for us after this. I had to decide whether or not I could ever truly forgive. Could I ever truly trust him again?

After weeks of misery I picked up the phone and called Ty and Sara's early one evening.

"Hello." Sara answered.

"Hey Sara, it's Holden. Is Parks there?" I said nervously.

"He sure is, hold on." I could hear a hint of elation in her voice, as she no doubt was in hopes that her mediation was paying off.

"It's Holden." I heard her whisper as she handed him the phone.

"Hello." Parks' voice was a mix of shock and nervous excitement.

It was the first time I had heard him speak in three weeks.

"Hey." I said, standing on the brink of a conversation for which there was no script.

After a brief silence he continued, "How are you?"

"Miserable."

"Me too."

"What are you up to tonight?" I asked.

"Whatever you want me to be up to."

"You want to grab some coffee and talk a little?"

"Yeah, that would be great...you want me to swing by the apartment?"

"No. How about we just meet there?" I responded.

I wasn't ready to have him stop by just yet. I still had lots of questions for which I needed answers. I needed to hear him say some things before I could allow myself to crumble.

"Uh....um, ok." His tone becoming more nervous after my response.

We decided on a place we used to go over on Sixth Avenue, a coffee shop with high backed booths that promised at least a minimal level of privacy. At 7:30 I walked in to find him sitting there waiting for me, my favorite Irish Creme Latte already steaming on the table, a gesture which made me smile in spite of myself. He stood as he saw me enter.

There I was, face to face with my greatest weakness, and the source of my greatest pain. In the aftermath of my traumatic childhood I had learned to take care of myself. My obsession with self-preservation and control had served me well through many turbulent seasons of life, a well employed defense mechanism. However, as is often the case, one's greatest strength can also double as a burr of weakness. That very defense, if not relaxed, could serve to leave me alone in this world with nothing to keep me company but my indignation and second guessed regrets.

After a brief hug I removed my scarf and coat, sliding into the booth across from Parks.

"You look good, Holden." He responded, unsure of what to say.

"Thanks, you do too."

"How are you doing?" He said, his blue eyes penetrating me to my soul as usual.

I simply shrugged.

"I've been worried about you." He continued.

"Well, you weren't very worried about me three weeks ago." My words piercing him like a dagger, my chief weapon of retaliation in times of personal pain. Immediately, I felt remorse. Here we were trying to talk through things and I was not getting us off to a good start.

"I'm sorry, Parks, I shouldn't..."

"No, I deserve it." He interjected.

"Will you just tell me why?"

With this my defenses weakened enough for my eyes to blur temporarily with tears, a response I fought with all the tenacity I could muster.

"I don't know what to say." He replied.

"Am I not enough for you? Am I not good enough to you? Do I not satisfy you anymore?" I couldn't believe I was asking these things, I felt so pathetic but needed answers.

"No, it's not like that, Holden. I couldn't ask for anything better than being with you."

"Then why?"

"It was just stupid...and it will never happen again...never, I promise you!"

"Was this the only time?" I interjected, a hybrid of heartsick lover and cross examiner.

"Yes, I promise you it was!"

177

I sat in silence, allowing him to take the lead.

"Holden, I never told you this because I didn't want you to get jealous or angry, but Conly and I were together for a while when I was at Chapel Hill. We were both closeted then and he was the first person I had ever been with."

"Oh my gosh, I don't want to hear this." I interrupted.

The last thing in the world that I wanted to hear that night was a recap of their sexual history. Hearing how much Parks loved me, needed me, couldn't live without me...I could handle that. In fact, I wanted and needed to hear those things. But hearing about Conly Rutherford and their college escapades...no, thank you.

"No, you need to hear this. There are a lot of things that you need to hear, things that I need to be able to say to you, because ever since we've been together I have been plagued with this gnawing feeling that I'm not good enough for you."

"What?" I said in a tone that showed just how ridiculous I thought such an idea to be.

"Holden, I have never met anyone like you. You are so pure, so good, so kind. I've never been with anyone like you. And I'm not like you. I've not been so perfect. I've been around, and it makes me feel guilty when I think that I have all this history and you have only ever been mine."

I just sat in silence listening as Parks poured out his heart. It didn't matter if his thoughts and feelings made sense to me, it didn't matter if I felt they were unwarranted, they were his reality and I understood in that moment that I needed to listen and try to understand.

"Holden, while you were preaching and helping people find their way in life I was snorting lines and blowing through hook-ups at Carolina. Then, I move back to the island and one April night Robert Guthrie says he wants to introduce me to his new preacher. I'm waiting to see some sixty year old, obese, gray-haired stick in the mud. To my surprise, he introduces me to the most gorgeous

178

guy I have ever met. Here I am, on my first week back on the island, lusting hard core after a preacher."

I couldn't help but chuckle slightly as a flattered grin spread across my face.

"It's not funny." Parks protested. I was beginning to see how heavily these thoughts were weighing on him.

"Parks, I noticed you too. Don't think that..."

"Holden, it's not the same." He interrupted. "You were a minister, doing great things and then came that day at Portsmouth. I couldn't control it any longer, and from that moment to this your life has spun out of control. You didn't want to leave Ocracoke, you had to. You loved Emilis and Robert and I know you didn't want to leave them, you had to because of me, because of something I started."

"Parks."

"I don't deserve you and I think I'm scared that one day you're going to wake up and realize that, too."

I just gave his words some time to sink in before responding. He was being vulnerable with me, not in a sexual way, not in a physical way, but in a deeper bearing-of-the-soul kind of way. For all the fun we had, for all the ways he had cared for me, that night was different. That night Parks was giving me deeper parts of himself than I may have ever known before, those ugly parts that we all would rather keep hidden. After a few moments of considering how unguarded he was being with me, I decided I needed to show my cards as well. The time was past for playing it close to the vest.

"Parks, from the first night I met you at that wedding reception there were deep feelings stirring inside of me, too. Yes, you leaned over to kiss me that afternoon at Portsmouth, but you never forced me to do anything. I had already fallen in love with you...I am still in love with you."

He looked down at his mug.

"Parks, you don't realize how incredible you are. I have

never met anyone as gentle, and good, and giving as you are."

"Me?" He interjected, looking up in unbelieving surprise.

"Yes you! Your heart is so much purer than mine. You are so compassionate, so unjudging, so willing to see the best in people. That is so refreshing to me. You don't know the times that you have challenged me to be a better man."

He smiled a subtle grin as I continued pouring my heart out.

"I'm scared too, Parks."

"What about?"

"I'm scared that I'm not enough."

"What do you mean? That's so not true."

"Parks, you've been with all these other guys before you met me, and I've never been with anyone else. It makes me really self-conscious because I'm scared that I'm not as good of a lover as they were, I'm scared to death that you're comparing me with them, that I'm not measuring up."

"Holden, I'm sorry. I promise you it's not like that..."

"And then I come home and find you with Conly and all of those fears come to the forefront. I knew you knew him from Chapel Hill and so I immediately thought that he was the one that got away, the one that you couldn't shake. Now, here I am losing you."

"Holden, you're not losing me....not unless you want me gone."

"I don't want you gone, Parks. But I can't live like this, not being sure that I'm everything to you like you are to me. It's not fair...it's not fair to me and I can't live like that. I won't live like that! I might be inexperienced, and insecure, and anything else you may want to call me, but I'm not going to be anybody's fool!"

"Holden, if you only knew how you blow every other guy I've ever been with completely out of the water. You are enough, you're more than enough. None of them could

180

ever touch you in my mind, Holden. You've made me see
what I've been missing. I think I'm the luckiest guy alive!
I like it that I'm the only one you've ever been with."
Then he continued: "Holden, I don't want to be with
anyone else, I promise you."

"Then, how do you explain the other day?" I said. I
wasn't crying now, I just wanted to know. I needed to
know what went wrong.

Parks began to explain to me how for weeks Conly had
been coming on to him at school, making innuendoes,
talking about old times, and even suggesting that I would
never have to know, just one time for old time's sake.
Evidently Conly wore him down. Add to this the fact that
Parks felt abandoned by me at times and kept in the dark
about what was really going on in my world, and we had
a recipe for disaster.

I had to admit that I had always been one to hold
things in. There was a time, when our relationship was
brand new, that Parks enjoyed the challenge of getting
me to open up and share my heart, to be vulnerable.
But after years of having to do that with me, it became
an arduous and annoying task for him. It made him
feel like I didn't trust him, like I was holding things back
which I didn't want him to know. He described how he
felt insecure when I would pull away and refuse to talk
about things. It made him feel like I was having second
thoughts about us. And then there was the Spiritual
component.

After Parks and I publicly began our relationship,
after the fallout, I had never been willing to discuss my
spiritual questions or dilemmas with him. I assumed that,
since he didn't share my faith background, he wouldn't
understand. I felt that he wouldn't get it, that he wouldn't
be sympathetic, and so I kept him completely shut out of
that part of my life. I never even gave him a chance to
process with me the pain of leaving the ministry and my
faith. For one thing, I didn't want to make him feel guilty,

181

to make him feel responsible.

As Parks opened his heart to me about this I began to realize that Parks didn't understand because I wouldn't let him understand. What I thought was protecting him from hurt and guilt was actually driving a wedge between us. I never realized what I was doing to him emotionally until that moment. Parks and I logged many hours that month in random coffee shops throughout the city. I was seeking understanding, Parks was seeking absolution. There was no doubting his remorse, I even felt sorry for him during those weeks. I had never seen Parks so broken, so humble, and at times pitiful, begging me not to call it off. To be honest, I never wanted to call it off completely.

As is the case in most relationships, our issues had not happened in a vacuum. I had hurt him in ways that I never realized, and vice-versa. It was a month of clearing the air. I, in no way deserved to be cheated on, nor does anyone! There is no excuse for that. But I had to humble myself in the coming months as well, accepting my role in our problems, a task that my pride fought with ferocity.

In the end we agreed that we loved each other too much to walk away, that we would put the past behind us and go forward. One night about six weeks after he began crashing with Ty and Sara, I was singing at a club across town and looked up during the second set to find Parks in the crowd.

When "Say It Isn't So" rolled around in our line up, I sang it with more emotion than I ever had before. It is one thing to just be singing lyrics; it is something entirely different to sing from a place of experience. With our eyes locked, I gave that song a sense of soul that only comes from living the lyrics.

In the early hours of the morning, after I had gotten home from the concert, Parks showed up at the apartment. I opened the door to find him standing there in his baseball shirt and blue jeans, his blue eyes begging me

182

for the new beginning we had been deliberating for well over a month. I know it sounds sappy, but in the beautiful silence of that moment it was time for us to come home to each other. Our eyes did the talking and that night I wasn't alone anymore.

Granted, there were still things to work through, things for us both to work on in order to care for the other, but we gladly made concessions. What sought to destroy our relationship seemed, ultimately, to solidify our commitment and fidelity. Conly was no longer a part of our lives and I began to be more open with Parks, sharing my hopes, my dreams, my fears, and trusting him to be empathetic.

Entry 36

It was during my time of soul-searching, of trying to figure out the trajectory of my relationship with Parks following his infidelity, that I got to more deeply know a guy who would become a life-long friend to both of us. Luke Clarendon was a fellow barista at the quaint coffee shop at Pike Place. Starting a new job is always anxiety producing. Coworkers can either intensify or allay those feelings. Luke was a Godsend to me on those early days of finding my way in a strange new city.

I absolutely loved Seattle, but I couldn't escape the ever emerging reality which echoed the famous line by Judy Garland, I wasn't in Kansas anymore. Life in the shadow of the Space Needle was a far cry from the way of life I had come to know beneath the Lighthouse at Ocracoke, and certainly different from the Johnston County tobacco fields of my earliest years. Even amidst my mother's pervasive dysthymia, she had instilled qualities in her three boys that set us apart as true southern gentlemen, qualities that some people in the northwest found strange and even annoying.

I have always been a people person, but a little on the naive side regarding the ways of the world according

183

to Parks. I found it uncivilized to pass someone on the sidewalk and not offer some form of salutation, a nicety that was second nature in the South. Some of these cultural differences really got under the skin of some of my coworkers, and before long I realized that some of them didn't really care to ever get to know me. To some of them I was a southern hick come to town and they took full advantage of every mistake I made, of every cultural nuance to which I wasn't privy, in order to poke fun and discount my intelligence. However, there was one person, from the first day I went to work on Elliot Bay until I left the Emerald City, who was relentless in genuine friendship...Luke.

While others looked at me with disdain when I didn't remember where a certain item was stored, or when I had questions about certain drinks, Luke was quick to take me under his arm and teach me the ropes. Like so many of us in Seatown, Luke was a transplant. He made his way to Seattle from Chicago, though he had grown up in Fort Wayne, Indiana. He and his wife, Tiffany, had moved to the Northwest after finishing college at Moody. They had a vision of planting a series of house Churches throughout the city, with a passion for "doing life and loving people" as he put it.

Even with friendship, there are people with whom you just have natural chemistry and those you don't. I felt connected to Luke from the beginning. He had an infectious warmth about him that began quickly chipping at my thick wall of guardedness. He was a Baptist and I was convinced that if he really knew me, if he knew that I was gay, the friendship would either be over or he would launch out on a quest to convert me. I had had my fill of religious people and of people turning their backs on me; therefore, any hopes of real friendship with him were eclipsed by mounds of suspicion and mistrust regarding the genuineness of his kindness and his motives. And so, I put Luke to the test.

184

I was so full of pain, anger, and bitterness at God, at the Church, at people in general, and Luke became the recipient of so much unwarranted misgiving and distrust. He had been nothing but good to me, but he represented everything that I felt had wounded me in my past. Luke became the scape goat upon which I placed all of the transgressions of every person who had wounded me in my fall from public approval. Unfair as it may have been, he was not starting with a clean slate. He would have to disprove every suspicion I had about him before I would let him in. Believe me, I watched closely to see if he was worthy of my trust.

When I think back to all of the times I pushed him away, kept him at arms-length, and gave him verbal lashings filled with the venom of a broken and jaded heart, it amazes me that he stayed around. But stay he did. His constancy was a curious and yet refreshing conundrum.

Parks always came down to the coffee shop on the evenings I worked, after he finished grading papers and doing lesson plans for the next day, and waited for me to close. One particular night I decided to test Luke and read his reaction. Luke usually worked the mid shift and left the shop earlier in the afternoon, before Parks dropped by. However, on this particular evening he had switched shifts with someone and was closing the shop with me.

That was the first time I introduced the two of them. Parks and I were never much on public displays of affection, especially in work environments. Admittedly, we had our issues, but with the exception of the couple of months following Parks' birthday, our relationship was largely drama free, unlike what we saw being played out in the relational lives of some other gay couples with whom we had become friends. In fact, we had a much more level-headed, peaceful relationship than most of the straight couples we knew.

Understandably, Parks was cautious at first in shar-

185

ing his sexuality with coworkers. After all, the last time word got out he found himself unemployed. Even though Seattle was a very different social climate from the Outer Banks, the sting was fresh. The coffee shop was more conducive to being out, but even then people acted surprised when they found out about Parks and me. I guess we didn't fit into the stereotype of the day regarding gay men.

Parks came in that night about an hour before closing and took his normal seat at the bar. I made him his standard venti hot chocolate, asking him about his day and what he wanted to do that night after I got off of work. As Luke made his way out of the back room, where he had been doing inventory, I made my move. I had no reason to hide and I loved Parks too much to try and deny that he was my boyfriend.

"Parks, here's someone I want you to meet." I said, turning to face Luke, who was smiling as he made his way towards us, a look of eager interest on his face.

"Parks, this is Luke. Luke this is my boyfriend, Parks." With that I just watched to see his reaction.

Parks, smiling, reached over the bar and offered his right hand in a hearty hand shake. Luke never missed a beat, meeting Parks' grasp, placing his left hand on Parks shoulder.

"Good to meet you, man!" Luke said.

"You too, Luke." Parks replied, "I've heard a lot about you."

"Well, you know what they say...Believe none of what you hear, and half of what you see!"

Parks chuckled, "So true! So true!"

"So," Luke continued, "are you from the Outer Banks too?"

The two of them stood there, engaged in a fifteen minute conversation about Ocracoke, surfing, and Tar Heel basketball.

"Well, Parks, it was really good to meet you. Holden's a

186

great guy, but I guess you already know that." Luke said, patting me on the back.

"Yep, he's the best." Parks said, looking at me, smiling. I was so confused. What just happened? I was expecting shock, discomfort, disgust, maybe even hatred. Luke gave me nada, leaving me a little dumbfounded.

That night as Parks and I walked home he mentioned what a nice guy Luke seemed to be. I told Parks about Luke's wife and their call to Seattle, mainly as a means of assuring Parks that there was nothing to worry about concerning mine and Luke's friendship. Nevertheless, my mind was still trying to process Luke's response.

"You seem suspicious of him?" Parks observed.

"I really like him. I just don't know how to take him. I'm still trying to figure him out."

"Why don't you just give him the benefit of the doubt, Holden?"

As months stretched into years I found myself beginning to take that advice, but the walls came down slowly. Luke never once mentioned my sexuality, and he continued to treat Parks and me with kindness and respect. As safe of a distance as I was committed to keeping from Luke, I did have some form of internal knowing that if I ever needed someone to turn to in Seattle, aside from Parks, he would be the first person on my list.

This exchange had taken place before Parks and Conly's rendezvous. In the weeks following the infidelity, I found that Luke was indeed a safe place for me to turn. I was in such a state of shock and total devastation that eating was futile, as it would come right back up again. I couldn't sleep without replaying the details of the discovery and the mental images over in my mind.

During the weeks of separation I was trying to hold down my job at the coffee shop, when all I really wanted to do was crawl into a hole and never come out again. I was living a nightmare from which I couldn't seem to wake. As much as I wanted to elude the entire experience

187

and wake up with it all behind me, the only option was to go through it with total uncertainty of the outcome.

I was closing the shop one night in late February, about a week after Parks moved out. The weather had reached an all-time high of 70 degrees and the day felt like spring, with people milling about the streets, enjoying the unseasonable warmth. At about quarter of ten Luke showed up and asked me if I had any plans.
"You want to hang out tonight? Tiffany's having a girl's night at our apartment."

I tried to evade the interaction, just wanting to go back to the isolation of my lonely apartment. However, Luke was persistent and after cleaning up we made our way to a little piano bar downtown. It was one of the few places still open which was conducive to semi-private conversation. There was so much I needed to say, so many tears that I needed to shed and have someone validate. Luke was there to share in whatever came out; but, for some reason, I couldn't go there just yet. I had some unfinished business with trust issues and Luke called me on it.
"Holden, I've been your friend for six months now, but you refuse to let me in."
I was shocked by his candor and a little embarrassed that my guard had been so obvious.
"Holden, I'm here for you man! I can see you're dying inside but you just keep pushing me away? What's the deal?"
"Luke, you've been a great friend, but I just don't trust you yet."
"Why not?" He said, as he leaned into the conversation. And so, I began recounting my story and the saga which prompted my exodus from Carolina. I had never before told him of my pastoral experiences, nor anything about my former faith. I didn't want to give him fodder for what I felt would be an intensified quest of evangelization, a fact that I also disclosed to him.
Luke's only response was one that I didn't want to hear.

188

"Holden, God loves you, buddy!"

"I don't believe that anymore." I replied, low and sharp, betraying how jaded I had become.

There at the corner table of the small piano bar, I spewed out long withheld feelings and questions I had never articulated until that night. I hadn't said these things to the Guthries because they were in a tailspin, nor to my friends from Bible College because they had disowned me, not even with Parks because, try as he may, he didn't completely understand. On that uncharacteristically warm February evening it all came rushing out. "Luke, you have no idea the hell that I have lived through. I loved Jesus with all my heart and wanted nothing more than for Him to love me too. I wanted to be the man He wanted me to be, but there was the unescapable reality of my attraction to men. And you know as well as I do what Scripture says about me, about my lifestyle. I feel condemned for something I didn't ask for; something that I tried to fight with everything I had, something that I prayed God would take away. Do you know what it's like to know that the God who you love sees you as an abomination? Do you have any idea what it is like to have your own flesh and blood look at you and talk about the Old Testament punishment of stoning for your sin? To hear people protesting and saying that people like you deserve to die? To be so despised for something you never asked for and didn't want? To lose almost everyone you ever loved because of who you're attracted to? To realize that you will never have a family of your own, no children to crawl up in your lap and call you Daddy?"

I rattled off this list without giving him a second to respond

"Luke, I didn't wake up one morning and just decide that I wanted to be gay. I wanted to be just like you, to be a normal, heterosexual guy. But at the end of the day, the struggle was still there and I didn't know how to beat it. So you tell me, what am I supposed to do?"

189

It was no-holds-barred as I gave open expression to my grief, my anger, my fears. Somewhere amidst my verbal tirade, Luke's eyes began to well with tears. I had never seen him cry. If I had ever known a man's man, it was Luke Clarendon. Yet, here he was sitting across from me, not enraged, not defensive, but with tears now rolling down his cheeks as he listened intently to what I had to say. I sat in silence and watched his reaction, never having witnessed someone extend such empathy to my pain.

In time he quietly and humbly spoke to me in tones so gentle that I couldn't mistake them for anything but love. In that moment we were connected on a soul level, like something was working below the surface, bridging the gap that had so long existed between us and our respective "sides" of the issue.

"I don't know, Holden." He replied. "There's so much of it that I don't understand."

We sat in silence for a moment longer and then Luke slipped his fingers inside of his shirt pocket and pulled out a small piece of folded yellow paper.

"Holden," he said, "can I read you something?"

"Sure." I said, hoping desperately that he wasn't about to give me a Scripture lesson.

"I have had you on my heart for a long time now and I wrote this the other night in my journal as I was thinking of you and praying for you and Parks," he said, still holding the folded piece of paper in his right hand.

After unfolding it he began to read. I've kept that yellow piece of paper in my wallet all of these years.

"Could we be friends, could we enter into life together… processing where we've been, the similarities and the differences? Could we be truly ourselves without fear of rejection, could we accept the convictions of the other? Could we be friends? Could we be a gift in each other's lives? Could we hold each other when life seems too much to cope with? Could we learn from each other and both be the better for it? Could we accept each other's

190

differences? Could you accept me when I disagree, and could I return the favor? Could we learn? Could you teach me...and could I be willing to learn from your experience? Could you be willing to learn from mine? Could we have a true friendship? Could we navigate these waters compassionately and maturely? Could we hold on and work through any awkwardness that may arise? Could we not walk away when it would seem easier to do so, teaching and learning a deeper lesson about real love? Could we let down our walls in a healthy way? Could we allow each other to challenge the other's preconceptions? Could we become true brothers and experience real connection in a lonely world that longs for such authenticity, a world often cruel? Could we?"

In the silence that followed his reading, he slipped the paper across the table towards me. I couldn't speak. I don't think any straight person, aside from the Guthries and Jane Anne, had ever made such a pure and vulnerable plea to be a part of my life, especially since my news became public. Words were few for the rest of the evening, as I chewed on the words that had just been read to me. The silences were full of a warmth that promised a new beginning in our friendship, a beginning void of walls and defense-mechanisms.

Luke would come to walk with me through that season of uncertainty with Parks. Our brutal honesty with one another was uncomfortable at times, but mainly refreshing. I never once went to his Church and he never pressed me to. Our friendship was free of pressure but full of genuine concern.

As uncomfortable as it may have been for him, he listened as I talked about my love for Parks. In time we discussed Theology and the host of questions with which I had wrestled for years. Luke came out to hear me sing at some of the clubs. And after Parks and I made amends, Luke and Tiffany even came out to some of Parks' soccer games.

191

I often avoided relationships with people who didn't agree with my lifestyle, but this one was different. I don't know if I can adequately describe it. Luke and I knew where the other stood on certain issues; and, though we had much in common, there were also some seemingly irreconcilable differences. Nevertheless, we were committed to this friendship, knowing that at the end of the day, all differences aside, we had each other's back. Reflecting on it now, I wonder if part of my connection to Luke was that he came to fill an important role, one abandoned by my older brother. Whatever the catalyst, Luke proved his loyalty and care over and over again. I would learn from him an important lesson: when it comes to friendships, loyalty is a much stronger foundation than agreement.

Entry 37

Parks and I had emerged from the nightmare of February '85 stronger than we were prior. I would never choose to relive the infidelity for any amount of money. The core-ripping pain of the now distant memory of Parks and Conly is still an unwelcome occasional intruder. Nevertheless, the crucible of that test left us more committed, more communicative, and closer than we had been prior.

Life was good in the Emerald City. Parks loved his teaching career and I had been promoted to manager at the shop. My work there, which I poured myself into following the exodus from Ocracoke, had been a crucial link to a sense of normalcy and productivity. In our spare time Parks accompanied me to the bar scene with the band and I cheered for him field-side during weekend soccer games.

Parks had joined a soccer league at the invitation of a couple of his teaching buddies, a really cool group of guys who treated us so well. On any given Saturday, you could find me there in the stands amidst the team member's wives and girlfriends. Parks was the only gay guy on

the team but they didn't seem to care, he was just one of the guys to them; and whenever I would join them for a team-night out at the bar, they extended to me the same level of camaraderie and acceptance. I think in some ways, knowing the two of us challenged many of their former thoughts and stereotypes of what a gay person was.

We hung out with friends, took the occasional camping/hiking trips to Mount Rainier, and fished and crabbed in Puget Sound from a small skiff we purchased from someone Ty knew, who was moving away to take a job in the mid-west. Life seemed to have a sense of normalcy for us on the West Coast. We were just two twenty-somethings enjoying our young lives.

From the time I left Ocracoke with Parks, Robert never wavered in his love for me. He had promised solidarity that day in my hospital room, but unlike so many others, he made good on that promise. I remember well the Thursday mail drop at our Seattle apartment. Every Thursday afternoon, when I would get home from work, there would be a cream legal-sized envelope with the navy J. L. Guthrie & Son Seafood Company logo at the top left corner. Sometimes the letters were lengthy, telling me about what was going on in the water that particular week, if there had been any shrimp, fish or whatever the seasonal fare of interest. Some were more brief, just a few lines to check in. Often there was a check for twenty or thirty dollars, with the instruction, "Go out and get you something good to eat." On birthdays or holidays the amount was more. Regardless of the contents, every Thursday the letters came.

I knew that Robert did not approve of how I was living my life. Contrary to the opinion of a great number on the island, he did not support my decision to be in this type of relationship with Parks or any other man. In the beginning this made me uncomfortable around Robert and I often ignored his questions, seldom ever writing or calling. No matter my lack of response, Robert wasn't deterred. On Parks' birthday, there would be a check for him as well, with a note, "Tell Parks we love him and wish him a Happy Birthday".

I never quite understood how Robert could disagree and yet still be so good to us. I guess love sometimes surpasses understanding. And although I seldom responded, keeping Robert and everyone else from my former life at a safe distance, each letter crept a little deeper into my heart with an assurance that, though so many in my world had discarded me, there was one who hadn't done so. When all was well in my world I gave the letters little more than a cursory read, sometimes only checking to see if money were enclosed. I feel a bit guilty even admitting that. However, on the dark nights of my soul, during the weeks following Parks' infidelity and in passing tides of homesickness, I sat with those letters, drinking deeply from the love Robert extended. I could picture him sitting there every Monday morning in the tattered swivel chair at his desk overlooking Silver Lake. His first order of business for the week: writing to his boy, as he so often referred to me.

I imagined him making his way to the little white clapboard post-office at the water's edge, before heading home for lunch with Emilis. No doubt the postmistress and other islanders looked on him with disdain as he posted his weekly letter, addressed to a young man in Seattle whom so many on the island had come to hate. Yet he did it, faithfully. It wasn't until recent years that I came to understand the full scope of shunning and complications which his commitment to me elicited.

Robert had been removed from his position on the administrative board of the Church. Approximately half a dozen of the men who had sold to him all their lives, and to his father before him, took their catch elsewhere. The crowd at Albert Styron's store no longer welcomed their golden boy on Saturday evenings.

194

After a couple of weeks of braving the social cold, the disapproving looks, and hurtful statements about me, Robert decided he would cease trying where they were concerned. From that point he spent the entirety of his Saturday evenings with Emilis, reading, talking, and watching Lawrence Welk on PBS. He loved me more than his own pride, more than additional wealth, and more than public approval.

For me, thousands of miles away from the sleepy little island I once loved so much, those years were filled with friends, laughter, love, and a deep sense that life was finally on an upswing for us. Sure, sometimes the money ran out before the month, and we certainly had our periodic disappointments, but overall life was good. The older I have gotten, I have come to see life as a series of ebbs and floods. Sadly, those two unsuspecting young men were on the verge of a change in the tide.

Entry 38

Lying here, looking back on the Fall of '87, I see more clearly a gentle progression which I missed in process. Amidst the host of ordinary days and the often thoughtless flipping of life's weekly calendar, autumn brought a turning point.

One crisp Saturday morning in mid-October, we went to Parks' soccer game as usual. Sitting in the bleachers that day I began to realize that Parks wasn't well. He had battled sinus infections with each season change all his life. In our time together, it was something I had grown accustomed to. He would feel awful for about a week until his system seemed to get adjusted and then he would bounce back. But, this morning was different.

Parks had been a goalie since his high school days, and a stellar one. So often I sat there grinning as I watched him block every attempt to penetrate his guard. Whatever his father's wounding jeers and abuses, Parks was a born soccer player. Intercepting the opponents' attempts

195

to score was as natural to Parks as sitting down to a piano was for me. Soccer was his music and he was incredible at it, but not on this day.

For the better part of a month, Parks had been battling a cold. But on that morning Parks was almost feeble, like he couldn't find the rhythm. It was as if there was a disconnect between his mind and his members. With every failed block and every fumbled attempt I saw his frustration mounting, accompanied by a pervasive sense of windedness.

He came off of the field before the first half was even out; and, with a quick jerk of his head signaling for me to come to him, I left the bleachers and joined him at the sideline. By the time I reached him he had leaned over, placing his hands on his knees. I came up to him and squatted down so that I could look him in the face.
"You've got to take me home." He said, completely winded, a look of worry in his eyes.
"What's wrong?"
"I don't know, but something's not right with me." he replied.
A couple of the guys came over to join us to see what was going on.
"I just don't feel well," he replied, presenting them with a more subdued sense of concern than he had indicated in our private discourse.
"Do you need to go the hospital?" they pressed.
"No, I think I just need to go home and lay down." he responded.
I looked on in silent concern, trying to ascertain what was taking place with him.

We went home and I helped him get undressed and into the hot bath I had drawn for him. I went to the kitchen and put on some soup while he rested in the hot water. After he got dried off and slipped into his pajamas, we spent the evening resting, slurping on chicken broth, and watching movies while curled up under blankets on

196

the couch. By nightfall he seemed a little better. We decided that we would call the doctor first thing on Monday
morning for a checkup. He would probably prescribe
some antibiotics to kick this upper respiratory infection,
the usual routine.

We slept in the next morning. I had taken the entire
day off weeks earlier so we could have the day together
before attending a Halloween party that evening. About
ten that morning I got up and made some french toast;
trayed it up and brought it back to bed. I could tell he felt
better that morning. He roused from sleep in a playful
mood that I hadn't seen in him the week prior.
"You still want to go tonight?" He asked with an energy
that let me know he wanted to.
"Well, I was going to wait and see how you were feeling
this evening."
"I think it will be okay, I feel a lot better this morning."
He said. "Maybe it was a 24 hour bug or something."
"Well, we'll see how the day goes." I replied.

We had found our costumes weeks before. Parks was
going as Blackbeard and I found an authentic looking
Ghostbuster costume, complete with back pack and gear.
At about six o'clock Parks said that he wanted to go, that
he thought it would do us good to get out and have a
good time, and so we started getting ready. Parks went
into the bathroom to begin the process of gluing on his
beard, while I washed up our lunch dishes.

As I finished, let out the water, and dried my hands on
the dish towel, Parks came back into the kitchen. I looked
over at him, eager to see his freshly glued on facial hair. I
just knew he had come in to show me; but as I looked up
at him, the only thing on Parks' face was a look of sheer
fright and panic. My eyes locked with his and we stood in
silence, my mind trying to figure what was wrong.
"What's the matter?" I said, worried by the look I saw in
his eyes.
He never took his eyes from mine, but simply lifted his

197

left arm over his head and turned his torso slightly to the right, placing the upper portion of his left rib cage directly in my line of view. With his right hand he reached over and there, just inches below his armpit, where side merges into back, was a harbinger that left me silent and nauseous.

A reddish-purple lesion, about an inch in length, interrupted our evening and our entire lives. As I stood there in silence, now casting my gaze down towards the kitchen floor, Parks spanned the twenty four inches between us and crumbled into my arms. As he buried his head on my shoulder and wept like a baby, I just stood there feeling completely detached. It was as if I was outside of my body, yet completely aware of everything that was happening. Here I stood, holding the person I loved most in this world, the one who had so often held me. He was the strong one, he was the one always stepping in to shield me from the full weight of cruel realities, and yet here he was, reduced to a sobbing child in my arms, making the types of moans and whimpers known only by those who have drunken deeply of life's most unwelcome tragedies. There's no telling how long we stood there frozen in our tiny kitchen, holding onto each other as our world began revolutions uncomfortably out of control.

As gay men coming of age in the eighties, we were not ignorant of the news washing over the United States and the world concerning a new epidemic that seemed to target homosexual men and Haitians. We had read the news columns, heard the public discourse on news channels, and even knew of some friends of friends who had died of the disease. But, somehow, call it youthful naïveté or tenacious hope; we had the idea that we would be unscathed.

The emotions and mental onslaught that evening were so overwhelming that, to this day, it is difficult for me to speak or write about. The heaviness and crushing pain returns so quickly when I recall that afternoon. Suffice it to say that this discovery forever changed our lives, plunging us from the height of boyish exuberance to the somberness of a death sentence in less than an hour. Granted, we had no formal diagnosis, no CD-4 count to confirm our fear, but we knew the score in a way that only those who have lived the experience could adequately describe.

That night we went through the yellow pages and found the number for Harborview Medical, hoping we could find the answers and help we needed. Of the few friends of friends we had known to die of the disease, they sought help here, and so it was the only place we knew to turn. We tried lying down that night, but neither of us could sleep. We passed the time rolling from side to side, staring at the ceiling, and watching the clock. There were many moments in which we simply held each other, an attempt to give and receive whatever sense of comfort we could muster. For the first time since leaving Oc-racoke, I actually prayed; though at the time I wasn't sure if God would even listen to my pleas. I was engulfed in a drowning sense of disaster as Parks wrestled with his own hurricane of emotions.

The morning came on slowly. At eight o'clock we made the call and took the drive across town, the car latent with silence. We were scared and alone, feeling as if we couldn't tell anyone because we feared the backlash, the ostracization, the threat of losing our employment, our housing...you name it...it was barreling through our minds.

The tests proved our worst fears to be our next chap-ter. Parks' CD-4 count was at around 150. The lack of stamina, shortness of breath, and ill feelings he had been battling were all part of a four letter word that pulled the rug out from under two robust young men, two young men that I can still picture in my mind. Parks had AIDS. What we had thought to be just a really bad allergy sea-son was the breaking down of his immune system and the

199

presence of pneumocystis. They wanted to test me that
day as well, but I refused. I was completely healthy and
felt completely normal, other than the pervasive sense of
nausea and anxiety brought on by the sight of the lesion.
Parks was the one who was sick, not me. After all, if I
were sick too how in the world would we make it? How
would we take care of each other? So in a strong-willed
refusal to accept any direction from medical authority,
and even Parks, I decided that when I was ready I would
get tested...and not a moment sooner.

The next five weeks were a roller coaster of emotions.
I had the uncomfortable task of supporting Parks through
the process of recalling all of his sexual partners, trying to
contact as many as he could to give them the news. Parks
had been the one and only person in my life that I had
ever been with, but he had been active in the years before
we met. In the end there were nine that he was faced
with the overwhelming responsibility of contacting, knowing all too well the type of tailspin his call was about to
throw them into. Some were married now with children,
some were in long-term relationships with other men, and
then, come to find out, there were two who were already
dead. There was no way of knowing who had given it to
whom, or when. There was also the inconvenient reality that, regardless of where the infection had occurred, I
was the last person in the chronology.

Before the shock wore off, Christmas had arrived. I
had no idea how to even begin celebrating Christmas
with this news looming over our heads, and yet there was
the somber thought that this may be Parks' last. With
that in mind, I tried my best to make it special.

Christmas 1987 was spent quietly in our little apartment near Pike Place, soaking up every moment of quality time we could muster, watching Rudolf the Red-Nosed
Reindeer and listening to Burl Ives singing 'Silver and
Gold' through a claymation snowman. It was a sentimental journey back to boyhood, to a place of nostalgic

200

innocence, a reprieve from the vicissitudes of life. Our Christmas gift to each other that year was a letter from the heart. I guard that letter with my life and have left clear instructions that it is to be buried with me, unread by anyone other than myself. There are elements of life that are meant to be private and special, and I intend to keep that Christmas Eve letter unadulterated from public view.

Entry 39

As the New Year passed, Parks' health continued to deteriorate. Everything was happening so quickly. Ultimately, Parks was admitted to Harborview, though there was little the medical professionals could do at that time other than palliative care. The days of visiting the clinic, learning how to care for him at home, and managing I.V. treatments and night sweats came to a close as his fever reached all-time highs and his health took a nose dive mid-January of '88.

I took off from work the entire first week after he was hospitalized, refusing to leave his side, but the reality of paying bills and the uncertainty of how long we were going to be in this position were weighing on me, adding much unneeded stress to the anxiety that was already threatening to overtake me.

About the fourth day into his first week in the hospital I went home to gather a few items. Walking into that apartment alone, quiet, I had my first real breakdown. I had refused to let myself fall apart to that point, knowing that Parks needed my strength. However, in the privacy of our tiny apartment, staring at pictures of me and my best friend, confidant, and love of my life, I couldn't hold back the heartache any longer. I was bent double with grief, sadness, fear, and anger, a young man scared to death with no one to turn to, no one to listen, no one to help. In the days following, I called Luke and Tiffany, and Ty and Sara, but on that evening I felt completely alone.

   After I collected myself enough to speak intelligibly,
I picked up the phone and dialed eleven digits that had
largely been neglected over the past several years, knowing the rotary phone on the kitchen wall of the little white
clapboard cottage would be ringing well after bedtime,
but I needed help and I didn't know where else to turn.
"Hello." Robert's voice echoed, still half-asleep.
"Robert." This was all I could manage to get out before
having to stop, trying unsuccessfully to keep myself intact.
"Holden? What's wrong?" He said, sounding instantly
alert.
"Robert, it's bad." I said through tears, then began the
process of disclosing the chain of events which led to this
late night call from the west coast.
When I finished filling him in on where we were there
was a period of silence on the other line, as Robert tried
to process news that would have far reaching effects.
"Do you want us to come? We can be on a plane tomorrow." He said with a calm assurance in his voice. Robert
loved us both and this news was an unwanted pill for him
to swallow.

   I was Robert's boy...I knew that. But Robert also
watched Parks grow up on the island. Parks told me
many times that the first money he ever made from commercial fishing came from Robert's pocket. One day,
at the age of nine, Parks had waded out on the shoals
around the island and picked up scallops. After opening
them, he brought his catch to Robert's office, so proud
of his quart-sized Ziploc bag full of bay scallops. Robert
reached into his pocket and gave Parks fifty dollars for
them, assuring Parks that he and Emilis would eat them
for supper that night. Robert knew the young boy finding
respite on Ocracoke needed to be helped and nurtured,
and this was one way that Robert could respond to that
need.

   I wouldn't find this out until years later, but Robert had helped pay Parks' tuition his last two years at Carolina, a secret between Robert, Emilis, and Parks' grandmother. And, after graduation, it was Robert who had gotten Parks a job teaching back at home. Love me as they may, their hearts also had a special place for the blonde headed, blue eyed little boy they had watched grow into a man on the docks of Silver Lake.

I knew that all I had to do was say the word and they would be right there by our sides. As much as I wanted to see them, I couldn't handle the visit at the time. I couldn't take on anything else, not even a visit from the Guthries...especially a visit from the Guthries. I needed to be strong, and I knew that as soon as I saw them walk through the terminal of that airport I would melt into a pile.

"Not yet, Robert." I replied, "But I promise you, I will call when I need you."

"Promise me you will!"

"Yes, I promise."

"It's Holden." I heard Robert say softly on the other end, a disclosure that Emilis had by this time made her way from the bedroom with sleep blurred eyes, curious as to what this untimely call was about.

"Is everything alright?" I heard her say in the background.

"I'll tell you after we hang up." Robert replied, then returning his attention to me he said, "What do you need right now?"

My pride, along with a sense of shame stemming from how lax I had been in my correspondence with him, left me nervous to even ask, but I had no other options.

"Robert, I am scared to be away from the hospital for any length of time, I just came home tonight for a second to grab some clean clothes. But with neither of us working right now, I'm scared that..."

Before I could finish my hat-in-hand request, Robert interjected.

203

"Have you got your banking information handy?"

"It's in the bedroom in one of my drawers." I replied.

"Go get it. Emilis, hand me that envelope over there and get me a pen real quick."

I got my paperwork and he walked me through giving him all the necessary information about my bank, my routing number, my account number.

"There'll be money in there first thing in the morning."

"Thank you." I said softly, overwhelmed and grateful.

"What hospital is he in?" he asked.

"Harborview, but please don't tell anybody on the island, please." I begged, "It would destroy him if he found out people back home were talking."

"We won't say a word."

"Thank you, Robert."

"Now you get on back to the hospital and don't worry about anything else, ok?" He said.

"Yes, Sir." I replied.

"And, Holden." He interjected.

"Yes?"

"We love you...both of you."

"Thank you." I replied.

The next day I called the bank from Parks' room to check our balance. When the teller responded, I was overcome. Robert wired three thousand dollars into our account that morning, enough to see us through the current month and probably the next. I could focus my attention on being with Parks, free from the fear of eviction and discontinued utilities. The following Thursday there were two letters in the mail, one for each of us, each one concluding with the same words from the Apostle Peter: "Casting all your anxiety upon Him, for it matters to Him concerning you."

Entry 40

It was during shift change one day at the hospital when Parks and I first met Annie Mae, who was to be our

204

nurse for the next several days. She was a middle aged
African American woman who stood about five feet tall,
of a larger build and incredible charisma, a welcomed
reprieve from the heaviness which settled upon us that
late October evening in our kitchen amidst cold linoleum
and drying dishes. She had a soul that seemed to wrap us
up and carry us through some of the most crucial weeks
of our lives.

"Hey babies, how y'all doin' today?" she said as she
entered the room.
I'm not sure if she ever called either of us by our real
names. It was always babies, or baby if she were speaking
with us individually.

Annie's accent let me know right off that she was not
native to the Pacific Northwest. Come to find out, she was
from Perry, Georgia, a small town just south of Macon.
She had lived through the Civil Rights Movement and
the end of segregation, going on to be the first person in
her family to graduate from college. Annie had worked
her way through nursing school with the same tenacity
and strength of conviction that led Rosa Parks to defy
second class treatment.

There seems to be a depth of caring which settles into
the wake of great suffering, an endowment of compassion seldom observed in those who have never plunged
the depths of heartache and ill treatment; and Annie Mae
became its chief ambassador to us in those trying days. I
don't know why it's this way, but as I've gone through life
I have found that there are people to whom you are immediately drawn, and those whom you would just as soon
not have in your life. Annie Mae belonged to the ranks of
the first. There was an immediate bond between us, and
the way she cared for us will be held in my heart until my
memory or breath depart.

As soon as she found out that we were southern boys
it was like old home week. We reminisced of the nuances
of southern culture, laughing at ourselves as we recalled

205

our many colloquialisms, even teaching her some new
ones from the unwritten coastal dictionary of the Outer
Banks. Then there were our conversations about food, of
boiled peanuts and Pepsi Colas, collard greens and fried
fat meat, fresh whipped cream and old-timey jelly cake.
Those conversations seemed a transfusion of normalcy,
lifting us above the often eclipsing news of CD-4 counts
and sarcoma complications.

One night, as Annie Mae was in the room hooking up
another bag of fluid onto the I.V. poll, Parks made the
statement that he missed his grandmama's fried chicken
and collard greens with little cornbread dumplings. The
next morning Annie Mae appeared at the door with a
platter of fried chicken and a serving bowl piled high with
collard greens, and little cornmeal dumplings about the
size of half dollars.

She was a God-send to us in more ways than I can
recount. Nursing for some people is a job, for others
it's a calling, and only those who have been in hospitals
for extended periods of time may understand the vast
difference between the two. The way she took care of
us showed that we were not just another name on her
caseload, not just another bag to hang, or another bed
pan to dump. No, to Annie Mae we were two young men
that she truly seemed to care for; we were human beings
to her.

When the institution, doctors with poor bedside manner, or the world with its cold toned venom, declaring that
faggots deserved to die, left us scared and injured, Annie
became the healing balm, taking us up in her arms and
allowing us to cry out our heartache. And then there was
Annie Mae's faith. It wasn't unusual for me to wake in
the mornings to the sound of her singing hymns as she
gave medications, or checked Parks' vitals; and she never
hesitated to tell us she was praying for us.

There had been others in my life, since everything had
happened on Ocracoke, who told me that they were pray-

ing for me; but, whether it was my own sense of jadedness or a sincere discernment of their motivation, it always seemed to ring with a sharp sound of misgiving guised in a thin veneer of compassion. I never had that feeling with Annie Mae. Whether or not she agreed with my life-style was nothing we ever discussed, but the genuine love and concern which she showed Parks and I gave me no doubt that her prayers were from a place of unconditional love. Faith like that has an effect on those around it.

It was during these last days at Harborview, with Annie Mae and me in the room, that Parks began asking more existential questions than he had ever voiced before. With the realization of his demise settling in, the threat of which grew more stark with every round of the medical team, Parks began to ask questions about life after death, about God, about Heaven, and about his own soul. I had long grown cold to this type of discussion, leaving that part of my life on the shores of Ocracoke when the ferry pulled from its moorings the day we began our journey west.

Parks began to ask me questions which made me very uncomfortable and I was glad to have Annie Mae around to help him in this transition. She had a grasp on Scripture and the love of God that I had never gotten in all my years of study and ministry. Annie Mae understood the heart of the Gospel, and it was good news of love and hope.

One evening as we were sitting in the room, Annie came in to check on us before leaving for the night. We sat around and talked for a while. She told us about what she was going to fix for supper that night, so we knew automatically that we would be having it for lunch the next day. That was just her way!

Mid conversation, Parks spoke up and asked if we would pray with him.

"I don't know how to make sense of all of this, or even to know if God will love someone like me, but I just want to

207

pray and ask Him to." Parks. said.

I was speechless. There was a time in my life when I would have had all of the answers, when I would have known just what to say, or how to lead him in prayer, but at this moment I was dumb-struck. We had never gone to Church after leaving Ocracoke, not even on Christmas and Easter. I wasn't comfortable talking about all of this again. Where was this coming from?

"Well, Baby," Annie Mae replied, "then, we'll pray!"

A smile stretched across Parks' face. We knelt, Annie on one side of the bed and I on the other, holding Parks' hands.

"Now I will pray for a few seconds and then you pray, Parks." She instructed.

"But, I don't know how to pray." He replied with a tinge of concern.

"Baby, you just say whatever is on your heart and I promise you, it will be music to God's ears."

I can't recall everything that Annie Mae prayed in those next few moments, but I will never shake from memory the words which came from Parks' lips after she finished, words poignant, precious, simple, and sincere.

"Jesus, I just give you me."

When we finished there were tears in all of our eyes. I held onto Parks' hand in silent support as Annie embraced him. I was torn inside. The faith that I had abandoned years ago was beginning to get uncomfortably close.

In the days following that prayer, I watched a Spiritual transformation unfold before my eyes unlike anything I had ever seen. In the years I had served in ministry I had become well versed in leading someone in prayer, in making sure they said the right words in order to make myself satisfied that they actually prayed properly to be forgiven, and in the hypervigilance of looking out for them following their conversion experience, trying to make sure that they did all the right things, wore the right clothes, and

208

attended services like I thought they should. But what I saw in Parks was so different, so genuine, private, and beautiful.

In the days following, Annie Mae bought Parks a Bible with his name embossed on the cover. Had anyone tried to give him or me a Bible before that night, I would have probably had an altercation with them. There was something different about Annie Mae, such gestures from her hands were respected, appreciated, and even encouraging. Looking back on it now, it's amazing how far I had swung in the opposite direction from the faith of my youth, how cynical, bitter, and jaded I had become with regards to faith.

Parks would sit and read that Bible for hours on end. He spent most of his time in the Gospels, fascinated by the words in red. He was like a child, experiencing the wonder of a loving Savior for the first time. Even his prayer life was oozing with a sense of peace and grace. It was a journey that I admired, but one that left me uncomfortably close to tears.

At night he would get me to help him out of the bed and to the chair beside his window. Parks loved studying the night sky. He had been that way since youth, prompting his grandfather to buy him a telescope for Christmas one year. Whether it was lying on the dunes at Ocracoke, on our skiff in Puget Sound, or sitting on the fire escape of our little apartment, Parks loved to steal away time to sit in silence beneath the stars. Something about the expansive serenity left him in reverential awe. He always said he did his best thinking in those moments.

After being admitted to Harborview, I went through the nightly ritual of getting him to his station by the window. After getting him settled I would turn out all of the lights in the room so he could see the stars. There we would sit together in the quiet darkness. I often sat on the edge of his bed, looking at his profile against the plate glass and city lights while he gazed up at the heavens.

209

On one of those nights Parks broke the silence, looking over to me he said: "Holden, I look up at the moon and stars at night and I pray, 'Lord, make it right, for everybody.'"

With the exception of words from Jesus' own lips, I don't think I've ever heard anything more beautiful before or since. That prayer did something to me. Even with all of my hurts and questions, this was one prayer that I could pray no matter how far I felt from God. And pray it I have, many, many times from that day until this. Those were special yet difficult times, caring for Parks and slowly watching him fade from my grasp. I was becoming painfully aware that Parks was preparing to die. Kick, scream, fight, and cry as I may, I was being dragged along towards a dreaded truth...soon I would be saying goodbye.

Entry 41

Over the course of the next two weeks, Ty and Sara came by almost nightly to check on us. Ty was taking it especially hard, which was difficult to watch since he was always the rugged non-emotional one. Every night as he hugged me before leaving, I saw tears in his eyes. The four of us had become very close in the three years since we had first met in their shop. We had shared countless meals, coffee dates, fishing trips in the sound, and camping excursions on Mount Rainier. In those earlier days we had been so fun-loving and free of care, but this disease had aged us all.

It wasn't just the disease that had slapped naive grins from our young faces, although that would have been enough, it was also the stigma. Before someone you love is gay it just seems like something out there, some detached subject that elicits laughter and even hatred. However, when it's your friend, your family member, your loved one...it's different. No longer do the gay jokes and AIDS related bigotry just roll off of your shoulders, suddenly it's personal, it's your loved one they are talking

210

about.

As long as we rob people of their humanity, replacing compassion and care with hatred and fear, we can justify all kinds of attitudes and actions. Just look at Nazi Germany. However, when we see the humanity of an issue, when it comes home to us, then somehow everything changes. This was the place Ty and Sara found themselves. Not only were their hearts broken as they came for nightly visits, but also when they overheard conversations about "the gay disease" or saw people on street corners shouting that "these queers are getting their due." What once had been white noise was now grievous.

Luke came by every day as well. He usually stayed for a couple of hours, bringing me lunch and smuggling in one of Parks' favorite lattes from the coffee shop. Sometimes Tiffany would join him, but having a one year old and another on the way kept her pretty tied up at home. Something that amazed me about Luke is that he never gowned up or put on gloves when he came in to see us. He was way ahead of the curve in his understanding of the disease's transmission. The way he would hug and touch us, skin to skin, extended a feeling of worth and dignity to us modern-day lepers. If Parks was thirsty, Luke didn't hesitate to help him sit up in bed and place the straw to his mouth. If sweats were getting the better of Parks, Luke was happy to relieve me for a few moments, taking the wash rag from my hand and continuing to wipe Parks' face and chest with the cool, damp cloth. As I sat in the chair by the window, eating whatever lunch he had brought me, Luke would take a seat on the edge of Parks' bed, caring for the two of us in any way needed.

Within two weeks after being admitted to Harborview, Parks slipped from consciousness. The beeping of his heart monitor and his belabored breathing replaced the familiar sound of his gentle voice. I knew the time was short and refused to leave the room for fear of him waking without me there, or worse, leaving without me to

211

see him off. Annie Mae kept especially close that week, her medical training made her even more aware of the proximity of his impending departure. Even on her days off she was up in the room visiting. She took my laundry home with her so that I would have fresh clothes to wear, cooked and brought me food, and held me in her arms as I cried my heart out.

For so many years I had wrestled through stages of dealing with my sexuality and the resulting ostracization; but, there was one stage in the grief process which I had not allowed to have its full reign...anger. With Parks now in a coma and my world crumbling to shards at my feet, completely unsympathetic to my cries for cessation, I found myself in a stage long fought and long feared. I was mad as hell.

I was angry at every injustice I had suffered, angry at the fact that I was losing the love of my life and best friend, angry that our plans were cut short, angry at a disease that left the Parks I had met that long ago Spring evening on Ocracoke racked with pain, covered with lesions, leaving me more and more with each passing day. I was angry at the world, even though I couldn't articulate all of the reasons why, and I was angry at God in more ways than I even cared to contemplate.

One evening Annie Mae became the receptacle for all of my pent-up emotion. She came in to check on us, but I had settled into silence as thoughts and emotions threatened to overtake me. Parks would have sought to draw me out of my private war, if only he could have opened his eyes or spoken.

"What's the matter, Baby?" She said, as she came and sat beside me on the small love seat at the foot of Parks' bed.

"I'm just so angry."

"Angry at what?" She questioned.

I knew she wasn't asking in a way which insinuated I had nothing to be angry about. Rather, it was a sincere way of providing me the space to spew out all of my

complaints, no matter how ugly or disrespectful polite
company may find them. With her open invitation, I began a tirade that went on for the better part of an hour as
I dispelled all of the welled up animosity, the fermented
by-product of years of stuffed anguish. My monologue
was punctuated by moments of pacing, at times my hands
waving angrily about like a lunatic. In the end I crumbled, resting my head upon Annie Mae's shoulder while
she held me like a wounded child.

I knew that some of the things I said may have been
hard for her to hear, especially when I expressed my
anger with God, the plethora of whys I held with regards
to Him. Once I composed myself, I sought to make some
form of feeble apology. I, in no way wanted to offend
her. Then, in her gentle way, she shared something with
me that I had never considered before, something that
would stick with me for the rest of my life.
"Baby, even Jesus asked the Father why." she said,
"There's nothing wrong with that. What matters is that
you run to Him with your questions, instead of away from
Him with them." With that disclosure, a peace settled
in my heart, assuring me that whatever I was feeling at
this moment, it was okay, it was normal, it was all a part
of the process, the process of watching the one you love
decimated by a terminal illness.

Sunday, February 14th, 1988 was much like every other
day of the preceding week. I spent the quiet lonely hours
by Parks' bedside reading, thinking, crying, and catching
an occasional cat nap between vital checks and occlusion
alarms from his I.V. pump. Luke stopped in for a while
at lunch, bringing me a card with money that the people
in his house church had given for Parks and me. I wasn't
sure what to say. I couldn't imagine a church wanting to
give money to us, but I was moved by the gesture.

Ty and Sara came that evening and brought me dinner. While I sat in the chair by the window, opening and
arranging the Tupperware containers in preparation for

my evening meal, Annie Mae came in and rubbed down Parks' legs and arms with lotion, talking to him just like he was awake and fully present with us. The scene was too much for Ty and he had to excuse himself into the hallway.

"I think it's wonderful how she cares for him." Sara said.

"I know, she never comes in without talking to him like that." I responded.

"I guess you never can tell how much he may be aware of." Sara replied.

After it was obvious that Ty wasn't going to be able to come back in that evening, Sara gave me a kiss on the cheek, then walked over and squeezed Parks' hand before slipping quietly out into the hall.

Annie Mae stayed on with us for a while longer. She wanted to hear the story of how Parks and I met, so I went over, sat on the bed beside him, and recounted to her the epic of our life together. It was good reminiscing. I was able to tell her some funny stories of our younger years, laughing as I thought about some of our ridiculous arguments and some of the crazy stunts he would pull when we would go out surfing.

That evening after she left I flipped through the channels on television, catching an episode of Designing Women before switching it off and taking a seat on the window ledge. There I sat, staring up in to the night sky like Parks had done so often through the seasons of our life together. And as I did, the words of his prayer echoed in my mind: "Lord, make it right, for everybody."

Eventually, I made my way back to my chair, exhausted and ready for sleep. That entire week I had slept in the bedside chair, leaning forward with my head and shoulders resting on the mattress beside Parks' legs. I wanted to be close in case he roused, in case he called out for me, as minute a possibility as that was.

On that night rest came quickly, the type of deep sleep from which one wakes to find drool running from the

214

corner of his mouth. However, somewhere mid-evening, my rest was violently shaken by the shrill, steady sound of Parks' heart monitor and the medical team busting through the door of his room. Annie Mae was the first one to enter the room when the alarm went off. I sat there in shock and half-consciousness as she and the team of doctors gathered around Parks' bed. There was no traumatic shocking with electric paddles or aggressive forms of CPR. Parks had signed a DNR a couple of weeks before and so the team performed the necessary checks and recorded his passing. I sat there in a state of horrified shock, watching as they unhooked him from the I.V.'s and the heart monitor.

"I'm sorry for your loss." The attending said, gently placing his hand on my shoulder before leaving the room.

Tears had missed their cue and I sat there in the interim in a blank trance, as if awaiting someone in the wings to feed me my next line. Annie sensed my need to be alone and simply rubbed me on the back before exiting. With everyone gone, I was alone in deafening silence with the lifeless body of the one who had been the main character in all my hopes and dreams for the future. Blue eyes that once twinkled, hinting of adventure, mischief, and deep abiding love, were now concealed behind closed lids. The strong arms that once held, assured, loved, encouraged me, now lay limp at his sides, lifeless. The chest that carried the heartbeat I treasured, and the breath that would tickle my neck as we lay warmly in bed in our cold apartment, now lie still and sunken, motionless. I rose solemnly to my feet and climbed into the hospital bed with my now departed companion. As I pressed my forehead close against his ear, nestling my lips and the tip of my nose for the last time upon the side of his neck, tears remembered their cue and rushed from the wings in unbridled torrents, embracing their curtain call. It was over, it was really over. Life as I had known it was forever changed and all of my hopes and dreams for the future

215

had taken their last bow along with the one who was the second half of them all.

Entry 42

That night after they came and removed Parks' body from the room, I began gathering our few belongings. The Bible Annie Mae had given him, the Outfield tape that he loved to listen to, my books and clothing. I began placing them into the plastic bag Annie had brought in for me.

"I'm so sorry, Baby," she said as she came in and sat down on the love seat, "I'm just thankful you had that one last moment."

"Yeah, but there's never enough time." I replied.

"Did he say anything to you, Baby?"

I didn't have a clue what she was talking about.

"What are you talking about?"

I was already in a tail spin and her words were making no sense.

"Didn't he wake up before he passed?" She replied.

"What are you talking about? No he didn't wake."

I could tell that she was wrestling with something at that point.

"Come here and sit down with me for a minute." She continued.

I walked over and sat down beside her.

"Baby, about half an hour before his alarms went off, I peeked my head in the door to check on y'all. When I did, you were sitting there in the chair with your head on edge of the bed, sleeping, like you've been doing, and Parks' hand was resting on the back of your head."

I sat there, silently processing what she had just shared.

"I thought you knew."

I just shook my head to the contrary, unable to speak.

Evidently, sometime in the night he had awakened to find me sleeping at his side, and like so many times before, he had rested what had once been his strong hand upon

216

the back of my neck. He had awakened and I had missed him. The weight of that threatened to shut me in. I couldn't bear to think that he had come out of the coma and I was so sound asleep that I didn't know it. I had missed a last smile, a last word, a last look into those blue eyes, a last interaction between the two of us, whatever that could have been. I had missed it. I had awoken so violently, to the sounds of alarms and medical personnel that I missed the fact that his hand had even rested upon my head. I had missed it and I was angry about it, and sorry, and tearful. As sick as I was that I had not felt that parting touch, the one thing that encouraged my broken heart was that in those last few moments he awakened to find me by his side.

After a time Annie left, giving me opportunity to finish packing. Before long, Luke appeared at the door. He had left Annie his number for this very reason and had rushed over to support me. Walking over to me, he wrapped me up in a bear hug and cried right along with me. Luke had come to love us both, and we loved him.

Luke was different than much of what we had encountered from the religious world. The Baptist house-Church pastor, who I was so skeptical of in those first few months, proved to be one of the truest friends of our lives. Wonders never cease.

Looking back on it, I would say that instead of telling us about the love of Jesus, Luke actually showed us Christ's love in tangible ways. Luke had come to express the very heart of God. I knew he didn't agree with me on any number of issues, but that didn't matter. As our friendship matured, I never doubted for one minute that he loved me. And, when it came time for Parks' memorial service, Luke was the one I asked to deliver the sermon. True to form, it wasn't some cold, impersonal monologue, but rather a message of hope from the heart of someone who had taken the time to know and love us both.

Eventually the tears ebbed and I pulled away from

217

Luke's embrace to resume my packing. Luke even had
the forethought to remove Parks' pillow case, shoving it
into one of my bags. That pillow case was my last tangible
piece of Parks, the last thing his head had touched
before leaving this world.

Luke helped me gather the last few belongings and
walked me down to his car. Nurses and techs lined the
hall that night as I left the hospital, mourning right along
with me. They all had fallen in love with Parks over the
course of our stay. His kind ways, his wit, his mischievous
grin had no doubt captured all of their hearts. Nevertheless,
there was probably another element at work here as
well. Had it been an older person, the sadness and deep
sense of unfairness may have been lessened. But, sadly,
Parks had died ten days after his twenty-sixth birthday.
Watching one so young die this awful death only intensified
the bereavement for us all.

Luke and I arrived back at the apartment just before
sunrise. Faced with the cold reality that he was actually
gone, walking into that apartment without Parks was one
of the hardest things I have ever had to do. Never again
would I hear his laughter reverberate from those walls or
see him walk through the door with his messenger bag
after a long day of teaching.
Luke stayed with me for the next day and a half until
Robert, Emilis, and Jane Anne could get there. Though
I'm sure he was needed at home, Tiffany knew my world
had just come unglued and that I needed the presence of
someone who truly loved me.

The next night, ripe with exhaustion, Luke and I
turned into bed shortly after nightfall. While Luke
crashed on our sofa, I curled up in our lonely bed. After
hours of restlessness, I flicked on the lamp and made my
way over to the closet. After fumbling through Parks'
side, I came across the navy turtle neck sweater he had
worn on our last night out. I pulled it from the shelf
above the hangers and drew it close. Everything had

218

come crashing down soon after that night. Thankfully, we hadn't had it dry cleaned. It still smelled like him, and as I held it I found a solitary long blonde hair on its shoulder. As a little boy clings to a teddy bear, this sweater became my nightly companion for the better part of two months.

Entry 43

The next two weeks were filled with unwanted tasks. In the course of Parks' sickness my focus had been on caring for him. Whether through preoccupation or avoidance, I had not given much thought to any funeral arrangements. I no longer had the luxury of evasion and now found myself standing amidst the showroom of urns and caskets at a downtown funeral home. I was fraught with the feeling that I was somehow trapped in the middle of a horrible nightmare from which I longed to awake, the type where you fall with a villain chasing you, yet cannot seem to move or scream loud enough to escape the impending doom. With every passing moment, the selection of an urn, the planning of the service, the writing of the eulogy, every decision an added reminder that he was actually gone.

Parks' service was a simple gathering of our closest friends. Emilis gave the eulogy, reminiscing of the spirited little blonde haired boy she watched grow up in Ocracoke Village, so many miles and years away. Luke gave an incredible talk from Parks' favorite Scripture, interlaced with personal memories. But, as is often the case with the loved one of the deceased, I felt like I was on auto pilot, simply trying to survive all of the formalities. My mourning would take full effect after the last plate of food had been delivered to my door, after the last prayer had been prayed, and everyone's life but mine returned to normal.

At the end of two weeks, Robert, Emilis, and Jane Anne were to make their way back to North Carolina.

219

Though Jane Anne and Robert seemed to have accepted the fact that I would not be returning with them, Emilis had her hopes set that they would need four seats on the return flight. I simply wasn't ready. Truth be told, I doubted if I ever would be. We all were a mix of emotions as I stood at the gate, watching them board the plane for departure.

With Jane Anne and the Guthries back in North Carolina and all of my Seattle friends settling back into their routines, I was left alone to begin picking up the pieces and assembling my new normal. We think we are so different, but we're not. Husband, wife, girlfriend, boyfriend, best friend, room-mate, lover....whatever...when you lose the one you've shared your life with, it's a void that cannot be described. Maybe the only ones who truly understand this are those who have joined the ranks of having their hearts broken with unwelcome goodbyes.

After Parks passed, I stayed in Seattle for just over two years, completely devastated and utterly terrified. Devastated because I had lost my best friend, terrified because I knew it was only a matter of time before the clinic, the doctors, and the medication regimen would become my world. I knew it was only a matter of time until I received a death sentence of my own.

I lived in a state of stubborn denial and fierce refusal for about eight months after Parks passed. I threw myself into my work, trying to distract myself from the gnawing sense of grief. As long as I could stay busy, I could avoid dealing with the full weight of my loss.

Ty and Sara stayed close by, having me over for dinner or inviting me out on weekends. As weeks turned to months following Parks' death, I began to join them at the local bars, but there was always a hole, a fourth spot unfilled. Removing Parks from the equation changed the dynamics of our relationship. Yes, we still loved each other; however, with Parks gone it was as if we struggled to strike a rhythm. Our interactions seemed awkward and forced; a painful reminder of the role Parks had played in our individual and collective lives.

While my relationship with Ty and Sara grew a little more distant, Luke seemed to scoop me up and carry me through those months. It was with Luke that I was able to pour out my deepest pain, and because he had remained so near during the storm, he was the one I could laugh with when the sun began to peak through the clouds. Often we would meet for lunch, or grab a cup of coffee in the evenings, just sharing life. He was as open with me as I was with him, which gave our friendship a refreshing sense of reciprocity. I didn't want to always be the focus of conversation, I didn't want every conversation to revolve around me, or Parks, or death, or sickness; and Luke seemed to understand that.

We talked about everything. Luke confided in me some serious relationship stressors he was facing with Tiffany, and even shared with me some problems he was experiencing within the network of house Churches he and Tiffany had planted. To Luke, I wasn't Holden... the gay friend, or Holden...the widower, or Holden...the sinner, I was just Holden...my friend. Rather than treat me like a project, he treated me as a full brother in the journey of life.

After about a year, I could tell that things were not okay with me health wise. I knew denial was pointless; but, I just wasn't ready to be sick. I wasn't prepared to have the diagnosis, to accept the fact that I had AIDS. I was just too young to die, as Parks had been too young. Nevertheless, when the first lesion appeared it was an unescapable reality check, leading me through the doors of the clinic I knew so well. I was 28 years old.

The clinic at Harborview had become a familiar place to me over the time between Parks' diagnosis and death, until inpatient treatment became the only option. Whether it was to meet with a case worker, physician, counselor, or for routine blood work and T-cell tracking, we were there frequently. I watched as this thing racked his young, strong body with unspeakable pain. I watched and wept as this disease stripped my protégé of his youth, his autonomy, and finally his life. I lived this with Parks, through the high fevers, the sweats that had me up throughout the night changing bed linens and pillow cases, through the diarrhea, through the morphing of a handsome, charismatic, robust, healthy young man into an emaciated corpse. The thought that it would soon be me was horrifying. However, I knew the longer I delayed treatment, the more rapid the process would take effect.

On June 4th I made a phone call which would chart a course I had fought to avoid. At 8:30 the next morning, Luke accompanied me to the clinic. My reintroduction to the staff was somber. Although the familiarity was somewhat comforting, we all knew too well where this path ended. June of '89 brought confirmation of what we all knew would be the score, ever since Parks had been diagnosed two years prior. I had AIDS.

Entry 44

I felt like an outcast all my life. Even as a child I was different. As the years stretched on, that difference led to painful rejection. I often isolated myself, buried in shame and an all-encompassing fear of being discovered. I knew well the pain of stigma, the wounds of shunning...they had pretty much been life-long traveling companions. However, being a gay man living with AIDS took ostracization to a new level.

At the time I still didn't want anything to do with Church. I was so bitter, still deeply wounded, and more angry with God than ever. Nevertheless, I still needed support, and so my case worker at the clinic suggested a group which met downtown twice each week. That support group, coupled with the friendship of Tiffany and Luke, was a lifeline during the emotionally turbulent months following my diagnosis.

222

Every Tuesday evening and Saturday morning I made my way to the community center, taking my place amidst the circle of metal folding chairs, joining a brotherhood of men living the same nightmare. We talked about viral loads, T-cell counts, and all of the normal medical jargon while checking in with the group, but usually, before long, we went much deeper, sharing fears of dying and the shame we felt in the context of the greater society. Together we mourned lost dreams and supported one another through the sharing of our respective stories, common and yet unique, laced with deep wounds from even our earliest years. We ranged in age from early twenties to late forties and represented a melting pot of cultures, ethnicities, and socio-economic statuses. Nonetheless, there was a sense of solidarity which transcended any external differences we held. We each had drank deeply from the same cup, belonged to the same team, shared the same fears, carried the same concerns, and many of us lived with the same severed relationships to families, families to whom we died the day we came out. For some of us, this group was supplemental to the care of loving friends and partners, to others it was the only beacon of hope in an ever darkening night.

As the year progressed, the circle would light candles and say goodbye to one fallen brother after another. Joe was the first one we lost after I started attending. He was twenty one years old...twenty one! Joe moved to Seattle from Montana, where his family were ranchers. Like so many of us, since a young age he had known that something was different. After graduating high school he headed for Seattle University, seeking to earn his Bachelors of Science in Nursing. It was here in Seattle that he came out; and during those years of trying to find himself, experimenting with all of the nightlife Seattle had to offer a young, handsome, gay man, Joe had contracted the disease. Before the year was over I watched him fall, as I had watched Parks, as I would watch five more of our

223

circle do before the new year.

One of the topics that Joe brought up frequently was his anguish of heart regarding separation from his family. Joe's mother died while he was still in high school, but he still had a father and older brother living in Montana. For the entire time I knew Joe, he made attempt upon attempt at bridging the gap between them. In the end he received one response from his father, a letter telling Joe they had nothing to discuss. That...that was the last message my young friend received from home before leaving this world.

Joe's obsession for reconciliation with his father and brother began to rub against my heart as we sat in session. In some ways, his story was mine. After Joe passed, I followed his example, sending a total of three letters back home to Johnston County. Mama and John have never responded.

Samuel, on the other hand, wrote back within a week. Since that first letter back from Samuel, we have kept in close contact with one another. I hadn't corresponded with him at all after our goodbye on the edge of the highway, as I left my native farming town for the last time. He now visits me whenever he has leave from the military. During these extended weekend visits we have been doing a lot of talking, laughing, and crying together, making our relationship the strongest now it has ever been.

As much as I would like to escape it, the reality is I am dying. As I watched my comrades fall, one by one, something happened inside of me. One chilly afternoon walking home from yet another memorial service, I found myself broken down emotionally in a way that I hadn't experienced since the diagnosis. Making my way down the sidewalk, I paused for a moment in front of the large arched doorway of Christ Church Cathedral. I had never been in an Anglican Church.` I hadn't been in any Church since Grace Chapel. I paused below the bell tower of the massive stone building and slowly, cautiously,

224

stepped inside.

The cathedral was unlike any Church I had ever attended back in North Carolina. The sheer magnitude of the place, coupled by the serenity of that vacant sanctuary, evoked a sense of reverence. I quietly opened the door on the pew box nearest the back of the Church and took a seat. I sat there in silence looking at the altar table with its golden Cross and candlesticks. I looked around silently at the huge stained glass depictions of Bible stories I had learned in my youth. I noticed the padded kneeling bench at my feet, but I didn't kneel. I just sat there, thinking, looking around, trying to find some sense of peace amidst the pain of my existence. I probably sat there for half an hour, watching others slip in quietly, kneel down in their pew to pray, and leave as unobtrusively as they had entered. I returned to this spot several times throughout that Autumn season, just to sit and think in the stillness and quiet.

Entry 45

Autumn pressed into winter and early December brought our first snow. No matter how many lights appeared in department store windows or how many boughs of greenery adorned the lamp posts downtown, Christmas that year felt anything but jolly. I was suffering from a bought of depression which left me more isolated than normal, though I realized that doing so only added to my blues.

I had lived so much of my life in a private internal war, sorting out the complexities of my experience. Now, I was left to wrestle with my grief in that same type of isolation. There were people around who no doubt cared for my well-being, wishing that they knew how to care for me in that moment; but aside from Luke and Tiffany, few seemed to truly empathize with the depth of my pain.

Parks and I never had much, in terms of material wealth, and even Parks' accumulated retirement was given to his father back at Hatteras, being his closest living relative. I didn't care about the money at all, that isn't the point. What bothered me is that in the wake of his death, at least where the financial and legal institutions were concerned, I was nobody. All priority went to a father who hadn't spoken to Parks in eight years, who used to extinguish cigarettes on his young skin, who made him run beside a moving vehicle until his legs buckled beneath him. This was who the courts recognized as Parks' next of kin, although we had shared a life for the past five years. I was the one who held Parks through the diagnosis and treatment, who cared for him through the decimation of his health, and, finally, through his death. Walter Eason was a worthless piece of shit who never even remembered Parks' Birthday, never so much as gave him a call on Christmas, and couldn't even find the decency to respond to Parks' letter, sent in the last months of his life. But he was the next of kin.

Infinitely more devastating was the paralyzing sense of loss. For weeks after Robert, Emilis, and Jane Anne returned to Carolina, I never got out of bed except to use the bathroom. People came by to bring cards or deliver food to the house, and I just pulled the covers over my head and ignored the knocks at the door. I didn't answer the phone, I didn't bathe, and somewhere in the midst of my deep depression over losing Parks, I had stopped eating and drinking altogether.

After I missed two consecutive shifts at work, Luke was no longer satisfied with well-wishing and came to my door with assistance from the city police. He found me in bed, breathing but unresponsive. I was taken to the hospital and treated for severe dehydration and depression. We still aren't sure if my lack of response was from physical malnourishment or if I was indeed catatonic.

My entire world died with Parks. He had been the one I built my new life around and with him gone I was utterly devastated. Emilis and Robert begged me to come home for Christmas, but I wouldn't do it. I just wanted to be left alone. I couldn't get up the energy to put on a front that would allow everyone around me to have a Christmas free of worrying about me.

I didn't feel like being chipper, I didn't feel like drinking egg nog and singing jingle bells and pretending like my world wasn't falling apart, because it was, it had. I was done with pretending, done with being strong. I wanted to just let it all out, the anger, the loss, and the pain of not being completely known by the people closest to me because there were things I felt I could never say to them.

How could they understand what Parks had meant to me? They had never lived their entire life in isolation and fear as a result of being different. They didn't know what it was, as I did, to find the one person in the world who actually got it, who understood, who cared so deeply. They didn't know what it was like for me, going from a life of utter isolation from even those closest, to feeling like I was no longer alone. That was my experience and, now, that sense of belonging had been ripped from me by this ferocious disease.

I just couldn't do it. I didn't have the emotional capital for social graces, or to pull myself up by my own boot straps. I just couldn't manage other people's emotions and their need for things to be hunky dory, and so I stayed in Seattle, alone.

Luke and Tiffany were going to Iowa to be with his family for Christmas. Ty and Sara were staying in town and told me to call them if I wanted to do something, but the season was painful enough without having to be reminded further of how much I missed Parks, which inevitably was the emotional outcome of every outing I had with the two of them after he passed. I simply called them on Christmas morning to give my best wishes.

On Christmas Eve, alone, sad, miserable, I made my way down the icy sidewalks to Christ Church for their

227

midnight Eucharist. I hadn't attended worship anywhere in five years, but it was Christmas Eve and I was alone. At a quarter to twelve, I slipped through the tall doors and made my way into my familiar pew box. The pipe organ music filled the cathedral as everyone took their places. The service was nice, I actually enjoyed it.

Following the benediction, the organist blew all the cob webs out of the organ with a recessional that let everyone know this was high Church. I remained quietly in my pew, nestled securely against the wall. By now I had lesions on my face and neck and wanted to wait for the congregation to clear out before I made my exit. I felt awful enough without having children point and adults hustle away from me in fear. With the final note sounded, the last parishioner out of the door, and silence settling into the sanctuary, I reached for my scarf and coat, placed beside me on the wooden pew, a subtle symbol which betrayed my fear of having anyone sit next to me. I wanted to be left alone. Being in worship made me anxious enough. The last things I wanted was someone pressuring me to come back, or asking me to fill out some visitor's card, or inviting me to join them for refreshments in the gathering hall. I just needed to take this at what-ever pace I could.

As I rose from my seat, I turned to see the Rector mak-ing her way from the entrance of the Church. I froze, not wanting to be rude but not wanting to talk to her either. I was scared and annoyed that I might not be able to get out of the building without having to speak. Within seconds the Rector was greeting me.

She was a very articulate lady, probably twenty years my senior. She seemed friendly enough and it didn't seem at all forced, which was refreshing. In my years of reading people I had come to be a pretty good judge of character, making my assessment within the first few min-utes. From what I saw and heard from her in the service, combined with the way she conducted our first encounter

228

I had a feeling that, even though I didn't want to be bothered, she was genuine and safe.

"How are you?"

"I'm hanging in there." I said, trying not to betray my depression, while also seeking not to lie to the Rector by telling her I was great.

"I'm Shannon." She said, reaching out her hand.

I hesitantly slipped out my hand to take hers, scared that the sarcomas would elicit a reaction I desperately wanted to avoid this Christmas Eve.

She looked down as she grasped my hand in hers. Noticing the lesions she simply smiled, the type of smile that comes more from a place of painful compassion than joy, then placed her other hand on top of mine, enveloping my extended hand in both of hers.

"I have AIDS." I responded.

She shook her head gently, as if my confession was unnecessary.

"My brother had AIDS." she replied.

We both stood there in silence, as she looked away batting her eyes to prevent tears.

"You want to go get something to eat?" she asked.

I didn't, but I did. I wanted to be left alone, to go back into the loneliness of my empty apartment, but at the same time I was starving for some form of meaningful interaction with someone with whom I didn't have to hide.

"I'm all alone this Christmas and could really use some company." She continued.

"Sure, I guess."

"Just sit here for a moment while I go change." She replied.

That Christmas Eve night Rector Shannon and I sat in a waffle house down the street from the Church until three in the morning. She was single and miles away from her own extended family. We helped ward off each other's loneliness that early Christmas morning, talking for hours about my life, her life, and her brother. From the sound of it, he and I would have made very good friends. It's a shame we never got to meet one another. There, amidst plates of greasy sausages, lukewarm toast, and piping hot coffee, we embarked on a friendship that has lasted till this day. It was also the night I realized what my next step would be.

Shannon began telling me about her own brother, how he had been ostracized from the family after he came out. She, like myself, had wrestled deeply with her faith, in relation to her brother's sexuality. She told of how she had always known he was different, but was scared to death to face it, to admit that he may be gay. In the end, she was the one who reached out to him, who stayed in touch, who went to visit, who wrote, his only link to his family. She spoke of how he died in a distant city surrounded by a group of friends who loved and cared for him around the clock until his departure from this life.

"I was so angry at him." She said, "Angry because he denied me the privilege of caring for him in those last days. He was my little brother and I wanted to be the one holding him when he passed."
Shannon had been the doting older sister, the one who changed his diapers, the one who carried him on her hip around their small mid-west farming town when he was just a toddler. And yet, he had chosen not to tell the family when he was hospitalized.

"I received a phone call from one of his friends, telling me that Brandon was gone. I remembered thinking: "...gone, gone, what do you mean gone? I just spoke with him last week and he said he was doing fine."

Brandon obviously hadn't been entirely honest with Shannon, and in the end, it was the voice of a third party that bore the news, news which left her world forever changed. Shannon had been torn apart by this, blaming herself for not having been a better sister, for not having been a good enough friend to him, for whatever she had done too little or too much of, causing him to leave her

230

out.

I could empathize with Brandon, though I never knew him. He likely didn't care if the rest of the family even knew at that point, but he probably didn't want his big sister to watch him die such an awful death. I had lived this with Parks, I know the things one sees when caring for someone in the final stages, and often it isn't pretty.

In part, that may have been why I had refused to return to Ocracoke. I didn't want Emilis to have to clean up my diarrhea. I didn't want Robert to have to bathe me when I didn't have the strength to support my own weight. I didn't want for them to see me waste away to a mere skeleton with lesions covering my body, or deal with the heart-wrenching pain, should I battle dementia.

Whatever Brandon's reason had been, I came face to face with the pain Shannon was carrying, having been denied the opportunity to care for him in his last hours. She had rocked him as an infant, doctored his boyhood scrapes and bruises, and I could tell there was a part of her that deeply mourned a missed opportunity to rock him again, amidst a different type of pain.

Sitting in the booth of that waffle house, I realized that not only did I want to be with the Guthries when my time came, I didn't want to deny them their desire to care for me in those final days, however messy and painful it may be. I really didn't want to be alone at the end, and, after all the Guthries had done for me, I owed them more than a telephone call from a stranger, informing them of my passing.

Entry 46

Although that Christmas morning brought a decision to return to a far-away strip of sand, bounded by ocean tides and gnarled oaks, I still fought it for months. The sheer thought of returning to the island made me short of breath. Pondering the transition brought up a great deal of anxiety as I thought about returning to that place.

231

I winced at the thought of facing those who had spoken words I felt my heart would never heal from, no matter how much I sought to forget. Just as fearful was the thought of facing those who truly loved me, those whom I had wounded and disappointed so deeply.

There was also another thought just as smothering. How would I handle returning to Ocracoke without Parks? The small seaside village was ladened with memories of him, of us. How could I stand it emotionally?

There was an even starker reality casting a shadow over my return. When I boarded that ferry, I would be doing so for the last time. This was the last scene of the last act of my existence on this earth. There was such a morbid sense of finality tied to packing up my Seattle life and moving back east. This would be the point of no return...and so I fought it.

One Saturday in early February of '89 I made my way down to Westport. After moving to Seattle, Parks and I had fallen in love with the place. Its little white lighthouse, crabbing fleet, and surf felt like a little taste of home. We went down there at least once a month, more when the weather was warm. Although it was a two and a half hour drive from our apartment in the city, it was the best surf spot around.

On this Saturday I just went and walked around the town, alone. It was the first time I had visited in over a year. I stopped by the little coffee shop we had frequented so many times, then found my perch on the rocks of the jetty, losing myself in the steady roar of the white water rolling in towards the beach. The ocean seemed to drown out all of the thoughts swirling in my mind and I welcomed the distraction.

A few short years ago those waves were the playground of two invincible young men in the prime of their lives. As I sat there, smack dab between what would have been Parks' birthday and the anniversary of his death, loneliness seemed my only companion. I did a bit of thinking

and even a bit of praying as I sat there that day. Don't
get me wrong, it wasn't some sentimental mush. Rather,
I took the advice Annie Mae had given me on the night
I ranted and raved in the room at Harborview. I had
questions, and anger, and more questions...and for the
first time in some time I actually brought those questions
to God.

In later years I have come to love how the 62nd Psalm
invites readers to pour out their heart before God. That
afternoon, sitting upon a bolder beside the Pacific, I did a
lot of pouring out. I had been harboring and stewing on
so many injustices, so many wounds, so much unfairness
in this life, and the bitterness had festered into a putrid
sore. With the sun beginning its daily descent, I began to
talk to God, but it wasn't in the polite, rehearsed, scripted,
learned, clichéd ways I had grown accustomed to in the
evangelical circles of my childhood and young adult life.
No, this was different, raw, real, a no holds barred expression of my deepest anger, regret, and fear. It wasn't
a conversation for the faint of heart, as out gushed long
unspoken words accompanied by a torrent of tears.
Afterward, somehow, leaving my perch that evening to
return to Seatown, I felt as though my release, my crying
out to God in such a unpolished way, had somehow left
me feeling cleansed, and exhausted. I had wrung out my
soul like a dish rag.

Entry 47

About a year after Parks' death, well-meaning friends
began trying to get me to go out again, seeking to lift me
out of my mourning, setting me up on random dates. In
time, I did go out on a couple; however, my heart was
never in it. When Parks died, something changed inside
of me, something in me died too. As I began to venture
back out into the club scene of Seattle, I was perpetually
reminded of just how different, how special Parks and I
had been. Sure, we were lovers, but more than anything

233

we were friends, best friends. It wasn't just about crawling into bed together when the mood struck; it was about having someone to come home to at the end of the day, someone to share your life with, someone with whom to share every meal, every heartache, every joy. As I began to venture back out into the dating scene, I came to a sober realization that I was no longer there...mentally, emotionally, physically, or spiritually.

There was the obvious reality that no one would ever be able to take Parks' place in my life or in my heart. In fact, I didn't have patience with anyone who would even try. But there was also this sense that I was facing something so much more serious than the frivolousness I saw in the bars around town. I was dying and my whole mental process was shifting. I was no longer sorting out what I was going to wear downtown on Saturday night. Rather, I was thinking about the fact that in a matter of some months, a year...who knows..I might be dead.

As can often be the case when facing the end of life, when a terminal diagnosis strips away the youthful sentiment of immortality, existential matters have a way of making themselves to the surface. Such was the case with me, particularly concerning life after death, and thereby revisiting, in a personal way, a faith which had served to be both the greatest of all comfort, and a stumbling-block with regards to the deep yearnings of my heart for affection from the hand of another man.

It goes without saying that my Christian faith was, at best, strained after the disrespectful disclosure of our love. Questions and wrestlings had long been held in the secret places of my heart, as I sought to hold in tension my deepening faith in Christ and the unavoidable, persistent realization that my relational and sexual desires were not directed towards women. Sure there were a number of girls I had dated through the years. Some I truly believe I loved, love that still finds a lodging place in my heart as I think of them tonight and wish them all the best.

234

However, try, fight, and scream as I may, I was never able to conquer my attraction to men. Then came Parks, the embodiment of my secret dreams, and my life took a new trajectory.

As exciting as it all was with Parks, and as much as I tried to conceal this for the years following coming out, I longed for a comfortable sense of reconciliation between my faith and my sexuality. I lived for so many years in the uneasy anxiety of suppressing my desires and yearnings for male intimacy, of following my faith convictions and denying myself the type of relationship most appealing to me. I was certain that to pursue it would mean my damnation.

After coming out I was placed in a new tension, different, but equally disturbing. In a matter of a few months I found myself fully embracing my love for Parks, and yet I lived in a sense of internal discomfort and mourning regarding a faith that I had left behind. I did a lot of reading when we lived in Seattle, exploring the developing body of literature promoting a pro-gay theology, as well as a number of religious pamphlets handed out on street corners telling me that I was absolutely going to hell. As much as I felt those curb-side pamphlets didn't contain the whole truth, I also found it extremely difficult to fully embrace a theology that found no discrepancy between embracing my sexuality and living faithfully to God. Believe me, I really wanted to embrace it, to be at complete peace with these two areas of my life, to be able to worship in Church with Parks, to take communion together without feeling like God was getting ready to strike me down at any moment. I had a deeply rooted conviction regarding the Divine inspiration of Scripture, and a high respect for it. Relaxing my fundamentalist upbringing was very difficult for me, as strange as that may seem. This stale mate brought incredible anguish, frustration and anger.

I was frustrated to no end by the declaration that what

seemed most natural to me was deemed unnatural and an abomination. I had a horrible time reconciling the love of God so evident throughout Scripture, with the sentence of stoning for those like myself found in the Old Testament. And, I could not read some elements of Paul's letters without feeling condemned. I just didn't understand. Even John, whose writing always filled me with such comfort and warmth, the disciple who rested his head upon the very chest of Jesus during the last supper, warned of the future of the sexually immoral, a category to which I feared I belonged. I was painfully and inescapably aware of the fact that I was gay. My attraction, fight it as I may, was toward men. Therefore, I was left to wrestle with these two enormously important and powerful parts of myself. To say that my confusion was soul-wrenching would be the understatement of the millennia.

This pain was further complicated by the number of people in my life who had further wounded me with their words. Friends had made horrible statements about gay people in my presence, long before they knew that their worst fears had come home to roost in their own circle of friends, statements like, "If my son was queer, I'd disown him." All the while I sat silently, absorbing the climate of the world in which I lived. It was this pain that ultimately led me to package the faith I had held from childhood and place it out of sight, too overcome with fear, anger, resentment, and sadness to even deal with it at the time. I convinced myself that God was finished with me, that there was no hope for me, and so I disengaged with this part of my life. It wasn't hard for me to arrive at the conclusion of being forsaken, especially since so many people in my life had made impassioned declarations that I was damned and, based on their tone, seemed very glad of it. I became an object of scorn and derision to those who once claimed to love me, I was abandoned by most of my family and friends, and I felt sure that I had been abandoned by God as well. And yet somewhere inside there

236

was a relentless, stubborn hope that God could still love someone like me, that somehow He would help me. Even as I write this I can see the tension in which I have lived, the proverbial tug of war, the torment of my mind.

The words I had been hearing from so many people in the Church made me doubt any inclination of hope, banning me to the ghetto of the unredeemable. And yet the question remained in my heart, are there any who are unredeemable? I couldn't imagine that from the God I loved and served, but the answer was coming so forcefully, so passionately, so angrily from those with whom I once served, "yes, and you're one of them!"

How can I recount the raging emotions and the onslaught of questions with which I have wrestled through the years? I don't know if time or my emotional health would even allow me to mine them. All I knew was that I was trapped in a suffocating vice between a faith in Christ that was the most core reality of my life, and fears related to my inescapable attractions towards men. I didn't believe I could have them both, I would have to choose... and yet I didn't feel I had a choice in the matter of my sexuality. It was a battle that sought to undo me.

After Parks and I first were intimate, I was so conflicted and overcome by it that I made a choice...friendship was all I could offer. I loved him and didn't want to lose him, but I couldn't see abandoning my faith either. It was awful and no one seemed to understand, a feeling that maybe only those who have lived it can grasp. Then came that fateful Spring day when my life was exposed before an empathy deprived world. In the minds of the parishioners and villagers alike, I was detestable. There was no room left for me to wrestle, no room to develop and grow, to come to my own conclusions. I was forced into view before I was ready, and this raping of my soul in the public square almost claimed my life.

Yes, I am gay, but at that moment in my life I wasn't ready to go public with it. When I reached my Pacific

237

home the force seemed equal from the other direction, forceful messages to accept who I was as a gay man, to free myself from my internalized homophobia, to dismiss any conviction that my lifestyle was somehow sinful, to either adjust my faith convictions or somehow adopt a form of spirituality that would allow me to escape my feelings of guilt. As much as I wanted to, I had such a hard time believing that God loved me. I wanted to know that so desperately. And since for whatever reason I couldn't, I just refused to engage religion and spirituality on any level. I felt like a man without a country. No one in the Church seemed to understand my struggle, nor did anyone in the gay community seem to empathize with my turmoil of faith.

I was angry at God for not healing me of this, for allowing me to be this way, and equally frustrated by declarations against it. I just couldn't deal with it any more. I had lived my life in constant turmoil since childhood, ever increasingly aware of my different-ness. I even remember praying for God to either heal me or kill me. Few people understand that type of pain.

As life progressed, I fell completely in love with Parks, bound to him by a deep interweaving of our hearts. I reached a point where I didn't give a damn what anyone thought, I was tired of hurting, wearied of loneliness, and determined to snatch whatever piece of happiness I could wrench out of the clutches of this sordid and patronizing life. Anyone or anything that stood in the way of my plan was deemed expendable. I was mad as hell and my modus operandi was the embracing of those who were for me, while telling all others to stay the hell away.

The first time I ever even prayed after crossing the Pamlico, in pursuit of our Seattle dream, was the day I realized Parks was sick, the beginning of what we fearfully knew would be the end. I could go on and on about my epic journey of faith. But what's most pressing on my heart today is this... How many are like me today, desperately wanting to be loved by God, wanting to belong to Him, to know that He will carry us through all of the pain and questions of our lives? But for so many of us, years of people telling us that God hates us, complicated by the shunning and abandonment we experienced because of our sexuality, left us feeling like there was no hope for us in God. In those first visits, sitting in the rear pew of Christ's Church in Seattle, I hadn't prayed, I hadn't knelt, I hadn't approached the altar because I felt a completely pervasive sense of shame and fear, as if I didn't belong, as if God had completely washed His hands of me. Now, as I read through Scripture, I realize that this was not true, but my own feelings and the words of others have been so very convincing.

Ezekiel recorded in the thirty-fourth chapter of his prophecy that the sheep which God loved were scattered. I, in no way want to take any passage out of context, but today that imagery captivated my heart as I thought of all those people, like myself, who truly loved God and wanted to be able to rest in the fullness of that relationship, but somewhere, somehow we were attacked, beaten, frightened by feelings and urges we were unable to end, driven from our childhood trust by powerful messages from those we respected, telling us that God hated us, that we were disgusting and detestable people, that the struggle we faced was too large of a debt for God's grace to cover. And so, we find ourselves scattered, wounded, and scared, left in isolation to wrestle with the deepest questions of our worth, our value, and our destiny. We are like scattered, fearful sheep.

The same little boys and girls, who stood in children choirs and sang of Jesus' love and walking on the Heaven road, the same knees which knelt beside childhood beds every evening, the same little hands that were folded in prayer, the same little lips which once faithfully uttered, "Now, I lay me down to sleep", are now scared, weary and silent. Silent because we don't know what to say.

The chill of our reality has robbed us of so much hope. Weary, because we have walked so much of this path alone. Scared, because we are deeply afraid that our first Love has no more love for us. Afraid, that all hope is gone.

And so, we sit alone in empty rooms, reading privately from the Book we sang about as children, trying to find some hope and comfort, some sense of God's presence in our lives. We slip quietly into cathedrals and hospital chapels, or kneel privately in living room floors...drawing near to God in the only ways we know how, hoping that somehow He will meet us there. And we pray, sometimes through tears, sometimes through the pain of jaded silence, sometimes through whispered pleas for mercy, forgiveness, and help. For some, even these private attempts seem too painful, and so we head back out, isolated sheep on the rugged cliffs of our lives.

Our prayers are simple and deep. We plead for mercy, for help, for understanding. We cling desperately to the grace of God and the shed blood of Christ, for we know it to be our only hope, we know Him to be our only saving Grace. We, painfully and gloriously, have been separated from any sense of moral superiority or self-sufficient holiness. And yet we are scared, scared that He hates us as much as society, as much as some within the Church, as much as some have told us He does. We pray through tattered faith, but we pray. We hold in tension a soul that yearns for hope and a heart numbed with the disappointment of supplications for healing left unanswered, wondering why He would leave us to struggle so, even amidst tearful pleas for deliverance, for a reordering of our deepest attractions and desires...wanting so desperately to be pleasing to God, and to escape the pain and misunderstanding that has been our lot in life.

We pray, though disillusioned by spiritual leaders who have literally and metaphorically turned us out of the synagogue without ever caring to know our hearts or understand our journey, though our eyes were wet and our hearts longing for a connection with God. We pray, though plagued with feelings of abandonment and fear... we pray. Though cowered in outcast corners, splattered with messages of failure, of not having enough faith, of not fasting or praying enough, of not trying hard enough to fight the feelings we held, we still cry out, we still look upward. Like a teenage outcast curled in a corner after being group mobbed in a high school locker room, we cower, bleed, and cry...we cry out, and we cry upward. Though laden with doubts and fears, with numbness and ridicule, with pain unspeakable and mental anguish to spare, with forces leveled against us, telling us there is no hope for us in God. And yet...in the war-ravaged ground of our hearts and minds, a tiny green shoot still stubbornly, remarkably reaches upward to the light, a private, desperate, and humble cry for help and absolution, for intimacy with God. Though all the world, and at times even our own hearts, condemn and tell us to give up... there's something inside of us that keeps reaching up. Our eyes, though misty and tired, still look toward the heavens and hope desperately for mercy, love, and grace... for a place of restful belonging in the arms of God.

And though confession, repentance, holiness, sanctity, and surrender are elements central to our faith, sometimes those words sting us and cause us to retreat. Sometimes the pain morphs into anger and jaded defense. Sometimes we don't care to hear the words of parishioner or priest, because we don't feel they truly care or understand. And, dare I say, there are times when we feel the same way towards our Father in Heaven.

Yet, gently, quickly, hopefully on the heels of such a feeling and confession is the remembrance that Christ, our elder Brother, drank deeply of the cup of our suffering. And even the faintest flicker of hope distracts our enamorment with the darkness of our own thoughts and fears, suggesting ever so quietly, in such a warmly

241

approachable way that He understands and cares and loves when no one else does, when no one else will, when no one else can. And a calming peace settles in amidst the torrents of frightened anxiety, a peace coming from the remembrance of His completed work and perpetual intercession on our behalf. A quiet encouragement to our souls.

I don't know why, but for most of my life I had a really hard time accepting or believing that God actually loved me. Tolerated me...maybe. Hated me...probably. But loved me...I couldn't quite grasp that. Was the catalyst of these feelings an abusive father? Flawed Theology? A pervasive sense of guilt and shame regarding my sexuality? Who can say? It has taken years for me to be able to begin to accept the fact that God could love me too.

I well remember one Sunday morning as I knelt in Seattle for healing prayer at Christ's Church, just prior to my return to Ocracoke. A female deacon laid her hands so gently upon my head and asked if I had any particular request. With tears filling my eyes, I told her that I was struggling so hard with my faith as it related to my sexuality. I found no condemnation there, no look of disdain...but, rather, a complete sense of grace, love and acceptance from her. Though I wish I had the prayer she prayed over me that morning in written form, so I could pour over those words of grace whenever my soul felt discouraged; fortunately, parts of it are firm in my memory. She prayed that my fear would be replaced with faith, and that I would rest in the knowledge that I am the beloved of God. I frequently return to those words, fanning those gracious embers into a flame.

I find comfort in passages like Ezekiel, when God declares that He will seek out His sheep, that He will seek the lost, bring back the strayed, and bind up the injured. And, slowly, quietly, gently I have come to embrace hope again, my only hope, the hope that Christ's work on Calvary extends even to me.

I have been blessed with Robert, Emilis, Jane Anne, Luke, Tiffany, and Annie Mae...people who became ambassadors of a love that helped to foster and renew this hope. People who gave me the space to wrestle, to fight, to cry and who always reminded me that, regardless of how I felt or what others said, God would never give up on me. This love helped provide me a safe place in these last days to pray as Parks did in his hospice room, "Jesus, I give You me."

But today I think of all those who fight this battle, whose lives are ravaged by this disease, whose minds are tormented in this struggle, and yet they breathe their belabored lasts without ever having someone show them the love of God...and my heart grieves. I, like many others, spent many years embittered, hurting, scared, acting like I didn't give a damn about things that had once been the primary and eternal focus of my life. But, in the end, camouflage it as we may, I think we all give a damn. My heart breaks as I think of all those who had no one to walk with them through those concerns. And yet, I don't believe they were alone, not forgotten, not forsaken, but wrapped up in the embrace of God in ways that we cannot imagine, and this gives me hope. I once read in Scripture that it's not God's will that any should perish, but that all should come to repentance...that whosoever shall call upon the name of the Lord shall be saved, and so I believe that God is going to move Heaven and earth to reach us with His grace, in a way we can understand, in a way we can respond to, however simple or private that may be. And yet I am reminded that, for all He is doing and will continue to do in each of our lives, He has moved Heaven and earth to reach us...with a Baby's cry in Bethlehem and an "It is finished" on Golgotha. And in understanding our Big Brother, Who walked a mile in all our shoes, Who paid the price for all our sins, Who lives to advocate and intercede for us, how precious to realize, like the lyrics of the hymn I used to sing so many years

243

ago, "whosoever surely meaneth me."

Entry 48

Finally, on May 1st of this, the first year of the last
decade of the twentieth century, I endured the painful,
yet needed, process of bringing closure to my Seattle life
and moving back east to the little island on the Outer
Banks. Robert hired movers to pack my belongings and
ship them east. Meanwhile, I went about the tear-stained
process of saying goodbye. It has always frustrated me
that folks here in Ocracoke have no way of appreciating
the huge strides of personal growth I had made while
living in Seattle for the last six years. To my friends
here on the east coast, they were supposed to be my life,
North Carolina was supposed to be my home. To mourn
returning to them, to my home state, seemed to carry a
weight of treason in their hearts. I have never been able
to adequately describe to them what my Seattle life meant
to me, how I was shaped and changed for the good by
people and experiences known beneath the space needle.
I came to know who "Holden" really was in those years
on the west coast. Seattle was both millstone and place of
rebirth.

As much as I loved Robert and Emilis, as much as the
waters of the Pamlico sometimes beckoned me, I had
built a life in Seattle surrounded by caring friends who
became a real sense of family for me. Somehow, leaving
all of this seemed like a death in itself. Had things been
different, my Seattle family and I may have been able
to exchange parting niceties of future trips to visit one
another; however, as I embraced each of them over the
course of those last two weeks of April, we were all well
aware that this really was goodbye.

Ty and Sara had me over for one last dinner, and as
we sat in their living room following dessert we wept and
laughed for the better part of two hours, recalling the first
time we met, the volumes of years and memories which

244

followed, and the things we wanted...needed to say to one another.

Throughout the course of those two weeks, I made my way through a steady stream of private goodbye dinners and somber coffee dates with friends and acquaintances who had played crucial roles in my life out west. Nevertheless, my last night in the city held the hardest goodbye of them all.

By that last day the apartment was all packed and shipped. Leaving it for the last time, I paused just inside the front door, staring at the vacant space. I stood there in the silence, key in hand, so many memories parading through my mind...good memories. I thought of the day we moved in, the last time I had seen the space so barren. I thought of all the laughter, all the dinners and movie nights, the quiet nights on the fire escape, the good times before the disease. Slowly I turned to leave, locking the door behind me. Slowly I rubbed my fingers across the brass 46 tacked onto the door's surface, my final farewell to what had been our home.

After returning the key to the landlord, I headed over to Luke and Tiffany's, where I would spend my last evening in town. My flight was to leave mid-morning on May first and Luke had asked if he could be the one to take me to the airport. It was a request easy to oblige, as he was the one I wanted to see me off, as I embarked on my final trip home.

Luke and Tiffany worked hard at keeping the evening light and jovial, telling jokes, and reminiscing of only good times and fun memories. Sitting around the table that night I fought off tears as it sunk in that this was the last time I would hear little Sailor call me Uncle Holden, or have little Molly bring me a picture she had colored for my refrigerator. We all had our teary moments that night, in spite of how hard we tried to keep the mood free of mourning. Yet, somehow, in trying to ignore the reality, we were being less than honest in our emotions towards

245

one another and the weight of that seemed to be robbing the night of its most needed expressions.

Tiffany put Sailor and Molly to bed; and after an hour of coffee and sitcoms the three of us turned in as well. It wasn't at all how I had anticipated the evening going. The labor borne by all three of us in keeping the mood light left me empty, disappointed, and sad. I wanted to know that my life had meant something to them in a deep way, I needed them to cry and I needed to cry in return.

As I finished packing my bag, the door to my room opened gently. The evening's dance of decorum and allaying raw emotions left Luke dissatisfied as well. There in that moment, my eminent departure settled in upon both of us.

There, on the edge of their guest bed, we wept together, speaking a language of affirmation, appreciation, and brotherly love that words, here, would only cheapen. Our hearts were broken on so many levels. We were mourning my leaving Seattle, we were mourning the miles that would now separate our daily communion, but we were also saying goodbyes of a more final and malignant nature. That night, Luke sat in the floor beside my bed, his hand gripping mine until I fell asleep. It was a brother's goodbye, and it touched my heart. I miss Luke so much. His wisdom, his compassion, the way he knew how to be a friend, these were gifts few others have matched.

The next morning we drove to the airport and said our difficult goodbyes. After a long, hearty embrace, I passed through the gate, unable to look back at him because of the weight of my emotions. I took my window seat and, within a matter of minutes, watched the city fade from view.

Entry 49

Late that evening, the plane tires screeched onto the pavement of the New Bern landing strip, rousing me from sleep and filling me with anxiety. I gathered my-

self enough to put on a good front for Jane Anne and
the Guthries, who were waiting and waving to me from
behind the chain link fence as I made my way down the
steps and onto the pavement. They were so excited, so
glad to have me home...and I felt guilty.

I didn't want to be here. I wanted to be in Seattle,
healthy, living my life. I wanted to wind the clocks back
five years and just stay there, a return to the days when
life was an adventure shared with my best friend.

After staying the night on the riverfront in New Bern,
we headed back to the island early the next morning. I
sat in the back seat beside Jane Anne, staring out of the
window, watching the quaint towns of Carteret County
pass by, a mirage of memories flooding my mind.

Just before lunch we pulled up at the Cedar Island
Ferry and got out of the car while we awaited boarding
time. Just yards away stood the Driftwood and beyond
the dunes lie the waters of the Pamlico. I made my way
down to the water's edge and found a seat on the old
breakwater which bounded the property line.

The only word that comes to mind which can capture
the essence of what I was feeling in those moments is
resolve. I was doing this because it was what I needed to
do...but I wanted none of it. I tried not to be too distant
from Jane Anne, Robert, and Emilis, but I was unmistak-
ably quiet and withdrawn. They, no doubt, were eager
for conversation and connection. I simply wanted to be
left alone with my thoughts.

In time I was shaken from my isolated trance as the
ferry attendant called for everyone to return to their vehicles, the blast of the loud speaker a startling distraction
from my ruminations. The metal clanking of the ramp as
we drove onto the deck of the vessel, once evoking excitement and a sense of adventure, seemed a piercing rever-
beration, as if a steel door had just slammed shut, locking
me inside this final chapter. The same feeling as when a
roller coaster car is making its initial climb and you realize

J.M. Styron

at that moment that you really didn't want to get on it after all, but your only option is to close your eyes and hold
on until the end...that's the feeling that swept over me as
we pulled onto the deck of the Cedar Island ferry for my
last voyage across the Pamlico.

In the years in which I had lived on the island, the
ferry division had provided lucrative employment to a
number of the young men on the island. The one-week-
on/one-week-off schedule allowed them a week to work
in the fishing industry, and a week on the ferry, thereby
securing a steady salary and much needed benefits. As I
peered through my back seat window, I could see that not
much had changed in that regard. I recognized several of
the island boys working on the boat that day. A few came
over to speak to Robert and even offered me awkward,
guarded greetings. Most stood at a distance, whispering,
occasionally looking my way. I just leaned back in the
seat and closed my eyes. It was just as I knew it would be,
and as I lay there with my eyes closed, my head leaning
back against the head rest, I felt the warmth of tears as
they ran across my temples from the corners of my eyes.
Jane Anne didn't say a word. She just slipped me a tissue
across the seat, keeping her gaze forward as to not alert
the others to my tears.

Though I no doubt had a multitude of things to cry
about on that particular day, one thing that was rubbing
me raw was the mixture of sadness and anger I felt regarding my family. I was so close to them geographically
and yet a seemingly unnavigable chasm lie between us. I
was saddened as a result of the absence of their love and
support, angered that they would shove me away when
parts of me didn't meet their approval.

Shouldn't family be a place of safety, a place of support, a congregation of open arms to hurting sons? My
sexuality had denied me the dream of a family, but had I
been blessed with a child I could not imagine doing such
a thing to my own. And yet, when I failed to perform

perfectly, the day my imperfections became visible, the moment I caused shame, they were somehow able to ignore and disown me. I just couldn't understand that.

I had been dying inside for so many years and no one ever seemed to take notice. Maybe they were oblivious to just how deeply I groaned from internal upheaval, or maybe they had suspicions that were too painful to acknowledge and so they chose to simply ignore them, to dance around the issue of me.

I cannot begin to tell you how hurtful and frustrating that was to me. Maybe it was their deep hatred of my sin, maybe it was pride and the fear of public humiliation, maybe it was discomfort in acknowledging and dealing with the reality that I was different; whatever the dictating principle, they loved it more than me, and that grieved my heart in ways that I cannot even articulate.

I never asked them to change their convictions. I wasn't asking for them to agree with me. I simply wanted them to love me. I wanted to be able to talk to mama about what was going on in my life, to let her know where I was in my journey, to have a sense of loving support and commitment. I wanted to be able to talk to John about the things I was facing, to ask him advice about everything from relationships to car maintenance. I just wanted to be loved. But, somehow my sexuality was too high a hurdle for them to scale, and so they simply stopped, they quit, they cut me off, they abandoned me. The weight of this struggle is heavy enough, without the added suffocating isolation of being an outsider to one's own family

Because of their refusal to know me and engage in relationship with me regarding any part of my life which they found uncomfortable or unacceptable, a wedge was driven between our hearts, making the rift deeper and more cavernous with each passing year, with each ignored plea for reconciliation and understanding. How could they go to their respective Churches each Sunday, sing

249

in the choirs, teach the classes, collect the offerings, and
yet have a son, now less than four hours away, dying with
AIDS, with whom they refused to speak? We had missed
so much of life, so much laughter, so much sharing, so
much love that I wanted to give and receive; however,
such expressions were stunted and inhibited by prohibi-
tions and fears more central to their hearts than any sense
of love and loyalty to me. I wanted to scream when I
thought about their refusal to engage me, to completely
ignore the very thing that had been one of the most desperate and impactful experiences of my life.

I guess, in no shortage of ways, I had been searching for a sense of belonging all my life. Somehow all of
that changed when I met Parks. He gave me a place to
belong. He took the time to know me, to hear the things
that everyone else had ignored or tried so desperately to
avoid. For the first time in my life I was at home...I was at
home with Parks. I finally belonged. Parks spent all the
years we knew each other reassuring me of that.

After leaving Ocracoke, that sense of belonging was
enhanced in Seattle. The urban setting came to be my element. Parks and I built a life in Seattle, a life of laughter
and friendship. A life of working and playing. A life of
commitment in difficult seasons.

However, here on this small island sticking out into the
Atlantic, this hamlet five or six hours removed from the
closest real metropolitan environment in the state, I felt
like a spectacle. I didn't belong here, not anymore. I realized that as we crossed the Beaufort Bridge on our way
east, and it was confirmed by the slight sense of nauseous
dread I felt while sitting on the break water at Cedar
Island. Slowly one fearful question made its way center
stage: What am I doing here?

In Seattle, I was Holden. Nobody seemed to care
about my sexual orientation. I was just another person
on the street. But here? Here I am a disdained novelty,
like a freak show in a circus. Here I am a "faggot" with

250

AIDS, who "has done this to himself". But as painful as this current reality is, the fact remains that I had nowhere else to go. It was too late to move back to Seattle, and my complete exhaustion from the trip betrayed a fact I tried to keep hidden, even from myself; my health is steadily deteriorating.

Growing up, I heard it said that there are things worse than death. In those moments on the Cedar Island ferry, making my final voyage to Ocracoke, I knew I had discovered the essence of that statement. The foreboding sense of being the object of active scorn and disgust made my chest tighten, leaving me to question the wisdom of my choice to return. The piercing glances from island boys working on the ferry were ominous foreshadowing of what lie ahead.

I didn't want to hurt Robert and Emilis, or Jane Anne. I wanted them with me, but not here. I wanted mama and John with me too, but, then, I was so pissed at them that I didn't want them within five hundred yards of me. I wanted Parks. He was the only one who knew what I was going through, the only one that I could speak candidly with concerning my deepest pains and fears of my heart. But, Parks was gone. I was absolutely suffocating in a smoke screen of isolation.

Entry 50

For about the first week back on the island I spent most days in bed. I was depressed, I was filled with anxiety about being back, I was ashamed for anyone to see me in this emaciated state, and I was mourning the life that I had left behind some three thousand miles away, as well as the life I once had known here.

It was about the fourth day of solitude when Jane Anne peeped her head inside of my bedroom door. She was getting ready to head back to Davis and wanted to say goodbye.

"Holden, what's going on?" she asked.

"I'm just tired...still worn out from the trip and all."

She simply shook her head in disagreement with a gentle smile on her face.

"That's not all of it. Is it?"

"No." I replied, my solitude exposed for what it was.

"Holden, I knew it was going to be hard for you to come back here."

"I feel like I'm smothering."

"You feel like you did before you moved the first time, don't you?"

"Exactly. Jane Anne, that's exactly how I feel and you're the first one who has gotten it."

"Except, this time you don't have Parks to share the pain." She continued, "Am I right?"

I felt my face get hot and my eyes well.

"Holden, I want you to know that you can talk with me about anything...anything. I'm not going to judge you or get defensive. I just love you."

"Thank you, Jane Anne."

"But you know what else?"

"What?" I replied.

"I've got a sister and brother-in-law downstairs that feel the same way as I do, and just want to love and be there for you.

I sat in silence.

"So, will you do me a favor?"

"What's that?" I asked.

"Don't block out the very ones who could be your biggest support."

With that, she rose from her seat beside my bed, kissed me on the forehead gently and pulled the door to behind her. She had brought to light what I had been hiding inside, and in a timely way helped me realize how I was hurting those I loved, and ultimately myself.

Entry 51

Today I felt much stronger than I have since returning to the island. Getting out of my room and actually sharing space with Robert and Emilis has helped to lift some of the depression, getting me out of my own head. One would think that after years of battling bouts of depression, I would become better at recognizing the things I'm doing that are unproductive. But to anyone who has been there, to anyone who has wrestled with overwhelming clouds of dysthymia, recognizing one's current situation and then actually doing something about it can often take more energy than we have.

In these moments, it's often the voices of those who love us most, who speak much needed truth into our lives...when they are secure enough to do so. Whether it was an Anglican priest in the pre-dawn hours of a lonely Christmas morning, Jane Anne seated on the edge of my bed, or letters from Ocracoke every Thursday afternoon, truth came to me in gentle showers when I was too conflicted to find it on my own. I think that's part of the beauty in how God works, how He will use others in our lives to help us see things more clearly and to get us onto the right path.

Jane Anne's words had shaken me from my isolated torment and given me the presence of mind to recognize that this monkey on my back, called depression, was pushing me to withdraw from the very thing I've needed most, engagement with people who loved and cared for me. And so, within a matter of weeks I've traded the private hell of my room for glasses of sweet tea on the front porch, Lawrence Welk on Saturday evenings, and meal time laughter with Jane Anne across the mahogany table in Emilis' dining room. All of these things have proven powerful doses of medication to lift my broken spirit.

For the past several weeks, the only times of intentional isolation have been my early morning retreats onto the front porch for devotions from the Book of Common

253

Prayer, given to me by Rector Shannon before leaving Seattle. That book has been a great blessing. The faith tradition I grew up in had no respect for written prayers or liturgy, actually, it openly berated them. However, for me, amidst deep grappling with my faith and an all too familiar sense of drowning in my own thoughts, the form and ancient rhythms bring me comfort. The written prayers give me words which I can pray from the depths of my soul, even when my own words fail me.

The past couple of weeks have had their moments. Last week my night sweats were almost unbearable. In some ways I wish I didn't know what was coming. Nevertheless, I would not trade my time caring for Parks for anything.

I wonder if elderly people resist being enrolled in nursing facilities with such vehemence because they fear being robbed of their dignity. I know that fear. I saw it often in Parks' eyes as the disease began to take its toll. I will never forget the look of fright and desperation in his eyes as his system began the painful downward spiral and he began losing control of his bodily functions. For a man in his mid-twenties this was even more difficult. I remember how he lay there and cried as I cleaned and powdered him following bouts of horrible diarrhea, looking at me through tears, apologizing for making a mess.

"You have nothing to apologize for, Buddy." I said, trying to keep from breaking down myself. There are such heightened emotions, frustrations, heartbreak, and exhaustion encompassing such devotion, an unspoken toll upon the care giver.

"I'm glad it's you, Holden." He replied in a whispered, wounded tenor.

"Parks, I'm right here. I'm not going anywhere."

"Please, don't." He said as he erupted in tears, "Please, don't leave me, Holden. I'm so scared."

Here again, the one who had been the bastion of strength and steadfastness, my own place of solace and protection,

254

reduced to tears in my arms. I realized that now it was
my turn. It was time for the man in me to rise up and
soothe the frightened little boy in Parks.

"I'm going to take care of you, Parks."

I made that promise in a moment when those words were
needed, needed to be said and needed to be heard. I
knew it wouldn't be easy, but it was required. No matter
how much a part of me wanted to run away and hide, to
wake up from this nightmare, I was never going to leave
Parks' side, especially now that he needed me so desperately.

"You always were the stronger one." He said.

"Me?" I protested.

"Yes, you." He replied. "You could never see it, but I
always could."

After a few moments of silence he looked me in the eyes,
tears now subsided, breathing now rested, voice calm:

"Holden, please take care of me. I don't trust anyone
else. I'd be ashamed for anyone else to see me like this."

"Don't give that another thought." I said. "I'll never leave
your side."

I remember smiling. That was it. It was never a question
from that point. Even when he was in the hospital, aside
from injections and other treatments I wasn't qualified to
administer, I took care of him. I fed him, when he was
able to eat. I bathed and shaved him. I changed his bed
linens every morning, and any time in between when
needed. I kept him turned so that he wouldn't get bed
sores. I cut his hair and kept his nails trimmed. I cleaned
him when his bowels broke down and wiped him with
cool, damp cloths when night sweats were at their peak.
I didn't want anyone touching him that didn't care
for him. I didn't want an ill-tempered nurse, who was
disgusted and inconvenienced by his soiled linens, to lay
a hand on him. And so, I stayed with him around the
clock.

  I have no regrets for that and would have had it no

other way. But now, faced with the same condition, I am soberly aware of what's taking place in my body. I know the high of energy and health I am feeling today will likely be followed by another ebb. But today things were good, and I used the opportunity to fulfill an obligation long postponed.

In the final days before Parks slipped from consciousness he had given me some instructions, necessary but hard to hear. There in Harborview, looking up into the night sky from his window-side seat, he told me he wanted to be cremated when the time came, and how he wanted me to take him back to Ocracoke, to our old surfing spot, and dust his ashes on the swells. This morning when I woke, I knew it was the day.

I had already spoken with Robert and Emilis about his wish. My strength, even though today was good, was still too depleted to handle this alone. As much as I wanted to lie on my board and paddle out through the breakers one last time, wishes and reality were at an impasse and I needed help in fulfilling this last request.

After eating an early lunch, the four of us boarded the Miss Emilis and made our way out of Silver Lake, through the inlet, north along the beach toward Hatteras, as seagulls sang their melancholic arias. Robert had gone out that morning and placed one of his large orange buoys atop the dunes nearest mile marker 78, helping to ensure that we laid Parks to rest in the exact spot he had requested. Eventually, we saw the orange dot on the shoreline and dropped anchor several hundred yards offshore.

The water was still warm from the summer sun, though autumn was quickly approaching. Robert helped me into the skiff we had towed behind the trawler, and we made our way closer to shore. As we got just outside of the breakers, Robert dropped anchor and stripped down to the board shorts he had worn beneath his khakis and oxford cloth shirt.

256

"You just let me know when you're ready, Holden."

I sat on the bow of the skiff for a few moments in silence as Robert sat on the edge of the stern giving me the privacy I needed, his back towards me, his feet in the water. It was good that we were doing this, but it held a sense of finality even the memorial service had failed to achieve. Following the service, I still had this urn, I had Parks with me no matter how morbid that may seem. Today I was letting go, no longer would I have a tangible part of him to hold onto, from today it would be only memories.

When I was ready, Robert helped me into the water and then onto Parks' longboard, which Robert had loaded into the skiff before we left the dock. It took all my strength to stay balanced on the board while holding onto the urn. Robert held the nose of the board with one hand and paddled with the other, pulling me in closer to the breakers.

"You tell me when." He said.

"This is good." I instructed, as we arrived at the spot where Parks and I used to sit on late summer evenings, bobbing in the swells so many years ago. My mind traveled back to that place, to those young energetic young men in the prime of life. So much living and dying had happened in the interim, so many tides had come and gone.

Robert swam a few yards away and left me to my task, keeping a close watch. I laid there on Parks' board, the salt water gently lapping onto the red fiberglass surface, mingling with the saline of my own tears. Today, I said my final goodbyes. Once I mustered the courage and strength, I sprinkled those precious ashes onto the sea's surface. With my mission complete, I laid my head face-down on the fiberglass and wept.

We quietly made our way back to the trawler and the warm blankets Emilis had awaiting us. We sat anchored in silence, the only appropriate response in such an hour.

257

After I gave the okay, Robert fired the engines and began steaming back down the beach towards Silver Lake.

As hard as this day has been, I feel at peace. Parks' wishes are finally honored, and with that I am pleased. There are so many questions to which I will never have answers, but for today I take joy in knowing that my life experienced a depth of friendship that few ever realize.

Entry 52

This morning I sat out on the front porch and got to thinking about Robert and how he pulled me on that surfboard yesterday, about all he did to help me honor Parks' last wishes. I fear I've taken him for granted through the years. I have always been much more comfortable with women. My earliest interactions with my father had proven men fearful, unsafe, and untrustworthy. Middle school locker rooms and high school gyms only served to reinforce my perception, and so I kept a safe distance from many of them. But there was something different about Robert.

With all of his brawn and ease in associating with the masculine fraternity, from which I often felt so ostracized, he was also such a good and gentle soul. In the early days he was a mentor of sorts, taking me under his wing and treating me like a son, a gift for which I may never be able to adequately express my gratitude. Nevertheless, it's the way he treated me after I disappointed him that had the greatest impact.

Although I always knew that Robert didn't approve of my choices, he never abandoned me and he never gave up on loving me. Through some heart to heart conversations with Jane Anne since moving back to the island, I've realized just what a price he paid in this community to love and stand by me through the years.

As I look back, it has been his expressions of commitment and love which have helped me believe the possibility that my Heavenly Father hasn't discarded me either.

I've done a lot of reading over the last several weeks, about all I have the energy for anymore. In one of Emilis' books I found a poem which I have come to love by Edgar Guest, summing up the way I feel about the love Robert Guthrie has extended:

"I'd rather see a sermon
than hear one any day;
I'd rather one should walk with me
than merely tell the way.
The eye's a better pupil
and more willing than the ear,
Fine counsel is confusing,
but example's always clear;
And the best of all preachers
are the men who live their creeds,
For to see good put in action
is what everybody needs.
I soon can learn to do it
if you'll let me see it done;
I can watch your hands in action,
but your tongue too fast may run.
And the lecture you deliver
may be very wise and true,
But I'd rather get my lessons
by observing what you do;
For I might misunderstand you
and the high advice you give,
But there's no misunderstanding
how you act and how you live."

Robert has been a living sermon on the steadfast love of God, a sermon that watered a long neglected faith, bringing it to growth again, inspiring it to stretch its wearied and withered leaves once more toward the Light. And today, much like Parks did years before on his bed at Harborview, I humbly called upon Christ, the Savior I

259

had known in the innocence of my childhood, the Savior of lost causes, asking for absolution, for remission, for the consolation of His Holy Spirit, and for His arms to hold me once again as I cry out for His love.

Entry 53

Although these months have seen increased engagement with Robert and Emilis, I still do not venture away from the house much. I tried in the beginning, taking evening walks around Silver Lake, but after Robert and Emilis received several calls in fear that I would "infect the community", I decided it best to just stay at home. The only exception being when Caryn comes to visit.

When everything hit the fan on Ocracoke I knew it was only a matter of time before the news crept upstate. People have always said that I was wise beyond my years, and I had already come to learn that friendships have varying degrees of depth and longevity. Of the probably fifty people who were closest to me through high school and college, there were only a handful of people who were of the quality and consequence warranting a personal disclosure from me. Coming out to them was a fearful proposition, wondering how they would take it, how I would phrase my disclosure, pondering the method and message of such colossal news, wondering how I would handle their reaction if it wasn't positive.

Caryn had been my closest friend for as long as I could remember. We had weathered many storms together through the years, supporting each other through the difficult seasons of life. Nevertheless, I had been unable to share this part of my life with her. Looking back on it, I think it's because I was never able to admit it to myself.

In the weeks following my discharge from the psychiatric unit, I called Caryn and broke the news. Though she had concerns, in the end she would stand by and love me in ways that few others have. Not only could I count on her to sit with me in the hard, tearful, anxiety-laden moments of life; but, I also knew she would fight for me. I smile even now as I think of her and her willingness to lay into anyone brazen enough to make a derogatory statement about me in her presence. That type of friendship doesn't come along every day and I am thankful to GOD to have enjoyed it for so many years.

Since I moved back here, she catches the ferry over at least twice a month for a weekend visit. On good days she'll help me into her car, open the sunroof, and head north on 12 to catch the Hatteras ferry. On those rides we share the type of fellowship known only to the most kindred of hearts, being completely comfortable to talk about anything, including the hard stuff, especially the hard stuff, the stuff I don't even feel comfortable telling Robert and Emilis. But some days we just ride in silence as the salt air fills the quiet car. Sometimes I think it's the friendships which are comfortable in the silence, the ones fluent in the unspoken language of complex emotions, that are rooted deepest in the soil of our hearts.

On days when I can't make it out of bed, she pulls up a chair, talks with me, reads to me, jokes with me, or brushes my hair. It is hard to think about leaving her, saying goodbye to the Hatteras excursions, the cups of coffee, and the sappy love stories we both enjoy watching. I realize that it is the imminence of my departure which leads her to the island so frequently, though tired from her own week's work. It is this same somber realization that makes each parting embrace on Sunday afternoons so difficult, understanding that each one may be our last.

Entry 54

Today I'm just so angry at my family. For so long I have tried to give them the benefit of the doubt, tried to be understanding regarding the duress they have experienced as a result of my sexuality. I have made excuses for them, shunned my own hurt, and not allowed myself to be overcome with feelings and thoughts that I deemed sinful or disrespectful towards my mother and brother. But today I'm tired of making excuses, tired of denying the fact that their silence, their unwillingness to engage me, and their refusal to get to know me as it pertains to this huge part of my experience and life has gouged at my heart.

I just do not understand how you can shun or shut out your own flesh and blood as they have done. I was the dutiful son. I was the one who always tried to take care of everyone's emotions in the house. I was the one who sought to console, to be the peace keeper, the mediator. It was my gentle and sensitive nature that took the greatest hits when angry words were spewed across the family table. I was the one who tried to care for mother in her loneliness. And now, when it comes to me actually having a problem of my own, there's no support available to me. There's absolutely no expressed interest in how I'm doing, or how I'm feeling. There's seemingly no concern for what it's like to be me, for what it's like to be a gay man living with AIDS in a time when the greatest response from society is fear and scorn.

I just can't get my mind around how someone could carry a child in their body for nine months, raise that child, watch that child suffer, watch that child hurt, watch that child try desperately to fit into the mold of his older brother and all the other guys around, watch him try unsuccessfully time after time to make relationships work with members of the opposite sex, watch him tormented by bouts of deep depression and isolation, and never seek to understand why. Worse yet, upon learning why, to turn your back, to refuse to engage, to refuse to discuss it, to refuse to love.

It makes me so angry. All of the love and nurture for members of her Church, all the Christmases and Birthdays spent reveling in John and his perfect little American Dream, while the queer son was banished to the island of misfit toys. In all the gift giving and cookie baking and

262

Christmas caroling, were there not five minutes for the little boy who once was your pride and joy. But I guess the shame I brought because of this struggle, that you have never sought to understand, was greater than any love you could muster for me. The scorn of society was too much a preoccupation for you to even realize that the child you once rocked to sleep is now excluded in a world as cold as ice crusted steel. How can you close off your heart so completely?

And it has been so long now, and so much hurt has occurred, that I don't think I could even begin to dialogue with mama, even if she wanted to, even if she began to open that door of discussion. Her denial of me, her exclusion of me and deep parts of my personhood, her refusal to get to know and understand me has left a jaded heart that on one front yearns for her understanding, and on the other could care less if she ever gives it. So much time has passed, so much hurting and crying in isola- tion, that I don't know how I would even begin to discuss things with her at this point.

Even now, after knowing of my diagnosis for months, she has not once tried to contact me. No card, no phone call, just cold, hammered silence. John has eclipsed me from his mind, or so one would think. I just can't under- stand that. Damn, I'm angry! How could they do this to me? How could they act like I don't belong to them, like they don't belong to me? How could they wall up their hearts, their emotions, their affections and leave me out in the cold to die alone?

A therapist once told me that the most intense anger is, at best, a thin veneer covering deep hurt. I guess she's right. I just can't believe that you can turn your back on your own flesh and blood, regardless of what they have done or been, regardless of how much of an embarrass- ment they have been to you. If I were a parent with a child who was dying of a terminal illness, I wouldn't let anything keep me from them...but not my family. They

263

go on with their Fourth of July picnics and Sunday dinners, their Labor Day cookouts and birthday cakes, as
if I had never been one of their number. Disowned,
discarded, abandoned by the very ones who should be my
sturdiest earthly refuge. And at this moment all I really
want to ask them is how they could hate me so deeply?

Entry 55

The return to Ocracoke has really been eye-opening
for me. Some of the ones who I would have thought
would be the first to visit me have never showed their
faces. Meanwhile, some of those who I thought would
treat me with contempt have been the very ones bringing
me pies or fresh fish they had caught, sending me cards,
or calling me on the phone to see how I was feeling.

I've definitely learned a lot about humanity, and my
misplaced judgments of others. I was so wounded by
some in the Church that I had closed my heart off to the
entire community of faith for so long, throwing out the
baby with the bathwater so to speak. But after returning
to Ocracoke I have come to see things differently. I've
realized that people are pretty much people. Some of the
most wonderful people I have ever known profess another
faith, or no faith at all. And yes, some of the most hateful
persons I have known are in Church every time the doors
are opened. But the Church is also full of some of the
best people anywhere on this earth, people who genuinely
love Christ and love their fellow man. I would be just as
wrong in judging all non-believers as horrible people as
I would in judging the bulk of my fellow Christians to be
hypocrites. In the end, I've come to see that we really are
all just people, and we all stand in great need of God's
grace, forbearance, and forgiveness. This doesn't excuse
hypocrisy or mean spiritedness, but it does put things into
perspective.

I've come to see that the most beautiful, the most
wonderful thing on earth, is love. It can alleviate fear,

264

chase away loneliness, remedy hopelessness, and soothe
the deepest tears. And although there are many types
of love, it's the type which lays down its life, its pride, its
right to be right for another that is the most Heavenly, the
hardest to give, and the most precious to receive.

Entry 56

I've started taking a new type of medication which
has been making me nauseous. To make it even worse,
I've been wrestling with the depression that comes from
being trapped in a body that is quitting on me. The rose
colored glasses are long gone. I know I am dying, and I
feel in my heart that it won't be very long now. It's hard
to describe, other than to say I have some sense of inner
knowing.

That being said, my stamina is greatly depleted. I can
hardly make it around the house on my walker without
having to stop to catch my breath. My appetite is almost
gone, but I force myself to eat in order to keep as much
strength as possible. The diarrhea is bad at times, and at
times I am so weak I don't manage to get to the bathroom
in time. I don't know if there's anything more humiliat-
ing than being a 29 year old man and having to rely on
Robert to clean me after such an episode. Now I understand more fully Parks' plea in those final weeks.

I'm so tired, so weak, so frail. Sometimes I catch a
glimpse of myself in the mirror and I can hardly believe
it's me. Where once was muscle is now a gaunt reminder
of how sick I really am.

Recently, I've been able to see the weight of my
deterioration in Robert and Emilis' faces; the concern is
evident in their eyes. Though they constantly try to carry
on as if things were normal, I can see them beginning to
weary under the pain. I see valleys of heartache etched
in lines on their aging brows. Nevertheless, last Thursday
night held a momentary sabbatical from the pain.

I was feeling particularly strong that evening, a stubborn surge of obstinance rising inside of me. I don't know where it came from, but all of a sudden the thought leaped from my mouth with a surprising air of determination.

"I want to dance." I blurted out, disrupting Emilis from her crossword puzzle and Robert from his weekly appointment with Top Cops on CBS.

Emilis looked up over her crossword puzzle book, from her lounged position on the sofa, as Robert shoved in the foot rest of the recliner, sitting upright to look at me.

"Dance?" Emilis replied.

"Yes, I want to shag again, like Jane Anne and I did that night at the wedding."

They just looked at one another in silent contemplation of my request.

"Do you think you're up to it? Do you think that..."

"I want to dance, just one more time." I said, interrupting Robert firmly and letting them know I would not be deterred.

I began to pull myself up onto my walker. Robert and Emilis sat frozen, trying to determine how in the world to fulfill this request. I leaned heavy upon the metal frame, trying my best to get my feet working like they once had in a not so distant age of youthful exuberance. My stance was feeble but I could still shuffle a little.

I tried turning loose of the walker to stand upright of my own volition, only to be met with the painful reality that my legs are no longer strong enough to support my weight. I am just too shaky. I tried to brace my falling body on the walker as Robert jumped up frantically to try and catch me. My moment of bravery and excitement passed as quickly as it had erupted, and I sat back in my chair, broken down by another reminder that this disease has robbed me of my life long before it has robbed me of my heartbeat. I buried my head in my hands and wept, my audible sobs interspersed with angry protests.

"This isn't fair! It just isn't fair!" I said angrily as Robert and Emilis looked on in silence. "I don't want to die; I'm too young...I'm scared." I said, settling back into the dialect of heartbreak. "I'm just so scared."

Robert and Emilis made their way over to me, offering the support of their presence; but, I was too broken to be consoled. They sat with me until the weeping slowly subsided, like a summer rain squall passing over the island and into the sea. In time I lifted up my head, the remnants of my soulful torrents fresh on my face.

Emilis reached up to wipe the tears from my cheeks in her gentle way. Unlike so many others, the entire time I've been sick she has refused to wear gloves as she touches me, and the feeling of her skin against mine, the fact that her love for me is even greater than her fear of contamination, touches my heart in ways inexpressible. In these moments I feel I catch a glimpse of what the leper felt in the eighth chapter of Matthew, when Jesus actually touched him before speaking forth his healing.

That night she looked me dead in the eyes, her deep blue eyes full of such strength that I felt her uninterrupted stare a channel of empowerment, steadying me, grounding me back into a place of stability.

"If you want to shag, my precious boy, then we're going to shag." she said, her gaze still fixed upon the windows of my soul as she remained at her post, knelt down on the hardwood at my feet. She turned her face up toward Robert, who was sitting on the arm of my chair, his hand upon my shoulder.

"Robert," she ordered in a soft, determined fashion, "Go put on my James Taylor record." As he rose, making his way to the chest record player which had sounded the Carpenter's Christmas Album so many years ago during my first island Christmas, she shifted her gaze back into my eyes and lifted both her hands, placing her palms on either side of my face. Gently rubbing my cheeks with her thumbs, she said:

267

J.M. Styron

"We're going to get through this, Holden...together."

With a gentle nod of the head and a quick wink of her left eye, she patted me on the leg and slowly pulled herself to her feet, a sign that the years were beginning to exact a toll from my heroin. She told me she would be right back and disappeared into the kitchen, while the sweet tones of James Taylor began filling the room. In the background I heard Emilis pulling out kitchen drawers and pushing them shut again. She reemerged with a bolt of her red satin Christmas ribbon and a pair of scissors.

"I've got an idea." She said.

In a matter of minutes I was standing with my feet on top of Robert's, our feet and legs bound to one another with satin ribbon, his torso flush against my back as he wrapped his strong right arm around my mid-section and placed his large, salt weathered left hand gently upon my chest to support me.

"Have you got him?" Emilis asked Robert, as she stepped back from tying the last ribbon on our legs.

"You better believe it!" He replied in his thick brogue.

With that, Emilis went over to the record player and picked up the needle, placing it on the track she had in mind. Momentary silence, touched only with the fuzzy sound of the needle dragging upon the vinyl, was quickly followed by the familiar piano licks of James Taylor's How Sweet It Is. Emilis shuffled and side-stepped her way across the living room floor to Robert and me, reaching out for my hands. I could feel her topaz ring against my palm.

For the ensuing four minutes we laughed more than we had in months, our spirits made lighter with every shuffled step and tambourine beat. It was as if for that suspended moment we forgot every burden and every care that weighed us down, the three of us dancing in stubborn defiance against all the sand spurs of life. We were dancing above the terminality, above the stress, above the gossip, above the mounding medical bills, and

268

the betrayals. We danced above those who had washed their hands of us, above the realization that I would soon say goodbye to the best sense of family I had ever known, above the imminent goodbye to their second son. We danced above it all with sheer joy on our faces. It was one of those precipice moments in life, and I am so thankful to have had the experience.

At the conclusion of the song Emilis and Robert sandwiched me in their embrace, each of us a bit winded following our four minutes of glory. Within seconds the needle drug on to the next song and the sweet, melancholic tones of Sweet Baby James filled the room once more, singing his ode to our home state. Slowly and quietly our bodies began a seamless and natural undulation while James sang of geese and omens. There I was, enveloped in the arms of two people who had consistently shown me a living picture of the love of GOD, a love which never gives up, never gives in, never stops, that never throws you away. Tears rolled down our cheeks without making a sound as the three of us swayed slowly from side to side. We were all aware of a most painful truth, this was my swan song.

Whatever had been or was to be, this was my family, this was my home, and somehow in times like these, those two things, apart from faith in Christ, are the only things that really matter. As we held onto each other, silent tears spoke a language of their own. We were silently saying our goodbyes.

Entry 57

I haven't written in a few weeks. I've been feeling poorly and haven't had the energy to do much of anything. Today, I miss Parks so desperately. For the weeks and months after his death, grief would come in waves, washing over me without a moments warning. All it would take would be a scent, a sound, a memory, any cue reminding me of him. As time passed those waves moved a little farther apart, occurring monthly, rather than daily as in the very beginning.

Today Caryn came over to the island to spend the weekend. I'm not sure how many more trips up the beach I have left, so I wanted to take advantage of the level of strength I felt today, to ride up to the north end and hopefully see some geese in the pond near the ferry terminal.

The autumn chill was thick today, sweater weather. Shells crunched under Caryn's tires as she backed out of the drive, onto the path leading towards the main road. I think we are both aware that our last ride may be sooner than we care to admit. We sat in silence as she drove, the top forty station providing a slight reprieve in the doleful quiet of the moment, which sat upon us like a heavy patchwork quilt. Heading north from the village, across Molasses Creek towards Hatteras, I shifted my attention to passing glimpses of ocean waves through breaks in the dune wall.

As we neared the old surfing spot, I lost my breath as my eye caught a glimpse of a ghost of sorts. The vision which lay just ahead on the edge of the sand dusted highway gave me cold chills throughout my entire body and a knot in the pit of my stomach. For a moment I was uncertain as to whether I would throw up or cry. The force of the moment left my mind reeling, uncertain if this entire experience were some form of disoriented dream. "Stop the car!" I demanded.

"What is it, are you sick?" Caryn replied in an alarmed, confused manner.

"Just stop the car, pull over right here."

She eased off of the pavement onto the shoulder and I made my way out of the passenger seat in as independent a manner as I could muster. By the time I had pulled myself to my feet, holding onto the car door, Caryn was there to help support my weight as I moved forward, silent, undeterred.

270

My hands shook as my fingers traced the names of Carter and Mondale on a bumper sticker clad tailgate. I knew this little red pickup. Though the years had faded the paint and salt had eaten away at the bumper, it was the same little Toyota that sat outside Robert's fish house so many years ago, waiting to take me on my first surfing trip.

I slowly moved towards the driver's side to the small cab, the window open, key still in the ignition. I opened the door as Caryn began to protest in discomfort. I paid her no mind.

I sat in the driver's seat, caught up in this surreal event. The UNC student parking sticker on the top corner of the windshield, the crack in the passenger side of the dash...this was all too much. As I grasped the wheel firmly in my hands, one of those waves of grief came crashing in upon me. Closing my eyes, I could see him again...like he was in those early days. I remembered his golden tan, his long blonde hair damp with seawater, his smell, my mind transporting me back to the days of our first summer.

The moment was interrupted abruptly by the sound of a young man's voice.
"Hey, what the hell are you doing? Get out of my truck!" Jordan came over the dune line from surfing to find a stranger sitting inside his vehicle.
"What do you think you're doing?" He protested angrily as he rounded the driver's side.

Nearing the opened door, he recognized the culprit. Though the winds of time and circumstance had no doubt taken their toll, as he looked into my eyes he remembered. Suddenly, I wasn't the only one facing a ghost.
"Holden?" He said in astonishment.
I couldn't speak.

Jordan was Parks' younger cousin. When we left for the west coast, Jordan was in high school. Parks had been his hero growing up. The one who taught him to play soccer, the one who taught him to surf. Parks had filled a crucial role in Jordan's life. One of the hardest things for Parks to deal with, concerning the way our news got out, was the impact it had upon Jordan. There's nothing quite as devastating to a young heart as the fall of a hero.

Parks went to see Jordan in the weeks after we were outed on the island, trying to console him, to be present to answer any questions he may have, but Jordan's parents wouldn't allow Parks to see him. Parks carried an enormous sense of guilt for the way Jordan was hurt in the aftermath, but there are some things you just can't do anything about, things that you just have to leave to God and time to resolve. On Jordan's sixteenth birthday, Parks had written him a long letter seeking to explain all the whys and hows, as best he could. He let me read it before sending it east. Inside the letter Parks enclosed the key and title of the little red pickup, which had been sitting in his grandmother's driveway since our exodus from Ocracoke.

Jordan and the rest of his family lived in Hatteras, and so I hadn't seen him or Parks' vehicle since my return to the island. But today I ran headlong into one of the most tangible memories I had of Parks. I cannot count the times I heard that horn blow from the driveway of the little cottage, or how many times I had followed it home from an afternoon of surfing.

Jordan didn't have much to say. I'm sure seeing me brought up a host of memories and emotions for him. We were all silent as I climbed feebly from the driver's seat, Caryn struggling to help support my weight as Jordan stood motionless with his hand atop the opened door.

He never replied to Parks' letter, eliciting a patch of sadness in Parks' heart which he took to his grave. As we approached the rear of the pickup, I turned back to look at him, still standing by the opened door. I didn't want to open an old wound, but as I watched him words flowed without hesitation.

"Jordan, your cousin was the best man I ever knew, and he loved you until his last breath."

Then, I turned to make my way, with Caryn's help, back to the passenger seat of her Honda. In that moment I felt I had done Parks an honor, I had helped vindicate his name to the cousin he loved like a little brother. Jordan now knew that his hero never stopped loving him. Whatever messages had been spoken around him concerning Parks would now have to collide with mine, now he would be left to wrestle with a different story.

I know that a relationship like mine and Parks' is disturbing to a great many people. In fact, I'm still wrestling with aspects of my faith regarding it. But love Parks, I did...more than any other person I have ever known.

Entry 58

Haven't written in a while. I've been so tired and really haven't wanted to. However, today was monumental. Today I was baptized in Silver Lake. All is well!

Entry 59

Not feeling well today at all. There's so much I want to say, to write down this morning, but I'm afraid I just don't have the energy. I've been having a hard time breathing over the last few days. My meds are making me really nauseous and I'm afraid I'm beginning with pneumonia.

Entry 60:

Lying in Greenville hospital. I fear I'm nearing the end and I'm scared. Jesus, I surrender to you!

Closure

In the weeks before Holden slipped into unconsciousness, Robert and I cared for him much as we had done for Robert Jr. in the final days before he left us. One day, while I was trimming his toenails and wiping his legs

273

down with lotion, he looked down at me from the head of
the bed where his frail and emaciated torso was propped
against pillows,
"Emilis, I'm sorry I'm sick." He whispered.
There was something so sad in those five words.   Hearing him say them broke my heart and I fought desperately
to choke back my tears. I tried to comfort him, to tell
him that I was the one who was sorry for all he had been
through; but, he continued undeterred.
"I'm real sorry for everything I've put y'all through."

   There were no tears, I don't think he even had the
strength to cry...just a frail and quiet request for absolution, one that wasn't needed, but which he obviously
wanted to offer. I feel guilty for even referring to Holden
in this way, but there is no other more accurate description of him in those last few weeks than to say that he was
pitiful. After he returned home to live with us I had gathered all the literature I could find on AIDS, which was
a precious little in those days in eastern North Carolina.
The public library didn't carry any books on it, as if to do
so would contaminate the whole building. Nonetheless,
what I did find did not prepare me for all that I would
witness first-hand as I cared for this precious young man,
day in and day out.

   I would make sure he had his medications and any
food or liquids he needed, although most days it was just
toast and ginger-ale, that's if he could hold those down.
I kept him groomed and rubbed his arms and legs down
every day with lotion. I had read somewhere about the
healing qualities of the human touch and decided this
could only help, especially since precious few people
would touch him after he contracted this panic shrouded
disease in the 1980's.

   Every afternoon Robert left the fish house early and
came home to be with Holden. This gave me time to
run any errands I needed to attend to on the island and
then cook supper. I've never been more proud of Robert

Guthrie than I was in those days when Holden returned home. Every afternoon Robert went up to Holden's room and helped him undress. Then, he would cover him in a bed sheet, pick him up and carry him downstairs to our bath, the only bathroom in the house which had an actual tub. He would get the water just the right temperature and bathe Holden while telling him about the day's events at the fish house, or about one of Joseph Wicker's newest tales. Many times Holden was so weak that he barely responded, aside from giving his gentle smile, or a faint whispered response. Robert was undaunted and kept right on talking, including Holden in the world from which fear, hatred, and the disease had isolated him. In the evenings Robert went up to Holden's room before bed and read to him from the Gospels, then he would talk some more.

He put on a good show of strength for Holden, but many were the evenings that Robert would sit on the edge of our bed and weep, his head buried in the strong, salt-weathered hands I had come to love so dearly. In those moments I watched Robert wade through a river of emotions. Some days he was broken and inconsolable, others he was angry, while others brought quiet contemplation.

Robert and I were getting ready to lose another son, and the pain of that realization was so heavy at times that it was all we could do to get out of bed in the morning. But we did get up, because we still had another day with him and were going to take full advantage of every moment. Our mourning would have to wait for another day.

It struck me, as I went back and read Holden's journal, that he had only devoted a couple of sentences to the day of his baptism. It breaks my heart to think that the pain of that morning was so deep that he chose not to recount it. But then, I can't say that I blame him. I am still grappling with some deeply lodged anger concerning some of that day's events myself.

One morning over breakfast Holden told Robert and

275

I that he wanted to be baptized. I thought for sure he already had been, but to my surprise that was not the case. Holden had told me of his salvation experience in adolescent years at a summer Vacation Bible School; however, he had never been baptized. With such a request upon our ears, Robert and I sought to make the necessary arrangements. Our first attempt was to contact my pastor. Holden had sustained so much hurt from some of the congregation at Grace Chapel, so many of those parishioners were adamantly opposed to his return to the island; and so we felt it best to seek another avenue. To our dismay, my pastor was in Durham doing a summer intensive at Duke and would not be back on the island for another two weeks. We discussed it with Holden, but he felt a sense of urgency, a sense that he might not be with us that much longer. He then asked that we contact the new pastor at Grace Chapel.

The current pastor had followed Holden in serving the church and was well aware of our situation, but Holden hoped compassion would prevail, as did we. At Holden's request, Robert made a phone call and left to meet the pastor at a home the Church was now renting on the island to serve as its parsonage. The pastor was agreeable but wished to baptize Holden at our house, in the bath tub, in order to prevent controversy over the use of the Church's baptismal pool. The main concern he voiced had to do with contaminating the pool and a fear of infecting others who would use it in the future. I was so indignant regarding that statement. It was Holden who calmed me down, assuring me that he would be fine with doing it this way. I realize now that, sadly, Holden's life had conditioned him for absorbing people's ignorance and fear. The baptism was set for eleven the next morning and I immediately phoned Jane Anne to tell her of the plans.

The next morning we got up and had breakfast together, awaiting Jane Anne's arrival on the first ferry.

It was a good day for Holden. The morning was warm with sunshine and he seemed to feel well, the best I had seen him in over a week.

In my home Church in Davis our custom was to be baptized in white robes, a symbol of purity and righteousness through Christ. Our entire family had been baptized this way when our time came to wade into the salty waters of Core Sound, following Christ in baptism. That morning at about half past nine, Jane Anne came through the front door with a white robe already starched and ironed.

"Where did you get that?" I asked.

"I got it from the Church, last night." She replied.

"Did they know what you were doing with it?" I asked, certain that they didn't. I had become jaded by the scorn and ostracization Robert and I suffered from so many since Holden left the island, and increasingly since his return.

"Of course they did." She replied, "I called the preacher and told him that I needed it, and why."

"Well, what did he say?" I pressed.

"He was thrilled." She replied, "By the time I got there to pick it up, he already had it starched and ironed."

I was humbled to the point of tears. Darts of hatred had pierced my skin and spirit over the past year to the point that I had begun assuming the worst of people. However, this one deed from the Davis Church gave me a spark of renewed hope in humanity.

"I'll go hang it in your room until time." She said. She made her way past me to the kitchen table where Robert and Holden were finishing their breakfast.

"Hey, my darlin'!" I heard her say as she walked over to Holden and gave him a kiss on the forehead.

"What's that?" He said.

"It's a robe for your baptism." She replied. Then she recounted the narrative of how our family had worn them for baptisms through the generations. "And you're family!" She affirmed.

"Thank you, Jane Anne." Holden said with a smile.

"The pastor sent this card for you too, buddy." Jane Anne said, handing Holden an envelope.

Holden opened the card and read it quietly, a gentle, warm smile appearing upon his face as he took in words from the Davis pastor. He then handed me the card with a look of peace and encouragement in his eyes which I hadn't seen much since his return to the island. I opened the card and found these works scribbled in black ink: "Holden, I just want you to know how proud I am of you and what God is doing in your life. I know that people can be very cruel, but you just rest in how good God loves you, cares for you, carries you, and keeps you. You just cling to the promise of Romans 10:8-13, come what may. Know that my wife and I love you, are praying for you, and are here for you should you ever need us.

-Pastor and Mrs. Elkhorn"

I had to excuse myself to the front porch. I sat in my rocker and cried as this one act of grace from my home Church invoked a disarming of my defenses. I carried such a burden through this entire experience. I had been accused of so many things that I had never done, never said, never known. I had watched as Robert's heart was broken, as the Church that he had loved and served since young adulthood not only turned its back, but aggressively attacked him, removing him from his leadership positions and all but taking his name off of the books. There were many people, once close acquaintances, who now shunned and ignored me when passing at the post office or in the general store. There were even the close, dear friends and Church circle members who refused to come to our house after Holden returned to the island. No longer were the women's circle parties and brunches hosted at my table. We had all become outcasts.

Through all of this, I had tried to maintain the grace my mother had instilled. I tried to keep my heart right, but my shoulders were weary and my spirit broken. I had seen the worst of people, in and out of the Church, since that infamous Spring day when the news of Holden's sexuality rushed through Ocracoke like a tidal surge.

But that starched robe, along with the words from Pastor Elkhorn, pulled the cap off of the well, and an artisan flood erupted. All of the pain I kept buried and hidden came to the surface and was purged. In a few moments Jane Anne slowly opened the screen door, stepping out onto the front porch and to my side. She knelt beside my rocker and wrapped her arms around me.

"Let it out, Sis!" She encouraged. "God is near to the broken hearted".

Jane Anne had been my sanity, my strength, my confidant, my sounding board during this whole ordeal. She knew my pain and shared the same unquenchable love for Holden that Robert and I held in our hearts. I have a shoe box full of cards she sent, each containing Scripture, like Psalm 51 and other words of comfort. She walked the road with us, and in times of testing those are the only people I really care to have around.

I continued my time of crying and ever so gently felt the dirt being cleansed, the pain being replaced with comfort only God can give. Henrik Ibsen, a Norwegian Poet, once said, "A thousand words will not leave so deep an impression as one deed." This line proved true to my experience on that autumn afternoon.

Pastor Elkhorn had extended a proverbial cup of cold water to a thirsty young man, the overflow of which had been used of God to wash my soul clean. Seeds of bitterness and caverns of pain were replaced with a peace which passes understanding. Jane Anne hadn't heard that they were going to baptize Holden in the bathtub. I knew this news would set her off like a nuclear missile, so I just let it lie for a while.

At about quarter of eleven we were all dressed and ready. Holden, clad in his baptismal gown, was sitting in

279

the wingback chair in the living room, 'the White House chair' as he always called it. Jane Anne was perched on the arm of the chair by Holden's side when the pastor from Grace Chapel pulled into the driveway. He made his way up the walk and to the front door. After entering he motioned for Robert to come to him. I could tell by the expression on his face that he was under some type of weight, some type of stress, and so I held my breath hoping for the best. Certainly not today, certainly not this precious boy's baptism, certainly we could have one day free of hatred and venom...these were my silent protests and prayers. It wasn't to be.

As it turns out, the pastor had made the mistake of disclosing the baptism to one of the members of the administrative council. This disclosure set into motion a grinding of the mill, culminating in an ultimatum, "Baptize him and you are done at this Church."
How could they? How could they be so cold as to deny Holden baptism? These questions filled my heart and mind with a sense of shocked disbelief, and still do. President Roosevelt once spoke of a moment of infamy, well this was ours. When I gathered enough of my own composure to be aware of what was taking place around me, I looked over at Holden, sitting there in his starched white robe. Where an hour before rested a countenance of hope, excitement, and peace, now sat shame and silent tears of sadness.

It was in the wake of this bombshell that I witnessed the greatest beauty I ever beheld. I watched as Robert stood in silence, his arms crossed, staring into Holden's face as the pastor made low, pleading apologies which were little more than white noise in the background of such a stinging disclosure. Robert never said a word. He simply raised his hand, placing it between his face and that of the pastor. His signal was unmistakable in the simplicity and seriousness of its message, a gesture that silenced the pastor and left the rest of us watching to see how he would respond.

Robert left the pastor standing in the foyer and made his way slowly, deliberately across the living room floor until he squatted down in front of his boy.
"Come here." Robert said, his eyes fixed upon Holden's tear stained face.
Holden slowly slid to the edge of his seat and Robert slipped one arm around Holden's back and the other beneath the bend of his knees. He then rose to his feet, holding our boy like a bridegroom carries a bride across the threshold.
"Jane Anne, get the door." Robert commanded, allowing no room for questions or hesitation.

With that, Robert made his way out of the living room, through the foyer, past the silenced pastor, out the front door, down the steps, beyond the picketed gate, and onto the drive leading towards the fish house and Silver Lake. Neither Jane Anne nor I spoke a word, we simply followed Robert, leaving the pastor alone in the house. He must have left at some point thereafter, because the house was empty when we returned. We haven't heard from him since.

All of that aside, I have never been more proud or more broken as I watched what unfolded between Robert and Holden, the two men I loved most in this world. They were bound by a love that went beyond anything suffering or ridicule could ever touch. Robert walked a good truck's length ahead of us, Holden's frail body in his arms, the hem of the gown occasionally catching the gentle breeze. We followed him in silence, down the road skirting the harbor, towards the entrance of the fish house.

Robert made his way to the cleared, sandy slip many of the fishermen used to launch their boats, wading unyieldingly into the warm late August waters of Silver Lake as the ferry made its way to the dock. There was such a sense of holiness and justice in this march that we

281

never stopped to worry about ruined shoes or clothing. The love of God was our anchor and inspiration that day, nothing else seemed to matter. Jane Anne and I followed until we were all standing together, the waters above Robert's waist.

There, beneath the Carolina sky, Robert baptized Holden in the name of the Father, and of the Son, and of the Holy Spirit. After a few moments of joyful tears and hearty embraces, we made our way back to shore. By the time we had finished, the fish house crew were congregated on the dock, watching in silence as we baptized our boy just yards from the ferry that had ushered him into our lives eight years prior. A sacrament had unfolded in the rippled reflections of the docks and boats, nautical trappings that had borne some of Holden's greatest memories in an age before life had reaped its toll, before his favor with the island had waned.

I know for a fact that most of those men had never seen him since the day the helicopter lifted him off to Greenville. Following that first shockwave of disclosure, and then later as news of Holden's diagnosis seeped through the island, the men of the fish house had kept their distance. Even those who dared to stop by the house after Holden's return home refused to come inside for fear of infection.

Nevertheless, here they were, face to face with a vision of Holden, the first in years. They had known a youthful, fun-loving, robust young man in the prime of his life. They had worked shoulder to shoulder with him on long-hauls in Pamlico Sound. They had stood chest deep beside him in the salty waters, pulling and tightening the nets. They had shoveled ice alongside him, into the hull of the Miss Emilis, on scorching summer days. Holden had laughed and bantered with them as they graded fish and headed shrimp beneath the tin roof of the fish house. They had known Holden in the springtime of his life, his gentle smile, his shy-laughter, the gleam in his eyes. But now they were seeing him near autumn's end, free-spirit-edness now replaced with the weight of mortality. Their mum gazes were a volumous disclosure of the upheaval taking place in their minds, minds that had long ago dismissed this young man with disgust and slanderous jokes.

It was a day of grappling between the long lodged hatred of Holden in their hearts, secured ever so indignantly by a label which erased his humanity in their eyes, and the almost palpable sense of pity etched upon the face of every man on those docks. The brine drenched white robe made painful revelation of the impact of the disease, of just how much Holden's health had deteriorated. His skin, once void of blemish, youthful, and beautifully tanned, was now marred with lesions. His once robust frame now revealed ribs, joints, and pelvic bones. But his spirit...his spirit....though burdened, it remained endearing.

I remember as we made our way past the docks where the men were standing, staring down upon the four of us, Holden asked Robert to take him up to them.

"I want to talk to Ryan." He said.

Though we didn't know what to expect, there comes a point when you do not argue with a dying man and his requests. The last words Holden shared with Ryan were on those very docks six years prior, the afternoon that Ryan helped to forever change the trajectory of Holden's life.

As we climbed the few steps from the sandy soil onto the docks, Robert called for Ryan to come to us. He slowly made his way from the assembly of his comrades to squarely face the scant frame of a young man who had lost so much following their last interaction. The interface was uncomfortable for all of us.

I have long believed that at the heart of every man is a certain level of goodness and compassion, products of the Imago Dei. Fallen as we may be, I have found that this goodness is there if we will take the time to look for it.

283

On this day, I didn't have to look long to observe it in the eyes of these salt hardened fishermen; and the pervasive sense of pity engulfing the crew had not eluded Ryan. I could only imagine that he may have been wrestling with a much deeper level of emotion, for his history with Holden had complexities unlike the other men.

"Ryan." Holden said, looking him in the eyes.

"Holden." Ryan replied, noticeably uncomfortable, uncertain as to how this interaction would play out.

"I want you to know that I forgive you." Holden said gently.

We were all silent until Holden spoke again.

"Robert," he continued, "I'm tired. Can we go home?" Turning to leave, I reached out and gently squeezed Ryan's arm, a humble gesture which I hoped would say, "Go in peace, all is well."

Tears began to flow down Ryan's weathered face as he bit his bottom lip in an obvious attempt to maintain his composure. We left in silence, walking back up the sand dusted road, beyond the lighthouse, back down the shell paved path of picket fences and fig trees.

   In all the many wonderful years that Robert Guthrie has been in my life, I have often been proud to call him my husband. I felt it as he launched the Miss Emilis from the railways, unveiling the name which he had kept a surprise until that moment. I felt it as I stood by him on the floor of the State House in Raleigh, witnessing his swearing in as a member of the legislature. I felt it as members of congress and governors would gather around our table, seeking Robert's help with a particular project or campaign. But all of those things dimmed to obscurity when compared to the sense of pride I felt watching him carry our boy from our living room, through an onslaught of scornful looks from neighbors and passers-by, and then baptizing him so tenderly in the salty waters upon which Robert had built his livelihood.

Life was pretty much our new normal for the next three months. There were the frequent visits of home health nurses Robert had hired to help keep close check on Holden's condition. Between the three of us, Robert, Jane Anne, and myself, we kept close by Holden. Robert spent his mornings conducting business at the fish house and his evenings with Holden, talking, joking, laughing, reading together, or, when Holden felt strong enough, taking well needed respites in the old four wheel drive truck on Ocracoke Beach, parking down by the inlet as the sea breeze blew through the cab.

An Anglican Priest named Shannon had been especially kind to Holden in his last months before leaving Seattle, and had given him a copy of the Book of Common Prayer with his name embossed on the front cover. It was a parting gift of Spiritual, eternal value which Holden cherished. He would rise every morning for morning prayers from this book, and once he was too weak to do much of anything for himself, he enlisted mine and Jane Anne's help in the Daily Office.

I had never experienced the Book of Common Prayer before, and I must admit, growing up in an evangelical tradition, I had little respect or use for written prayers. However, after those morning devotional times with Holden, it has become my own practice until this day. Though laughter and small talk were always a part of our home and interactions with one another, especially with Jane Anne now taking residence in our spare room to help care for Holden, his mind was now fixed on eternal things.

Holden especially loved one of the traditional collects: Of the Reign of Christ. This is the prayer he loved to end morning prayers with every day. Even in his lowest and most painful mornings, I can almost see that sweet, peaceful grin broaden across his face as he would close his eyes and take in the words that I prayerfully read at his request:

285

"Almighty and everlasting God, Whose will it is to restore all things in Thy well-beloved Son, the King of kings and Lord of lords: Mercifully grant that the peoples of the earth, divided and enslaved by sin, may be freed and brought together under His most gracious rule; Who liveth and reigneth with Thee and the Holy Spirit, one God, now and for ever. Amen."

I later sent a note to Priest Shannon, letting her know what an eternal, endearing gift the book had been and what an impact it had made upon our boy. I am so grateful to her for the love she extended to Holden at a very crucial time in his life, and am hoping that one day she will visit us on the island.

In early October Holden's health made a turn that we knew was coming, but hoped wouldn't. Within a week he was incoherent, comatose. It began with some belabored breathing, which was a tale-tell sign that he was developing pneumonia. His doctor had informed us that this was a likely possibility.

We wanted to make sure that he was getting everything he needed in those last days, so we had him taken to Pitt Memorial on the mainland. We kept vigil at his bedside around the clock. Even Robert never left the hospital during those last days, content to let the business fend for itself as more important matters took precedent.

Every morning we gathered around his bed for morning prayers and every day Robert massaged Holden's arms and legs with lotion, talking to him about his memories of growing up on Ocracoke, sharing funny stories and good memories of the years when they had worked together in the fish house. In those moments Robert reassured Holden of the love of God, and on several occasions he made tearful admissions of his own love for this second son.

Jane Anne read Scripture and, true to form, told Holden jokes just like he was understanding every word...and maybe he was. Whenever life got too serious, too hard, whenever the pain would get really bad while we were still at home on Ocracoke, Holden would look over at Jane Anne and make a standard request: "Tell me something funny." Jane Anne always rose to the occasion.

Even in the somber gloom of a hospice room, Jane Anne could still elicit laughter to the point of tears. Several times, every day, she would get up and grab her purse, stop by the foot of the bed, squeeze Holden's foot and say:

"Now, Holden, I'm goin' out to smoke. Don't you go anywhere while I'm gone or I'm gonna be pissed off." Then she would make her way out for about fifteen minutes. He never left us while she was out.

One day she was reprimanded for smoking in an "undesignated area". Even in the Tobacco State, the public tide was shifting against the use of the product, a fact that Robert gloated over and Jane Anne despised. I remember that evening well, as she came back to the room in a huff. "This state was built on tobacco money, now it's a four letter word." She protested. "I'd rather have prostitute tattooed across my forehead than light up a cigarette in public anymore."

I don't know how she could come up with this stuff so quickly, so off the cuff, but suffice it to say, Jane Anne had a gift of wit unparalleled by anyone I have ever known.

One evening she was by Holden's bedside telling him the story of an interaction she had with one of the parishioners at Grace Chapel. The lady had long been of compromised health, or at least she always complained of being so, and had asked Jane Anne to pray for her at some point during the years.

"Every time I would run into her when I was visiting the island, I would always say, 'Honey, I'm still praying for you.'"

"Well, Holden," she continued, "one day about a year

ago I saw her on the porch at Albert Styron's Store and I said to her 'Honey, I'm still praying for you.' And she lit into me."

"What did she say?" I interrupted, having ceased my crossword puzzle as I tuned in to Jane Anne's tale.

"She looked at me and said, just as curt as she could, 'You say that every time you see me and I'm still sick.'"

"Are you serious?" I interjected, "She really said that to you!"

Jane Anne looked at Holden, unconscious in his bed, "You know how she is, Holden."

"What did you say to her?" Robert inquired.

"I looked back at her and said, 'Well, you better be glad I was praying, you might have been dead by now."

Robert and I laughed until our ribs were sore. This wit was Jane Anne's trademark. Things can't always be heavy. We would never make it if they were. Thank God for people like Jane Anne who have the gift of making others laugh, helping to lift burdens, if ever so briefly.

On the morning of October 20th, Samuel arrived at the hospital. Robert had called in some favors and secured him leave so he could be with Holden in what we all knew would be the final days of his earthly life. He made it just in time.

Changes in Holden's condition through the night piqued the attention of his nurse and she called in his doctors well before sunrise. Samuel walked into the room to find the three of us standing around Holden's bed as his breathing became increasingly belabored. From the looks on our faces, I'm sure it was easy for Samuel to deduce that this was it.

Ever since Holden had returned home from Seattle, Samuel had become a frequent guest at our house. He and Holden were very different people, and having never met his family I couldn't ever quite say where the favor lie in their looks. Samuel was much larger in stature than Holden, his hair was lighter, and his way less affable;

288

however, one thing I always noticed was that they had the same eyes. There was the same type of light, the same twinkle. But this morning, the twinkle in Samuel's eyes quickly turned to sorrow.

We stood by as Samuel, in full uniform, crawled into bed next to his big brother. This strapping service man now reduced to sobs of grief. I worried how it may be affecting Holden, but a larger part of myself realized that this was needed.

There were no words for a long time. We stood silently around the bed and allowed Samuel the free expression of his grief. In time, Samuel began to talk. He told of bedtime stories read to him by Holden when their mother worked nightshift at the mill, of a time when Holden had sold some of his belongings so that Samuel would have shoes for basketball, of folded up fifty dollar bills slipped into his little brother's hand on every visit to Johnston County. Samuel told of Holden standing up to teachers and peers on his little brother's behalf, how he washed and ironed their clothes, and how he would cook their meals when their mother was too tired or too depressed to get out of bed. When Samuel was struggling in school, it had been Holden who tutored him and helped him with his lessons. It was so sweet to me, hearing these stories and watching Samuel hold his big brother's hand while he told them...both sweet and heartbreaking.

At half past eleven that morning, Holden's breathing became noticeably more shallow. I began to pray that God would take him quickly. I couldn't bear to hear him suffer and fight for every breath.
At seven minutes past twelve, Holden breathed his last.

With Holden's last breath taken, his mouth gaped open and life-less, all the strength we had been mustering over the past months left us. We all grieved and grieved deeply. He meant so many things to each of us, and the weight of that moment fell hard upon our shoulders. Once our crying ebbed, there seemed an indescribable

289

peace which filled the room that morning. It was like the serene quiet after a summer squall.

On October 20th, 1990, Holden laid down a life of pain for an eternity of grace and peace with God. God's loving and peaceful presence was so real to us in the room that morning, and ultimately, as with all who have come to Christ for His free gift of Salvation, Holden was received into love that none of us can completely fathom until our time comes to experience it. Nevertheless, it was a time of deep mourning as we said goodbye and returned to the island without him.

Two days later, Holden's body arrived on the afternoon ferry. I remember standing beneath the gnarled oaks of the Methodist Church, watching as they pulled the cherry casket from the back of the dark grey hearse. Though I had watched the entire process unfold, it still seemed surreal to be standing here watching this, to think of what that wooden box contained.

After the casket was put in place before the altar rail and the lid raised, the undertakers left us to ourselves in the piercing silence of the sanctuary. We each made our way to the edge of the casket, looking down into the lifeless face of one so young, two weeks shy of his thirtieth birthday. Robert took it hardest. He stood at the side of Holden's casket, his hands resting on its edge, staring down at Holden for the better part of an hour. There were ebbs and flows of silence and sobbing as Robert said goodbye.

As night fell upon the island, Robert let it be known that he was going to stay at the Church. It had long been customary on the outer banks to 'sit up with the dead', as we called it. I guess it started back when the body used to be brought to the family home the night before the funeral, and the casket placed in the parlor. Though many people had stopped doing this as the years progressed, for Robert it was one last night to spend with his boy before the cold, unforgiving earth separated him from sight. I

290

simply left him to it and made my way back down to the Church a couple of times throughout the night to take Robert coffee, or a blanket. After sunrise, Robert came home to shower and dress for the funeral.

The service was held the next morning at 9 am. Holden loved morning. He once told me it always reminded him of new beginnings. We had talked often of his service in the months following his return home. He had three firm requests: 1.) he wanted beautiful music, 2.) he wanted Jane Anne to speak, and 3.) he wanted his service early in the morning. We did our very best to honor all of those wishes.

The fall morning left a chill in the small sanctuary, as a handful of people on the island began to enter, quietly taking their seats. The room was quiet, reverent. Robert, Jane Anne, Samuel and I sat on the front pew, the candles upon the altar table flickering gently.

Holden had requested his service be simple and brief. He had heard the piercing words of those in the community who never would accept his trust in God as genuine, and internalized so deeply the disdain held for him by so many on the island that he expressed how he wanted to just slip away quietly. I understood the sentiment; however, from my standpoint, a life that had given so much love to others deserved to be honored.

The bell tolled, announcing that the hour had arrived. The cherry casket peeked out from beneath a spray of white calla lilies, Holden's favorite flower. Caryn brought a mutual high school friend, Leah, who had since gone on to study vocal performance at the Boston Conservatory. Leah had been a dear friend to Holden in the turbulent and formative years of high school, sharing the spotlight with him in a handful of musical dramas. Holden had always loved "Somewhere" from West Side Story. He had played the part of Tony, opposite Leah's as Maria, during their senior year of high school. Holden once told me that those moments on stage provided his first sense

291

of being in his element, of finding his place. As Holden's hopes for a so called normal life dissipated and he was left to wrestle with indescribable pain and isolation, this ballad from a simpler time came to hold an even deeper meaning for him. Today, it was Leah's turn to sing it to a fallen friend.

After the song ended, Jane Anne made her way to the pulpit. I had always enjoyed hearing her speak about the Lord. She seemed to grasp His grace more than I was ever able to, and she possessed such a unique gift for expressing it. Today, Jane Anne was serious. It was a time to honor Holden's life and she was the one he had entrusted with that task.

I wish I had a manuscript of her comments, but she decided to speak extemporaneously. All I have to rely on is my memory of that morning, the sense of overwhelming peace I felt as Jane Anne celebrated his life so beautifully. She honored Holden in a way that I don't feel anyone else would have been able to.

Jane Anne and Holden had a very special bond. It was as if there existed an unspoken language between their souls. She understood Holden and the complexity of his life in a much deeper way than Robert and I were ever able. Her empathy came from a place that found no fault, a place that sought only to love. It was this understanding of her unwavering love that, I feel, solidified the bond between the two of them. It was that love which caused her to advocate on Holden's behalf when necessary, and it was that love that undergirded Jane Anne as she ascended the steps to the pulpit of the small island Church. Holden always said that he would rather sit at Jane Anne's feet and hear about Jesus, than sit under the instruction of any Doctor of Philosophy he had ever met. I have to agree.

The service was brief and beautiful. We concluded with the burial, in our family plot, right next to Robert Jr. I can't help but weep even as I write about it. It was so beautiful, very sweet, but there's still a deep part of me that is angry, that feels like it was all wrong, that screams out that Holden was too young, too good, too precious to go like that.

After the service concluded, Robert needed to just get away. He headed to the fish house and left Silver Lake in the skiff Holden and Parks used to take out fishing. Robert was wrestling too. Wrestling with the same stew of emotions and thoughts simmering in all our hearts. Robert told me how he rode around the back of the island, pulling the bow of the skiff onto the edge of the marsh, the spot he had taken Holden that first Christmas to harvest juniper. It's funny how in times like this we just want to be close to anything that reminds us of the person. For Robert, that day had been a very special memory. In some melancholic way, he must have been seeking to relive it, to draw close to the feeling of having Holden with him again.

He told me of how he sat there on the bow of the skiff looking out over Oyster Creek, allowing himself to come completely undone in the solace of nature and the absence of onlookers. As he gave expression to his grief, something rose above the volume of his own wailing, a sound he knew so well. As he looked up through tear blurred eyes, a V of Canadian geese made their way over the mottled autumn pre-dusk sky. For Robert, and for me, it was a sign, a sign that all was well, that Holden is at rest, that God is near.

About a month after we buried Holden I had an unexpected encounter that was both insightful and heart wrenching. It was three weeks before Christmas and I had just returned to the island from a trip home to Carteret. In by-gone days that time of year would have been spent in a whirlwind of shopping and decorating, planning my holiday social calendar and organizing the

293

menus of the dinners and receptions we would host during the month. This year my heart wasn't in any festivities.

I didn't care to see a Christmas tree. I didn't even break out my Christmas albums to play on the old turn table in the living room. Just months before, I had laid to rest my second son; and I just couldn't seem to recover. There were so many emotions that would wash over me without warning, leaving me reduced to tears in the middle of a department store, driving down the highway, walking through the fish house, or standing at the sink washing dishes. I could be washing a glass that Holden loved to drink from, catching a glimpse of his Helly Hansens still hanging on the fish house wall, coming across a scarf or purse he had purchased for me and mailed home from Seattle; whatever the spark, it would ignite a brushfire of tears, sadness, or anger.

I was mourning desperately for a life that I felt was too soon extinguished, and I grieved with everything in me. Jane Anne and I made a trip to Beaufort while I was home, but it wasn't for holiday shopping down on Front Street. I didn't enter Stamper's Jeweler, Miss Sarah's Dress Shop, or even Mary Elizabeth's Boutique. Instead, I was at Ernest's Florist picking up two large white poinsettias, one for Robert Jr.'s grave and one for Holden's. His death reordered our worlds and even Jane Anne couldn't seem to find her humor for months following his departure.

We knew where he was, that wasn't the problem. The issue was that we missed him. We missed his gentle smile, his voice, his bear hugs, his fun-loving, youthful exuberance. Every time I went into that upstairs bedroom to clean, I secretly hoped that I would open the door to find him sitting there on his bed reading, just as I had seen him do so many evenings after he first came to us. I wanted to see that signature smile one more time, to watch the twinkle in those precious eyes, to once again hear his contagious laughter. But time and again the door creaks open to confirm our stark reality. The only tangible pieces of him left are the drawers full of clothing that I refuse to discard. As far as I am concerned, that room will remain just as he left it. When the separation gets too much, I slip into that room and weep as I run my fingers across flannel shirts and corduroy pants that still carry his scent.

On the day I returned to the island from Davis, I drove straight from the ferry dock to the cemetery. Normally, I have Robert join me when I tend their graves, but on that day I just wanted to have some time alone. I felt a good cry coming on and wanted a private moment in which to unleash my emotions. Parking along the sand path encircling the cemetery, I gathered the poinsettias from the back seat and made my way to our family plot. The greatest pain I have ever known is outliving my own child; and now I have done it twice.

As I walked gingerly through the plots, trying to avoid stepping on any graves, I noticed a couple of people around Holden's marker, one standing, one kneeling. Drawing closer I recognized Samuel's tall, large frame; however, there was one kneeling whom I had never met.

As I approached Samuel greeted me, offering to help with the flowers, while a thin framed, dark haired woman traced the etched marble with her fingertips. Samuel and I stepped a couple yards away, giving their mother some needed privacy. I looked on as she began running her fingers through the island sand which served as a gulf between her and the body of her fallen little boy.

She hadn't seen or spoken to Holden since the day she closed the door in his face, after his news went viral. She had ignored his letters from the west coast, his pleas for reconciliation. She had even declined to attend his memorial service. Nevertheless, she was a mother, and being one myself, I suspected it would only be a matter of time before the reservoir crumbled and she would rue the days

295

of missed opportunities.

"So, you're Mrs. Guthrie." She said, looking towards me from her seat on the ground beside Holden's headstone.

"Yes." I replied, not sure of how to address her, and still battling my own feelings of anger towards her regarding her abandonment of that precious child.

"Holden thought the sun rose and set around you." She said with a gentle smile, a smile that I had seen so often before, now knowing its origin. Her words served only to bring another wave of grief upon me. Tears flowed down my cheeks as I struggled to articulate a response.

"I thought he was the special one." I muttered, trying to retain some shred of composure.

"He was special." She said. "He was always special."

I made my way over to where she was and sat across from her on the cold December ground. I spent the better part of the afternoon there, as she poured out so many things long bottled in, ranging from tears, to laughter, to fits of anger...all appropriate responses to grief, especially when tainted by regrets.

"He was always different, special." She began. "John, he was the rugged outdoors one, the jock. But Holden, Holden was my boy." Her speech trailed off into silence as she cast her attention back to the marble, once again tracing the indentions of his name with her fingertips.

"I'm sure he told you about how awful his childhood was." She said, breaking the silence.

"No, I'm afraid he didn't." I replied.

With this she began to recount the events of those early years in graphic detail, my heart breaking inside of me as I learned of the turbulence Holden had known, even from early childhood. As she told of the beating, I literally felt sick.

"That whole incident happened because Holden was different." Then she continued. "He loved pink. Every time he would tell someone his favorite color when he was a little boy it was always pink. We would try not to show

296

our shame. But it wasn't just a color; I mean who cares about a color? But when John was out in the yard with a football, Holden was in my closet trying on my high heels, clomp clomps as he called them. I guess we all knew it. I think I just tried to ignore it, but his father just couldn't take it and so..." tears broke through, as she continued, "I guess his whole life he was beaten up for something he never asked for, or wanted."

As we sat there, the cool dampness of the soil seeping through our clothes, she showed me pictures of a little boy whom I had only seen in grown-up form, those dark eyes dancing with life and energy, that gentle smile present even from the beginning. She shared all the good memories of Holden before Ocracoke, seasons that had passed before he entered our lives. And she shared her regrets of not being there for him, of the severed relationship, of missed opportunities and moments forever gone.

Just before Samuel helped her up to leave, she propped a tattered, gray, stuffed animal against Holden's tombstone, a furry little dog with a red collar. She didn't explain. She didn't have to. There is an unspoken language which exists between mothers in moments like these. I just looked at the faded and tattered dog, thinking of the innocent, care-free little boy that must have carried it tirelessly under his arm, who slept with it after bedtime prayers. I thought of the light, unencumbered little guy with sparkling eyes and an infectious smile who would all too soon come to grips with life's harsh realities, and my heart grieved. Too soon was the innocence lost, too soon was his playfulness replaced with the weight of something that threatened to undo him, too soon would those wonder-filled eyes be closed in death. And yet, there was a strength in that little boy, a vibrancy that persevered against devastating odds, and a depth of faith and compassion which affected every life he ever touched.

We offered each other a sturdy embrace, and Samuel helped his mother back to the car, the harshness of the

297

years showing on her tired frame. There were no ever-
green wreaths, no red satin ribbons, no trees, and no garlands at our house that Christmas Eve, just two candles
glowing on the mantle. And in the oak shaded cemetery
down the lane sat two white poinsettias, a tattered,
stuffed, red-collared puppy beneath one and a worn, one-
armed, black teddy bear beneath the other.

In a letter Holden wrote to Robert, Jane Anne, and I,
just about a week before he slipped from consciousness
and into the arms of Jesus, he penned these words:
"I've come to believe that we each can be used either to
give life or to destroy it. Thank you for being used of
God to give it." There are few things in my life that I
cherish more than that letter. I pull it from the family
Bible and read it frequently now that he's gone.

There will never be another Christmas season, another
fourth of July fireworks display over Silver Lake, another
silver Honda passed on the highway, another surfer carrying his board, or another flock of geese flying low in the
Autumn sky which will not evoke memories of a young
man with starry eyes and a beaming smile, who climbed
my front steps one chilly October afternoon and forever
changed my life...our lives...for the better. And so I'll
close this remembrance of Holden, my precious boy, with
words prayed by St. Francis long ago:

"Lord, make us instruments of Your peace.
Where there is hatred, let us sow love.
Where there is injury, pardon.
Where there is doubt, faith.
Where there is despair, hope.
Where there is darkness, light.
Where there is sadness, joy.
O Divine Master,
grant that we may not so much seek to be consoled, as to
console;
to be understood, as to understand;

298

to be loved, as to love.
For it is in giving that we receive.
It is in pardoning that we are pardoned,
and it is in dying that we are born to Eternal Life."

Until we meet again, my precious boy!

Your Emilis

Made in United States
North Haven, CT
29 June 2024

54210022R00167